Praise for *The Story*

"A riveting tale of right, wrong, and vengeance. Restless souls (on Earth, as well as from the spirit world) can find peace only through justice, and at times, only by working together. Ann Hite writes brilliantly about the human condition—in this world and the next."

—Amy Hill Hearth, author of *Miss Dreamsville*
and the Collier County Women's Literary Society

"Transports you high atop Black Mountain, North Carolina, smack in the middle of a gothic tale so haunting and with characters and voices so authentic you'd swear you were living amongst them. Ann Hite's ability to weave the reader through the pages of the story catches you off guard with each and every spooky twist. Impossible to put it down. Brilliant!"

—Lisa Patton, bestselling author of *Whistlin' Dixie in a Nor'easter*

"There is a powerful new Southern voice sweeping across the literary landscape, and it belongs to Ann Hite. . . . She is a born storyteller who has crafted a mesmerizing and haunting tale. *The Storycatcher* is one that you'll want to put at the top of your reading stack and savor."

—Michael Morris, author of *Man in the Blue Moon*

"Steeped in lushly drawn landscapes and teeming with mystery, *The Storycatcher* is a beautifully rendered story of the journey for redemption and justice that drives the human heart, even beyond the flesh—and the knots of family we tie, and sometimes must untangle, along the way. I was utterly absorbed from the first, riveted and captivated, and no more able to leave the side of Ann Hite's haunted characters than the ghosts that are leading them toward their impossible secret."

—Erika Marks, author of *The Guest House*

"Haunting and daring, *The Storycatcher* grasps readers by the wrists and pulls them into a world where the only boundary is the one of unfinished business. Ann Hite is a fearless writer who leaves her readers breathless, always looking back over their shoulders, unaware of the turn up ahead. *The Storycatcher* is riveting Southern gothic literature. Hite has written an unforgettable novel that is lyrical and beautiful, absorbing and graceful, proving that she herself is a master storycatcher."

—Karen Spears Zacharias, author of *Mother of Rain*

Ghost on Black Mountain

"Multiple female narrators add dimension and perspective to Hite's first novel, and the sightings and visits from the spirits are often appropriately eerie. . . . Artfully woven."

—*Library Journal*

"Will intrigue readers eager for a Southern Gothic tale, and suggests a promising future for the Black Mountain novels to come."

—*Publishers Weekly*

"Twists folklore with the genres of Southern Gothic, paranormal, and literary fiction like a fine, fat pretzel, a guilty pleasure after midnight. . . . A richly layered tale of haints, hoodoo and heebie-jeebies, mayhem and murder, love and betrayal."

—*Press-Register* (Mobile, AL)

"Hite paints a loving portrait of rural mountain life in the early twentieth century, and characters are nuanced and true."

—*Atlanta*

"A haunting Southern gothic tale . . . wonderfully crafted."

—*San Francisco Book Review*

"Pull up a rocker and gaze into the hills at sundown. Old-time front-porch storytelling unfolds in this dark, twisted tale where hardscrabble lives, murderous secrets, and ghosts intersect on a mysterious mountain."

—Beth Hoffman, *New York Times* bestselling author
of *Saving CeeCee Honeycutt*

"Haunting, dark and unnerving, Hite's brilliant modern gothic casts an unbreakable spell."

—Caroline Leavitt, *New York Times* bestselling author of *Pictures of You*

"The authentic voice of Nellie Pritchard, who comes to Black Mountain as a new bride, wraps around you and pulls you deep into this haunted story. I couldn't put it down."

—Joshilyn Jackson, *New York Times* bestselling author of *Gods in Alabama*

"An eerie page-turner told in authentic mountain voices that stick with the reader long after the story ends."

—Amy Greene, author of *Bloodroot*

"The inhabitants of Black Mountain live side-by-side with the spirits of the dead, throw spells and dig for treasure, solve their problems with careful alliances and the occasional murder. This is a story where the spookiness of a mountain village comes to life through gritty characters whose feelings and motivations seem all too similar to our own. Ann Hite captures their voices so well, you'd swear they're whispering into your ear. . . . Captivating."

—Rebecca Coleman, author of *The Kingdom of Childhood*

ALSO BY ANN HITE

Ghost on Black Mountain

THE STORYCATCHER

ANN HITE

GALLERY BOOKS

New York   London   Toronto   Sydney   New Delhi

G

Gallery Books
A Division of Simon & Schuster, Inc.
1230 Avenue of the Americas
New York, NY 10020

First Gallery Books trade paperback edition September 2013

GALLERY BOOKS and colophon are registered trademarks of Simon & Schuster, Inc.

For information about special discounts for bulk purchases, please contact Simon & Schuster Special Sales at 1-866-506-1949 or business@simonandschuster.com.

The Simon & Schuster Speakers Bureau can bring authors to your live event. For more information or to book an event, contact the Simon & Schuster Speakers Bureau at 1-866-248-3049 or visit our website at www.simonspeakers.com.

Designed by Davina Mock-Maniscalco
Map by Jerry Clifford Hite

Manufactured in the United States of America

10 9 8 7 6 5 4 3 2 1

Library of Congress Cataloging-in-Publication Data

Hite, Ann.
  The storycatcher / Ann Hite.—First Gallery Books trade paperback edition.
    pages cm
    1. Young women—Georgia—Fiction. 2. Family secrets—Fiction. 3. Ghost stories. 4. Mystery fiction. I. Title.
  PS3608.I845S76 2013
  813'.6—dc23

                                  2012050508

ISBN 978-1-4516-9227-3
ISBN 978-1-4516-9231-0 (ebook)

Ella Ruth Hite
I miss you each day.

Jeffery Swafford
This is my love letter to you, brother.

Aileen Swafford Brown
The sister I haven't met and would love to know.

MAUDE TUGGLE

DANIELS
CEMETERY

BLACK MOUNTAIN
CHURCH

PARKER

DOBBINS

House

JCH

BLACK M

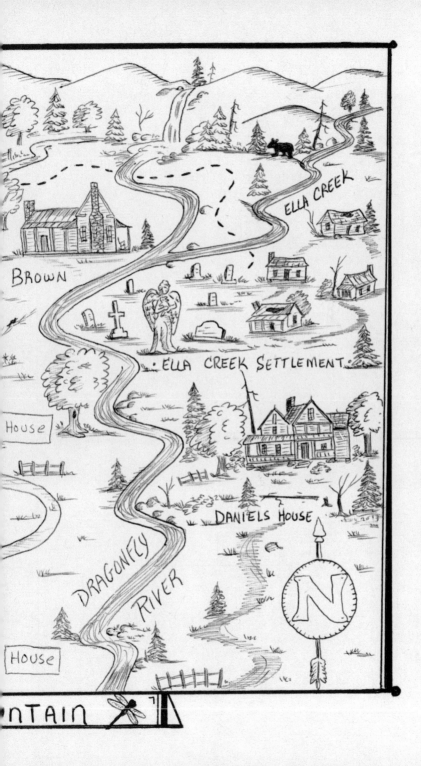

ELLA CREEK

BROWN

ELLA CREEK SETTLEMENT

House

DANIELS HOUSE

DRAGONFLY RIVER

House

N

ntain

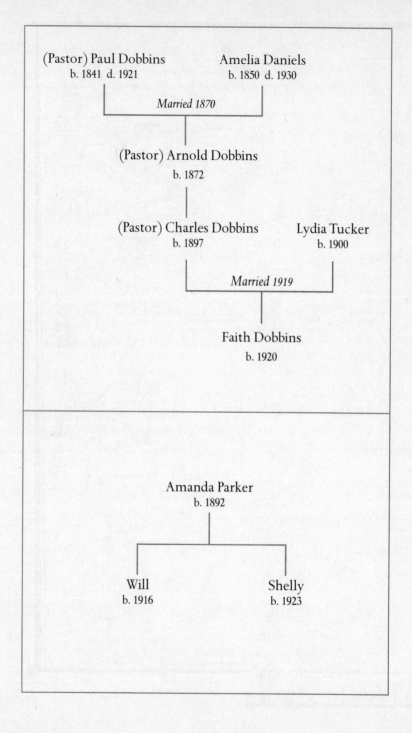

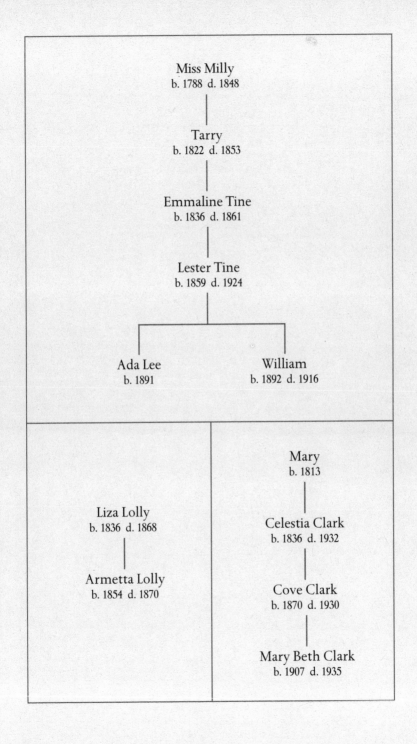

Miss Milly
b. 1788 d. 1848

Tarry
b. 1822 d. 1853

Emmaline Tine
b. 1836 d. 1861

Lester Tine
b. 1859 d. 1924

Ada Lee
b. 1891

William
b. 1892 d. 1916

Mary
b. 1813

Liza Lolly
b. 1836 d. 1868

Celestia Clark
b. 1836 d. 1932

Armetta Lolly
b. 1854 d. 1870

Cove Clark
b. 1870 d. 1930

Mary Beth Clark
b. 1907 d. 1935

Dayclean

September 1935

Dayclean: The space between the shadows of night and the first rays of sun. A time when almost anything might happen. Tides change without warning, love hatches between the most unlikely people, a ghost devours a person's soul.

—Old Geechee saying

Ada Lee Tine

THE SALT FROM THE OCEAN hung thick and heavy in the air. The only breeze came from the boat moving. Roger and me stood together side by side at the boat's wheel, him driving, me watching.

Ebb tide gave me the creepy crawlers. Ebb tide was unnatural, bad, nothing but bad.

"That sorry fool Mr. Benton is bringing his colored mistress to stay for two weeks. Mr. Tyson be letting them sleep in his house. He never struck me as one to put up with that mess, but by gosh he is. Just shows you how you never know a person. Ain't nothing but trouble going to come. You mark words." My shoulder brushed his.

"How you know all this, girl?"

"I heard the missus talking," I explained. "Mr. Benton's woman be colored all right, and missus be raising Sam Hill about it too. She done told Mr. Tyson he's bringing shame and sin to their family, letting them two stay there. Didn't stop him. He shooed her away, saying things were done and over. I hear Mr. Benton and Mr. Reynolds is the best of friends. Ain't no chance Mr. Tyson will turn his back on Mr. Reynolds. He'd be some kind of fool."

Mr. Benton T. Horse, from New York City—he couldn't stand being called his last name 'cause it didn't get him much respect—was a big, fancy banker and best friends with Mr. R. J. Reynolds, known throughout our parts as the tobacco king. Mr. Reynolds was one rich man because he bought and paid for Sapelo Island right smack in the middle of the Great Depression. Mr. Benton was a whole story in himself. He was one of those sneaky fellows. The first time I laid eyes on him back at the start of summer, I knew he was a mule, just a plain old mule. Now, there ain't a thing wrong with mules—they be hardworking animals—but when a man takes to being uppity and trying to hide behind some fancy words, it sticks out like a sore thumb. Mr. Benton was a sweet-talker and wore one of those big old smiles. He was the kind of white man that made a woman have to look over her shoulder lest he might give a sneak attack. Being around this man was like putting a big spoonful of sugar in my mouth. I drew up every time.

"I think this Mr. Benton better be careful. He ain't in New York City," I said. "White folks down here don't take kindly to sporting a colored woman around like she be the same. And him being a Yankee ain't going to help a bit either."

The shrimp boat scooted across the water just as smooth like we was moving on some lazy lake surrounded by big fancy homes. Whenever I worked at the Ridge, Roger gave me a ride from Sapelo Island to Meridian Dock each Monday, and then back to the island every Friday. The Ridge was a strip of marshy land that ran from Darien along the coast of the mainland where all the rich folks lived in their big fancy houses. Our arrangement went on the whole summer long. But it was the middle of September, and I should have been tucked away on my front porch or cooking at my stove, not headed for the mainland, Darien. I should've been weaving my sweetgrass baskets like Mama and Grandmama did before me. But Mr. Tyson needed me, and I went. My family had always worked for his, and the extra money didn't hurt.

"Mr. Benton's wife will fly through him and jerk a knot on his head if she finds out about this woman. That much I know. She's one mean soul, always screaming for me to bring her something or another."

Roger never took his stare off the water. "You in a mess. You in a mess," he sighed.

He guided *Sweet Jesse* through Doby Sound into Hudson Creek, where he docked just for me before he made his way out into open waters. That morning the marsh was quiet like Roger, who never had a lot to say on any given day. All that could be heard was the putt, putt, putt of the gasoline engine. Gray clouds built in the southeast sky. A big storm was headed our way. Normally we saw signs of a storm in the motion of the water and tides long before it reached us, but ebb tide was hiding what was taking place out at sea.

"He's paying good. I don't even have to work next summer. I could stay on the island."

"What in the world would you do with yourself, girl?" Roger looked at me sideways.

We'd been knowing each other since we was little things, running around Hog Hammock in our bare feet, seining in the canals, climbing trees, and scaring the fire out of each other by telling stories of haints and such. A hammock was a high place in a low area, and that was just what me and Roger was. We lived in a place higher than everybody else without being uppity. Nope. Just plain old happy and simple, that was us. Before Mama passed, she had a hope that I had me a husband in Roger. I never had the heart to tell her we wasn't nothing but good friends. Of course, there wasn't no law that said a man and a woman had to be in love to be married. Lord, that kind of thing was only for folks who didn't have to worry about making a living. Mama died thinking her oldest child had her a husband. This gave her peace. But I was alone, while my brother took out to live a fine life on the mainland. He didn't last hardly no time before he got himself in a mess and died. Times was enough to choke a horse, so I couldn't fault him none for leaving. But if he had stayed put on the island, I would've had him to lean on, and he would have stayed alive.

"I'd weave baskets," I replied. My sweetgrass baskets were asked after in Darien.

He nodded. "You should, but you won't. You can't stay away from Mr. Tyson and his family." He kind of smiled. "I'd like to see you weave all summer. You make the prettiest baskets."

Roger and me was Geechees, Saltwater Geechees. We lived where Geechee slaves broke their backs growing rice and cotton for the big plantation. Slave blood was our blood. Geechee stories was in the sweat that poured off our heads. The salt marshes made up our bones. Our lungs wouldn't work without salty air. We was happy to die right there.

"Maybe I'll just do that." I couldn't look at him, 'cause if I did, some sweet feeling showing in his eyes might ruin things between us.

"Just smile and do what this Mr. Benton tells you to do. We're both good at that." Roger studied the sky in front of us.

I cut him a look to make sure he was pulling my leg. "I don't like smiling. It's one thing to wait on Mr. Tyson and his family, but some big-bellied white fool and his uppity woman is a whole other thing." I shook off a cold chill that walked up my backbone.

"Shadow passing over your grave?"

I nodded. "It's this dern ebb tide. It takes the life right out of the air."

"Now, don't go blaming ebb tides, girl. They're made for resting. Mr. Wind takes a few hours off. The water pushes back; even the old fish keep still. It's a good life." He looked dreamy, like he just told me some fairy story with a happily-ever-after ending.

"Ebb tide means bad is coming. Everybody knows that." I watched the thick, gray clouds. We worked our way over the water to the dock.

"Just a little storm, not no hurricane, but we could get some higher tides and flooding." He shook his head. "I sure hope there's some decent fishing today."

"I wish I had me a boat with no one looking for me to wait on them hand and foot. It'd be just me and the ocean."

Roger owning his own boat was like buying a piece of land, something to be proud of. He was a practical man. No root or ghosts for him. That's where we was different. I had me a bit of whimsy passed on from my daddy's people.

"What you talking about? Ploeger-Abbott seafood owns my soul along with all the fishermen's whether they be colored or white. One day they're going to decide not to take our catches no more. Then what? Watch what I say. But they can't beat me. I get up every morning and do what Daddy and Granddaddy did. They fished with seining nets made by their own hands without a fancy gasoline boat. The catch was pure and plentiful. Fishing is part of me like baskets is part of you."

I took a quiet breath and relaxed into his words.

MR. TYSON LEFT THE OLD TRUCK at the dock for me just like he always did. His house was too far for walking. Most of the homes on the Ridge was prim and white like the snooty folks that lived in them, but Mr. Tyson's house was big and brown, practically built in the marsh like it had sprung up from the mud during a low tide. Sometimes I liked to stand on the top floor in the little attic bedroom and smell the salt. I saw myself back on the island, walking the beach, the water churning around my feet on the pure white sand, or better yet, weaving my baskets. I loved the way my fingers worked the sweetgrass. Weaving was like thinking hard. I'd get lost in another place. My body went loose and rested in the movements.

I passed Mr. Tyson's house on Cowhorn Road and cut on over to Darien, where I had to get some supplies. The old houses and churches along the way gave me something interesting to look at. Behind each door was a story, whether the family was rich or poor. We all had a tale.

I figured more than one tragedy happened in Darien. Babies was born and people passed on just like anywhere else. During the War Between the States, the federal troops burned down the little town for the pure sport of it. They even burned the homes of the very slaves they'd come to free. Now, what sense did that make? Spirits roamed those old roads, especially right before dark, a time of day we Geechees called dusk-dark. Those from long ago believed it to be a sacred time, a time when a soul stood between two worlds.

I heard tell there was a colored woman's ghost who walked the Ridge. She was what the old-timers called a storycatcher. Her job was to set life stories straight, 'cause the Lord only knew how many were all twisted in a knot. Her story was a big question. No one knew where she came from. Maybe it was lost or forgotten or one of them hidden stories, put away on purpose. It was said she wore a long skirt and a bonnet on her head. Folks said if she looked a person in the face, she'd own him or her for a night. In that time she'd work a story that had gone wrong. Sometimes good came, but mostly not, 'cause it was the bad stories that got wrapped in lies. One tale has a mama that beat her daughter every day for no good reason at all, just out of pure spite. The mama lost her mind the night she seen the spirit and tried to kill her neighbor with a butcher knife. The sheriff hauled the mama off to jail. Last I heard, she was still at the state penitentiary. The daughter went on to be a decent person. Thank goodness, I always left the Ridge before daylight was gone, and I'd never had the pleasure of seeing the old woman ghost in person. See, I had me this gift called sight. I saw spirits who was stuck to the earth for one reason or another. Most of them wanted to give me a visit and tell me all about their troubles.

I got my shopping done and headed back to the Tysons'. Sometimes I was sure that house sighed out loud when I came in the door, but that was pure whimsy on my part.

Just before lunch, Mr. Benton's shiny black car pulled in the gates and around back of the house. I opened all the windows because ebb tide was gone and the wind was blowing right nice. Mr. Benton bounced out of that car and threw open the door where that woman sat, like he was some young fellow. Well, Lordy be, no wonder he was all happy. That colored woman unfolded into a tall, slender frame about twenty-something years younger than him. She had the longest legs, them Hollywood kind. She wore a snooty city suit, complete with this little hat perched sideways on her straightened hair. I'd seen it all. The seam up her nylons was a perfect straight line. I couldn't help but wonder how long that took. I'd never even touched nylons, seeing how the women in the Tyson house had the good sense to know how hot and sticky summer and fall could be. The silly heels that colored girl wore sunk into the soft, dark earth. So she slid them perfect feet out and left her shoes where they was. I had to chuckle at that. She was light-skinned but not so light she could pass. No, she was colored. Anyone could see it.

"Lou?" Mr. Benton yelled.

Now know this: Lou had never been my name or even a nickname, but that's what Mr. Benton called all the colored womenfolk he came to meet in Darien that summer. Me, I just answered. It made life easier, even though there wasn't one good reason for him not to remember my real name. I pushed open the screen door, and there between Mr. Benton and the colored woman was a misty-looking spirit not fully solid, a woman hunched over like she'd been down too many times to stand tall. She raised her head and looked at me straight. Not even a chill went up my spine. I was looking at her, the woman spirit that made everyone stay off the Ridge at night.

Mr. Benton's colored woman laughed while the old woman spirit shook her head and walked between the two. Mr. Benton reached right through the haint and grabbed on to his woman's hand without flinching. That was a good sign he be mean underneath all them grins, 'cause otherwise he would be feeling the old woman.

"Lou, this is Miss Mary Beth Clark." He looked the woman in the eyes, and Lord help me, it was plain he was smitten by a bad spell.

"Lou here is the best cook on the coast. I'd be willing to bet in the whole country. I'd take her to New York, but she won't have no part of leaving that little island of hers. Says anywhere else is godforsaken." He winked at me like we was some kind of friends.

"Maybe if you could remember my name, Mr. Benton, I might work for you, but until then, no sir, I won't." I nodded at Miss Mary Beth Clark, and a look passed between the two of us. It was the kind of look folks give each other when they know more about a subject than they be saying. "You can call me Lou too." I clicked my tongue.

The old woman spirit planted herself close to me, but I just ignored her. I didn't want this fine new couple thinking I'd gone around the bend. In those days, I still wanted to swear ghosts off like Grandmama swore off dipping snuff. "What would you like for your supper, Mr. Benton?"

He held Miss Mary Beth Clark's hand like she might scoot away. "What would you like, honey?"

I guess we was going to playact like they was something real instead of pure sin.

For a second, greed flashed across the face of Miss Mary Beth Clark. A want so deep and thick it couldn't be hidden by the best of playacting. That girl had gone plumb without. Maybe that's why she was with someone like Mr. Benton. Times were getting worse each day. Had she left that look as it was and gave a decent answer, I could have found a reason to like her, but that little snip gathered herself back into them uppity ways and looked down her nose at me. "Just something light." Her voice was a whisper.

"What do we have that is light, Lou?" Mr. Benton winked at me again.

I started to tell Miss Mary Beth Clark to go graze on the marsh grass—that ought to be light enough—but I pulled them words right back before they got out. "I'm cooking some fresh crab with red beans and rice. Maybe some of my greens too. It's a recipe from the island." I smiled real sweet at Miss Marsh Grass.

"Sounds like a good meal!" Mr. Benton whooped. "Her crab is astounding."

The wind kicked up, tossing the tree limbs draped in moss. The clouds gathered across the sky. I needed to go get the fresh crab before the rain.

Miss Mary Beth Clark stared out at the marshes with a worried look on that perky face. "Those clouds are dark."

"We got a storm coming our way. This morning was an ebb tide."

Miss Mary Beth shook off a shiver. "I want to explore the house." Then she turned to me. "Where will you sleep?"

"I'll be spending the nights in town and back in the mornings." Great-aunt Hattie always let me stay with her when I was on the mainland. There was just so much I could stomach of white folks before I got purely sick of them. "And I go to the island on Fridays and come back on Mondays. You'll have to fend for yourselves."

Mr. Benton grinned like he knew some big old secret. "Lou here, like all the help, is afraid to be at the Ridge after dark. Tyson warned me they're afraid of a ghost who prowls the area." He laughed like Miss Mary Beth Clark and him was the same color, like she didn't have stories. The woman spirit stood right next to her and him, watching every move they made.

"You'd be surprised what be real around here, Mr. Benton." I tried to keep the pure hate out of my words.

Miss Mary Beth Clark raised her eyebrows at me. "Sounds like some of the stories my grandmother told when I was a child." She looked over at Mr. Benton, and in that look, I could see she didn't care for him no more than I did. This was the same look coloreds used to speak to each other without being heard. The girl came from a family that taught her right, even if she was trying to outrun them.

"Come on. This is a grand place. Been in Tyson's family forever." He guided Miss Mary Beth Clark through the kitchen. The last thing I wanted was that woman prowling through Mr. Tyson's house.

Once I was alone, I turned to the old woman spirit. "What you doing here? Mr. Tyson ain't done nothing to you or anyone. He be a good man and don't need your trouble."

"You right about him. I'm here for my own reasons." She pointed her head at the kitchen door.

"I don't want to know. Leave me out of it." I grabbed my crab basket.

"Now, that little old girl has a story that needs fixing. Poison, pure poison. Ain't nothing like a young'un that shuns her family and takes things that don't belong to her."

"Don't tell me. I just cook and clean. I don't want to know one thing. I got to be here for two weeks, and then they're gone and out of my mind."

The old woman cackled. "You ain't never going to forget those two, girl. I be talking to you some more. You got to listen whether it suits you or not." She walked right through the kitchen wall. The thick, gray clouds moved over the Ridge.

THAT EVENING AUNT HATTIE met me at the door. No one really knew how old she was, but it was old, probably close to ninety. In her hands was a little lacy handkerchief. "Something is about to happen. It's in this storm." The rain pelted her tin roof, and this made her shout. "It's been whispering in my ear all day. Tide be high tonight, way too high."

I put my arm around her shoulders. "I saw the old woman spirit out at the Ridge in the daylight. It's about them folks that come to town, not any of us." I didn't dare tell her the old woman's last words.

"Lordy, you seen the old woman in the daytime? It's got to be bad." She led me into her small, tidy house made of tabby. "That ain't good, even if you got sight, child."

"The old woman spirit is here to tell the colored mistress's story. That's all. That little prissy sure has that ghost stirred up."

"Did you warn her?" Aunt Hattie gave me some of her Russian tea. The fresh orange flavor was the best in weather like we was having. I was right content to sit there all evening listening to the rain.

"What good would it do? She done looked down her nose at me. She's way too smart and fancy for the likes of a cook who knows some root and lives on Sapelo. The spirit said something about her not owning up to her family and stealing."

Aunt Hattie nodded. "You know she's got a name."

"What you know about the spirit, Aunt Hattie?"

"Not much. Mama said her name was Emmaline and she was a slave here in Darien. That's all."

"Why didn't you ever tell me?"

"No reason. Now, you just don't get caught up in it."

"What's for supper?"

"That nice Roger of yours brought me a mess of crawdads, said you loved them best in white sauce. I boiled them in the stuff."

"My mouth is a-watering."

ONE MINUTE EVERYTHING is scooting along in happiness, and then a big, fat gator comes slithering through the water and flips over the boat, upsetting the whole balance. But one would have to believe life held a balance. That's exactly what happened that rainy night while I slept away. Aunt Hattie and me heard a pounding on the door. We busted into the hall at the same time, 'cause there wasn't nobody who would come calling at midnight.

I'll always remember the sweet moment of peace, of life as it should be, with only those little problems that take up people's time.

Douglas, a man who worked for Roger, stepped in the door. He took off his cap, wet from the rain, and twisted it in his hands. Little drops of water fell on Aunt Hattie's fine hand-me-down rug, seeping into the rose pattern. The wind lashed the trees outside. "I'm awful sorry, Miss Hattie, for bothering you so late, but I got some bad news for her." His look landed on me.

My mouth went dry. I was actually thinking maybe he was there because of Aunt Hattie's son, who had never been right in the head and took out wandering a couple of years before. My stomach turned sick.

"Spit it out," Aunt Hattie fussed.

"It's Roger, ma'am." He finally looked away and studied his cap.

A dark shadow pulled at me. "What?"

"Roger wanted to catch you before you headed on out for the night. He had a nice big basket of shrimp that could be cooked for their dinner tomorrow." Douglas shook his head like he was trying not to remember. "Roger took himself right up to Mr. Tyson's door, and that would've been fine except that crazy man from New York City was there. I don't know what Roger was thinking, having a talk with that colored woman like she be one of us. That Yankee had Roger put in jail for trying to have his way with her." Douglas passed his hand over his face. "The deputy came and took Roger right off of *Sweet Jesse*."

I couldn't get a breath.

"A mob of white men took him from the jail. I was right there, and that deputy didn't do much of nothing. Oh, he threatened, but he didn't even draw his gun. I tried to tell them they was wrong, but they just hit me in the head." He lifted his hand to his forehead, and I noticed the lump on his hairline. "These white men be crazy and don't give a hoot about justice. Everybody in Darien knows what kind of man Roger is. There's talk this was the KKK 'cause someone was complaining over Roger having big catches. Said he's grown too uppity. I'm afraid for Roger, ma'am."

That bunch of words rattled around in my head like a bag of bones. The bottom let out of the sky just as I thought it couldn't rain any harder. My heart beat in my head, thump, thump, thump. My blood was pure ice. "A mob? Mr. Benton's mistress? KKK?" I looked around the room like I'd find Roger standing there. "I'm going to kill me Mr. Benton and that Miss Mary Beth Clark just for good measure." The words came out like I was slicing away at the air.

"You hush, now." Aunt Hattie tugged at my arm. "That talk will only get you in a heap of trouble. That be a white man from New York City. You can't talk like that."

A deep sorrow tangled with crazy rage formed around my heart. Emmaline, the old woman spirit, was behind this.

"Let's go to church. Folks will meet. We'll figure out what to do." Aunt Hattie pushed me to the door. I grabbed my coat from the fancy hall tree some white woman passed on to Aunt Hattie. I was still wearing my nightgown. The rain fell in sheets. But this wasn't the worst of the storm. Roger always believed that the ocean was a woman to be treated with complete respect. That showed how good he was. Now the sea was throwing a fit.

"I got my truck," Douglas offered. "I'll take you to St. Cyprain." The Episcopal church was one of the oldest in those parts, the first colored church to start up after the emancipation. The slaves had been taught white folks' ways, but when they started their own church, they mixed in some of the old beliefs. Me, I didn't have one bit of use for a white church. I'd seen too many so-called good folks use the cross to hide their judging, hateful ways. I prayed on the beach. That was the best church in the world.

The lights from St. Cyprain spilled out the double doors into the rain like the lighthouse on St. Simons; the bright yellow glow cutting through the storm, offering help to those in trouble. Inside the church, folks was milling around. All of them buzzing at the same time. Was there something they could do to help? Could they save Roger—such a fine man—from a crowd of determined white men? All the people in that part of the county knew of Roger and his hard work. My heart settled in my chest. A tiny sliver of hope rested on my shoulders. Those men couldn't punish Roger for something he hadn't done. It wasn't right. It wasn't just. The mistake would sit with them forever if they did. All that mess was just a bad dream, waiting to be shooed away by the morning light. I went over to stand by the wall.

A bunch of voices, louder than the others, began at the door and spread across the church, moving through the crowd like a wave rolling into shore. Mark Tinker's sister, Halo, wiped at her eyes and came running at me. "Lord!" she screamed. "Lord have mercy, girl!"

My look settled on her.

"They shot him on the way to Savannah on Highway 17. Right there in the middle of the road. They done killed him. They didn't even try to hide their intentions. Like he was bad and not worth the effort." She gripped my wrist with her thick fingers.

Her words turned my heart to ice and something broke inside me. Something cold and hard. I yanked my arm back, turned, and walked out the door into the night. It was like my life was being told in a different way, a way not intended.

"You get back in here!" Aunt Hattie used that voice she always used on me when I was a little thing and took off mad at the world. My heart was dead. I died with Roger.

"Let the girl be. She needs to mourn. She loved him best of all." This was old Harper's voice, the voice of a newfound truth.

I wandered in the hard rain without looking, without thinking. Emmaline walked out of a big twisted oak, and for a minute she looked part of the gray moss swinging wildly. It was like our souls were set for the same purpose. I followed her.

FUNNY THING ABOUT BAD STORMS, they leave their mark and then they're gone. This storm—no one would ever remember—touched us with its fingers, moved up the coast, and then swung inland across the North Carolina mountains, where it stirred up some more trouble.

When I woke up in Aunt Hattie's extra bed the next morning, the sun stretched across the room, beating on my body. Another hot day. And just like on any other morning, for a minute I wanted to live in that time before my feet hit the floor to go to work. A shadow hung in my mind, but I didn't want any part of it. Then I thought of Emmaline, her magic, the way she took a story and turned it inside out. The way she made me follow her.

Aunt Hattie flung the door open and looked more ruffled than I'd ever seen her. "You going home now. Get up! I got you a ride back to the island. You ain't got much time." She looked into my soul with them watery brown eyes that was fading to hazel as she grew to meet death. "Don't be coming back here anytime soon. Understand? We ain't losing you too." She put my clothes in my hands. My gown was gone. I wore some old housedress of hers. "They won't bother with Sapelo. They be too scared of stories and that Mr. Reynolds to do that."

"What are you talking about? I can't go nowhere until I let Mr. Benton know I won't be back, not that he should get my respect. But I want to look him in the eyes and tell him what he caused." The pain stuck under my rib and grew worse like I'd eaten some bad fish. See, some things are too bad for a mind to handle. Mine had shut out most of the night.

Aunt Hattie watched me close for a minute. "She got you, didn't she?"

"Who?" Some soft scream built in my head.

"You know who. Emmaline, the old woman spirit. Don't play dumb with me. Somebody killed that Yankee man and his woman. They don't know what happened up there, only that it's a bloody mess. What you know about that?"

I looked away as the pain moved down into my stomach. I couldn't remember what happened after I met up with Emmaline, only that she took me to that house.

"Roger be dead too, child. You can't change that." Her words sat there between us.

"I don't want him to be."

"You hush, now," Aunt Hattie whispered. "Get on out of here. Douglas has you a ride back."

I pulled my black shift over my head. The world outside the window had come out of the night all fresh and clean. Water drops hung on the leaves.

"Go on, now, before I start believing you didn't have nothing to do with that mess. If anyone asks you, you be right here with me all night, crying your eyes out."

"Yes, ma'am."

She put her hand on her hips. "Right now the police is asking all kinds of questions. I just pray Emmaline didn't work through you. The police be saying Roger was innocent all along 'cause of what happen to that Yankee man and his girlfriend. That's what the chief is thinking, anyway." Aunt Hattie handed me her Bible. "You read on that. Keep your mind clean. Get some good root on the island to wash that Emmaline away. Stay there until this mess is over."

I closed my eyes, managed to nod, and tucked the Bible under my arm.

"I love you, girl." Aunt Hattie nudged me out the door.

"They both be dead?" I asked, because for the life of me I couldn't see what happened in my mind, only Miss Mary Beth Clark's face stayed with me.

"Both."

I climbed in the truck with Douglas.

"Let the island heal you!" she yelled.

Those kind of hurts never heal.

WHEN DOUGLAS LET ME OFF at the dock, he held out a soft gray cloth. "I thought you'd like to have this."

It was Roger's old cap. "He gave you *Sweet Jesse*. Left it in writing. She be yours free and clear."

I glanced over at *Sweet Jesse,* rocking at the dock with the other boats. "What am I going to do with a shrimp boat?"

"Fish." He shrugged.

I got out of the truck.

"The whole town, even the deputy, say they real sorry for Roger's death."

"It don't bring him back." I watched the boat.

"No, ma'am, it sure don't." He nodded. "Can you drive her?"

"I reckon I can." I'd watched Roger too many times. I could take *Sweet Jesse* back to Sapelo with my eyes closed. I walked off toward the boat.

"Hey."

I turned around.

"I think if you did kill them two—and I sure hope you did—you be the bravest woman in these parts. Roger would be proud of you."

I walked down the dock without looking back. Roger didn't believe in killing for any reason.

THE SALT OF THE OCEAN mixed with the salt of the marshes was one of those smells I couldn't get enough of. I watched Sapelo get closer. My island was there, telling me to come home, calling me. I felt Roger standing over my shoulder, and the feeling sunk in that I might never go to Darien again. I was a Saltwater Geechee that loved a man without knowing until the story went way wrong. I learned something hard and cold.

The high tide spilled into the canals and onto the banks. That's when I seen him, Biali, the father of the slaves. The African slave that taught others to survive and live a good life on Sapelo. He dropped to his knees and prayed his prayers of freedom, of strength, of life. I watched him until he became part of the grasses and left me alone to take *Sweet Jesse* into dock.

PART ONE

Hailstorm

Late Summer 1935

"A lost soul always finds its way around on the mountain."
—Shelly Parker

Shelly Parker

NADA BIRTHED ME RIGHT THERE on Black Mountain. A Christmas baby born with a caul. Nada called it a face veil. Either way, the thing was supposed to give me power through a special gift. That's what Nada told me, and she was the smartest woman I ever knew. So, I watched for my gift like a girl at her own birthday party. It wasn't until I was ten years old that I understood there wasn't bows and wrapping paper involved.

I lost my big brother Will the last week of August that year. Just after Arleen Brown was buried in the cemetery, he up and left without a good reason or even a word. I cooked and cleaned just like Nada. It was expected. Will had turned nineteen, a grown man. That whole month he had brooded around, having words with Nada more than once. It was like all of a sudden he just couldn't find his footing on Black Mountain, like he was headed off that mountain.

There was a secret hanging in the air at our cabin, and I figured it had something to do with the way Faith—that was Pastor and Mrs. Dobbins's prissy daughter—followed Will everywhere. Stupid old girl caused more problems than she was worth. I'd seen her and Will with their heads together, hushing every time I came near, shooing me away. Faith loved Will. A colored boy could die for anything a white girl said—didn't matter one bit if it was true or not—but especially if that white girl's father was Pastor Dobbins. Faith had turned into a beauty, or so everyone on the mountain said. But seeing how she was the pastor's daughter, what was they going to say? I thought she was downright ugly 'cause pretty is as pretty do. And that girl didn't do one thing pretty.

The morning the folks were supposed to view Arleen, I slipped over to the church for a peek in the window. It was the last place in the world Nada would have me be. The most mournful music floated out the windows. That old piano made a sound that stopped me right there in my tracks. Sweet and all tangled with some unspoken words, begging. And who was sitting there playing? Pastor. Lord have mercy, one look at him and I forgot just how mean and hateful he was. He was so lost in sadness. His fingers was long, pretty, like one of them paper-thin plates Mrs. Dobbins was always making me wash. In that music was the man a woman would want to marry, the softness, the person who could mourn a young dead girl. Everyone had a decent side.

That whole afternoon Will didn't show his face, Nada festered like something had crawled up under her skin and was burning her from the inside while she worked in the kitchen of the main house. "This mountain be turned sour over this here death," she mumbled under her breath.

"What did you say, Amanda?" Mrs. Dobbins was hovering over the silver, touching each and every fork, spoon, and knife so I had to polish the dern stuff again.

"Nothing, ma'am," Nada lied. Lying to white folks was just necessary. A colored couldn't always guess what actions they might take next.

So, it didn't surprise me none when Nada went to our cabin before

I finished washing all them dern dishes we'd messed up. There was a turkey cooking in our oven. Lord, the food that would be placed on that dining room table would be enough to feed the whole mountain and still leave some. A lot of to-do over some old white girl that looked like she might break in half. Shoot, when Arleen looked at a person, it was like she wasn't really seeing them but something way off.

The sun was gone, and all that was left was the grayness that spread from the sky to the ground. The water was almost too hot to scrub the mixing bowls, but I tolerated the burn just to be finished and out of the house. A flicker in my side view made me look out the back door. A black shadow passed by the glass. One of the tin measuring cups on the counter clattered to the floor.

"Shelly, why are you still here?" Pastor stood in the hall door. Nothing about him seemed like that music he was making earlier.

"Washing dishes, sir. We made us a right big mess getting that dinner ready for tomorrow."

He stared me down and then looked outside. "Have you been moving things around on the porch?"

"No, sir. Been right here most of the day."

"I left my prayer book there on the porch rail."

"I haven't seen it, sir." What in the world would I do with his prayer book?

Meanness was written all over his face. "Let me know if you do see it, and Shelly, if you're lying, I'll find out."

"Yes, sir."

By the time I got to the cabin, Nada was sound asleep. Will still hadn't come home. Pastor had made him dig Arleen's grave earlier. Lord help, Pastor might have met his match with Will, who looked real calm and sweet, but if a person made him mad, it wasn't a pretty sight.

On my bed was a little green book I'd seen a hundred times. It wasn't a funny joke. The dern thing was opened to a prayer called "Lost Sheep."

When in need, one only has to look to the Shepherd, the caretaker, the trusted one. Who will tell the truth. He will point you in the right direction and keep you close, safe.

Maybe Faith put the prayer book on my bed. She was known for slipping around. There was only one way not to get blamed for the mess.

I cut across the field through Daniels Cemetery and then scooted in the back door of the church. The room was dark except for the two gaslights on the wall near Arleen's burying box. The thing wasn't homemade like most burying boxes, but shiny as a pond of water on a clear, still day. Store-bought from Asheville and delivered by truck. All the fine church ladies had been chewing on this since the truck drove away, a dead girl in a shiny box while her whole family was so poor they struggled for food. And no one was sitting with the body. Somebody always sat with the body before a funeral. It was mountain tradition.

I ran to the pulpit and placed the book where Pastor kept one of his Bibles. Now I could get home and in bed. But no, oh no, that burying box drew me to it, pulled me like it had hands and arms. I ran my fingers over the smooth wood. The lid squeaked. Arleen looked like she was hurting with her mouth drawn up. Death caught her in the middle of a horrible pain. In the curve of her arm was a tiny blue baby boy. Smaller than one of Faith's old baby dolls.

"This was a mean thing to do," I whispered to the Jesus hanging on a little gold cross.

"It's not his fault." A girl's voice spoke out of the shadows. "Don't go blaming the wrong one."

I dropped that lid. The sound echoed through the dark, causing the gas flames to jump. I ran out of that church without looking back. I never did tell a soul about hearing that voice, not Will or nobody.

THEY BURIED ARLEEN and that baby of hers the next day while I set the dining room table in the main house. Each fork was put in the right place. That big old fancy dinner for people who loved plain and simple seemed silly. The sky turned black like a storm was coming. The mountain was mourning Arleen Brown, a simple mountain girl. Her death brought a push of wind that started and never stopped. A whisper scooted through the air. *"My story ain't been told."*

BY THE TIME THAT BIG HAILSTORM found Black Mountain, Will had been gone almost three weeks. Me, I was wishing I could go to school like other kids, make some friends, learn to read better. But there weren't no colored schools for miles. Nada ordered me to sit on the front porch of our cabin while she gathered clothes from the line. I'd been underfoot and no help that whole day. The pure white sheets from the main house snapped in the hot wind. Nada wrestled to free the clothes before the rain let loose, and it didn't take a smart person to see the bottom would drop out any second. One long, angry black cloud stretched as far as I could see across the sky. The air turned thick and sticky, and the light became a yellow-green. On the edge of the woods stood a woman bent over hobbling along, wearing a dress of blue ticking that was long to the ground. "Get up from there, silly girl!" She pulled a cane out from behind her back and waved it. What had I gone and done now?

"Go in that there house!" The woman narrowed her eyes, and when I didn't move, she bared her sharp witch's teeth at me.

I jumped to my feet, thinking I might cut across the porch and head for Nada, but then I thought better of it. Just as I ducked in the cabin, a flash of purple light splintered the wooden boards where I had been. Lord be, I thought I'd never hear again. I thought I was dead. The noise shook the cabin under my feet, and a charred hole opened smelling of a crackling fire. I was sure the cabin would burn down to the ground with me in it.

"Shelly!" Nada screamed, and then she ran faster than I'd seen her run. She'd been right slow and quiet since Will left. Lordy, that woman who always bossed the world had lost her footing, worse than when Daddy was killed in a moonshine deal gone bad.

"Nada."

She ran up the steps, stared at the hole, and came to me. Her look stayed on me for the longest, like she was counting all my fingers and toes. "I do believe you be the luckiest little girl I know." Now, Nada didn't cotton to Pastor's god. She believed mostly in hoodoo, with a little Jesus nailed to the cross on the side. She wanted no part of a god that made a person rant and rave like Pastor was known to do when he was on a roll. But that afternoon she looked at the sky and said, "Thank you, Lord God, for my girl."

Me, I believed in God and figured Pastor had just conjured him a bad spirit to listen to. He was always talking about souls being crushed for their sins and all. God didn't crush souls. He loved them. Anyway, Pastor never knew a thing about Nada's gifts. He wouldn't have tolerated any magic in his house, but Mrs. Dobbins—now, she be a different story—liked the spells Nada conjured. They made a fine pair, Nada and Mrs. Dobbins. Nada always said hoodoo wasn't about good or bad magic. It was about working out your own life, the story we live on this earth. That kind of story was powerful no matter if it involved money, health, or sweet, sweet love. Nada's magic could bring bad on folks who were bad and good on those that walked the right path, but her spells couldn't fix everything 'cause Will was gone, and nothing, nothing Nada tried brought him back.

"No, ma'am. Ain't luck or God that saved me. A scary woman with sharp teeth told me to get." I was ten, almost eleven, and had a habit of sucking two fingers when something on my mind went to worrying me silly. I slurped and pointed at the woman still standing near the porch. The woman turned and hobbled back to the woods.

Nada took a breath like she might tell me I was fibbing. The sky turned pure green. "You seen a spirit, Shelly." The words tingled in the air. "She be a person that passed on."

Now, that ain't what I wanted to hear, but it told me why the old woman was wearing clothes from a long time ago. I'd always saw me plenty of people—strange and a little off to look at. Only Will and me could see these folks, but he told me they was nightmares and not to worry over them. So, I never thought on them too much until he wasn't there no more.

"A soul without her body. They can look just the same as you and me." Nada spoke softer.

My slurping got louder. "A haint." I spit the words out around them two favorite fingers of mine.

"She saved you, Shelly. That means she's been with you for a while. See, these spirits can be attached to you without your knowing. You been seeing ghosts?"

"I don't know," I whispered.

"You best act grateful. She's probably one of your daddy's peoples. They lived all over this mountain at one time." Nada rubbed my cheek like I might just be something real special. Then she pulled soft-like on my two fingers. "Don't be fretting. Be thankful. You be way too old for this sucking mess." She looked at my fingers. "See there"—she pointed to dark spots on my skin—"you be leaving marks. Ten is nearly grown, child."

I hugged her tight like some kind of dern old baby and buried my face into her bosoms. The smell of talc powder mixed with spices from the supper cooking on the stove in the main house eased me. In that place, I was grateful. Time, the storm, everything, stood completely still like we didn't have nothing to worry on.

"You got sight." Nada sounded proud.

So if I had this so-called gift, Will did too, and since we both had different daddies, that meant we got our abilities from Nada and I liked that part.

"Sight be the best gift of all. You got to show it respect. You'll find a place to rest in it. I promise." I almost believed her sweet words as I played with the loose threads on her white work blouse. I guessed maybe I'd known for a while this mess was with me.

"Amanda!" That hateful Faith Dobbins ran toward the cabin. Her white dress blew in the wind.

Just that week while Faith was downstairs in the front room visiting with her mama's company, I went upstairs to straighten her bed and collect the dirty clothes for washing. That's when I slid that white lacy dress right over my head like some kind of dumb fool. I don't know what got into me. It was way too big, but for the longest time, I stood hungering after the thing. What in the world could a colored girl do in such a dress? I took me a deep breath and moved in front of the long looking glass. Lordy be, what a poor sight stared back at me! Some old dark-skinned girl dressed in lace with nappy hair that couldn't be tamed, much less combed decent. Nothing would ever change who I was. I studied the girl a minute more. The last person in the world I wanted to be was Faith Dobbins. I yanked on that dress, and a button popped off. For a minute I got scared, but then I figured I'd be the one to sew it back on, anyway. "No more of this mess," I told myself. "You be just fine like you are. Amen." Then I got on my hands and knees and looked under the bed. There it was. Not the button, but Nada's sewing basket, the one that belonged to my great-grandmama. Nada had hunted for it since Will left. I stood up and brushed off. I figured I had me something to tell if Faith started whining around about the dress.

And there she was running to Nada like she be hers instead of mine. She tumbled down the grassy hill that separated her world from mine and got back up. She ran so hard I could have sworn the devil was licking her heels. Hate be a strong word, but Lord, I hated Faith Dobbins all the way down to her old lacy doll babies lined up against the pillows on her bed. All I ever had was corncob toys and blisters on my hands from scrubbing those fancy clothes on the washboard out back of our cabin. Faith had everything a girl ever dreamed of. Everything but my Nada.

The sky turned pitch-black. She scrambled up on the porch with us. Nada pushed me from her. "Miss Faith, get over here."

Faith buried her face in my Nada's neck. Stupid old cow.

"What you thinking, leaving your mama and heading over here in this weather?" Nada asked.

"Who did this?" Faith looked into the burned-out place on the porch. I wanted to rip out one of her yellow curls by the root. Nada said she was one of the rare white folks who could tolerate sun without burning. Mrs. Dobbins only clicked her tongue at Nada and would yell to Faith to cover her arms and wear a hat. Ladies did not allow their skin to turn brown. My skin being a fine shade of brown let me have all the time I wanted outside.

"A bolt of lightning came out of the heavens and nearly hit my baby. Then what would I have done? All my children would be gone."

I could have pinched Nada for calling me a baby in front of Faith.

"Your daddy would say someone on this mountain made God angry," Nada said.

Faith clicked her tongue like some grown woman. "Daddy would say it was Shelly who did the bad thing. Mama says God gets blamed for way too much that people bring on themselves." She looked at me with that smirky smile of hers. She thought she was grown at fifteen and tried to boss me as much as she could.

"I wish your mama could act as sensible as she sounds sometimes." Nada shook her head. Her look landed on me. She was telling me to keep my mouth closed and to quit having such hateful thoughts about Miss Faith. And she told me not to say a word about my sight or the haint that saved me. She kept that stare on me long enough to know I got her message loud and clear, then patted Faith's ugly, prissy head like she be a puppy. Only Nada and me could talk without speaking. It was our secret.

I was Nada's treasure, better than Will. 'Cause I was still here. Daddy's own flesh and blood, not that that counted for much. I was Nada's reason to keep working for folks like Pastor and Mrs. Dobbins.

Without warning, hail poured down, bouncing off the ground.

Maude Tuggle

THE MORNING ARLEEN DIED, I sat on my porch looking at the mountains. A storm brewed in the air, but there was no physical proof. It was one of those rare days when I could see forever with no mist or clouds. If I were a painter, I would have painted the mountains, layered one row after another. No, the storm was more of a feeling. I was Black Mountain's granny woman in the days when granny women were still sought out and respected. My mama was a granny woman, and so was Grandmama, who was part Cherokee. I was born right there on the mountain, but no one would have guessed. Plain and simple with a head filled with science, thanks to Mama. No spells, tales, and omens for her. After the Spanish Flu came in 1918, Mama finished my education at home. I turned into a bookworm. By the time I was twenty, I had two options: leave the mountain or follow in Mama and Grandmama's footsteps. I chose the life of a granny woman just as the mountain picked me for the job. I knew silly things like how Cherokee believed a rock was alive and could give a person wisdom. Up until that hot, still morning three weeks before the storm, I hadn't lost one soul to sickness, accident, or birth complications. But all that was to change.

One of the Brown twins—I wasn't sure if it was Robert or Andy—ran up the path. "Miss Tuggle, can you come?" This twin pulled off his cap and twisted it in his hands. "Sister's having her baby." He knocked at the dirt with his worn shoe. "Ma said we ain't got a thing to give you right now."

"You tell your mother I'll be right over and not to worry about payment. Babies have to come into this world on their own time. This one is coming a bit early." I tried my best to hide the worn-out feeling creeping into my voice. "I'll be right behind you. Which one are you, anyway?"

This won a sparkling smile. "I'm Andy, ma'am."

"You boys look too much alike." I stood. "Go on. Tell your mother I'm on the way."

He nodded and took off like the devil chased him.

I decided to walk, rather than drive or pull Sweet Gay, my gelding, out of his pasture. It was no telling how long I'd be with Arleen before the baby came. Babies had a way of doing what they pleased, and rushing around like a chicken with its head chopped off wouldn't get me any closer to delivery. It's always a humbling moment when a new soul enters the human race. This is a holy time, a still space, a wrinkle. For a few startling seconds, it's as if the spirit lags behind, dragging her feet rather than entering a place full of struggle and strife. I saw this in the tiny faces. That need to just remain pure and at peace. But their souls always caught up with the body, always. And I'd seen my share of new babies being born.

I took Mama's old doctor bag, black worn leather with cracks here and there. The clasp had broken years ago. Inside were herbs and powders for pain, a needle and thread, a stethoscope I ordered from Boston, and the hook tool—if a baby didn't make it, I would have to remove the poor little soul. I hated keeping the instrument with me. The others on the mountain would have said its very presence brought bad luck. But being a midwife or granny woman wasn't about luck or superstition. It was about skill. Arleen was frowned upon for having a baby out of wedlock. Folks didn't talk about the circumstances, but their disapproval, the belief she brought a grave sin on her family, floated in the air. Those on the mountain didn't mean harm. But these beliefs cut into the very core, bringing judgment to settle on the surface.

ARLEEN WAS IN FULL LABOR and pushing when I got there.

"That baby is way too early, Maude." May Brown frowned.

Mama always told me not to promise something I couldn't deliver and to give thought to every comment before I made it. So with these lessons in mind, I only nodded. Arleen was propped in her parents' old rope bed, looking too much like a young child. Her stomach was tight enough to pop. She clinched her fists as a pain swept over her like an old-time baptism in Dragonfly River.

"This baby is in a hurry." I smiled.

"I'm worried, Maude." May's hair fell loose from her always-neat knot.

"Babies will do what they are going to do, May." I touched her shoulder. "You go gather some clean sheets."

"Look after my girl." Her words were calm but stern.

I nodded. That simple. I nodded as if I were the one who decided the fate of others.

Arleen let out a war whoop of a scream.

"We're going to work together, Arleen."

She twisted her head and looked directly in my eyes. "I don't want to die."

Something cold and unfamiliar settled into my bones. "You're not going to die." The mountain would have called this an omen.

A gold cross, with a tiny diamond in the middle, sparkled at her throat. Where would Arleen get such an expensive piece of jewelry?

Arleen pulled me close and said in a hushed voice, "I didn't want no baby. I didn't cause it. Tell everyone when I'm gone that he did this to me. He tricked me. I didn't have one bit of say."

The terrible confession pushed my breakfast up in my throat. I closed my eyes and concentrated. The baby had to come into the world safe. It was my job to make sure it was healthy. I couldn't listen to stories.

The sheets turned a deep red in one crystal-clear moment. Arleen cried out in such pain I nearly jumped out of my skin. "Stay with me, Arleen! We have to get this baby here." I pulled the top sheet away, and blood smeared my palm.

"He did this to me," she whispered.

Red was everywhere. Worse than when I treated Marvin Blank for his chain saw accident. "May!" I had to save Arleen.

"I hate him, Miss Tuggle, and that be a sin." Her eyes were dull.

"You listen to me. You're going to be fine. I've never lost a mother."

Arleen watched something beyond me. "He did this to me." She groped her hand in front of her like she was reaching for a person, but no one was there. I took her hand, a link, a braid. Arleen went limp.

"Dear Lord, God!" May dropped the fresh sheets on the floor and fell to her knees by the bed.

"I have to get this baby here." I let go of Arleen's hand.

The baby's shoulders were out. I pulled, and he landed in my hands, lifeless and blue. I whacked his bottom. "Come to me!" I screamed for his soul. "Breathe, do you hear me? Breathe!" I looked into his tiny face. His weight was nothing in my hands. "Please." I used two fingers to clear his mouth. Nothing.

"Give him to me, Maude. Let him go." May took the baby from my grasp, tears running down her cheeks. "He is a beauty, just like his mama."

My hands shook so bad I clasped them in my lap. "I'm so sorry." That's the only three words I could manage.

My knees went weak, and the room turned hot. "I have to step outside." Arleen's life was over, and somehow I didn't prevent this from happening. Somehow all my experience failed me.

The hot, sticky air hit me full force. Three steps from the front porch I lost the contents of my stomach. I collapsed on the grass and folded my knees into my chest.

Later a shadow fell over me. "Miss Tuggle." It was one of the twins. The sun hovered over the treetops. Soon the orange and pink of the day's end would swish across the sky.

"Yes."

"Mama wants to know if you'll come sit with her for a while. She's called Pastor and wants you to be with her when he comes."

I sat up knowing I looked like a fool out in the front yard, but Arleen's brother didn't seem to care.

"Yes, of course." I thought of the cross. "Where did Arleen get the necklace she was wearing?"

The twin shrugged. "Don't know, Miss Tuggle. Mama asked after it too, but Arleen never gave a good answer."

I HEARD THE ESTEEMED PASTOR before I saw his face. "May, this is God's will." But his normally loud know-it-all attitude trembled slightly. Funny how he wrote off this tragedy on God. "I know it's hard." His words were lifeless like a frozen tree in the winter.

The man made me insane. I left Arleen's body wrapped in fresh, clean sheets and went into the front room. Pastor Dobbins gave me a hard look but kept speaking.

"Arleen was having a bastard child, May. This is God's judgment on her soul."

Those lies twisted around me. "May, I need to talk to you about Arleen's last words." I hadn't intended on repeating Arleen's story, but something had to be said to counteract the horrible opinions of that man.

"What did she say, Sister Tuggle? I'm sure May wants me to hear this too."

"I'm not your sister, Pastor Dobbins. I'm not even a member of your church." I touched May's shoulder. "Could we talk alone? Then you can tell anyone you want. I'm sure Pastor won't mind waiting on the porch."

His face clouded. "I'll step out." But he gave me a look to kill before he left.

May slumped down into a rocker.

I squatted in front of her. "Arleen told me she was forced to have relations with the father of the baby. She didn't sleep with him on her own free will."

May looked at me with a spark of life in her eyes. The mountain washed away so many good women with burdens way too big to carry. "Who was this man? I should have known. I should have."

I tasted the name that came to me. It was gritty and refused to be swallowed. I had no proof. Only my gut. He was a man I hated just because of his judgments. That was no reason to believe he would commit a crime. "I don't know. She didn't get a chance to tell me."

A board creaked on the porch.

"Tell Pastor what Arleen said. Maybe he won't think she's damned anymore." May stared out the window.

"Pastor doesn't get to decide who is damned and who isn't. Only God has that say-so, and he knows the truth. Not my truth or yours or even our good pastor's outside. May, Arleen was a good girl."

She turned to me and took my hand. "But Pastor belongs to God, so he knows what is right and wrong."

I CROSSED THE MEADOW behind the cabin headed home to find some sleep, to put all the thoughts racing in my head to rest. That hot wind pushed me along. Each step was quicker than the last. Zach Walters came into my mind. He was Asheville's sheriff and an old friend. I guess one could say we had been an item. Many gossiped that we were romantically involved. But that wasn't so. I just couldn't allow myself to be serious. My life was on the mountain as a granny woman. His was in Asheville. Those two worlds would not come together without someone giving up what they loved most of all, but I missed our once-a-week dinners. In that moment, I wanted to talk with him as a friend.

The lantern provided a circle of light around me. The stars shone in the sky. My lantern lit her face, a Negro girl. "You got to pay attention. You be messing with fire, ma'am." Then she was gone.

"Who are you? What do you want? Is this about Arleen?" The air tingled with the sound of wind in the trees. I hurried through the yard. My heart beat in my ears, and I had a great urge to run through the darkness before something touched my ankles. The girl looked real enough. Now I was seeing the mountain haints that I refused to believe existed. I smiled for the first time since Arleen passed.

THE HOT WIND BLEW for three weeks without stopping. All the folks on the mountain saw it as an omen, something bad coming our way. I didn't believe in omens, but even so, the wind unnerved me. Then one afternoon a big black cloud came rolling over the valley right at us. I heard the hail—a pelting sound that approached through the woods—before the blinding thickness took over, surrounding my cabin. I sat at my mother's desk, under my bedroom window, writing about the most recent baby I caught, but became distracted by the thought of Faith Dobbins, who I had seen earlier in Daniels Cemetery. She was an odd young woman, and that was exactly why I liked her so much. She reminded me of how different I was at that age: all arms and legs, inside my own thoughts while others looked for husbands, made their own clothes, and cooked.

The sound of the ice vibrated on the tin roof, straight into my whole body, and all the way down into my fingers. This new addition to the house grated on my every nerve no matter the weather. It was an eyesore, to say the least. The glaring brightness on a sunny day announced to all the mountain my cabin had a brand-new roof. The horrible tin affair came to me as payment for delivering the Hawkinses' baby just as my old faithful roof threatened to fall in. The Hawkinses' baby daughter was one of those infants who took her sweet time coming into the world, all red-faced and screaming when she finally arrived. So, Mr. Hawkins felt obligated to do something more than give me fresh eggs for a month. I would have preferred the eggs.

The hail made such a racket I wondered if the tin would hold, half-way wished it wouldn't. Fall storms could blow up out of nowhere with a vengeance. But I'd felt this one coming since the day Arleen gave birth and died. And I wasn't one to believe in such things. The folks on the mountain were a peculiar lot and lived their lives around superstitions like planting by the signs—even Mama took the planting signs serious—but not me. I never believed in the good people's mountain magic or the punishment issued by their god. This storm was a sign. I just had no idea for what.

My plants would be pounded by the ice, but they were hardy. Some like lemon balm and yellow dock Grandmama planted when she was young and first beginning her practice. Herbs were my tools like a hammer and nails completed a carpenter. At barely thirty-five, I knew more about the human body and what made it work than some doctors with their fancy degrees. But as happy as I was, I still dreamed of going to medical school. Impossible, so I made it a practice to read every modern medicine book I could find. Some I ordered all the way from Boston and New York City. I always saw a much wider picture than just my mountain. Right before Mama died, she urged me to move away, go to a city, find a different kind of life. Caring for the sick was a selfless practice that ran a person into the ground. But it was too late by then. The time for me to leave had come and gone. Healing was my husband, my good marriage. It gave me a reason to move through life. It was my expression of love, a love that resided in the valleys, rivers, and the tall spruces that scrubbed the sky. On Black Mountain I saw what was coming at me, except for the day the storm came rolling in on us. Something dark was hidden in the tingle of electricity, something that had been with us for a few weeks but we just ignored.

The hail lasted for about five minutes and then stopped as suddenly as it began. In the pause of complete silence, I released a breath I didn't even know I had been holding. "Enough of that," I whispered to the emptiness. The sound of a train rushing down some invisible track came straight for the cabin. The leaves were motionless. Sweet Gay, my gelding, was pushed against the barn wall as if he expected to be run over.

The tops of the maples, oaks, and spruces began to wave in a frenzy. Whole trees popped in half. Snap, snap, snap. Still I stood watching, hypnotized. A large limb hit the porch, and I shot out the back door, fighting the wind as I ran. The pump house roof flew over my head and smashed into a large oak tree at the edge of the woods. I pulled open the root cellar doors out back of the cabin and entered the dark coolness, safety.

The doors shuddered so hard I was sure they'd take flight. The sound of metal against metal came from every direction. The smell of fresh-cut wood filled my lungs. A sickening pressure sat in the air. All went quiet, and then rain beat on the doors. Glass shattered somewhere as I sat with my back against the canned tomatoes, squash, and beans put up for winter. Then suddenly the rain stopped and a bird sounded in the woods.

The door didn't give. I shoved my shoulder against it and pushed with all my might. By gosh, I wouldn't be stuck in the cellar. It opened. A large limb had fallen across the doors. Sun peeked in and out of the gray clouds. The air was cooler. The wind was gone. Sweet Gay still stood against the barn, safe. Metal glittered in the sunlight from atop some of the untouched trees. The hideous new tin roof had been peeled back and torn away. A long, crazy laugh escaped into the air. But there was no time to lose my mind. Someone might be hurt. I was the granny woman. This was the life I had chosen freely, caring for the mountain's people.

Armetta Lolly

ME AND PASTOR CHARLES DOBBINS was stuck to each other from the first day he stepped foot on this mountain. I was that little whisper in his ear just as he fell off to sleep, letting down his fight. I was the moan in the wind, the chill on a hot day. I was his lifelong worry. I wasn't making every move he made because I thought highly of him. He was a devil walking around in a human body, and I'm sad to say he was considered a man of God by some. His heart was easy to read 'cause the Dobbins family had a dark streak that ran way on back to the time when I lived and breathed.

There I was in Pastor's church when the bad storm hit. He was standing in front of the big gold cross that hung on the brown wall behind the pulpit. He'd been there all morning while that girl of his wandered around the graveyard like that be the place for a fifteen-year-old. He didn't even notice. He wasn't fooling most on the mountain, even if they acted dumb. Them bruises and so-called accidents that cursed the Dobbins women proved there wasn't no God in him, but the holy churchgoing folks in the congregation never said a word. They could have been scared of him and for good reason, 'cause he had a way of punishing those who stepped out against him. Take what happened to Dig Wilson three farms over. He pointed out Pastor was spending the church fund on his new car. Wasn't long after that Dig's whole family got real sick, nearly died. Pastor claimed right from the pulpit that God had given Dig and his family just what they deserved for lying, that they was proof of the wrath of God. What he didn't tell was how he poisoned their well water. Them churchgoers had paid in a big way for playing dumb, not just Dig's family, but the whole lot of them. They was so stupid they hadn't figured a thing out. Yet.

The sky broke open and hail pounded the roof. And even me, who had been dead longer than this man had been alive, got a little itchy to run. Pastor's eyes got big and his hands went to shaking and he stared at the ceiling with them big blue eyes of his like he half expected the thing to open and God's mighty hand to reach in after him.

"God in Heaven. Is this my punishment? Am I to witness your fire and brimstone?"

Always he was searching out some punishment from God. I never bothered telling him that God didn't have to do too much of that business 'cause folks was always sticking their own big feet right smack in the middle of the biggest troubles in the world. We was our own worst enemies.

The hail covered the grass and made me think of snow. I sure did miss snow. Since I died, I could only see it, not smell it. There wasn't nothing in the whole world better than the scent of snow. Daddy used to tell me I was pure crazy. That snow couldn't smell. But Mama would shoo him away and tell him to let me be with my dreams. But it was more than a dream. Snow smelled like those soft peppermint sticks that melted in my mouth on Christmas morning. One fine pink striped stick of sugar.

"Take me off this earth! I can't live on this godforsaken mountain anymore. I need to live a new life," he cried out.

Right then—like God was listening to him—the hail stopped. Just stopped. What came next was a black stillness. The kind that fills up a space when a soul leaves a body. I squeezed my eyes shut, as if a haint could die again. Somewhere way off came the sound of a steam train. Crack, crack, crack. Wood splitting along with a rumbling that came straight from the pit of Hell. It was bubbling over into the living world. My good man of God took him a dive right under the first pew in the women's amen corner and stretched out on his stomach. Lord Jesus, if only his church could have seen him. Time tiptoed and Pastor stayed in his safe place. His breath went from fast to slow to fast again. He was thinking on being a boy and hiding from his daddy under a bed. I wasn't fond of knowing that man's thoughts, but there wasn't nothing I could do about it.

Rain beat against the walls of the church, a decent church if not for pastors like him. Windows dripped and then poured. Still he kept out of sight in the dark room. No one had ever bothered to give the walls a good whitewash, and that made for a gloomy place.

"My retribution is too great!" he cried.

This was one big word, but I figured he was going on about what God expected of him as a man. The rain came to a stop. And there we were, quiet, listening. Not much time went by before the sound of a wagon crunched on the path outside. Someone had come to ring the bell. The same bell tolled seventeen times for me. Me, a colored girl from Ella Creek. That was because Amelia wanted to say good-bye. Otherwise a colored girl's death on this mountain would have gone unnoticed.

Pastor crawled out from under his pew and brushed off his pants.

Mr. Harkin removed his hat and walked in the front door. He bowed his head and mumbled some words.

Since I died, sometimes I could see a person's story, the real one, not the one made up in their heads. Mr. Harkin had lost his daughter to murder—except he didn't know it was murder; instead, he thought she got turned around in the woods—and he rang the bell himself that day. I shook off the vision. At least the daughter's murderer would die, be killed in a bad way that he deserved, by his wife. She would get clean away.

Mr. Harkin reached for a rope dangling from the opening in the ceiling.

Pastor stepped into the aisle where there was some light. "Peal Harkin."

"Pastor." Mr. Harkin gave him a right irritated look. "You should let your whereabouts be known."

Pastor frowned. "Where else would a good pastor be? Who was hurt?"

"Loop Wilkins was in his field." Loop was a mean drunk that beat his poor wife all the time. The Lord only knew the last time he stepped foot in a church. But he could have been the most honest person on that mountain, seeing how he let everyone know just who he was. "He's dead. The storm picked him and his tractor up and turned them over. He was crushed." Mr. Harkin's cheeks were pink from hurrying. "Took his head right off. Mary, his missus, found him."

"Anybody else?" Pastor came closer so his face could be seen clearly. There was them wishes about Mrs. Dobbins dying again. He looked right at me. Sometimes I was sure he could see me, wished he could. He needed to know that nothing he did was ever truly hidden.

"Some hurt. Maude is headed to your house. You best be on your way."

If the locals knew what I'd seen walk across Pastor's face, they'd run him off the mountain, scared or not. A black, oily smoke gathered over his head and shot through the room like a living thing. The desire be powerful. Lord, someone needed to put a stop to him before he did some real harm. But nobody knew my story. If I could find the right person—one that could see and hear me—all this mess could be stopped before it got way out of hand. That white girl who died knew part of my story, but she didn't get to tell. She was coming with a story of her own, and together we were going to stop this terrible meanness. This I knew down to the bottom of my toes. 'Cause what's right is right. And us two both was looking to make better of our time on earth before we moved on.

Faith Dobbins

WHEN A GIRL LOSES SOMEONE they love most, someone who knows them inside and out, something goes missing inside her soul. That is the girl I had become the summer of the hailstorm, the summer Will left. A large square of silk, folded small and pushed down the front of my dress, my second skin, soft and smooth, gave me a promise, an escape. The crayons that Miss Tuggle gave me, dark green and black, were in the sides of my slippers.

"Where are you off to?" Mama stood at the kitchen window with her back to me.

"Just going to take a walk in the woods," I replied. I opened the back door and slipped out before she tried to stop me. I hadn't been in the woods since Will left, but Mama didn't notice this. That summer she spent most of her time staring at our side of the mountain, as if it spoke to her in a voice that only she could hear.

"Watch the sky. It feels like a storm."

And it did, a bad storm; one that had been brewing for three weeks. The day Will left—and his last words, his request—was something I pushed out of my head each and every time an image showed up. My whole world collided with the unthinkable and spun out of control. Gone. He was gone.

The day he left, I stole the sewing basket from Amanda's front room. Will's great-grandmother, who was a house slave on a big plantation in Louisiana, not far from where I was born, had come to me in a dream. She told me the basket was mine to use. Amanda told the story of how her grandmother was the best seamstress and hoodoo woman in New Orleans. I had heard her tell this so much, I longed for it to be part of my history. So me, a nearly grown white girl, soaked in grief over a colored boy leaving, stole her colored maid's sewing basket. Amanda never took the basket from its place under the black ladder-back chair near the fireplace, the very chair her grandmother sat in to sew clothes. When Amanda had sewing to do, she used Mama's kit. So, while she worked in her garden out back of the cabin, not even knowing that Will had left for good, I walked in her door and took the story as my own. I hid the basket under my bed, way underneath, where only a young child would think to look.

I had never pushed a needle through cloth, but when I opened the basket and touched a pale-green loop of thread, I saw the woods the way Will loved them, lush, soft, wet with a fresh rain. I ached to create something of my own. At first I used old clothes I'd planned to put in the ragbag. I cut them into squares and stitched them together in a nine patch I'd seen the ladies on the mountain sew at their quilting bees. In and out, in and out, the needle slid through the fabric. The cloth gave off little sounds that could be heard in the silence. Spiders spun webs like stitches in a fine quilt. Then, one day I found the silk deep in the back of Mama's old wardrobe like she had planned on making something special. Mama, of all people.

When I wasn't sewing in my room with the door locked—that

pesky Shelly was always knocking and yelling to come in and clean—I walked through the graveyard. The markers reminded me of quilts, the beautiful flower borders and intricate details chiseled in the granite, no marble there. Families on the mountain worked hard with little to show for their effort. But still they managed to create art in their own way. All I had was a blank length of silk and a closet full of new clothes but nothing to honor my existence. In the cemetery a peace settled over the graves. Thoughts came to me clear and crisp. This was my place.

So the morning of the bad storm, I was in search of a special headstone. Just the right one. Miss Tuggle told me that if I covered the stones with paper and used a crayon, I could take the design for my own. Only Miss Tuggle would know something like that. She was so smart. If I had a friend on that stupid mountain, it was her. I told her mostly everything, even how I ached for Will after he left. But some secrets were never meant to be told, so they festered inside like an infected cut on a finger.

The stone chose me, pulled me there. A new stone. August 25, 1935. Fifteen years old. Fancier than any of the others even though the Browns were one of the poorest families on the mountain. I know this because their daughter took my hand-me-downs. The polished carving read: ARLEEN, A DAUGHTER AND MOTHER. TOO YOUNG. The silk draped over the stone like an A-line skirt fitted to Mama's body. I smoothed the wrinkles away and held the cloth with one hand. The dark-green crayon moved over the fabric easier than I thought. The words formed in the scribbles. Curly leaves, flowers, and a hand holding a broken chain link. What could that mean? That Arleen was a link in the world's chain and God broke her away? I bore down harder. Bits of crayon flew through the air and it broke. My fingernails ran across the hard surface, and one tore to the quick. I pulled my hand away in time to keep the blood from dripping on the silk.

The sky turned yellowish-green. Something was in the air. A loud clap of thunder shook the ground and I jumped to my feet. My head spun, but I ran, ran so hard a stitch of pain took my breath. The smell of burnt wood nearly knocked me down as I got closer to Amanda's cabin. Was she okay? I reached the porch just in time and flew into Amanda's arms like some little kid. The sky let go of the ice.

As soon as the hail stopped, Mama came running across the yard with a scream caught in the expression on her face. "Amanda! Do you have Faith?" Like I was a little girl.

Amanda pulled both Shelly and me to the steps. "You be losing your mind, Mrs. Dobbins. You know she either be with me or you."

"Go to the root cellar! This is a bad one. I grew up with twisters." Mama stopped in front of us just as the sound of a train barreling toward us shook me to the bottom of my feet.

"Run!" Amanda screamed. The trees swayed in a frenzy. Mama ran in front of us to the root cellar door. She jerked on it over and over like a crazy person, but the thing was stuck fast.

"There she be, Nada." Shelly pulled at Amanda's arm and pointed to the woods.

An old woman leaned on her cane like she wasn't afraid of the storm at all. She was odd and out of place. Almost like a dream.

"The woman is pointing for us to go over there."

The woman swung her cane in the direction of the trees.

Amanda herded us to the spot where the cane was pointed. "Best be coming with us, Mrs. Dobbins. Now!"

Mama ran after us. "You're going to get us killed, Amanda."

"In the hole," Amanda ordered. Shelly and I ran past the old woman and jumped into a deep ditch made by an uprooted oak. I held Shelly's hand tight even though she tried to pull it away. I didn't care whether she was hurt or not.

Mama and Amanda locked their fingers together in one solid link and put their bodies on top of ours. Their weight took my breath away. The wind turned loud. Trees began cracking and popping all around us, and then, in a rush of sound, one fell on us. When the storm passed, Amanda and Mama still held each other's hands. That's when I thought of my silk and crayons. Ruined.

"My foot hurts something horrible, Amanda," Mama said in a whisper.

"You two got to help push this limb off of Mrs. Dobbins. It be on her leg."

Me, Shelly, and Amanda shoved as hard as we could, and it rolled out of the way. I crawled out of the hole more than a little stunned to be alive.

Miss Tuggle rode into the yard on her horse. "You got hit hard. Is everyone all right?" She held her doctor bag on her lap.

"My mama is hurt!" I yelled.

She swung off her horse in one smooth motion, like a dancer. "I saw you at Daniels Cemetery just before the storm moved in. I'm glad you made it home." Her long, dark hair hung around her shoulders.

Daddy was a shadow behind her, making his way toward us.

Mama allowed Amanda to hoist her from the hole. "We're so thankful. If not for our Amanda, we'd be dead." Mama's face was scrunched in pain.

Shelly crawled out last, looking so much like Amanda it made me sick. She wasn't a bit afraid. That trait she got from Will.

"Mrs. Dobbins has a bad broke ankle, ma'am." Amanda held on to Mama, and I grabbed Mama's other arm.

"Let's sit her down over here." Miss Tuggle frowned. Mama's ankle was a horrible shade of purple, and her whole foot dangled in an odd way.

"Don't you think she needs attention now?" Daddy touched Miss Tuggle's shoulder.

She flinched and moved away. "I'm trying to give her just that."

"But the ground?" Daddy cut a sideways look at me like I had disappointed him. My daddy was the handsomest man on the mountain. But this didn't seem to impress Miss Tuggle in the least.

"I need to give your wife some medical attention, Pastor Dobbins. It seems to me your home took quite a hit." She nodded at the house.

I looked at it for the first time. Part of the roof was missing, and a tree had cut down the middle.

"This is the safest place for now. Do you want me to look at her ankle or stand here and argue?" Miss Tuggle stared Daddy down.

A vacant look washed over Mama's face. "My mother died one year after I married Charles. Only two months before Faith was born. Isn't that right, Amanda?"

Miss Tuggle looked directly at Amanda. "Did she hit her head?"

"A big limb fell in the hole on us. She got the worst. Can't say if she hit her head. It's a wonder we lived." Amanda looked at me and then at Shelly.

"Why didn't you take Lydia to the root cellar?" Daddy's voice had that mean edge.

"Charles wouldn't let me go to my mother's funeral. Said we lived too far away. Said I shouldn't travel. I never got to say good-bye. I could have taken a train. Charles sat on his high and mighty throne like he was someone pure and holy. But he's not, not after Georgia." Mama looked at Daddy. "We arrived at Black Mountain, North Carolina by way of Georgia. Didn't we?"

"Shut up, Lydia." Daddy looked at Miss Tuggle. "She's talking out of her mind."

Miss Tuggle knelt down in front of Mama. "I'd like you to go down the mountain to Asheville. This break is too bad to be treated by me. You need a hospital."

Here was an adult admitting she didn't know everything.

"He should have let me go," Mama continued. "I would have stayed, and then nothing, nothing would have happened. My life would have turned out better." Her words slurred, and then she slid very lady-like onto her side.

"Shut up, Lydia!" Daddy yelled.

"You shut up!" I stood as tall as I could, balling my fingers into fists.

Miss Tuggle touched my shoulder. "I need you to go to the Connors' cabin. Tell Mr. Connor you need his truck. Tell him to come quick." She waited a second. "Don't worry. Pain makes people talk out of their heads. Your mama will be fine."

I looked at my father, and wished I were a man. If I were, I'd kill him. Men were strong and could justify the taking of a life. But I was a fifteen-year-old girl, who missed a colored boy so bad she was going crazy a little at a time.

MAMA HAD TO STAY in the hospital down in Asheville. I refused to leave her side. Amanda told me to go on home with Daddy and she'd stay, but I only gave her a mean look. "My mama needs me." I nearly spit the words at her.

Amanda never seemed a bit bothered. "I'm going home to Shelly, then. That is, if you don't need me."

Of course I needed her and she probably knew it, but Shelly needed her worse, being all alone up there. "How you getting home?"

"Miss Tuggle. She said I could ride with her." Her face was soft, and I wanted nothing more than to place my head on her shoulder.

I nodded and rubbed Mama's hand. She was sound asleep. "Maybe she can come home tomorrow." I looked at the cast on her foot.

"Maybe, child." Amanda touched her fingertips against my shoulder. "I'll be back with your daddy tomorrow."

I nodded. Divided. I was the child in the Bible the two women fought to keep so bad that the judge decided the baby needed to be cut in half for each woman. I was two halves. "She'll get better tonight."

"Yes, ma'am, she will." And Amanda was gone out the door, but not before she ran her fingers through my hair one time.

MAMA WOKE THAT NIGHT, stroking my hair where I fell asleep with my head on the bed. "Faith, get up here beside me."

In my sleepy state, I didn't pretend to be too old to cuddle to my mama. My body fit right next to hers. Her eyes were clear. "You're going to be okay."

"Yes, sweetie. I'm touched you stayed," she whispered.

"I couldn't leave you alone."

"Amanda would have stayed."

I shrugged. "Shelly would have been by herself in that cabin."

Mama nodded. "Yes, I guess you're right."

"Do you remember anything?"

"I know the storm was bad. I can still hear that tree falling."

"Do you remember any of the things you said to Miss Tuggle?"

Mama was still. "No, what did I say?"

She smelled of antiseptic, but underneath was a hint of her flowery perfume. "You talked about how Daddy wouldn't let you go to my grandmother's funeral."

"I did?"

"Yes."

"I guess I must have been out of my mind in pain."

I placed my head on her shoulder. "How did you and Amanda meet, Mama?"

Mama relaxed. "Well now, that was a story, Miss Faith, a story you've heard too many times." She grinned.

"If you're too tired."

"I'll talk for a while." Mama adjusted a pillow under her head. "It was right after I came to live in New Orleans with your daddy."

"You were from Atlanta." I finished for her.

Her laugh was like a whisper. "Yes. Atlanta is the best place in the world."

"But Daddy made you go live with his family."

"It was never a question." She took a breath. "The first time I saw Amanda, she was bent over in the bishop's flower garden, weeding. The sun stretched over her sturdy back. A strong posture meant an upright person. Or so my mama always said. I stood on the edge of the perfect rows of daffodils and purple irises. A small boy played in the dirt, probably catching hookworm or something, close to a goldenrod bush in full bloom."

"That was Will." I breathed in deep, avoiding the ache.

"Amanda looked up and a flash of knowing crossed her face. Her hair was relaxed into soft curls. The copper color of her skin warmed her features. She settled back on her knees, not a bit surprised I was there.

"I gave her my name and told her the bishop's wife suggested she might be interested in a new position. I offered to pay her whatever she was being paid plus more. I wore my dark-brown dress with the white Peter Pan collar. My shoes were tiny little leather affairs. It was like I was the one who was looking for a job.

"Amanda told me she had seen me coming in a dream she had and then went about digging her bare hands into the black soil. She was put out that the bishop's wife hadn't told her to find a new job. I was pretty sure she wasn't going to take my offer when she looked at Will and said, 'Go find that rabbit hole you was playing in yesterday.'

"He turned a white-toothed grin on me. 'Mama says I can keep that rabbit if I catch him.' Lord help, he was the cutest thing."

"Will always had a softness for animals." I laughed just to keep from crying.

"Now, Amanda was exactly like she's always been. She gave him a firm look and shooed him off. I was so taken with his open, sweet manner, I told him he had to promise to show me if he caught the rabbit. Then I gave my best smile to Amanda, whose face turned softer around the eyes.

"'Don't give him hope,' she said. 'The missus would take offense with him if he came wagging a rabbit to the door.' But she didn't really sound mad at me. Will ran off in the direction of the shed. That's when Amanda asked me what kind of job I was offering.

"I touched my stomach that pushed tightly against my dress. I was backward in many ways. Amanda laughed at me and cut right through all the properness, telling me she could be a good maid and nurse.

"See, the cook at your grandfather's house claimed Amanda was a witch. I needed a witch with the way my life was turning out. I told her I was new in New Orleans and who your father was.

"Amanda tilted her head and seemed to pull me into some kind of warmth. 'All the maids in town be knowing about your husband, Mrs. Dobbins. I be knowing him just as good.' Amanda gave me a real smile that revealed perfectly straight white teeth. 'There be things about me you don't know, wouldn't like. I'm to myself and need my own place. I'll not live with you in your house.'

"Had I been older, more experienced in running a home, I would have understood Amanda had stepped over the line, but I needed her and was so stupid I didn't even notice. Instead, I offered her the rooms above the carriage house.

"'We might be good together. Time will tell,' Amanda told me. She had the softest smile, not like now, strained and put on for us."

I shifted on the hospital bed so I could see Mama's face. "Tell me about the night I was born." This was my favorite part of the story.

"It was late summer when my little baby came into the world. Your daddy was away in Georgia on a revival trip. A hailstorm just like we had today broke several of the windows in our fine house. That beautiful baby came into a world with a blind fury of horrible pain, so bad I came in and out of consciousness. Amanda stood right with me almost the whole night, giving me her spells. Finally, I passed out cold. Amanda was left to bring the baby into the world on her own."

I couldn't help to think about how Mama said we came to North Carolina by way of Georgia.

"I woke with a dizzy head. Amanda stood over me, smiling. The baby girl was wrapped in a blanket, clean as she could be. Her face was round and plump. She had your daddy's nose and eyes. A sweet version of him. There was no denying who she belonged to.

"'You swore I was having a boy, Amanda. Your spell didn't work.' I laughed at her. But I had so wanted a girl. The door creaked open and Will eased up to the bed. He wore a worried look like a little old man.

"'Here's this baby just as fine as can be!' Amanda held the baby girl close to him." Mama stopped talking.

I breathed in this part of the story, imagining Will worrying over me.

"He looked at you for the longest and then touched your cheek. See, Amanda was sure he was what she called a reader, someone who can see people's futures. She asked him what he saw." Again Mama waited, as if she might have been finished for the night.

This was a new part to the story. I held my breath, praying she would continue.

"'I see me two girls in one.' He always sounded like a grown-up and he was quite sure of himself. Now his prediction scared me to death, and it must have shown on my face.

"'He probably sees her as a grown woman too. He still be young,' Amanda said as she placed you in my arms. Then she issued one of her warnings. 'Mrs. Dobbins,' she said, 'the hail be the omen tonight.'

"But I was humming some silly little song with no name to my daughter and didn't even have omens on my mind." Mama smiled at me.

I was quiet a minute thinking about the new part of the story. "Maybe the hailstorm today was part of the omen."

Mama's breathing was heavy. "Who knows? I've come to know Amanda's magic quite well. She always knows what she's talking about." Mama patted my shoulder and fell off to sleep. I snuggled close to her, pushing my thoughts about Amanda, Will, and all that had changed over the past three weeks right out of my head. For that moment I was with Mama and I was safe.

Ada Lee Tine

I SHOWED UP AT THE DOCK that afternoon because a voice came in my dreams and said a boy was coming to meet me. I learnt a long time before to follow that voice wherever it pointed me. It was two weeks after them white folks had been murdered in Darien, and everyone talked about it so much they forgot who else died for no dern reason at all. Those on Sapelo didn't breathe a word about the mess. We just swallowed down the story and pretended to forget. We all was hurt to the bone because of our own dead man. So I knew when that boy arrived he'd be walking into a mess of sadness.

He came on Mr. Reynolds's shiny new boat, the one he used for trips to and from the island. When the boat came pulling up, I thought it didn't mean a thing. Mr. Reynolds was always bringing folks over for a visit. They was the busiest people I'd ever seen. The boat driver was Cotter, who called himself working for Mr. Reynolds in one fashion or another. He was nice enough when he felt like it, but some days he was meaner than one of our wild hogs. He docked the boat, pushed his fancy captain's hat back on his head, and pointed at the hungry-looking man next to him. "This here boy didn't lie. He said someone would be waiting on him."

The boy smiled. "Yes, sir. I don't lie." He walked off that boat and came right up to me like he knew me his whole life. Who in their right mind would let a young man like that go hungry? His face was so thin it was scary.

As soon as we was away from hearing, I placed a hand on his shoulder and looked him dead in the eyes. "Who you be, child?"

"I ain't no child, ma'am. I'm William Tine, eighteen years old. My daddy was William Tine too. He came from this place, but he's been dead so long I never even saw him."

I studied him. He didn't seem like no liar, maybe he believed the tale he told. But I knew my brother, William—or Willie—never had a child with his wife. She was a root woman with powerful hoodoo. This I knew 'cause of Willie's letters that came from New Orleans. Seen a photo of the happy couple together right before he passed on. Never had a baby. "What's your mama's name?"

"Amanda. She be from New Orleans. That's where she met my daddy. He was playing cards and she worked as a barmaid."

Willie was a drinker and a card player. But I couldn't for the life of me remember that gal's name he married.

"My mama was and is one of the best hoodoo women around." He stopped talking and stared off. "She lives on Black Mountain now. That's in North Carolina."

"Well, boy, lots of mighty strange things take place. You showing up here is one of them things, and I don't know what to think."

"I can do any work you have, ma'am."

I couldn't help but laugh. "I'm sure you can. But one thing you got to know. William Tine was my brother." I let that settle with him.

He looked at me funny and looked away.

"He died three weeks after he married your mama." Something about the voice in my dream the night before made me think of Willie. I took them dreams dead serious like any smart person would.

"My aunt. That be strange. I didn't think family would meet me at the boat."

"Ain't nothing too surprising on the island."

"Mama never told me a thing about my daddy. Just said he was William Tine from Sapelo Island, a Saltwater Geechee. How'd he die?"

I wasn't about to start discussing them matters with him. It wasn't right. Eighteen or not, he had him a mama with her own truth. That pitiful excuse of a boy needed a place to stay, and I had me a empty room. "I got a room. You come on, now. But I got to know what kind of mama lets her eighteen-year-old boy just up and leave North Carolina while the whole dern country is struggling with the Depression?"

"My daddy died a bad death, didn't he?"

There wasn't no going around this boy. "I don't like talking on it, but he was buried out in New Orleans somewhere. Only your mama knows. My brother was supposed to live on this island and live out the old ways. It's our place. He didn't believe in such and now he's gone. Don't know what happened to him, not really. Only your mama has all them answers."

"I got run off of Black Mountain." The words were hard around the edges. This was a grown man talking.

"You call me Ada, Ada Lee Tine."

"My daddy's spirit stopped me on the road off of Black Mountain. He told me to find family. Said someone would be waiting at the dock for me on this very day. He told me the truth." He said this like he sure wasn't used to truths.

Who was I to argue with my dead brother? "Come on. You need to eat." That mama of his could have been with child. It didn't take but one time. She wasn't a truthful type, so why would she have told me about a baby?

"I got this for you, ma'am. Made it from some nice maple a man let me have for pay. It took me two weeks of working to get this done." He shoved something smooth and shiny at me. "I worked for a man who made real nice furniture. He fed me and showed me how to make this. Then he put me on a train in Macon, and I rode it to Savannah. He was a special white man. They don't come around too often."

It was a little box—square, shiny, and perfect in every way.

"I figured anybody could use a nice trinket box. See, I'm useful."

Them tears I'd held in way too long came out of nowhere. "This is beautiful. I don't reckon no one has ever gave me something so pretty." I swiped at the tears as he looked off, pretending not to see. "You like crab?" I asked.

"I ain't never had none."

I hooted. "Lordy Jesus! You call yourself a Tine? Tines have crab in their blood, boy. You'll like mine. I've been told I'm the best cook in these parts." Maybe Willie Tine did one thing right. Maybe he sent that boy 'cause he knew how bad we needed each other. I touched his shoulder. "You come on home with me. I'll teach you all I know. Is anyone looking for you?"

"No, ma'am. I don't reckon a soul will come."

I studied the shiny box in my hand. What kind of mama lets a boy like this slip away? "I can use help. I be your aunt that never married. You be my boy now."

"Pardon, ma'am. I'm not a boy. What you do for a living here?" He looked around at the palmettos and tall oaks. The moss hanging out of the trees, waving wild-like in the wind. The rows of stones marking family after family of folks that lived on the island for longer than most could remember.

"I make baskets. I used to work here on the island when I was real young, but now I work every summer on the Ridge for a white family my mama worked for. It be real rare any of us work off the island unless we fishing. And that's what I hope I'm going to do. I just got me a boat. You think you could be a fisherman?"

He grinned big.

"I got me a shrimp boat by the name of *Sweet Jesse*. We both going to learn us how to fish. It's in our blood. What you say to that?"

"Yes, ma'am. I reckon I can learn real fast."

I had no doubt that Will Tine could be anything he set out to be. And there it was. Sometimes a loss be so big a soul felt like she was going to die, and then along came something good to take her home in the right direction again.

PART TWO

The Bottle Tree

June 1939

"*A old, dead cedar tree be best. The branches are cleaned smooth. Bottles of all kinds are slid on. Get you some red, yellow, blue, and brown ones. Mr. Sun shines through the glass and draws them haints into the pretty colors, trapping them before they know what happened.*"

—Amanda Parker

Shelly Parker

THE SUMMER FAITH TOOK HERSELF down the mountain without telling no one—you'd have thought she escaped from jail—the whole house was in a tither. Now, it was the plain truth that I didn't like the girl, but she'd been acting strange, odd—that was a new word I read in one of her magazines. Even Amanda noticed how she fretted whenever Pastor and Mrs. Dobbins came in the room. It was catching, 'cause then I started watching them, especially Pastor, too. Anyway, Faith had gone against Pastor and Mrs. Dobbins. She wasn't even real smart about it. Didn't try to hide a thing. She went to the mercantile to buy thread for that silly quilt she was working on with my great-grandmama's sewing basket that she stole and flashed in front of Nada's nose every chance she could. Four years of that mess, and still Nada hadn't brought it up to Mrs. Dobbins, like the basket just be worthless. And Nada turning her head stuck right in my ribs and twisted like a knife. Anyway, "unchaperoned" was the word Pastor kept shouting. He shouted and shouted, but Faith refused to tell them how she made the trip. I guessed it was the first interesting thing she'd done in her life. She stood up and did something other than whine for more attention. There wasn't a bit of love between me and her, that was for sure, but a person had to admire her gumption.

When Pastor led Faith off into his study, Mrs. Dobbins started wringing her hands. Lord, she was a mess. Nada kept that cold stare of hers on the study door, and when it opened she stopped cutting up the chicken for dinner.

"What happened, Faith?" Mrs. Dobbins asked.

Faith didn't have no choice but to stop, 'cause Mrs. Dobbins blocked the door.

"That Tuggle woman took her down the mountain without permission. I want to see her today! Here!" he roared. Then he gave Faith one of those "you going to die" looks. "If there's not a good reason for this, you won't be going to her house again. Now, go on to your room and stay there." He gave his whole attention to Mrs. Dobbins. "I've never cared for Faith working like some farmhand, anyway."

So it was agreed in no extra words that whether Miss Tuggle wanted to or not, she was to come in front of Pastor. And I'd never known him not to get exactly what he wanted out of folks. Everybody on the mountain, including Mrs. Dobbins, knew Miss Tuggle hated Pastor all the way down to her toes. Nobody knew why. They didn't have to. Miss Tuggle was her own woman, and what she thought was given honor. I cut out humming around the front room dusting Mrs. Dobbins's stupid doodads. No cleaning up after Faith for a few days. No, I figured Miss Prissy had got herself in so much trouble she wouldn't be in my way. They'd probably lock her in the attic with only bread and water. She had to be the neediest white girl, always yelling for me to go fetch her some book or a glass of water like her dern legs was gone. *Shelly, sew on this button.* Her being a fine seamstress. Even Nada made over them awful quilts. *Shelly, I need*

*me some apples, peeled and sliced, mind you. And don't be walking in
the woods. I seen you the other day. I'll tell Amanda. Can you clean the
spot off my shoe? Shelly, Shelly, Shelly."* Trying to always boss me like
she's some kind of grown-up. Nada said she was, but I knew better.
Shoot, I was more grown at fifteen than she was at nineteen. I knew
how backward she was even if nobody else wanted to stand up and
take notice.

Mrs. Dobbins was beside herself when Pastor walked back down
the hall and slammed his study door. She followed Nada from room to
room for at least an hour.

"Mrs. Dobbins, you got to get out from under my feet. I can't tolerate it no more. You best go see Miss Tuggle yourself."

"Oh, I can't do that. It's not proper. Charles would be very upset."

"She ain't nothing but some old granny woman, not a thing special.
So stop your fretting before you drive both me and you crazy."

"I just can't face that woman after I talked out of my head that day.
She knows too much."

"Shoot, Mrs. Dobbins, she's probably heard worse."

"I just can't."

Nada took a deep breath. "I'll send Shelly over to get her right now.
Just to bring peace to this house."

"What if she won't come? You know she hates Charles."

Nada rolled her eyes at the ceiling. "You just a trouble borrower.
That's all you be."

I slid into the kitchen, but Nada followed me.

"You stop trying to get out of this mess." Nada watched me close.
"Take yourself over to Miss Tuggle's and tell her she has to come see
Pastor and why. And ask her if she can give me plenty of catnip and
chamomile. I'm running low. I got to either calm this white woman or
take a dose of my own tea."

Now, the last thing I wanted was to go to Miss Tuggle's house. I
didn't have nothing against her, but she was a quiet woman. And I was
pretty much a quiet girl. I was afraid we'd quiet each other to death.

"Don't give me that look, Shelly. I see what you thinking. Just do what I say."

"I don't know why you care so much, Nada. Let Mrs. Dobbins go after Miss Tuggle herself. We're just the maids."

Nada's face turned silent and still. "Shelly Parker, I ain't putting up with your stuff today. Now go, do what I say."

"Yes, ma'am." Half the time I believed Nada cared more about Mrs. Dobbins and Faith than me.

"Count yourself lucky to be out of this house on such a pretty day. I'd give anything to just go for a walk."

I hung my head and scooted out the back door into the sun.

"Watch yourself," Nada whispered.

Somebody was always, always warning me about being careful.

I took me a big breath of air clean down into my chest. Outside the main house my thoughts floated right off in different directions. I could make believe one day I'd leave the old mountain, maybe go to school too. I was smart, just not book smart. You had to have books to be that kind of smart. Mostly I only read the Bible and a torn-up copy of *Little Women* I snitched from Faith's room. She be the one who taught me to read so she could play teacher with me. I was always getting my hand slapped with the ruler. I wanted me a real schooling. President Roosevelt said every person had the right to a decent learning. I heard him on Mrs. Dobbins's radio. Mostly she listened to the gospel station down in Asheville, but when Pastor was out of the house, that woman might listen to anything. The house was full of showing something one way when it was really a whole other set of circumstances. Anyway, I had me two one-hundred-dollar bills tucked under a loose floorboard in my room. Nellie Pritchard—I guessed she was as close to having a friend as I had come—gave me the money after she up and killed that no-good husband, Hobbs. I never told a soul, not one, about the murder or the money. Everyone but me and Mrs. Connor—she lived down the mountain a ways and came to Nada for all sorts of spells, right decent for a white woman—thought Nellie had died. Folks claimed to see her ghost roaming the woods. Silly stories. All that mess made me laugh. Nellie got herself right on a train and took off, but that was a secret I kept tight to me. Nada sure didn't know nothing about no murder, money, or me leaving the mountain. Me hiding all that stuff was Nada's fault, anyway. She's the one who made me work for Nellie. Secrets weren't nothing but untold lies.

The sun hit the yard in places, leaving long shadows, reminding me of fall in summer. In the side yard stood three spirits. Ever since I came to understand my gift the year of the hailstorm, they appeared any time they felt up to it. I walked right by them 'cause I didn't have time for their foolishness, always needed me to listen to some story or another. "Leave me be today," I said. "I already got to go to Miss Tuggle's house. I ain't messing with the likes of you too."

A girl stepped out from the line and looked at me dead in the eyes. I got me a good look at that sour face. She was a colored spirit about my age, and that was downright spooky. "You talking to me, gal?" And mouthy too.

I walked me a straight path to the road without looking back. Something told me that haint could come right along with me if she chose.

Faith squatted in front of a gravestone in Daniels Cemetery. It looked just like she was drawing, but Nada said she was stealing the pictures and words on the markers, using them for her quilts. If ever there was a witch, Faith Dobbins was one. She'd done sneaked herself out of that house right under her mama's nose. But that ain't what made her a witch. Anybody could probably fool Mrs. Dobbins. Nope. It was the stuff she stole when she thought nobody was looking. Stuff like hair from Pastor's hairbrush, a button off her mama's nightgown, herbs from Nada's garden. All those things was makings for a spell of some kind. Wasn't no telling what she took from the cemetery besides words and pictures. I got out of her sight before she spied me, but knowing her, she done knew I was there.

Black-eyed Susans, scarlet beebalm, and yellow cornflowers dotted the grassy patches along the dusty road. They swayed like dancers in a hot wind. It hadn't rained in weeks. Dust hung on the trees and coated them in a dull tan color. Nada fussed over her garden, hauling water from the well. There wasn't nothing so sorrowful as looking in a creek bed and seeing nothing but rocks. Even the birds saved themselves for better times. Only the heat bugs hummed in the evening. This was the sound of the mountain thinking big thoughts. Black Mountain was alive and collected souls for sport. When it got riled, no telling what might happen: Fresh milk turned sour, a calf came out with two heads, and mules went wild for no good reason. People were known to turn half-crazy. If the mountain was stirring, it was a lot more to worry over than a few ghosts, even if one was a colored girl with a mean look on her face.

I was so deep into my thinking that I got to Miss Tuggle's in no time. Because she was the granny woman, she brought just about all the kids on the mountain into the world, including me. But if the truth be told, I was scared to death of her. She wasn't like all the other folks. She was smart, book smart. I could tell by her talking. This was a woman who did some reading. No man ever wanted her, and that was purely a shame, seeing how she was so pretty.

"Can I help you with something, Shelly?" Miss Tuggle stood waist-high in lemon beebalm. All around her stood purple and lavender butterfly bushes with orange butterflies the size of my hand flitting in and out. They moved like little fairies from one flower to the next. Miss Tuggle's hair hung loose. Most of the women on the mountain kept their hair tight in a ball on the top of their heads, even dumb old Faith.

"Sorry to bother you, Miss Tuggle."

"No bother at all. What can I do for you today?" She stepped out of the balm. "You look in a turmoil." No one on the mountain ever used words like Miss Tuggle.

"Well, we got us plenty of turmoil over at the main house. Mrs. Dobbins be wringing her hands and pacing around. Pastor wants you to come see him today about taking Miss Faith off the mountain without his say-so. He ordered Miss Faith to her room until he finds out what happened, 'cause she ain't talking no more than she has to. But she ain't listening 'cause I seen her at the cemetery again. He'll give her the worst kind of punishment."

Miss Tuggle huffed real loud. "That man. She's a grown woman and needed some thread from town. He doesn't own her."

I shrugged. "Pastor pretty much does whatever he pleases. He says if you don't have a good enough reason for taking Miss Faith, she won't be allowed to work in your garden no more. He don't much care for her gardening."

Miss Tuggle gave me a long, slow look. "He did, did he?"

"Nada asked if she might get some chamomile and catnip. This dry spell has been hard on her garden." Lord, that woman was wearing men's work boots.

She kind of smiled. "I've been watering mine every morning and evening. We've got to get some rain. Does she need mint too?"

"She's got plenty, ma'am."

Miss Tuggle walked to the homemade pole fence, gray with years of standing, mended here and there. "Come on in the garden. I'll show you Faith's part."

Was that woman crazy? The thought of Faith lifting her hand to do any kind of work knocked my shoes off my feet. "No disrespect intended, ma'am, but are we talking about the same Miss Faith? I figured she wasn't really working in the garden. I don't think that girl ever got her hands dirty."

Miss Tuggle had a little smile on her face. "I guess we let different people see different sides of us."

That didn't make a lick of sense.

"Faith is a hard worker."

I didn't have one bit of belief in Miss Tuggle's story. "If you say so, ma'am. I ain't fond of those quilts of hers either, but everyone else, Nada too, says she works hard on them and those folks see pretty where I don't."

Miss Tuggle scrunched up her nose. "She works hard at a lot of things. I love her quilts because they are unusual. They're like paintings."

I held my tongue on that one.

"Faith has taken a lot of cuttings to Amanda for her garden."

Well, there it was. That girl knew I hated working in the garden. She was always trying to get on Nada's good side.

Inside the fence was some red clover for the croup, two long rows of chamomile, a row of boneset and pokeroot, and large rosemary plants lining the fence. Each corner held the biggest bushes of lavender I'd ever seen. Butterflies fluttered and glided from one flower to another as bees joined in their dance. In the middle of the garden sat a wooden bench.

"I like to sit here and think. Don't you like to think, Shelly?"

"Yes, ma'am." Thinking was real important.

Miss Tuggle squatted and clipped the chamomile. "Most of these plants were started by my grandmother. She was a granny woman too and part Cherokee." She touched the boneset. "This was planted by her. She called it Agu-weed." The white flowers moved in the breeze. She touched another plant. "This is yellow dock." The red blooms were something else to look at.

"What's it used for?"

"Cleansing. It takes the waste out of the body. Grandmama used it to purify the blood." She smiled and moved to the catnip. "I guess your mama plans a nice calming tea. She's good at what she does."

My heart nearly flipped over with pride.

"I remember the first day I met Amanda. It was cold. And your brother was angry because he had to stay at home alone on Christmas Eve. You were born before it turned Christmas, and your mama walked home early that morning with you tucked close to her in a sling. I never even knew she was carrying a baby until she showed up at my door. I can't tell you how many times I'd seen her here and there on the mountain. She gathered plants like me. A woman not showing she's with child happens sometimes. It was three weeks before Mrs. Dobbins figured out Amanda had you, even though she wore you in the sling she made. Said she made it when your brother was born. It was quilted from scraps of clothes. Beautiful work." Miss Tuggle was quiet for a minute, like she was thinking. "Faith isn't so bad, Shelly. She is an intelligent young woman and pleasant to be around. Troubled. You strike me as a self-sufficient young woman, yourself." When I didn't say a thing, she went on. "Come with me. I have some homemade chocolate cake. Do you like cake?"

Did winter always come to the mountain? "Yes, ma'am."

The front room of her cabin wasn't a bit fancy, but it was beautiful all the same. Every inch of the walls was covered with books, all sizes and colors. All I could do was stare.

"Do you like to read, Shelly?"

"Yes, ma'am." I waited a minute, taking in the sight. "I love books the best."

She walked right up to one of them shelves and pulled a skinny book off. "I read a lot. I can live the rest of my life out alone if I have my books and garden. Both feed me, Shelly. The garden teaches me I am part of this mountain, the dirt, the air, the trees, even the insects. It humbles me into something so much smaller and insignificant. My books nourish my soul. When I open a cover and begin to read, I go to new places, to worlds I never knew existed. I time-travel into the past and up into the distant future. I'm never Maude Tuggle, the spinster and granny woman. I'm a woman with her own life." She looked at me. "And all of that from a bit of dirt and a few words." She placed the book in my hand.

When I was three, I touched the warm eye on the stove of the main house. The heat moved through me so fast my hand was burnt before I understood what was happening, before the pain set in. That's how this book felt in my fingers.

"*The Weary Blues.*" She smiled.

The name floated on the air like music falling from the old pump organ in our front room.

"It's a poetry book." Miss Tuggle's words were a whisper. "Here." She took the book back and opened it. "This poem is called 'The Negro Speaks of Rivers.'" She read the poem as we stood in the middle of the room with all her books around. The words rocked me like a baby in its mama's lap. The poem sang to me deep in my bones and talked of rivers like they was some kind of living, breathing thing. Dragonfly River was just like that, singing and moving down the mountain. Ever since I was a little girl, I'd go sit on the mossy banks and close my eyes. Will always called it being with God. I liked that. Being with God. Just being. Nobody wanting nothing but stillness. That poem was all about muddy water and sunlight, about coloreds throughout time being part of the rivers, as if rivers and coloreds was one and the same.

When she finished, she shut the book and gave it back to me. "Langston Hughes wrote this book. He's a Negro."

Those words caused time to stand still. A Negro. What a fine word. Much better than "colored." I closed my eyes tight and hugged the book to my chest. "Yes." That was all I could get to come out of my silly mouth. Nada would say Miss Tuggle didn't have no understanding of coloreds. That it wasn't her place to put a Negro's book in my hand. And she was probably right, but I was still proud to hold them words close to me.

"You should help Faith and me in the garden for book loans."

"Yes, ma'am. I will." I didn't even pause, knowing full well it would be like having my teeth pulled to be around Faith and in a garden.

"Good."

We moved out on the porch. Me hugging that book tight in one hand and holding a plate of cake in the other. It was like a birthday party. I looked out over her yard happier than I'd been in a long time—wondering why I had been so afraid of Miss Tuggle—and seen them two gravestones under a great oak. There stood that mean colored-girl spirit I'd seen in the pastor's yard earlier. She'd done followed me to Miss Tuggle's.

Miss Tuggle looked in the same direction. "Those are family graves."

That colored girl sure wasn't no family of Miss Tuggle's. "Most folks be buried next to the church, in Daniels Cemetery." Nada would have called my words sassy.

"I've never fit in with the church, never will." Miss Tuggle kept her look on them graves. "Mama is buried in the cemetery. I don't know where I'll be buried."

"My daddy be buried in the colored part of the old cemetery up the mountain a piece. He grew up on that side of the mountain."

"My family always did things their own way, not like the rest of the mountain, much less the church. One of these graves belongs to my father. He hung himself from that very limb." She nodded at the tree. "I was your age. The mountain never forgave him. When he was alive, he roamed the dark each night, searching for something to settle his mind. Now, that's a story for another time. The folks on this mountain could tell it better than me, anyway. I don't believe in magic or ghosts." She said this with a firm voice.

I looked away from that colored girl. "I learned two things from Nada: catch a story and throw a spell. Those be the two most important things in a person's life. I have to believe. If I told you what I was seeing right now, you might believe. It's no secret how straight and tall you are, Miss Tuggle. But that don't make the haints just fairy stories."

"Straight and tall, am I? I like that. I'm sensible. Go ahead and tell me what you see." I heard the mocking in her voice.

"I have what Nada calls sight. That's what folks here on the mountain call conjuring spirits. 'Cept I don't have to conjure the dern things. They show up all on their own without a invite."

"I know what sight is supposed to be, but Shelly, it is just a silly superstition. You're way too smart for that kind of thinking."

"I sure wish it was a bunch of fairy tales, Miss Tuggle. But it ain't. My life would be a lot happier if it were."

"You don't have any special power, Shelly. I know your mother believes that because you were born with a membrane, you're bound to be touched. I helped bring you into the world, remember? You're just plain Shelly. A beautiful, smart young woman."

And wouldn't it have been real nice if that were so? "Yes, ma'am." I pointed to the graves. "Who belongs to the other grave?"

"A friend who couldn't be saved from illness, even by Mama. That was a long, long time ago." Her face turned sad.

"No coloreds are buried on this land?" I blurted.

Miss Tuggle gave me a sharp look. "Why would there be?"

I shrugged. "'Cause I see a colored girl right there by the head-stones." Stupid ghost was going to cause me all kinds of trouble.

Miss Tuggle walked down the steps into the yard. "I don't believe in such stories, Shelly." She was real put out. "When you come back, we will work on gathering some of the herbs."

"Make sure you choose a fruitful day, not a barren one." See, I did learn something from Nada about planting signs.

Miss Tuggle frowned.

I guessed she didn't believe in signs either. "Might not get to come back if Pastor doesn't get what he wants."

"Hide that book from him. Now, run on and tell Faith I'll be over later this afternoon to explain things to her father. I'm glad you're coming along with Faith to work the garden." Her smile was real. "Now, go on before they come hunting you."

My visit with Miss Tuggle was finished. I looked over my shoulder. A warm light glowed close to her, around her. That was the light of someone who was part of the mountain now. Someone she was tied to. Then I heard that sound of the mountain whispering in my ear. *"You'll always belong here, Shelly Parker. This is your home."*

THE SPIRIT OF THE COLORED GIRL stood waiting in the backyard of the main house. She was madder than a wet hen.

"Who are you?" I asked before she could say a word.

She glared me down. "What you asking me questions for? I'm here to talk to you."

"'Cause you be in my yard bothering me."

The girl threw her head back and laughed. Around her neck was a thick scar. "It not be your house, girlie."

"I work here."

"Well, la-di-da."

"Get on out of here! I ain't got time for you!" I yelled.

"I ain't listening to some old uppity girl with sight. Lord, I've been stuck to Pastor for too long now. But if you seeing me, then you be useful, part of the story. Better watch out. Something going to happen." She nodded at the main house. "He's bad and he be watching you, but you too dumb to see." She was quiet a minute. "I got you something. It be important. I left it in the lost graveyard. You'll know where to look. Watch yourself. Live folks aren't always welcome there."

A coldness ran down my head. "You need to leave me be."

The girl turned her whole anger on me. "I'm Armetta. I grew up on this mountain. Listen to me, girl. I left you something in the lost graves. Are you too dumb to know where that be? But understand you can't make me leave. I'm part of this mountain. And I'm going to save you from Pastor whether you like it or not."

Faith picked that time to walk out the back door. "Did you talk to Miss Tuggle? Mama is about to fall over from worry. Come in and tell her what Miss Tuggle said." Faith folded her arms over her chest.

I tucked the book in the back of my skirt. "I thought you was sent to your room. You don't listen, do you? And Miss Tuggle be wanting me to come help in the garden from now on too." I took a real delight in rubbing this in on Miss Faith.

"You're awful smart-mouthed to be my maid." Faith stomped into the house.

"There be trouble, nothing but pure trouble," said Armetta. "That white girl done got herself all wrapped up in a story that don't be hers. She be stirring up the woods and those stuck there." She watched the place where Faith had stood. "Don't forget to find what I left you." And she was gone.

If I slapped Miss Faith Dobbins, Nada and me would be kicked off this mountain. Even though Faith stole the sewing basket. Wasn't nobody ever going to care about some colored maid and her sewing basket from Louisiana, anyway. Well, at least that mean old spirit was after Faith and not just me.

THAT OLD HAINT got under my skin. I knew exactly where she hid this thing she wanted me to find. Only one lost cemetery on the mountain. The path took me into the haunted woods. Now, I'd seen haints a lot, but I knew better than to linger in that place. A girl couldn't see the light of day 'cause the trees was so close together. So, I moved it on up the mountain, trying not to feel like someone was watching 'cause they probably was.

The lost cemetery sat on a flat place not far from Ella Creek Settlement, the only place on the mountain where coloreds were put to rest. I don't think a live soul remembered it was there. My daddy was buried in there, so the girl didn't have nothing on me. And what would a haint have to give me? Nobody ever visited them poor old graves anymore except me. And half the time I just went to get away from work. The air was thick and hot. And thunder rumbled in the distance.

"I see you, girl."

Lord, I nearly jumped out of my skin. Over near a headstone stood a little colored girl. Couldn't have been more than nine.

"Where'd you come from?" There wasn't no real colored girls on that mountain but me.

"Georgia." She was right pitiful looking, with a ripped dress and only one shoe. That was one sad-looking haint.

"You followed me out of them woods."

She shrugged. "I'm just here to talk to you and help you find Armetta's gift." She giggled like she had said something real funny.

"Well, show it to me and get it over with," I fussed.

"Not so quick. You can't boss me. I'm here because of him. He's got a few of us stirred up."

"Who?" But something twisted in my stomach.

"That fellow who calls himself a preacher." She stepped close to me, and I could see bruises all over her neck. "He's got to be stopped."

Now I was thinking of walking away while the getting was good.

"You ain't going nowhere, girl. You got to listen to me and to Armetta and the other one that's coming. You got to. Understand? If you don't, you'll die." She looked off into the spooky woods.

"Are you going to tell me where this thing is I'm supposed to find?" Talking to her was pure silliness.

"Ain't you going to ask me what happened? How I died?"

"Nope, 'cause I ain't getting into that mess." I looked around the graves, searching on my own. I was one stupid girl for coming.

"I got beat bad, real bad. I didn't even know what he was going to do to me. He was sweet and quiet."

"Hush up. I don't want to know no more. It ain't my story to take care of."

She laughed. "You be wishing before it's all over you knew the whole story. He done away with my sister too. Down in Darien, Georgia. You don't know about that place. But you will."

"It was stupid to come looking for something a haint hid." I had to get out of there and forget about the whole trip.

"You ever heard the sound of a neck breaking? A pop and a crack." Her words choked the air.

"I don't want nothing from you haints."

She went over to a tree near a gravestone. "Here it be." And she was gone.

For a minute I just stood there, not running, not moving. The wind picked up and shook the tops of the trees. "I ain't doing nothing to help you!" I shouted into the air. "Nothing."

The grave marker was part covered with kudzu vines, and I didn't bother to look at it because there was a book with a leather cover stuck in the leaves. Lord, the thing was old as the dickens. Now, as much as I wanted to just leave there, a book was a book, so I picked it up. Armetta was some kind of haint if she could move things. I shook off a chill.

The printed writing was decent, and I could read it real good even though there was water stains here and there.

Armetta Lolly
April 1869
Ella Creek Cemetery could be found a half of a mile southwest of the settlement with the same name. That's where I was birthed, Armetta Lolly.

I slammed the book shut.

"You better read it, girl. If you know how to read. This here will save a lot of trouble." Armetta's voice seemed like it was part of the wind.

"Hush up," I mumbled.

The treetops shook, and I took the stupid book with me on down the mountain. But I sure, sure wasn't going to read a bit, not a bit. I was going to get rid of me a haint.

LATER THAT NIGHT when Nada and me was back in our cabin and the book was safe under the floorboard with my money, I decided to talk to Nada. Maybe she could help me. "What do you do about a spirit that won't leave folks alone? How you get rid of it?"

She was busy conjuring a spell for one of the young girls on the mountain that wanted to be rid of warts. "What kind of trouble this spirit be? Different ways for different spirits." She never looked up.

"Just sassy and bothersome."

Nada watched me for a minute. Questions crossed over her smooth, copper-colored face. "When I was young, Granny had a young white boy's ghost following her each and every place she went. It was a boy she watched pulled from the river because of drowning. She didn't know him none, but he came to her 'cause of her sight. He was the saddest spirit, and just looking at him nearly broke her heart in half. And it was that reason alone, she had to get rid of him. Haints like that can wear on a soul and bring a person bad things. That's how come you got to know what be bad in a spirit and what be good. It ain't always plain." She looked at me with her mama look. "Some old woman on the plantation told Granny about making a bottle tree. They be best for catching them simple spirits that need to move on. See, a bottle tree can be made out of that old dead cedar out there in the yard. You clean them branches so they are nice and smooth. Then you start collecting the bottles we use at the main house. Get you some yellow, red, green, and blue ones. Slide them on the branches. The sun shines through the bottles, and them simple spirits get sucked into the colors and trapped there for all time." Again questions scooted over her face. "You build you a bottle tree. That might solve your problem."

So there it was, a bottle tree would rid me of that mean haint, Armetta. I looked out the door for the purpose of inspecting the dead cedar. There she stood in the yard right by Pastor.

THAT NIGHT AFTER I WENT TO BED, Mrs. Dobbins came to our cabin, tapping on the door. It was bad enough I spent each and every day around her. Nada creaked it open as quiet as she could.

The smell of honeysuckle beat that woman in the kitchen. "I'm worried about our girl," she whispered.

Why in the world did Nada put up with her mess? "Go sit at the table, Mrs. Dobbins. You don't look good. I'll make you some calming tea."

"Where's Shelly?" Mrs. Dobbins asked.

"She be asleep in her bed, like she should." Nada bumped around the kitchen.

Laying there was kind of a lie, since I wasn't letting nobody know I could hear.

"I'm worried about Faith and Shelly too." Mrs. Dobbins cleared her throat.

This I had to hear. From my bedroom right off the kitchen, I could see a lot. I always went to sleep with my head at the foot of the bed so I could watch the moon pushing up in the sky.

"I be thinking on both of them too since he threw a fit about Faith leaving the mountain. She be a grown woman. Ain't nothing wrong with that." Nada was just out of my sight in the far corner of the kitchen, but the worry was in her words. Faith wasn't nothing but a job to keep us living. That girl sure wasn't nothing to worry on. Maybe Nada had noticed Faith gathering conjures. That sure, sure be a reason for concern.

"Charles has black moods." Mrs. Dobbins stopped a minute, looking in Nada's direction. "They are getting worse. I don't want him to go after them."

Nada let out a disgusted huff. "We just got to watch them real close, Mrs. Dobbins."

"Can't we call each other by our given names by now, Amanda? We've been through too much. We're family. I like you better than some of my real blood."

Nada marched past my door. That woman was going to bring out Nada's worst. "We not ever going to be family, ma'am. We're together due to circumstances. It's best to remember such things." Her words were colder than a January night. "I work for you. That be all. I'm your colored help. Sometimes the pets be in better shape than me and Shelly." Nada stomped back past my door again.

Mrs. Dobbins breathed hard like she might break into one of her crying jags she'd taken to doing in the last few weeks. "I'm stuck, Amanda. I'm stuck." The words sat quiet in the room.

Somehow I almost understood what she meant by stuck. There were times in a person's life when she couldn't see which way to go.

"I've had my stuck times too." Nada rattled teacups—little things with purple violets painted on the inside—that Mrs. Dobbins gave away when she didn't like them no more.

"I've been pushed and pulled. All I've ever done is try to please people I care about. Half the time I walk around taking the blame for other people's mistakes. If there is a God, I have one question for him. What is enough? What? When do I say no more? The problems in my life were not caused by me. I'm innocent, except I never put my foot down when I should have. Mama always said I just refused to see what was in front of me."

That woman didn't have one problem I could see. Well, maybe being married to Pastor. That would be a pain in the side 'cause he was all slick and nice in front of the church members, but in his own house, he was another story altogether.

"Lots of times you got to let water under the bridge just flow, ma'am. Damming it up will hurt someone."

Mrs. Dobbins sucked in a big breath. "I guess that goes for Will leaving too. Is he water under the bridge? Or Shelly, is her future here on Black Mountain water under the bridge?"

Nada moved so I could see her. "You be bothering me now." She got quiet for a minute. "Mrs. Dobbins, you got a bad habit of walking a fence. One side of that fence ain't got a thing to do with you. Leave it be."

Mrs. Dobbins clicked her tongue. "You're wrong about that. It is my business because I was brought into this without my consent."

They was talking about something way bigger than Will leaving or me and Faith in trouble. The unspoken words hung in the house like a cloud blanketing my valley.

"Maybe. But you got yourself hemmed right in a corner when you married the man. Don't know how you can get out of that fix."

"He will not hurt me anymore." Mrs. Dobbins was firm. "Haven't you noticed?" There was a long silence before she started talking again. "You're right. I should have made a better choice, but I was young and stupid. Things would be a lot different now if I had."

"Yes, ma'am, I know all about young and stupid. Look at my life in New Orleans before I came to work for you. I married Clyde Parker when I got here, didn't I? Can't be much stupider than that." Nada laughed. It sure wasn't no secret how much trouble my daddy stayed in while he was alive, but it still hurt to hear Nada say things like that. "But we do have our girls." Nada's words were soft, soothing, like she just might care about Mrs. Dobbins.

"Yes, you're right, Amanda. We wouldn't have our girls if things had gone different. Faith is worth any amount of pain. And now, now he's watching Shelly. He's turning his anger on Faith. He wants to swallow her like he did me and anyone else he comes in contact with. But it's the look he has on his face when he's watching Shelly that scares me the most."

I was fine. Pastor wasn't coming near me. I hadn't seen one bit of change in him, except maybe he was nicer.

Mrs. Dobbins was silent a minute. "I could kill him." The words slid right out as if they belonged between the two of them.

"If you're going to do that, you got to be careful how. Men like Pastor don't kill easy. You don't need to go to the gas chamber." Nada didn't have any teasing in her voice.

"I'd probably lose my nerve at the last minute."

"And he'd get you." Nada laughed. "He's turned brave. I got to say that. Brave and stupid."

The old mantel clock ticked and we all listened. Heat bugs hummed outside.

"I told Charles I knew all about what he did." The words wound around the ticking: ticktock, ticktock.

"That wasn't so smart." Nada's words were a straight, flat line.

"Maybe, but he stopped hitting me. And I told him I'd tell his father, the grand bishop, all I know."

"You completely crazy, woman."

"No crazier than you." Mrs. Dobbins laughed.

"I guess you be right about that. I'm still here too."

"I sinned."

"How did you sin, Mrs. Dobbins?" It was Nada's turn to laugh.

"I listened to Charles talking to God. I know everything, Amanda. He confessed." There was a thick silence. "Much more than circumstances."

"That's dangerous. I'd be willing to bet he's done way more than you know." Nada kind of laughed, but it was her mean laugh. "You be stronger than I thought, Mrs. Dobbins. But he might be meaner with something held over his head."

"He won't hurt me. We just have to watch Faith and Shelly, even you."

The last thing I wanted was that woman putting her attention on me.

Nada padded across the kitchen in her soft house shoes. "Shelly will be watched, Faith too."

I could stay out of Pastor's way.

"It's coming, Amanda," Mrs. Dobbins whispered.

"What be coming, ma'am?"

"The bad. It's been in the air since the storm four years ago. It will come walking in our yard any day."

Now, I was used to Nada talking like this, but not Mrs. Dobbins.

"Yep. I'm afraid you be right."

"I might have lost my mind if I hadn't come here tonight to talk, Amanda. I feel better knowing you're watching them too. And I wanted you to know I understand."

"I be watching every move that man makes, and Mrs. Dobbins, I'm glad you understand, 'cause I'd do it all again. Now, we can break breath anytime you see fit." Nada was asking her to come back and talk. Lord help. And what did she do that Mrs. Dobbins understands?

Mrs. Dobbins scooted her chair back. They had finished. She cut a look into my bedroom, so I closed my eyes, even though she couldn't see nothing but a shadow in a bed. I had me a passel of questions. But one thing I knew for sure. Nada had a big old secret that she shared with Mrs. Dobbins. And whatever it was, it had Mrs. Dobbins all stirred up.

THE FIRST DAY I WENT TO WORK in Miss Tuggle's garden we gathered rosemary, just like she promised. When Faith thought nobody was paying attention, she sneaked into the cabin and snitched hair out of Mrs. Tuggle's hairbrush. When I got home, I added my fifth bottle to my bottle tree. They was right pretty: a fine blue, a red, a yellow, and two deep brown. One for every time Faith did something crazy. When the wind blew hard like it did on most days that early summer, the bottles clinked together and made music.

I followed Faith to Miss Tuggle's each and every time she went. Gardening sure wasn't my favorite, but the books handed off to me was treasures. By the end of two weeks, I had read me a bunch of books. And my writing was getting better. Once Faith caught me writing on my tablet Miss Tuggle gave me. I held my breath because I figured that was the end. She would go tell her daddy. But instead, she took the pencil away from me and corrected my spelling. If I hadn't known way better, I would have thought I was liking Faith too. Of course, that was pure craziness, because I sure couldn't like some girl who took to roaming Daniels Cemetery like she lived there.

One morning Faith took out to steal words on the gravestones, and I had some free time. My problem was that free time wasn't free if Nada saw me, so I had to find me my own place to go, kind of like Faith. As much as it pained me, I headed through the woods to Ella Creek, to the lost cemetery. I sat beside Daddy's grave and read him my newest book. Not a soul bothered me, and I figured all that other stuff was just a haint trying to keep me from starting a bottle tree.

That was the day change whistled up the mountain, 'cept I didn't even notice 'cause I was out in the afternoon sun hanging the clothes on the line in the side yard near the cabin. My mind was on my own sweet business caught up in a good case of thinking. Chores were good for that. The air was just as hot as any summer day could be.

"You be one stupid girl if you think you're going to catch me in some old bottle tree. It be a right fine tree to look at, though." Stupid Armetta stood behind me, wearing the same old fancy yellow dress she had worn the last time I seen her. It was the kind of dress a white girl might pass on to her colored help. I figured Armetta must have been buried in it.

"Nada says a bottle tree is just the thing for unwanted haints." I pulled the sheet over the line.

"A stupid ghost, maybe. Your mama didn't tell you it can't work on spirits that have a good reason to be here? I ain't one bit confused. I was born right here and never left. You read what I sent you after?"

I popped a pillowcase in the wind. "No, and I ain't going to read the silly thing."

"You be one stupid, stupid girl. Sight might be your gift, but you sure don't use your own eyes."

"I use them, all right, but I ain't helping you."

Armetta laughed. "It ain't me you be helping, girl. It's you. Can't you see how he looks at you? Don't tell me you're that dumb."

"Hush up. How do I know you're not some haint bent on hurting Pastor?"

Again she laughed, but this time it was pure mean. "I am bent on hurting him before he hurts you and that crazy daughter of his. Didn't you listen to that little girl spirit from Darien, Georgia, up in the cemetery? She told you part of her story."

"How do I know any of it is true?" I said.

Armetta stood there for a minute before she spoke again. "I lived in that cemetery."

"The lost one?"

"Well, Prissy, I sure ain't talking about Daniels Cemetery over there. My cemetery be way older than that one hooked to the church."

A cold thought walked through my mind. "You ain't here to look out for me. You be lying. Why you here?" I hung a pretty pink tea towel in the sun. "Faith be conjuring you?"

"She's a sad excuse for a conjurer, but she's smarter than you. At least she knows what I know and she has her a plan." Armetta shook her head. "Still ain't figured on how she came up with it, but she's got her one. You ain't doing nothing to stop Pastor. You be pretending he's nice." She studied me. "You're scared of me. That's why you made a bottle tree. The old girl who can see haints is scared. I be here all the time, all along. Don't you know that by now? I'm stuck with him. I follow him. Never can get far from him."

"Pastor?"

She looked at me like I was crazy. "Well, I sure ain't talking about Abraham Lincoln."

"Did you know him before you passed?"

"Who, President Lincoln?" She laughed again. Then her look turned hard. "That ain't none of your business, girlie."

"Just leave me alone," I told her.

"Can't. Trouble be walking right in the door, and you ain't even paid it no mind." Armetta looked out toward the woods. "This be nothing like your everyday haints. You best watch. Look at what is around you. And take care of those dear to you. Stay out of them woods where the lost cemetery be. They haunted with the worst kind of spirits and they ain't always dead, girlie."

"I ain't listening to you." I threw another sheet over the line. "You just trying to scare me."

"You be one dumb girl thinking you all alone up in that cemetery. That be where they're buried."

"Who?" I tried to act like her answer wasn't no skin off my back.

"Not who. What. The stories. They all be there." And she was gone.

DEATH KNOCKED ON THE DOOR of the main house around evening time. A death that was felt deeply but had settled and slipped to the back of folks' minds. See, the mountain took this death so personal it closed its heart. Now the door to the truth began to crack open, the air turned hotter and was hard to breathe. Nada walked around our kitchen gathering the makings for a spell. I went to sit on the porch to cool off some. There stood Arleen Brown on the back porch of the main house. Lordy, after four years, she showed up to get her answer—not from God, but Pastor. Why in the world would she hunt him out? He didn't have no good answers. His struggles with God sure wasn't going to hand Arleen any peace.

She never moved. When Pastor walked out the door and straight through her, he didn't even flinch. That's when a cold chill walked up my spine, and for some reason I heard Armetta's warning from earlier that day. Arleen wasn't looking for him. It was something more, something bigger, but what, I wasn't sure. She stood with complete stillness while we both watched the sky turn orange and pink as the sun dipped into the tops of the trees. Me, standing on the front porch of our cabin, and her, right there on the back porch of the main house.

"Shelly, what you doing out there on the porch so long?" Nada stood in the door.

Wasn't no use trying to fool her, because Nada could most of the time smell them untruths out. "I see Arleen Brown standing on Pastor's back porch. She showed up a little while ago."

Nada sucked the air. "Lord, why now, after all this time?"

"Don't know."

Nada held up her hand. "Some things are best left alone. Arleen Brown be one of them things."

"Yes, ma'am." I waited a minute for her to settle. "But Arleen's here now. Maybe it's because her mama is still mourning after her. I hear tell at the last ladies' gathering that Mrs. Brown is worse now than when Arleen left the world." I waited just a second. "And Nada, I remember how mad Will was when word came she died."

Nada frowned. "I don't want to know why that girl be waiting on Pastor. We best forget her."

"Like how you forgot Faith taking your sewing basket?" There was some things a girl couldn't put behind her. "And I don't think Arleen be waiting on Pastor."

Nada gave a little puff like maybe she'd been waiting on me to bring the stealing up one more time. "You still thinking on that basket?"

"It was my great-grandmother's."

"And who is that girl waiting on if she not be waiting on Pastor?"

I shrugged. "Just a feeling."

Nada came close to me, so close I could see sweat on her upper lip. "Never trust nobody, Shelly. No matter how nice and caring they seem."

"You mean white folks?"

"Anybody. Folks most of the time tell their own truths, but that don't mean they be honest." She looked out the door again.

"I can trust you, Nada."

She looked at me a minute and then nodded.

That pause got under my skin. "The bottle tree didn't work," I blurted.

Nada took a sip of coffee. "Some spirits be too smart to be caught. They've come to finish what they started before they passed."

"This one is stuck to Pastor. Says she has to be with him."

Nada raised her eyebrows. "What's her name?"

Part of me wanted to keep this to myself. "She's mean and bossy."

Nada watched me as her coffee steamed. "Will talked about a ghost he saw out near Ella Creek. Said she told him she lived in the lost cemetery. Told him she kept up with Pastor, knew his thoughts, his stories." She shivered.

"Her name is Armetta." I fiddled with a thread on the skirt of my dress.

"Don't talk to her. She ain't nothing but trouble." Nada's back went straight.

"I'll try, Nada, but this girl's not a spirit to be pushed aside. She be my age and colored. I don't have to open my mouth. She keeps coming back."

"She said something to Will. I know she did." Lines of pain crossed Nada's forehead. "You don't bother with Arleen either. It can't be good she's back. A bad thing is headed our way."

My throat closed. Nada sounded like Armetta. "Okay." Wasn't nothing I could do if them haints lined up to talk to me.

Nada looked out the door. "Is she still there?"

The porch was empty. "No, ma'am."

Her shoulders relaxed. "Good. Them two ghosts are stirred up at the same time. We got to be careful. You remember what I said."

"I don't have a lot of say-so with this here sight, Nada."

"Just leave them be."

That was a lot easier said than done.

Faith Dobbins

L
AVENDER PETALS FELL all over the grass, fluttering down like snow-
flakes onto the back porch stairs as I stepped down into the grass. The
wisteria vines grew way up in the trees, and huge clusters of blooms
hung here and there. They were blooming in June, two months late.
The mountain had skipped spring altogether that year. A melody played
through my mind. My dance began as a two-step, and then I caught the
wind and twirled. My skirt whipped out around me. I threw my arms
out to each side looking like a foolish child, but the moment to dance
was too strong to resist. For just a second I was happy. Had I been a
young girl, I would have expected a prince to enter at that very moment
if I believed in such things, but I wasn't—and didn't. I was nineteen and
too old for such fanciful ideas. I danced. The blossoms fell around me.
A sleek black car topped the driveway. I froze where I was. No one off
the mountain ever came to our house.

A man emerged from the car who looked so much like Daddy, only younger, I had to do a double take.

"I'm here to see Charles Dobbins." He stepped closer. His fingers were long like a girl's, like Daddy's.

"He's at the church." I nodded my head in the direction.

"Why doesn't that surprise me? I bet he's preaching to the air, ranting and raving." He smiled. "Some things never change."

I had to smile.

He laughed. "You have to be Faith. Goodness, I haven't seen you since you were just a baby." He held out his hand. "Now you're a woman."

"Yes, I am Faith." I didn't touch his hand.

"I won't bite. I promise."

His hand was warm, almost hot, but the squeeze was gentle.

"I really need to have a word with your father. I've come from New Orleans just for the pleasure."

"He doesn't much care for interruptions." The lavender snow fell heavier.

Even the man turned to take a look. "This is a fine place to live. Why is it he's always writing letters about how terrible the place is?"

"Daddy doesn't like it here. He's more of a city preacher, or so he says. I like it just fine. Daddy says living here is God's punishment for something bad one of us in the family did. He probably thinks it was me."

The man grinned. "We need to be formally introduced. I'm your uncle Lenard."

"I'd like to say I've heard of you, but Daddy doesn't talk about New Orleans or anyone there."

This brought a loud laugh from my uncle. "I just bet he doesn't." The man looked at the church. "I'm going to surprise him. Pray for me." He winked. "I want to see that fine mother of yours too." He strolled off with the blossoms catching in his blond hair, the same shade as mine.

I let him get around the corner of the church and I cut down behind Amanda's cabin into the woods. Amanda would throw a fit if she
knew I was there because she believed they were haunted. I'd heard
the spirits calling at night, too, but of course I never told anyone.
Mama would have thought I was crazier than she already did, and
Daddy would have sworn a demon was in me. The thing was, a tiny bit
of Amanda's magic had moved into me when I stole the sewing basket.
Once I sent Daddy a bad thought and a glow showed all around him for
hours afterwards. Other times the knowledge of a spell would pop into
my thoughts, as if my mind always contained the directions. The magic
sat in my chest and ached for use. It settled in my joints and made
them stiff. And when I didn't use the suggested spells, the magic
floated through my head, creating an unbearable pressure that pushed
against my temples. A losing of one's mind was not a pretty thing.

I knew if I stayed on the edge of the woods I'd be safe enough. The
daylight washed the fern-covered ground. I didn't have to walk long before I came to the back of the church. I stood under one of the open
windows.

"You're not welcome here, Lenard!" Daddy's voice boomed.

"Come now, brother. We haven't seen each other for too long.
What, almost nineteen years now."

"What have you come for?" Daddy barked.

"Father has a deal. He realizes he can't keep you trapped on this
mountain forever."

"Really," Daddy said skeptically.

"Father wants you to walk away from the idea of preaching, from
this church, and he will give you the new mercantile he bought last
week in New Orleans. Imagine, Charles, the city, home. It would be an
honest living and there is an apartment on top. I've seen the whole
place. It's wonderful. It would be a healing life, Charles. You would
be safe."

Daddy's anger seeped out the window where I hid against the wall.
The thought of losing my mountain made me sick.

"Tell him I refuse!" Daddy yelled.

"Be reasonable, Charles. It's only a matter of time before you make the wrong choice again. Your letters prove that. The last letter sounded like a madman. Of course your maid and her children will have to find another life besides living off of your income." My uncle raised his voice on the words "maid" and "her children."

I balled my fingers into fists. Amanda could not be sent away.

"You don't need her anymore. The child is grown."

So I was "the child."

"Times are hard, Charles. A store is truly a gift."

"A gift. A gift. To strip me of my calling, my God. A gift."

"Was that night in Georgia part of God's calling, Charles? Is that God giving direction?"

Glass shattered in the window three down from where I stood. I swallowed the scream in my throat and took a step back.

"Your temper hasn't improved, has it, Charles? Father requested I speak with Lydia. It's over. If you stay here, it will be of your own accord. Father will wash his hands of you."

"You won't speak with my wife!" Daddy's voice was strained and twisted in a way I'd never heard before.

"I will." Uncle Lenard's voice was quiet and sure.

"Leave. Leave now! I will not leave Black Mountain. Tell Father he will have to expose me for what he thinks I am. I will not leave my church. I will not."

Footsteps moved across the old wooden floor. "I will have my visit with Lydia and then take my leave. You can't stop me from speaking with her. I'm not afraid of you, brother." Uncle Lenard's footsteps moved down the steps.

I stood still. If Daddy caught me, he would beat me. He had it in him to do anything, and that was exactly why his brother had come. He knew what my father was capable of.

* * *

I WAITED UNTIL DADDY LEFT the church, his boots crunching on the path leading through the cemetery. The cemetery wouldn't be safe, and the last place I wanted to spend much time was the woods. So I went in the back door of the church to wait out my uncle's visit and what it would bring.

If Daddy loved anything at all, it was the church—the actual building, not the people. The walls of the sanctuary were nothing but blackened wood. The windows didn't provide any brightness, even though when I looked through the old, wavy glass, the daylight was still there. I chose to sit in the women's amen corner. My body relaxed on the hard wooden bench as if I hadn't slept for days. I hadn't, not well. Strange dreams had plagued me since my last visit to the cemetery.

A shadow moved into the one source of light, the vestibule where the bell ringer swung from the rope each Sunday morning. A woman moved down the aisle toward me wearing an old-fashioned cotton dress with lace around the throat and hem. Most of the folks on the mountain wore clothes that were old and out-of-date, so I didn't give her much thought. The woman had red hair wrapped in a knot on top of her head.

I stood so as not to scare her since I had been sitting in the shadows. But the woman only looked through me. Around her neck was a cross just like the one Daddy kept in a velvet bag, just like the one Arleen wore when she was buried. In the center was a tiny diamond. When I was six, Daddy told me one day I would receive the necklace, but he never mentioned it again. What I would have given for some real light at that moment.

"Excuse me, ma'am. Can I help you? My father is pastor of this church."

The woman didn't say a word, but her soft look lingered on the walls. "Have you seen my Armetta?"

"I've never heard of her." My voice echoed off the high ceiling.

She looked at the cross of Jesus hanging on the wall. Then she turned to me. "I need to find Armetta. It's so important. I can't leave without her."

"I'm sorry. I don't know her."

A horrible sadness soaked the air in the room.

"If you see her, please tell her Amelia Daniels is looking for her."

A loud popping noise like a rifle being shot came from outside the window. A large limb fell from the big oak tree, narrowly missing the corner of the church. "My goodness." But I was talking to thin air. The woman was gone. She must have left through the back door.

By the time I walked into my backyard, I was thinking only of the limb. I never mentioned the woman to Amanda, who stood on the back porch. Uncle Lenard's car was gone.

"Where have you been, Faith?"

"Walking," I lied.

She raised her eyebrows. "You best not be in the woods. Remember what I told you."

I opened my mouth but closed it again.

"It's full of bad spirits."

"I know. I know," I said.

"Don't act all sassy with me. Have you seen Shelly?"

"No, ma'am."

Amanda smiled. "Your uncle was here."

"Really."

"Didn't stay too long. Your daddy made sure of that. Your mama went to her room and locked the door. Must have been a bad visit."

"Sounds like it."

"Your uncle was driving a big old fancy black car. You sure you didn't see it?"

"No, ma'am." Another lie.

"Nothing good comes from wisteria blooming in June." Amanda watched the lavender petals fall to the ground. I just kept quiet. The time for talking would come, and when it did, I could only pray something good would come from all I had to say.

*　*　*

THAT NIGHT I HEARD a girl's voice call to me from outside. This would be enough to make most people pull the sheets over their heads. I felt the pressure against my temples, the ache of an unused spell. I stopped in the kitchen for a glass of water. Thump, thump, thump, the pain continued. I fumbled with one of Mama's good crystal glasses and shattered it on the floor. I began to gather the larger pieces when one sliced into my thumb. Red flashed across my hand. The pressure in my head left and was replaced by a light feeling, relief.

The girl's voice, now in the room, called out to me.

"What did you say?" I asked.

"Make a charm quilt."

The pain in my head was gone. I went back to bed.

MY BODY WAS LIGHTER, better, when I didn't eat, but I couldn't tell Mama or Amanda such a thing.

"Look here, Miss Faith, I made your favorite red velvet cake to go with your lunch." Amanda held out the platter with the beautiful white frosted cake on it.

"Thank you. I'll have a slice after supper."

Amanda frowned. "What's got into you, girl? You're not eating a thing."

I forced a laugh. "I have to watch my figure. You'd make me fatter than a laying hen if I let you."

She gave me her look. "You look on the skinny side to me."

"Amanda, I have a question."

"What that be?"

"What is a charm quilt?" I looked away.

Amanda grew still. "Why you ask about such a thing?"

I shrugged. "I don't know. I heard one of the church women talking about making a charm quilt."

Amanda clicked her tongue. "I just bet you did. Them holier-than-thou ladies." She placed a tea towel lightly over the cake and put it away. "It ain't no quilt you want to make, Faith. Charm quilts ain't nothing but trouble. They can be one thing or another, but most of the time they all have meanness in common. Can't think of no other reason to make one."

"How about protection? Can you protect someone by making one?"

Amanda gave me a sharp look. "Well, I reckon, but I ain't never heard of such around here."

"But I could do it?"

"You need to get your mind off any charms. You know how I feel about such things. They ain't made for children."

I laughed. "I'm not a child."

Amanda gave me a real smile. "Leave magic to me. A charm quilt ain't nothing but hurt, Miss Faith."

"Yes, ma'am."

"I mean it."

"Okay." I left for my room. The voice said a charm quilt.

LATER THAT AFTERNOON when the heat was the worst, I went upstairs for a nap. I had the strangest dream. Nana Tyson stood in my room near the window. I had only seen pictures of her, but I knew her instantly. She wore a white suit, the pricey kind found in cities. Her body looked frail, and I rushed from my bed to support her so she wouldn't collapse. Her smile was sad. "Your mother isn't here to meet me? She sent you instead?"

"She's not here. Only me."

"She never chose to see what sat right in front of her, never. I'm so sorry you were pulled into their mess, sweetie." Nana Tyson's words woke me up. The room was empty, but I swore I smelled her perfume, a light lavender fragrance.

I had slept all afternoon and it was night. I tiptoed through the hall to Daddy's room. The door was cracked open and his bed was untouched. But in the dark corner stood the ghost I saw with Shelly in the backyard, the one who seemed angry, a colored girl. She wore the same stained, old-fashioned yellow party dress. Shelly called her Armetta. Of course I never told Shelly I could see her ghosts. No. She'd use that fact against me. In that moment I remembered the woman in the church, the one who asked after Armetta. The spirit stood in the shadows looking at me as if this wasn't the first time she had come to Daddy's room. "There be a price to pay. A way to live and a way to die. What will you pick, girl?"

I jerked awake, this time to my room flooded with late-afternoon sun. The dreams sat with me on the bed, too real. A sharp knock made me jump. Daddy pushed open the door. When I was younger, I used to wonder how many plain white dress shirts he owned. Probably a closet-ful. Each one crisp and clean.

"Your uncle Lenard was here this morning. Did you see him?" His voice was soft but stern. When I didn't respond, he ran his fingers through his thick blond hair. "He upset your mother. Don't bother her."

"Was it him or you?" My words were quiet but sassy, almost hateful.

"You don't want to be punished, Faith." His voice turned mean.

"I am a woman, a grown woman. You can't punish a grown woman."

His face turned hard. "You are my daughter. Is that understood? You will not disobey me. You obviously do not know what is good for you."

"You can't keep me from being grown. Most girls my age are married."

"Really, Faith, is that what you're looking for—a husband? Didn't you learn your lesson with that boy? Don't you understand what kind of girl you are? You can never marry." His voice grew louder. "You are an abomination in the eyes of God. A sinner of the worst kind."

"Stop. I'm not," I cried.

He stepped closer. "You have sinned in more ways than one."

"Will is that boy's name and you know it. I never did anything wrong and you know that too. I just wonder what Mama would say if she knew the story Will knew."

Daddy grabbed my arm, squeezing until his knuckles turned white. "You are a tramp, trash. You make me sick." His face was bright red. "Your colored boy will walk with you the rest of the way to Hell. You're just like him. You are the devil, the mark of the damned is on your soul."

I only stared at him.

He shoved me so hard, my head bumped against the wall. "You're a whore." He spit on me and left the room.

The pounding pressure began. I pulled open my drawer and took out the knife. The thump at my temples slowed. I sat on the bed and stared at the wall.

Shelly barged through the door into my bedroom without knocking and stood stark still. Her gaze settled on the paring knife in my hands, so perfect for peeling the skin of an apple. I pressed my thighs together like a child trying to hide her worst deed. Shelly moved through the space separating us and took the knife right out of my fingers while all the time staring at me like I was some crazy person. I was. For a minute Shelly and I just looked at each other. I guess I could have explained how making the cuts helped me breathe better, took the pressure away, helped me from using the magic, but shame formed a knot in my throat.

She studied me a minute more. "You got one mean spirit following you. Probably all stirred up from you stealing pictures off them stones at the cemetery. You crazy putting them on quilts. That's just asking for a haint to smite you down. You're one strange girl. I know what you really are. I've seen what the others haven't. Something worse is going to happen if you don't stop that mess." Her words clipped the air like sharp shears used for cutting hair. "The spirit be a colored girl. She's part of this here mountain, and that makes her a haint to worry after."

I swallowed the crazy laugh building in my chest while the warm blood trickled down my thigh. "I don't believe in ghosts, Shelly," I said in my most hateful voice. "And really you don't know anything about me."

"You go ahead and poke your old hatefulness at me. This spirit is mean. Don't mess with mocking her. She'll not have it. And I know all about you being a mountain witch. You can't deny it. I been watching you."

Oh, how I wished I was a witch.

"You ought to ask Nada to help you before you make a mess you can't clean up alone." She looked at the blood dripping on the small handmade rug.

The warm moistness on my thigh kept me from ripping out her hair. "You're crazy with all your magic and talk of ghosts."

"You ain't the one to be calling nobody crazy, girl. You know it be a real spirit. I seen you looking at the one that saved us from the storm. You was right there and seen it all. I know you can see them. Your face tells the whole truth just like now. You know what you done to your legs is crazy. You know it."

I looked out the window. Those woods were haunted. I'd heard the cries myself on some nights.

"You might be mean and spoiled but you ain't never been a liar. I'll tell Nada you're coming tonight."

I thought of clawing out her eyes. "Will wouldn't like how you're acting right now."

She sucked in air. "Will ain't here, and if he was, he sure wouldn't like what you be doing one bit." With all her mean ways, I still understood the truth floating between us. He would hate what I had become. "I be special. You remember that. I have the most special gift on this mountain as far as Nada believes. Go on and see her after supper." And she was gone out the door.

Sometimes I wondered just what she knew of Will leaving. She spoke out about everything but him. It was as if he died.

* * *

AMANDA WAITED AT HER little wooden table. Shelly wasn't anywhere to be seen. This fact helped me relax. Amanda crushed pieces of what looked like brick into red dust. "Sit, child." Her voice was sweet enough, but I heard the sternness. She wasn't putting up with excuses.

The chair I sat in creaked with age.

Amanda swished her finger in the dust. "You be too thin." The heat bugs hummed outside. "Pastor's real put out with his uppity ways and ran him off. Your mama had a nice long talk with him. I don't know about what, but it couldn't be good. Lenard Dobbins ain't never been nothing but pure trouble, more so than your daddy. I promise you." She looked at me. "Mrs. Dobbins said she didn't believe you talked to your uncle. She's comfortable with that. But me and you know that be a lie."

"Yes, ma'am." The words hurt my teeth.

She nodded. "What you see in this here dust?" She fluttered her fingers at the tabletop. Amanda was pretty. Her face was soft and gentle, and her hair was relaxed in big curls. Most of the time she kept it tied in a bright-colored scarf.

"A shadow shaped like Shelly's ghost girl, the one from my dream. Armetta." The words popped out of my mouth like someone else was speaking for me.

Amanda nodded like I made perfect sense. She pushed some of the red dirt around so it made another design. "What now?"

I shrugged and turned away. The pressure in my head threatened to begin.

"Look hard, girl, or you be wasting my time."

Letters formed in the dust: "W-I-L-L."

Amanda sucked in a sharp breath. "Don't mess with me."

Anger bubbled up from way down deep inside, but I managed to shove it back. *Remember, Faith, you got to keep this a secret. You can never let on you know.* Will's words rang in my head.

"I didn't come here for this. You asked me to tell you what I saw. I did. I see his name."

Amanda moved my skirt up my thigh. "Will ain't got a thing to do with any of that."

Some of the cuts I made earlier in the day were trying to heal. The new one looked bad, deeper. "Why did you ask me if you didn't want to know? I'm sorry you don't like the answer. Next time I won't even bother coming to see you."

"Never you mind now. Stay where you be. How Will got a thing to do with this? He's been gone too long now." Her voice sounded strained, like she was holding back.

The truth was that Will was behind more than Amanda knew. He left me when I needed him most. I looked out the front door into the yard. "I don't know anything about him leaving," I lied. It was the untruths that ate at my soul.

Amanda watched me close. "I guess. But I don't like thinking on him. His very name hurts to the bone." Her touch on my arm pleaded for a better answer. "I just need to know what happened that last day, Miss Faith. You don't owe me a thing, but what happened to my boy?"

She thought he was dead. Maybe he was; at least the Will that walked off our mountain died. Sweat broke out on the back of my neck, and my head began to pound. I promised. "I don't know." The silence in the room took me over.

"How you don't know, Miss Faith? How? You two was closer than any souls could be. Drove Pastor crazy. I seen that. I knew. I always warned Will to stay arm's length of you, but he wouldn't listen."

The words were stuck in my stomach, twisting and turning.

"You know. I know you do."

The hum of the heat bugs grew louder. I swallowed the thick feeling down my throat. "I don't know." Each untruth tasted easier.

She squeezed her rough fingers into my arm. "What happened? He wouldn't just up and leave like he did. No good-byes. He was my boy. How can you tell me you don't know? Now look at this mess." She nodded at my scars. "Something happened that day. You've been like my own girl. Why won't you tell me?" The pleas pulled at me. I loved

Amanda. It would serve both her and Will right if I told her everything that happened that afternoon. Just screamed it at the top of my lungs. He wasn't ever coming back to the mountain.

The familiar knock began inside of my head. I had to concentrate and wait for the feeling to pass.

Amanda released my arm. "You wasn't nothing but fifteen. You can't be blamed for anything that happened when he left. What drove him from me, Miss Faith?" She looked back at my scars. "Them things have a story to tell me. Each and every cut." She covered the marks on my thighs with my skirt. "Something is driving you to this. Something you know."

She was right about that.

Amanda picked up a bottle and sprinkled white powder over the dust on the table. With her eyes closed tightly, she moved her lips in what looked to be a silent prayer. She scooped the dust into a small sack with a drawstring. "Sprinkle this in front of your door and cover it with the small rug near your bed so it won't be noticed."

I nodded.

"As long as the dust is there, you be protected from your father. He can't come through that door. You should have come to me earlier. I should have known you was in trouble. Your mama came here worrying over you. I should have known. He can't hurt you if you do what I say."

My hand tingled and burned when I touched the pouch. I wanted to believe in its protection. I had to believe that Amanda's magic was real.

"You do what I say, and the bad can't come. I've been good as that mama of yours to you. Rocked you in my lap alongside of Will. You crawled in my bed when you was sick. You tagged after me all day long. You remember all that? You know how much I love you." She pointed to the drawstring sack. "This be my best conjure. It's a strong spell. But what follows you might be bigger than any of my magic. Time will tell. The one condition on this spell working is you got to believe, girl. You can't doubt." She reached behind her and took a small brown jar off a low shelf. "Here, keep this salve on those places. They'll heal without scars. No more of that mess. You hear?"

A jagged line cut through my heart. I loved Amanda that much. I knew my cuts marked her. "Yes, ma'am." I hung my head.

"Now, it's not shame I want to see on that face of yours. You be the best girl I know besides my Shelly. You got to stop walking that grave-yard. It's not a safe place. All matters of haints looking at you. This whole mountain not be safe for you. Something is chasing your soul. Winter be here soon. Nobody has to run in the winter. If we can make it until then, my time with Mrs. Dobbins will be over. We got to man-age until winter. Then we'll see."

"Mama will always need you, Amanda." But the truth was I needed to know Amanda would be right where I could find her.

Amanda gave me a dark look. "Lord, your mama be the thorn in my side since the day I chose her."

"I heard Mama chose *you*."

Amanda laughed. "Don't believe no stories that woman has told. I picked her, sent her a dream."

Those two had something. It wasn't love, and it wasn't hatred ei-ther. Something strange, still, and turbulent all in the same movement sat between them.

Amanda touched my hand. "If Will comes to you, leave him be. He don't need to be in this mess. Leave him. Understand?"

"If he came to me, you'd know 'cause I'm not going anywhere. I wish I could." I was stuck on the mountain. Shoot, I couldn't even go to Ashe-ville without a scene. "Will was smart enough to never come back."

"You'll be right here for a while. Just a while, though." She looked out the door like she could see something I couldn't. "Go on, now. Get on to your house before it gets too dark." Amanda sat at the table as if all the energy had drained out of her. She stared where the dust had been. "It's going to be a hot, hot summer, I suspect."

* * *

WHEN I GOT BACK to my room, I found a note:

> *Faith:*
>   *That bottle tree in the yard is for the colored spirit that don't like us.*
> *But it didn't work. It ain't going to work 'cause she's way too smart. This*
> *colored girl is going to cause a bunch of trouble. Be careful.*
>
>   *Shelly*

Part of me knew this was Shelly's way of saying she halfway cared, but I wouldn't have admitted that out loud.

Mama and Daddy came to say good night just like always, like I was some little girl instead of a grown woman. Daddy stopped at the door like he had run into a wall. I held my breath. He made no move to come across the threshold. Mama didn't even notice. She was blind just like Nana Tyson said in the dream. Behind Daddy stood Armetta.

My newest quilt was spread over the armchair near my desk, waiting for me to gather the most important pieces. It was going to be my charm quilt. A death quilt. This quilt would be for protection. It was sewn to make those included in the stitches safe and give death to the one who threatened them.

Mama hugged me. "I worry about you, Faith. What will I do when you find a husband and leave home? I can't let you leave me," she whispered. But what she refused to see was I had already left.

THE NEXT MORNING I set off for Miss Tuggle's garden, with Shelly following at a distance. If only Will could see what kind of girl he left me to protect. The only reason she tagged along was her true love for the books Miss Tuggle loaned her. I understood. As mean as Shelly was, she still deserved to go to school. To read. It wasn't fair. Mama said life was never fair and you couldn't help everyone. But wasn't it our job to try?

Many of the plants we were gathering were for healings Miss Tuggle performed. While she refused to believe in mountain magic, I wholeheartedly believed in Miss Tuggle's powers. She called it science. Amanda called hers conjuring. I saw their abilities as freedom from those who would, given the chance, control them.

The sun was pulling slightly away from the east when Miss Tuggle met us on the porch. "Hot today, ladies. Hope we don't die of heatstroke." She wore a big, floppy straw hat to block the sun off her face.

I loved how she referred to us as ladies. Shelly even softened around the edges and loosened the ridge that was her shoulders.

"Have you finished *Tom Sawyer,* Shelly?"

The girl grew quiet and humble whenever she was in Miss Tuggle's company. "Yes, ma'am."

"Good. What did you think?"

Shelly kind of smiled. "That Tom was a rascal but brave. I'd want him on my side if I was in trouble."

Miss Tuggle laughed. "I have some more books, but first we will gather the rosemary today."

A stubborn look went across Shelly's face. "No, ma'am. Today is a fiery day. Rosemary that is picked today will hurt instead of help."

Miss Tuggle clicked her tongue but smiled. "You know what I think of that nonsense."

Shelly hung her head. "Yes, ma'am, but it still be barren."

A barren day was perfect to gather the rosemary I needed. Just a little, along with some hair from Miss Tuggle's brush. Of course she couldn't know. I had taken her hair a few times for practicing some spells with no results, but this new spell, the death quilt, was powerful. This one would work. There were many things Miss Tuggle didn't believe in that I thought of as real. I'm not sure she'd ever change her way of thinking even if proof waltzed right in front of her. Miss Tuggle had to be part of the death quilt, the map to the destination where I would find freedom.

Shelly ran her hand down the stems of rosemary and pulled gently on the leaves just like Miss Tuggle showed her. The air filled with the musky fragrance.

We stood nearly shoulder to shoulder. Miss Tuggle stood between us, slightly taller, straighter. She looked from me to Shelly. "You two are so much alike, whether you want to admit it or not."

Both of us huffed at the same time. No two girls could be further apart. But the garden held the magical peace I sought, so I didn't speak. Within the aging, homemade pole fence, I was worthy, whole, important, and full of courage to bring changes my way. We worked until lunch. Miss Tuggle insisted we take a sack of her homemade biscuits and salty ham. Shelly left with three new books.

I SLIPPED AWAY FROM THE HOUSE while Shelly hung clothes on the line and talked with that ghost Armetta. What an odd life I had. Our maid carried on conversations with the dead, and I took the gravestones as mine. My square of silk, hidden in a bottom dresser drawer since the tornado, was clean and ready for a new rubbing. This time there wasn't a cloud in the sky. I knew just where I wanted to go without hesitation. I knelt on the thick grass in front of the stone, and for a minute I traced it with my finger: ARLEEN PATRICIA BROWN. I draped the silk over the marker. The etching would be the perfect centerpiece for the death quilt, an essential piece. The crayon moved smoothly across each letter. The silk grew warm under my fingertips, almost hot, the kind of hot that calmed a sore muscle. A shiver ran over my head and a fuzzy feeling worked through my chest. Arleen. It had been four years since her death. Why had I waited so long to retrieve her design and create her quilt? It was her quilt.

"What are you doing?" The sun blinded me, but I knew Daddy's angry voice.

I continued to rub, not wanting to lose the warmth, the tingle. To give up would break the spell working through me. Freedom. The heat in my fingers raced up my arms and shocked my mind.

"Stop!"

The design was perfect, the letters crisp.

"Did you hear what I said? Are you crazy?" Daddy touched my shoulder.

Something worked inside of me. I jerked away. "No."

He raised his hand in the air and let it fall across my face with so much force a tangy, bitter taste filled my mouth. The wind kicked up and turned from hot to chilly. Several drops of my blood sprinkled over the silk and marred the design.

"Go home. I don't want to see you doing this again. You're of the devil."

I pushed back into a kneeling position without a tear in my eye. Empty.

"Get out of my sight! Stay away from this grave. You've no business here."

The air had a touch of coolness. He left me on the grave. The etching was complete. I bowed my head. Because I was his daughter.

PART THREE

Tangled Truths

June 1939

"Some stories try to tell the truth, but they become tangled in all the hearsay."

—*Armetta Lolly*

Faith Dobbins

W HEN I WAS JUST a little thing, after we moved to Black Mountain but before Shelly came along, I would take Amanda's hand and smell it for no reason. The musky scent of hard work mixed with lemon kept me safe, showed me I was loved. A darkness with no name or shape hung in the air, something thick and fearful, always threatening in a heavy sort of way. Amanda never asked me what I was doing when I smelled her. Instead, she acted like this was the most natural thing a white girl could do to her colored nursemaid. But Amanda was so much more than a maid to me. She was my calm in the worst upheavals. I felt her unconditional love even in the smallest of things. When I was old enough to understand Amanda wasn't really part of our family, I would pretend she was my mama.

So the first time I saw Shelly curled up in a sling that hung next to Amanda's body, I knew that place should have been mine. I threw a fit, the granddaddy of fits. Even then I knew that Shelly had everything I longed after. My tantrums went unnoticed by Mama, who seemed the most tolerant of mothers until one realized she was detached. It was simply not in Mama's mind to see I was tortured. At times my fits were so intense I would bite myself and leave a ring of deep teeth marks on my chubby arm. Sometimes I couldn't even remember throwing the tantrum. I would break my favorite toy, and in one case, I cut a beloved dress into pieces with Mama's sewing scissors. The only person who could settle me was Will. He would walk into the room and put an arm around me, pulling me close.

Amanda always clicked her tongue and would tell him to let me be. I would bury my face, hot with tears, in his chest. There I would stay until my heart slowed and the anger seeped from me.

"Come on." He'd pull me out to the garden or the edge of the woods. "Look at that there red bird, Faith. You be as beautiful as him. You be way too loving to act like you do about Shelly. One day you'll be looking out for her." In so many ways he was an extension of me.

Where was Daddy? Oh, he was ever-present, even when he was physically removed from our house. In many ways he was the problem, but I was way too young to understand that back then.

Mama loved me best of all. I was her treasure. She told me I was the child she almost lost but found—whatever that meant. But when she spoke those words, music went off in my head. So Mama taught me the lessons of loyalty and avoidance. In her example, I found a way to escape much of what Daddy thrust on us while still remaining in my flesh. It was a magic trick, really. To remove my essence in front of his very eyes, a sleight of hand, and he never noticed.

While Mama presented her valuable lessons, and Amanda taught me love, Daddy schooled me in how to lie. I was a liar not by intention but by circumstances. My favorite Bible story was Joshua and the wall of Jericho. There was proof people could win in the worst of conditions just by shouting something bad to the ground. Faith. But how could a young girl have such beliefs when the one she trusted, who should have protected her, opened the door to the darkest of times? How? Lies. Daddy told lies just by breathing the air in and pushing it out.

THE AFTERNOON DADDY HIT ME at Arleen's grave something inside my chest snapped. A cracking of bones. To say I was shocked by his action wouldn't have been true. He was a contradiction that parted my soul like the Red Sea.

As I knelt at Arleen's grave, tasting my own blood, a power moved through me, a rush of emotions so strong I thought I might kill him right then and there. And with this thought flooded a deep dark guilt. I was the same as him.

Somehow I had to stop the whole business. I ran home and locked myself in my room. No more. No more. These words beat in my head.

"*Look,*" the girl's soft voice whispered.

The hairs on the back of my neck stood up. My heart fluttered in my throat. "Who is there?" I called.

"*Be still, girl. Listen.*"

Then I heard him. Will. His sweet voice. "*You have to stay here and be clear of him as much as you can.*" Our final conversation before he left the mountain. He smelled of the woods on a rainy day, fresh and clean. His soft face was fading from my memory. I loved him. I always had.

"*Do you remember his words?*" Maybe this was the mountain's whisper that Amanda talked about. "*Take his warning. He was smart. Good. He always, always told you the truth.*"

It was his truth that nearly finished me off. Down in the shadows of my soul sat the whole murky story, the reason Will had to leave, the reason I had to stay. And this truth could never be put aside no matter how hard I tried.

I unfolded the silk and gave it a pop in the air before I spread it on the bed. I smoothed the wrinkles. A shiver of expectation swept over me. I brought the quilt from the trunk and placed it on the bed alongside the rubbing that would be stitched in the center. The quilt edges were scalloped and covered in tiny rosebuds, stitched in red, bloodred, new thread purchased at the mercantile in Asheville. In longhand I had sewn the name "Arleen." The letters were pale green, a satisfying shade. My charm just for Arleen's truth. A girl my age should be married or close to it. Instead of gathering items for my future wedding, I collected old buttons, lace, ribbons, and handkerchiefs, personal possessions. I was the crazy quilt girl of Black Mountain. But a needle sliding through the cloth with ease, grace, a looping delicate satin stitch, was better than any human relationship. I could trust the thread to always produce the beauty I saw in my mind.

My fingers shook and the dull pressure built in my temples. Not again. "Help me accept what is true and move through it." I prayed these words, but still the urge to cut was strong, overwhelming. I said the chant over and over, hoping if I said it enough times without messing up, the pain would leave. Arleen's face floated into my thoughts. The last time I saw her, I handed her a sack of my used dresses. Her stomach had been large, and her face reflected a true hatred, as if it were my fault she was pregnant and unmarried.

Daddy had forced me to bring the clothes. He said a good God-fearing girl would want to minister to this poor soul. Then he shoved me against the car door. *You will take these dresses to Arleen and tell her they are for her to wear after the baby comes. Tell her you will help in any way you can.* Daddy never left the car. So, I told Arleen to have a safe delivery. I wanted to be kind. I never intended to look down on her.

These memories pounded in my head. I should have taken time to speak longer to Arleen. I lifted the sewing basket from the drawer. "Help me accept what is true and move through it."

A glint, a shimmer from the sunlight on the table next to the bed, drew my attention. The room turned ice-cold. The twinkle of something near the lamp pulled at me. The tiny gold cross hung from the bedpost.

"How did that get here?" But I knew the cross. I knew the tiny diamond had sparkled around Arleen's neck in the fine new casket Daddy bought in Asheville. I knew it belonged to him, and thinking how Arleen might have gotten it made me sick. Arleen's face had been frozen in pain, and in her arms, a tiny baby. A boy.

I was seeing things. Crazy. One little slice, just one, a movement really. Maybe just the coldness of the blade next to my skin would bring peace, certainty, even if it was short-lived. The thought of cutting was so sweet my teeth ached. I closed my eyes at the sight of the necklace and squeezed them so tight little stars danced bright red, the color of blood when it hit the air.

"Help me," I breathed. The razor was buried in the top dresser drawer under my cotton panties. I felt around and rubbed the cold, hard blade with my thumb. Just one slice and relief. The cross dangled on the gold chain, a delicate, pretty thing. The necklace didn't even belong to Arleen.

"I paid for it, girl. Your daddy put it on my neck. Said I was his, like he was really giving me a gift. The devil's gift was more like it."

I dropped the razor.

Arleen sat on my bed. She touched the cross with her finger. "Pretty, ain't it?" She wore a red dress I had given her. Her long hair spilled over her shoulders in thick curls. She waved one of our church fans. Her lips were painted a deep red. She was prettier than she'd ever been alive.

"Why are you here?" My voice sounded calm, distant.

"You wished me here, girl." Again she touched the cross. "We got to take care of you, seeing how you're so tired and strained to keep going. I'll protect you. Let me fight him. I'm strong now."

I looked at the razor on the floor.

"No more, Faith. If you cut yourself this time, he wins. He'll own you for life." Arleen clicked her tongue like Amanda did when she wasn't happy with one of us kids. She dangled the cross on her finger. "This here is our prize, our one and only prize."

"I'm sorry I brought you my old clothes. Please go away and let me handle this."

"Oh, girl, you thinking on that?" She stood. "It wasn't you I was hating that day." My old dress fit her perfect. She held out the hand with the cross.

The knocking in my head began to blind me. I just needed the razor. Just one cut.

"No more." Arleen could read my thoughts. She was so close. "Use me, Faith. I'm better than some old razor any day. You got to take my hand. I can't help if you don't."

"You're a spell from Amanda," I whispered. The pounding in my head began to slow. The sun had disappeared behind the trees, and outside the window was the lifeless gray of in-between.

"No, ma'am. I'm a memory you long to throw away, to be safe from. Ain't no safe in this situation, and you know it."

I looked into her deep brown eyes and reached for her hand. Electricity ran through my arm.

"That's me. I'm with you now," Arleen whispered. "I promise to do all the things you've wanted to do. I promise. You and me, we're the same. You took my words from the stone and wished me here. We're going to finish us a quilt with a death spell. God help the soul that is sewn inside of a death quilt because if that soul touches the quilt, it will be damned forever."

Arleen Brown

I STOOD IN FRONT of Faith's looking glass. She would be just fine now. I picked up that mean old razor and dropped it out the window into the rosebushes below. I had a job to do. My soul was tangled up in the making. I pushed the cross into my skirt pocket. Wouldn't do a bit of good for one of those fine women downstairs to notice it. Then me and Faith's secret would be out. I had just a little time to sew a soul into that death quilt before the nightmares began.

Shelly Parker

WHEN A GIRL'S MAMA TELLS HER not to do something, most of the time she busts a gut to do it. That was me. Arleen Brown standing on that porch for a whole afternoon stayed on my mind. Something told me she hadn't disappeared at all. I was about to bust from wanting to find out why she came in the first place. The heat had turned off so bad in the afternoon I finished off them clothes, helped Nada with the melons for supper, and went to dust the fancy dishes in the pantry. One square window allowed me a look at the bottle tree as the sun sprinkled the colors over the yard. Nada polished the already shiny silver. We worked side by side quiet as could be.

Then Mrs. Dobbins came into the kitchen with her face dragging on the ground. "Faith is locked in her room and refuses to come out for supper. I think her and Charles had a fight. Did you see him with her, Amanda?"

"No, ma'am. I ain't seen him all day. But she ain't been right since that brother of Pastor's came."

"Amanda, see if you can get her to come out for supper. She listens to you."

I twisted around, and my elbow caught a stack of dishes just as Pastor came walking in the back door. The gravy bowl fell to the floor, shattering into a bunch of pieces.

All was silent for a second.

"You've broken the best piece. Those dishes belonged to my grandmother." Pastor fixed his dark stare on me. "See me in my study." He never raised his voice.

Mrs. Dobbins looked at Nada like the world was coming to an end.

Nada showed me her "be careful" look.

I picked up the pieces, swallowing silly tears.

PASTOR LOOKED OUT THE WINDOW in his study. "Where I come from this isn't even hot." He said this without looking at me. "Do you like summer, Shelly?" His voice was soft but held a sharp edge.

"It be okay. It ain't my favorite."

He chuckled. "All young ladies love snow. I bet you love snow." He stared at me. "When the worst snow comes in the winter, I feel smothered. Trapped."

This was a strange talk about a broken gravy bowl.

Armetta stood in the far corner where the thick shadows hung. I hadn't never been so happy to see a haint.

She frowned at me. "You ain't read a word of that book I left you. How we going to help anybody?"

"So you've become clumsy, Shelly?" Pastor's words curled around the room like some big old black snake. On his face was a soft smile that might fool some but not me 'cause I knew that man. He wasn't nice to nobody.

"If you don't read it, things are going to get worse than you ever dreamed, girlie." Armetta moved close to me. "Don't let no show of his softness fool you. He be tagging you right now, and if you don't read that book, you going to end up like that haint who stood out on the porch the other night. You listening?"

"Clumsy and deaf too, Shelly? Or are you afraid of me? I hope not. I wouldn't dream of hurting you. That's not who I am."

"I'm not scared, sir. I broke the gravy bowl twisting around in the pantry. It be awful crowded in there."

"So you're blaming it on me, Shelly? That's not respectful."

I looked at my old shoes with run-down heels that rocks poked through when I hiked to the cemetery or over to Miss Tuggle's.

"Do you need anything, Shelly? I can get you whatever you might need."

"I could use me some shoes," I said.

"He be trying to trick you. Careful. You don't want nothing from him," Armetta whispered.

"How old are you now?" He looked me up and down.

"Fifteen."

"A woman." He nodded. "And do you like boys?" He drummed his fingers on the desk.

"He's crafty as a dern fox." Armetta was so close I should have felt her breath.

"None around here to like. And I don't want to end up like Arleen Brown."

Armetta cackled. "See, that's why I picked you, Shelly. You be brave."

He cleared his throat and looked away. "You're not like your brother. That's the only reason I've let you stay on. I won't have disease and abomination in my house."

"Don't pop off. Don't say a word. It be a trap. He wants to hurt you. He wants you to give him a good reason." She looked over at Pastor. "Killing him would be a pure pleasure. Don't you think, girl?"

"Did you ever hear Faith talking to your brother?"

"He's a snake." Armetta glared at him.

"No. I seen their heads together but they always hushed up when I came near." The thought of Will and Faith whispering still sent anger through my body.

"He contaminated my daughter."

A scream went off in my head. I balled my fingers into fists.

"Go on. I don't want to think about your brother. Leave me. Maybe we'll take a walk soon, Shelly. I would like that."

"Get on, now. Be careful." Armetta moved to me, and the breeze sent a icy-cold chill through my bones.

FAITH STOOD on the edge of the woods just looking.

"What are you doing?" I asked.

She didn't move.

"Mrs. Dobbins is all stirred up about you. Don't you care?"

Faith turned and looked at me. That's when I understood Mrs. Dobbins's worries. Something wasn't right with that girl.

"I want to go to Miss Tuggle's tomorrow." Her voice sounded different, lower.

"I guess we could, but we gathered pretty much everything yesterday. I ain't even started my books she gave me."

She tilted her head to the side. "You can read, girl?"

Faith had done gone around the mountain with craziness. "Well, I guess I can, since you be the one who taught me how. What's wrong with you? You been messing with cutting again? I thought Nada fixed that."

Her face turned quiet. "No, that mess got stopped before it started." She wasn't talking like Faith at all.

"Mrs. Dobbins said you and your daddy had words?"

A shadow moved over her face. "He ain't my daddy. You got it?" Her fingers were balled into fists.

"What's wrong with you? Of course he be your daddy. I don't blame you none. He's crazy. I got to go find something to do. Pastor done told me to get on out of the house." I walked off toward the cabin. Wasn't one reason why I couldn't go home.

Faith stayed by the woods, looking like something was coming for her.

Armetta scooted along beside me. "That girl be hurt deeper than you'll ever know. She's gone. Won't be back anytime soon, but she's close by. She wants her truth to be known. Ain't that what we all want?"

A flash of Nada went by the kitchen window. She knew Pastor's words were all over my body. "Why you always around me?" I asked. "How long you been here? Did you know my brother?"

"You be full of questions, seeing how you won't read my book. What you think I showed it to you for? It be important. You just going to let folks die?"

A cold chill ran along my arms like she had touched me. "I ain't reading it."

"You got to 'cause you be important to what will happen. And bad is going to happen whether you read my book or not. It's going to happen to you, but you be so dumb you won't see. The girl that can see haints won't open her eyes. Ask your mama why she be afraid of Pastor. Ask her what she knows about all his doings."

My stomach flipped over. "I don't want you around, haint."

"Well now, girlie, you be stuck just like me. It's the way life gathers to you. But you need to read that book if you care about that granny woman friend of yours. 'Cause she could be the one that dies. Somebody always has to die, but your granny woman might just die a early death." And she was gone.

"So we'll go to Miss Tuggle's tomorrow?" Faith stood right beside me.

I turned to look into those deep brown eyes. Something just wasn't right about that girl.

* * *

NADA DISHED UP OUR FOOD that evening flinging bits here and there, sloshing part of mine on the table. "Have you noticed a change in Miss Faith?"

It near drove me crazy to hear Nada call that girl Miss when she up and raised the mean old thing. "Naw," I lied.

Nada glanced at me with that squinted-eye look. "You mean to tell me you didn't see how she acted this evening? Like she be a stranger now?"

I scooped up the pinto beans on my plate. "She talked different this afternoon."

"Something ain't right about that girl," Nada fussed. "Something has happened. You sure you don't know nothing, Shelly?"

I shrugged. "No, ma'am."

"Eat, Shelly," Nada snapped.

This all had to do with Arleen Brown's ghost standing on the porch. Now, that was something to think on. The spirit had left and Faith changed. "Faith is grown. You don't have to look after her no more. She ought to be marrying this summer. She's the right age." Now, I knew that was plain silliness, 'cause Faith didn't have one boy even interested in her. Her beauty was there for everyone to notice—and that's one of the reasons I didn't like her none—but she was part of a package. No boy wanted to come calling on the pastor's daughter, especially if it was Pastor Dobbins.

Nada's steady stare washed over me.

"She's old enough to do what she wants. Miss Tuggle even said that."

"You been spending too much time at that woman's house." Nada stomped to the door and stared at the main house. "Them storms be big on the horizon." She was quiet a minute. "You're jealous of a white girl."

I laughed. "That'd be like taking a stroll through a blackberry thicket. I'd be bound to get more than one thorn."

Nada turned to look me dead in the eyes. "I know you be jealous. I been watching that girl since she was born. I look after her. What you thinking, gal? You want me to have a hard heart? That's what you want from your own mama?"

The pinto beans were pushed to the side of my plate, hidden under the potatoes, like I was still some little girl. "I just want you, Nada."

"Lord, Shelly, you've always had me. I'm right here, but you almost grown now. You got to stand up and be that woman you going to be. You can't cling to me. If you do, I've failed as a mama."

"Yes, ma'am." I knew I'd never really had her. A soul can stand right next to you and still not be with you.

"You think them books you got hid in your bedroom is going to teach you something you don't already know? You looking to be something more, and I can't stop that. Maybe I should get me a jealous bone."

I stared at my plate.

"And don't go thinking you got some kind of big old secret. I know all about that money under the floorboard, been knowing you had it since Nellie Pritchard ran off this mountain. I ain't one of those dumb enough to think she died. The girl had too much smarts. That knowing didn't come from magic. No, that is one mama talking to another. Mrs. Connor told me that part of the story. You hold on to that money. It'll be running money one day."

I felt like a heel of three-day-old bread was better than me.

"A mama don't have to make over the child closest to her heart, Shelly. You're all I have." Her voice broke in half.

But I was second 'cause Will left. She had to want me. I scooted the beans around on the plate. Lord, sometimes what a girl asked after was too much, way too much.

"You run rings around Miss Faith and she knows it. That's why she treats you so sassy. She got a whole lot less than me and you."

A grunt escaped me.

"What you thinking? You thinking something over there?"

"She got everything any girl would ever want, Nada. I can't run rings around her or nobody else. She's pretty, rich, and white."

"So you think that's what life is? You sure I raised you?"

My food sure got a lot of notice.

She shook her head and clicked her tongue. "It's my job to stand right here and open my arms. I just hope you try and see it that way. It's what I get paid for. There ain't no talking about it. If we don't have Miss Faith, we don't have a living." She touched my shoulder. "You think I don't know how you feel? I know how you ache after Will and worry on losing me too. But, girl, we all lose someone. That's all the comfort I can give. I'd be lying if I gave more."

Silly baby tears came into my eyes.

Nada moved to the other side of the kitchen. "And don't keep that money under the floorboard. It ain't no good place. Find a better one. Like I said, that be your running money."

"I ain't running, Nada."

"We all say that in our lifetime, child. It be the biggest lie we tell."

I LOOKED UP from scrubbing the clothes on the washboard and saw Faith walking in my direction.

"Shelly."

I didn't even bother to look at her face or make a sound.

The air turned cool, and seeing how it was hot only minutes before she came walking up, I got uneasy. Now, I'd been mad, hurt, and downright bothered with Faith, but never scared.

"You know who I am, don't you? You done figured it out even if you ain't admitting up to it. You came to see me and my baby, to peek in the box. You know me. We watched the sun sink into the trees together. You know me." The sunlight hit the bottle tree just right so blue stained the grass.

My heart jumped in my chest. "You be crazy."

She shook her head. "No, ma'am. I know just what I want. Do you know what I want?"

A dark shadow moved in behind Faith. "I think we're disturbing Shelly's work, Faith." Pastor's words were too sweet.

Faith never turned around; instead, she smiled at me like she knew something real important, a secret that could save both of us from him. "I'm talking to Shelly. Please leave us alone, Pastor."

Pastor's cheeks turned pink. "You need to learn your place, girl."

"You done taught me all about place, thank you. I don't need no more lessons."

"You've gotten too high and mighty for me." Pastor came close to her. "I can correct that problem."

What happened next is the kind of stuff that starts a story on the mountain. Faith whipped around and looked Pastor dead in the eyes without shaking a bit. "I'll kill you if you ever touch me again. I promise. You understand. I will."

I held my breath 'cause I figured she was going to die. Pastor stared into her face and left. Yep, left us both right there.

Faith squatted down close to me. "You know me. I'm not Faith. I'm here to put a end to all this big bunch of a mess. And Faith is going to help me."

"You trouble. You going to get Faith in trouble."

"Nope. I'm going to look after her. Somebody needs to. She was hell-bent on hurting herself. But I need your help, Shelly. You can see and hear that ghost who roams the mountain. You can hear them all. You got to protect me from the living while I do what has to be done. Can you do that? Can you help me take care of Faith? Can you keep my secret?"

"Nada and Mrs. Dobbins ain't going to see one thing Faith does wrong. She be the most special. You'll be fine. Just don't talk much. You sure don't sound like her. What you going to do anyway, Arleen?"

"You got that spirit's book. You best read it."

A shiver ran over my back. "What you planning to do?"

"Kill. That's what a death quilt be for, girl. Didn't you know that?"

THAT AFTERNOON PASTOR KNOCKED Mrs. Dobbins to the kitchen floor for no good reason. So much for him not hitting her no more. Something bad was in the air. Something was going to happen.

Mrs. Dobbins came to our cabin after it turned dark.

"Lord, Lord, he's started hitting again, Mrs. Dobbins."

"Yes, Amanda, I have to do something. He wants to send Faith to the state hospital. We have to do something."

Again I was on my bed, listening like some dern old spy.

"I'm going to talk to Tyson, my brother, Amanda. The family summer house is on the Georgia coast."

"Will Pastor look for you there?" Nada whispered.

"Maybe. He knows we have a house there, but I'm going and taking Faith. I have to do it when he's not around."

"You can't drive that good," Nada hissed.

"I have to drive us there." She was quiet a minute. "I want you and Shelly to go too. We're not safe."

That woman was crazy if she thought Nada and me would go.

"I'm not going but you can take Shelly."

I sucked in air.

"You're stubborn, Amanda."

"Yes, ma'am. When you leaving?" Nada asked.

"At the right time. Tell Shelly to keep her things ready. We may have only a minute's notice."

"I will."

Nada was going to make me go. What was she thinking? Mrs. Dobbins didn't even want me to eat from the dishes she ate from. How was Nada going to make me go to another state?

"What's the name of that town where your brother live, ma'am?" Nada spoke louder.

"Darien."

I turned sick. That little girl haint up in the lost cemetery had said something about Darien. Lord, what kind of mess was I in?

WHEN NADA GOT UP the next morning, I was sitting at the table with my book *Mules and Men* by Zora Neale Hurston, pretending to read, calming myself as best I could.

"I know you was listening, and you got to go with them, Shelly." The lines around Nada's eyes fanned out.

"I ain't leaving, Nada. Why I got to go? Let Mrs. Dobbins and that crazy girl go by themselves. Me and you could use my money and leave here."

Nada looked out the door at the dew-covered grass. "You going. Be ready. When the time comes, there won't be no messing around."

"Why I got to go? Did you hear me? We can use my money."

"A person can't run from someone like Pastor. Mrs. Dobbins is thinking she can. Someone has to stay behind and fight him off. It ain't going to be you. He's got his eyes on you." It was quiet in the room. "You smart enough to know what that means. You got to go with Mrs. Dobbins and Miss Faith. It's what I can do to take care of you."

"He's mean. He might hurt you."

Nada laughed. "I know just what he is, Shelly." Her words didn't have one bit of wiggle room. "You going, Shelly, so you be safe. That's the end. I'll use my magic on him. Don't worry."

"Miss Tuggle says there ain't no spells or magic and she sure don't believe in spirits."

Nada puffed up. "That is a smart white woman for you. She doesn't even know our kind of life. She gives you some old book, but what does she know? White women don't always tell the truth. She's lifting you way high, and sometime you going to fall down. That's going to hurt, but we all got to fall sometime or another." Nada sat down at

the table with me and took my book. "Have you seen any spirits lately?"
She opened the book and pushed it back at me.

"Naw."

Nada nodded at the book. "Read to me, Shelly girl. I know you love
this old book. I've watched your face when you study in your room. Tell
me what them words say."

And that cracked me open. I took her gift. We read until the sun
streamed into the kitchen, way past time to go to the main house.

Then she stood. "I love you, girl," she whispered and left the
house.

There wasn't nothing, nothing like a mama's whisper in a girl's ear
to help her feel at peace, even if it wasn't real.

Maude Tuggle

W HEN SHELLY SHOWED UP leading the way two mornings after their last visit, I was surprised. Faith held her shoulders straight and tight like she was marching into battle. Her face was void of the emotions that usually appeared, providing a window to her heart; instead she looked guarded, as if she wore a carefully crafted mask of the features—the perky nose, freckles sprinkled on her cheeks, the crease in her forehead when she was angry. Shelly was on the porch before I got the door open.

"Well, good morning, girls. It's good to see you again so soon."

Faith stopped at the foot of the stairs and watched me close.

"Faith here needs to speak with you today, and I'd like to gather some more chamomile for Nada."

"Go right ahead, Shelly." She left us standing there.

"Well, Faith, what can I do for you?" I studied the girl in front of me. "Would you like to come in?"

She looked away. "Yes, ma'am." Her hands were pushed down in her skirt pockets.

"How have things been at home?" I walked into the front room, trying to begin the conversation.

"Different."

This made me look at her. "Different?"

"Yes, ma'am."

"Is that what you came to talk about?"

"Yes, ma'am. I guess." She stepped close to me. "I've always trusted you, ma'am. That's why I talked to you."

"I'm glad you feel free to." A shiver went over my arms. "Is everything okay?"

"I don't know." She looked at her feet.

"Is Pastor Dobbins bothering you?" I watched her close.

"He has."

"What has happened, Faith?"

Her eyes turned cloudy. She pulled her hand out of her pocket, grabbed my hand, and dropped something inside. "You got to watch this close. It's part of the truth, ma'am, and I only trust you. You'll know what to do. You're the only one strong enough to do it." And she left me standing in the front room.

In my hand was the tiny gold cross with the diamond in the middle. The last time I had seen it was on Arleen in her casket. I couldn't believe Faith would steal it.

Maybe it was time for me to eat my words and go make up to Zach so we could talk about this. He'd probably think I was crazy, but he might be interested in finding out how a beautiful young woman stole a necklace off a dead girl.

"MAUDE, YOU LOOK like a picture." Zach Walters sat on the corner of his desk watching as if I were a snake about to strike. "When's the last time I saw you?"

"A year ago." The sky was blue as could be in Asheville. "We've had the hottest weather."

"Don't try to change the subject. A note, Maude. A note?"

I took a deep breath. "I didn't come to talk about last year, Zach."

He slapped his knee. "Well, you made it clear my pretty face didn't bring you back here today, so what can I do for you?"

At least he was joking, maybe. "It wasn't you, and you know that. You'd never be happy with me. You want more than a supper once a week."

He frowned. "You don't know what I want. But tell me why you're here."

"I have a dumb question."

"I really doubt it's dumb. I don't think you have dumb in you."

"I need to know about someone's past."

"Ask them." He laughed.

He wasn't going to make my visit easy. "Funny."

"Who is the somebody?" He watched me closely, still seated on the corner of his desk.

"I want to know what brought our good pastor to Black Mountain."

"Charles Dobbins?"

"Yes. I just want to know how he came to live here."

"You haven't started going to his church, have you?" He was grinning.

I would not be pulled into his warm smile. "No. I haven't changed, Zach."

"Then why so curious? He's been on the mountain nineteen years."

"He hates being there and strikes me as one of those slick city preachers. Why would he stay here that long?"

"There's more to it than that. I know you." He looked at me and winked.

"I think he might have done something bad, but I don't want to talk about it until I have some proof."

He frowned. "So you're going to play sheriff? I don't think so. What do you think he did?"

"Don't ask. Please. I promise to tell you when I find something that says I might be right." It was a low blow, but I reached out and touched his hand.

He looked at my fingers and then me. "If this were anyone else but you, I'd say no way." Zach stared at me. "He baptized my niece, little Mary." He nodded to the corner of his desk, where he had a framed picture of his sister and her family and one of his parents.

"How did that happen?"

"He was visiting Maggie's church the Sunday Mary was to be baptized. He just took over. Maggie was right put out with the whole affair. The man invited himself to Maggie's for supper. She said he was strange."

"How so?"

"Well, she said he was oddly out of step with the rest of us. Our grandma used to call this 'a dill pickle that was too sour.'"

I smiled. "I want to know how Charles Dobbins ended up on Black Mountain."

"I know his daddy is a big preacher in New Orleans. If I'm not mistaken, he told Maggie he had family that once lived on the mountain."

"Really?"

"I could have sworn Grandma talked about a Dobbins who lived up there for a while, some kind of to-do over him. But I can't remember the story."

"My family goes back before the Civil War, and I never remembered Mama speaking of a Dobbins."

Zach ran his hand through his sandy-colored hair. "Could be my bad memory." He stood. "I could make a couple of phone calls to New Orleans. I know an old boy in the police department there. He'd oblige me."

"Could you, Zach? That would be wonderful. Maybe it will prove my feelings wrong."

"I'm not one to take feelings for granted." He winked and touched my arm. I did miss him. "Why don't you check with Tucker Platt for the church records? He got them when his daddy passed on. Maybe you can find that story I was talking about." His face lit up. "I remember now. A piece of jewelry and a Dobbins. I'm sure that was the story Grandma talked about."

I rubbed the cross in my pocket. The last thing I wanted to do was get Faith in trouble for stealing Arleen's cross.

"Take a look at the records."

I nodded. "Thanks for your help and time."

"Take care, now, and don't go getting into something you can't handle." Zach smiled.

The door rattled when I opened it. "Me?" I laughed.

"Maude." Zach frowned.

"Yes."

"At least you have to come back to see me now."

TUCKER STOOD NEAR THE BARN when I pulled into his yard. He threw his hand in the air like all folks did on the mountain when they saw a neighbor. "What brings you my way, Miss Tuggle?"

"We're having a hot summer." I walked to meet him.

"Yes, ma'am. Hope it'll rain for my corn." He smiled.

"Zach Walters says you have the old church records."

"He's right. They're down in the root cellar in Daddy's old trunk. Been there for going on nineteen years now."

"Could I look at them?"

He gave me a tolerant shrug. "I don't see why not. They're yours as much as anyone else born and raised on this mountain."

"Thank you so much, Tucker."

"Why are you so interested in them old books for?" He nodded in the direction of his house.

"I'm hoping they hold some history, not just birth and death dates.

Don't you ever wonder about all the people who have lived on this mountain?"

Tucker was a thirty-five-year-old man who looked fifty. "I don't think I ever gave it much thought, ma'am. But you'll find all kinds of things in them books. The keepers couldn't help all the stories they knew and some that wasn't even truth." He grinned.

"How far back do the books go?"

"All the way to right after the War Between the States."

"Really, that far?"

"Yes, ma'am. The first preacher was a Daniels, you know. He was a book-learned man who wrote lots in the books he took care of."

"The cemetery is named after him."

"Yes, ma'am. The Danielses used to own nearly all the mountain. Lived in a big old house up on the east side with its own graveyard and keeper. They didn't have much to do with anyone else. Lonely life, if you ask me." He pulled open the big double doors leading into the root cellar.

The temperature dropped ten degrees. "Why did your daddy have the church books?"

Tucker laughed. "When Daddy got word a Dobbins was coming to be pastor, he took it on himself to save the records." He popped open the lid to an old wooden trunk. "Here they be." He pulled out the first of what looked to be four large leather volumes.

"Your daddy had heard of Pastor Dobbins?"

"I reckon he did. The pastor's family, anyway. Said they was nothing but a troubled lot." Tucker placed one of the books in my hands. "But Daddy was always funny about outsiders." He took out the other three.

"I promise to take good care of them."

He snorted. "I ain't worrying over them books none. Most folks don't even care anymore." He frowned at the ones he carried.

A chill walked through me.

"Daddy said they even kept track of the coloreds by name. That wasn't done much back then."

We walked up the stairs into the sun. "This should be helpful."

He put the three books he held on the seat of my truck and then took the one I had, placing it on the seat with the others. "You enjoy yourself, now." He laughed like he'd made the funniest joke.

ARLEEN BECAME A GHOST in my cabin that afternoon, not one of Shelly's spirits, but a haunting all the same. I kept that gold cross close to me. Funny how a bunch of names and dates could keep me sitting at my desk until the last of the sunlight slid in the window. I picked a tattered old diary out of the pile, and a paper fell into my lap.

LOST

ARMETTA LOLLY

A colored girl age sixteen or thereabouts

Disappeared from Ella Creek Cemetery on Black Mountain

February 1870

If she is seen, please let Miss Amelia know.

She is desperate to find Armetta.

The Lollys have worked for the Danielses

since before they were freed by the war.

How curious. I opened the book to the page where the paper had been.

Today Amelia's gold cross with a small diamond in the center came up missing. Paul thinks it could be Armetta since she's come up missing too. I have a hard time believing this accusation. Armetta and her parents have been a part of our family since they were purchased by grandfather way before the war. Amelia loves Armetta dearly. Until Paul came here, Armetta was my sister's only companion. Armetta never left Ella Creek Cemetery. This I know for sure. Not on her own. I fear

*something has happened to her. I hate that Amelia has to leave
for New Orleans without knowing where she is. But Paul is
wanted at home. I say good riddance to him. Never have I met a
man quite like him.*

The cross lay in the palm of my hand, the tiny diamond twinkling
in the one last beam of sun stretching across the desk. Arleen wore the
necklace in her casket. Could the cross in the book be this cross? And
if so, how in the world did Arleen get it? Wouldn't its age and history
prove Charles Dobbins didn't own the cross?

I looked out the window. Folks on the mountain would swear the
mountain knew the whole story and kept it close to its heart.

Arleen Brown

MY SOUL WEARING FAITH'S BODY was like putting on a dress two sizes too small. I was busting at the seams. She was spoiled and demanding, while I was hardworking and quiet. I just had to finish what I came to do before I was found out. I had to protect that silly girl and Shelly. And I knew I was supposed to leave the revenge part to God, but it just wasn't in me to do that. I wanted to see Pastor suffer like I did and have his life cut short. Nothing good in what I wanted. The death quilt was going to make it happen. Some folks, like my daddy, didn't believe in charm quilts. But I did.

Faith's mama slipped out after Pastor when it turned dark. There was something in the air, had been since he slapped her in front of Shelly the afternoon before. I slid between the rosebushes and the house. Wasn't no sense in me getting in their mess. I had other things to do. And there in the moonlight was the razor, the one I took away from Faith. I slid it into the pocket of my skirt 'cause it might come in handy if the charm quilt didn't turn magic like I hoped. Pastor stood in the yard staring at my woods, like maybe he could hear them spirits calling him. He would be trapped right there with them if I got my way.

"God, I know what you want me to do. A man has to be the master of his own home."

Lord, he was always using God as an excuse to show his bad.

"I'll take care of the women, bring them back to their places. I will not tolerate any more disrespect."

Missus stepped out of the shadows behind him and into the moonlight. "Really, Charles, what do you plan to do? What do you think God is telling you to do? It's not God telling you to hurt your daughter and wife. You know that. It's you." The hate in her words shined like a lantern. I was liking her better and better.

Pastor swung around. "Lydia."

The light from the back porch lit up the side of his face. That jaw of his was set in a straight line.

"I won't let you hurt me or Faith. Is that understood?" Missus came near Pastor.

He stepped toward her. "Lydia, your threats mean nothing, nothing. I'm the boss in my own home."

She threw her head back and laughed right there in his face. The fool woman didn't even see how dangerous he had turned in that minute.

"I will accept your father's offer on behalf of Faith and me. We have to get away from you. And I will take Amanda and Shelly back to New Orleans too. You can't stop me. I don't want to risk living with you anymore."

His fist moved through the air and struck her in the jaw. The look on her face made my heart ache. She really thought she could fight him. I knew what it felt like to be on the other end of his meanness. There wasn't no fighting clean with him.

I stepped out of the bushes.

"I won't keep quiet if you lay another hand on me. I'll call the sheriff." That woman was still running her mouth. I had to admire her courage.

I took another step forward.

He went at her in a blind madness, beating at her face.

The razor felt warm in my fingers. Cutting him would be simple, but I didn't want simple. I wanted him to suffer, to see just what he did to me. Missus was grunting with each thud of his fist. The moon caught the razor, turning it shiny and dangerous. My steps came quicker. I could see his neck, smooth. I brought the razor up to my chest and came so close I could smell his sweat.

"I think you best stop right now." Shelly's mama stood there with a hoe over her head. Them words curled through the air like a snake about to strike. Half of me believed she was talking to me. "I'm going to kill you if you don't leave her alone, and that would be something I should've done a long time ago."

Pastor's fist stopped in midair. He turned around to face his threat, looking at me and back at Shelly's mama. "You don't scare me."

"Really, sir." The words came at him in a mocking tone. "You know my soul is just as black as yours." She nearly whispered this.

I raised the razor in front of me, walking closer to him.

Shelly's mama shook her head at me.

Pastor stepped away. "You deserved a beating, Lydia. Go on to your colored woman and your crazy daughter. You make me sick, all of you." He stomped off without even noticing the razor. I put it back in my pocket. I was the worst of his worries, and he didn't even realize it.

Shelly's mama threw the hoe down. "Come on. I need to doctor your face. He beat you bad, fool. You should've shut up." She helped Missus up from the ground.

"I didn't want him to notice Faith out here," Missus said.

"Your help wasn't needed. I could have taken care of him. I'm not afraid. He knows I have the power to hurt him."

Shelly's mama knew I wasn't Faith. She was a true mountain witch.

I heard a voice come up beside me. "You be exactly right, girl. But you ain't going to stop one thing from happening with your plan. You ought to work with me." I looked over and saw that mean colored ghost who followed Pastor everywhere standing to my left.

"Come on, Faith, before he comes with his gun," Shelly's mama said, frowning. "We got to get you off this mountain. I don't know what kind of spell you're under, but you're under one and we both know it. You got to leave this mountain tomorrow."

"Amanda, you have to go with us." Missus grabbed her arm. "Who's going to protect you if you don't?"

Amanda laughed. "You don't worry about me. I'll take care of myself. I always have. You will take my girls and watch over them. Somebody has to be here to send him in the wrong direction." She shot me a stare. Her love for Faith was right there between us. I started humming.

"What's that song, Faith?" Missus asked.

"Just a bedtime song."

Amanda clicked her tongue. "You come on."

But I had me one trip to make before we made a run off the mountain. They was all fools, but I had to go wherever Faith was supposed to go. I slid away while Amanda helped Mrs. Dobbins into her cabin.

WHEN I WAS A LITTLE THING, I wouldn't have been caught dead in those haunted woods. Mama taught me way better than doing any such thing. But seeing how I was dead and wore Faith's body, it didn't bother me a bit. See, I was one of them haints. But I was obliged to take care of Faith. The good thing about being a spirit was I could see just as good in the dark as I could in the day. And all those souls stuck in them woods was easy to spot too.

When I came out on the other side of the woods, my favorite

meadow was washed in that big old moon that hung in the middle of the sky. There sat the little house, still just as sad as it could be, leaning and peeling. I could have stood there in the tall grass forever, looking. That's all I wanted. Sometimes a girl just didn't know what she had right in front of her. She went looking for more, bigger, fancier. Dying wasn't half as hard as being stuck on Black Mountain as a soul with a story to tell. Wasn't but two people left on the mountain that wanted to know the truth. One of them was dead, Pastor's ghost Armetta, and the other was alive, Miss Tuggle. My story was under her skin, and she didn't even know it good yet.

The little barn out to the side of the house leaned worse than ever. Something about that pitiful building made me want to cry, just howl into the air, to sob for all those times gone. The swing on the front porch of the house rocked back and forth in the wind that was blowing just for me. Way up in the big oak—it took me and the twins, holding hands, to circle the trunk—sat an owl. Now, that was an omen. Owls brought messages. They wasn't bad like lots of folks thought. They was good medicine.

Shoot, them boys was twenty, grown men, probably gone. When they was little, they was more than a handful. Mama left them with me when she worked the field with Daddy. That was a long time before I lost my whole world.

A yellow glow lit the front room. If the boys—Andy and Robert—were still home, they would be in the corner playing checkers, arguing over some move one or the other made. Mama would be nodding off to sleep as she did her best to sew on missing buttons and patch holes in the boys' pants. Daddy would be pretending to read some old paper he picked up in Asheville while working his delivery job, if he still worked there. Farming on the mountain had turned so bad he took to hauling rock for the quarry the year I passed. Purely shamed him to work off the mountain 'cause his daddy and granddaddy farmed that piece of land. He couldn't do much else with it. Nothing grew. Not that year, anyway. Some might say that was a warning. I should've heeded it, but I was working on leaving too early in my life.

My dying nearly put Mama under the house and was one of the reasons the mountain held on to my spirit. Or maybe she understood that my story wasn't finished.

A loud bark came from the backyard. Blue—Andy's dog—shot around the corner and ran right at me. And then, there he was. Daddy stood in the open door staring right at me. "Who's out there?" His voice sounded like the gravel he hauled, rough.

I couldn't make that Faith say a word.

"I see you there. What you need, girl?"

Blue stood right at me, growling. He knew something wasn't right.

Daddy came down the steps of the front porch.

"It's me, Faith Dobbins, Mr. Brown," I lied.

He stopped walking. "What you doing out this time of night? You had to cut through them woods to get to us. Is something wrong?"

Now my plan, if I ever had one, was to just look at the house and maybe catch sight of one of them. "I was walking and got turned around," I lied again.

He kind of shook his head. "You are a strange one, just like folks say."

This didn't hurt my feelings a bit. "I'm not afraid of the dark."

"Maybe you should be." Daddy ran his hand through his hair. It looked thinner.

"Angus, who are you talking to?" My mama stepped onto the front porch. Her hair was pulled back in a perfect knot, just like always.

I couldn't make Faith's body take a breath. Mama.

"Pastor's girl is out wandering around them woods." Daddy was tired of the whole mess.

Mama walked down the steps as Daddy came back up. "Child, what in the world are you doing out here in the moonlight for? Are you charmed?" She came closer. "Hush now, Blue. Go on." Blue looked at me one more time and ran up on the porch.

And I took that breath. "Just walking."

She looked at me for a minute. "No girl in her right mind would be out walking in them haint woods. Pastor wouldn't like it."

"I don't care what Pastor thinks." And the words sat between us.

Little threads of hair fell here and there around her face.

"You don't look right, Miss Faith." Mama moved up to the pole fence that stood between us. "Is something wrong with you?"

"No, ma'am. I'm leaving here soon, and it's likely I won't be back." Because something was going to happen and either way all would be finished.

"Pastor's leaving?" That special smile she always used for Pastor, the one that said he was someone to look up to, had faded to a blank face.

"No, ma'am. Just me and Missus."

She studied me. "You seem different."

"I am. A girl changes once she's not pure no more." I was talking way too much.

Mama stepped so close to the fence she touched one of the poles. I smelled pork chops and gravy on her. "What did you come to say?"

"Arleen, she loved you a whole lot, ma'am. More than she ever told you." And there was those words I held inside with all the hurt 'cause Mama never guessed what he did to me. Didn't keep him from hurting me. 'Cause I thought she was supposed to always protect me and know what I never said.

Her breath caught. "I always knew she loved me. She was a good—a pure—daughter, no matter what others said. She needs to be in Heaven resting with that beautiful baby boy."

"Yes, ma'am. I think she will be before too long."

"I surely hope so. I'd hate to think she's caught in them woods out there. Nothing that happened is worth being stuck."

And she was right. "Things ain't that simple, ma'am."

She nodded.

"A truth has to be told and souls saved."

She smiled. "Well, I'm proud you came here to see me. It soothes my heart." Tears was in her eyes.

"Mine too." I turned and walked back to the woods. She didn't call out, but I felt her watching me leave. I was her only daughter, and she loved me with every bone of her body. And I loved her too.

Armetta Lolly

THAT SHELLY WAS GOING to get herself killed, and there wasn't no denying it. She turned her nose up at my book when some of the answers be right there if she'd just put it all together, but not Shelly. Nope. Instead, she went and built some dumb old bottle tree like a fool. That girl was dumber than I thought, but she was all I had. She had to listen before Pastor got just what he was after.

When that old white girl inside of Faith stood up to him, he stomped back in his study and sat around thinking on the time in Georgia that put him up on this old mountain. Bad stuff only a few knew, and they was dead. The man wasn't a bit sorry for his actions, not one bit. Not one person on Black Mountain knew what Pastor could do, except maybe the white granny woman. She be smart, but she was headed down a long road without a map. I couldn't talk to her. I tried. She seen me, but she wasn't having none of it. Shelly had to be the miracle to stop him this time. And that thought scared me to death.

He went to stare out the window into the backyard, watching that cabin.

Miss Amelia taught me how to write pretty decent. So while Pastor was away from the desk, I took me a pencil and did my best sentences. The lead broke on the pencil, and that's when he turned back and seen my writing.

Just a little while longer and the truth be told no matter what you try.

I whispered in his ear, "We in for some dark times, Pastor."

He gave a little shiver, wadded up the note, and threw it in the trash.

KNOWING A BAD PERSON'S THOUGHTS is like watching a storm bearing down on the mountain. There ain't one thing that can be done to stop the damage. All I could do was try to protect those around the terror barreling their way. I sure wished that old haint in Faith's body would have spilled Pastor's blood. My worries would have been finished. My story could have finally come to a rest. But I knew better than that. Some things had to happen to get my story told. That's the part I didn't tell Shelly about reading my book.

That dirty skunk Pastor went to stand outside Shelly's cabin and watch them women through the window. He'd done lost his whole mind, not that he ever was in his right mind, but he had come unhinged.

"You stupid woman." He watched Shelly's mama the closest, like she was his worst enemy. "I gave you a home and food. Now this. You think you're going to run over me, run the rest of my life with all your threats. You've taught Lydia to stand up for herself. No. I won't put up with either of you." The bitterness in his voice could have rotted through the wood on the porch, but them women never even heard him, didn't sense a bit of danger.

I went through the front door of that cabin so fast I tipped a pot of chamomile sideways. Both women looked at the table. But I headed back to Shelly's room. Dern fool was sound asleep.

"Shelly. Hey, Shelly, wake up, girl. It be important."

She opened her eyes and gave me a hateful look. "Get on out of here."

"You listen."

"What you want?" she whispered.

"Get out there with your mama. Pastor done beat that wife of his, and now he's on the porch watching them through the window. They ain't even seen him. He's done gone completely crazy, Shelly. Bad stuff headed this way. You can't stop it now. It's too late. And here you are sleeping like some doggone princess."

Her mouth turned into a thin, straight line, but her feet hit the floor. "Nada." She stopped cold, staring at the Missus's face.

Her mama looked away. "Remember what we talked about, Shelly? Be ready."

"He's out there watching right now, Shelly. Go throw the door open." For once the girl listened and darted across the room, opening the door.

There was a clatter, and we both seen Pastor jump off the porch.

"Pastor was looking in the window, Nada. He turned over our churn. No telling how long he's been there."

"You got to make your mama leave too, Shelly." But somehow I knew Shelly's mama couldn't be made to do anything. "Now you understand about my book? You got to trust me and read. Will you?"

Shelly nodded, and I knew she'd read it without any more of her mess. I just hoped it wasn't too late.

PASTOR WAS ALL STRETCHED OUT on the grass looking at the moon like he was some boy star-watching.

"You be losing your mind," I whispered in his ear.

He turned his head toward me. "And you're just a ghost who can't help anyone. You couldn't help yourself."

I lost all my words. Shelly stood on the porch watching me. The ghost girl was out there on the edge of the woods looking too. A spirit with a body.

PART FOUR

Heat Lightning

June 1939

"Flashes of lightning without thunder, signaling a storm is coming."

—*Amanda Parker*

Maude Tuggle

The NEXT MORNING the sky looked like it would dump rain on us. I woke up thinking about what I found in the church records. There wasn't any time like the present to go find that cemetery. Maybe there would be some answers there. I left a note in case anyone needed me and set out. There must have been something in the air, something driving me to get away from the cabin, some forewarning. The woods were like a ghost story. A cloudy white mist blanketed the area. As I moved up the path, I could see a splash of sunshine in the clearing ahead. A large old house, now covered with vines and surrounded by mountain laurel, stood alone. A ghost house. The church records indicated Ella Creek Cemetery was less than a mile behind the old Daniels place.

I almost missed the graveyard because of the years of neglect. Headstones were barely showing, and in some cases totally hidden behind the forest's growth. The sun hit and glinted off something in the brush. I pushed away a pile of leaves and branches. An angel appeared in graceful beauty on her side, fallen, tangled in kudzu vines, wounded. What a silly, romantic thought. The angel's face was finely chiseled. I was content to look at her. Something in her eyes made her seem alive. Another fanciful thought. I pushed my hand into the undergrowth and touched the cold marble. Even when something rustled, I stayed put, staring at the elegant face. "Who are you?" I whispered. A shiver ran through me along with an urge to dig her out and take her home.

I stood. That's when I saw the words LOST and ARMETTA LOLLY written on a marker. Was this the colored girl I read about in the church records? A cold breeze moved over me and a mist blew in from the woods, spraying my face with fine droplets of water. A deep sorrow rushed through my chest. Silly. If I were Shelly, I would claim the mist, the emotion that twisted my insides, proved there was a spirit, a ghost, a lost soul.

"Lost." It wasn't totally uncommon for a person to become lost on Black Mountain. Patty Harkin had come up missing and was found dead. Nellie Pritchard walked off from her house and was never seen again. Maybe this Negro girl lost her way in the woods. They were thick and dark from spring until late fall. But all the mysteries could probably be explained with diligent snooping.

Again the wave of sadness swept over me. I moved to another group of headstones close by. The Danielses. The low cloud pushed and pulled its way through the cemetery, dropping the headstones one by one into sudden darkness. The birds were silent. A few feet away I found a smaller stone, PAUL LAMAR DOBBINS. My fingers tingled as I traced the letters. Dobbins wasn't exactly an uncommon name, but my heart knew this was the connection to Pastor Charles Dobbins.

Fear slammed square in my chest, taking my breath. Something moved through the mist in my side vision. A fleeting shadow, maybe a fox or a bobcat, scooted through the trees. I began to run, nearly falling over the angel to get out of the place. How stupid of me. By the time I could see my cabin the sun was out and I felt like a young fool. Thank goodness no one knew. Zach wouldn't think I was totally crazy. I had to tell him about what I found in the books and cemetery.

I WAS STANDING by my truck when George Connor, a good friend and farmer from down the mountain, came barreling up the drive in his old pickup. He smiled as he climbed out.

"Maude, you look like you've been running around the mountain."

Sweat rolled down my face. "Everything okay, George?"

"Well, I met Mrs. Dobbins driving down the mountain. Lord, I always give her room. She's not the best driver, but today she was in a bigger hurry than usual."

"Really? Doesn't sound like Lydia. She seldom goes off the mountain."

"I know." He shoved his hands in his pockets.

"The mist was bad in the woods today."

He nodded. "That part of the mountain scares a lot of folks. I'd stay clear if I were you." He smiled.

"Well, I can see why they make stories up about the place." I tried to laugh.

"You mean the old ghost house. It be scary, all right."

"It's the old Daniels house, right?" I tried to sound casual.

"Yep. I wouldn't go there."

"Mama said once that the Danielses were wealthy."

He laughed. "I reckon, but money sure didn't help them none. Nobody liked them. They had one decent child, a son, who helped start the church. The rest of the lot was touched in the head. That's what my mama said. But you know how rumors are on the mountain."

"Really, mentally ill?"

He shrugged. "That's what was said. The Danielses never used planting signs, and they always turned their backs on folks down the mountain. They liked to make fun of hardworking people. Mama said they died out because of their scorn."

"But who was mentally ill?"

George cocked his head to the side. "The father kept the young daughter holed up in the house. Wouldn't let her leave for no reason. He made one of his housemaids live in the cemetery. When he died, the daughter got out and made friends with the housemaid in the cemetery. They say the daughter nearly grieved herself to death over her daddy. Finally she got married off and left the mountain, but she be buried up there."

"How horrible."

He grinned because it was just like George to spin a good story. "But I didn't come up here to tell you all that, Maude. I just came from Asheville. The sheriff says he needs you to come see him. He has an answer for you." George watched me. It must have been killing him to know what I asked the sheriff. And of course the whole mountain knew at one time I had dinner with Zach once a week.

"Good." I didn't even tell him a thing. "I'll drive down."

He tipped his hat. "I'll take my leave since you won't give me a juicy bit of gossip." He laughed.

"George, all kidding aside, what do you know about that Negro housemaid that lived in the cemetery? I found her grave today and she's mentioned in the church records."

He gave me a long look. "You been digging around, Maude?"

"Yes," I admitted.

His face turned quiet. "What I told you is the truth as I know it. See, I just know enough to stir things up."

I laughed. "Oh, that is so true, George."

"You have a wonderful day, Maude, and tell the sheriff I'll see him again soon. Then he can tell me all about your meeting." George would go home and tell his wife how crazy I was getting, living all alone like I did. A new rumor to begin floating around the mountain.

"It's a pure pleasure, George, as always."

Out of the corner of my eye I saw the Negro girl in the yellow dress standing in the meadow near the woods. In a blink, she disappeared.

* * *

ZACH WAS SITTING at his desk when I opened the door to the sheriff's office. "You got my message fast enough." He grinned.

I took the empty chair. "You know George Connor. He couldn't stand to hold it in long. You found out something about Charles Dobbins?"

He pulled a folder out of a pile on the desk. "Yes, my friend proved your concerns. I think you need to tell me everything you know."

"First, what have you found?"

"I know why Charles Dobbins came to be a pastor on Black Mountain and why he hasn't left. And Maude, you were right. He never would have chosen this place on his own." Zach drummed his fingers on the paper.

"So tell me." My stomach fluttered. Would he believe what happened to me in the cemetery that morning?

"His father is a big guy in the Episcopal church in New Orleans. Pastor Dobbins was pulled out of the class he taught at the local seminary and sent to run a revival all over the Southeast. He wasn't a pastor but a teacher, but a lot of the students were complaining to the head dean about his beliefs and theology. So Pastor Dobbins ended up on the coast of Georgia. His father sent the youngest brother, Lenard, along to keep Charles in line. Lenard was and is known all over New Orleans for his taste in card games and losing money, the black sheep of the family. Anyway, he took off the first night to play cards somewhere on a dock in this place called Darien. When he came back early the next morning, Charles was missing, so he reported the disappearance to the sheriff. That's when he found out the police had discovered the body of a young Negro woman in the warehouse near the bank of the Altamaha River where Charles and his brother had pitched their revival tent. Then the story gets more interesting. My friend says there was another Negro girl found but the story went cold there. No one pressed charges against Pastor Dobbins or his brother, not even a report by the sheriff. The way my friend found out about this was Lenard himself, talking after a few drinks and a card game. Two witnesses put Charles with the first Negro woman before she was found dead. Lenard confided that he believed his brother was very capable of killing. My friend said you could chalk Lenard's story up to differences between brothers, but still. It's something to think about."

I never saw myself as a woman scared easily, but that was the second time in one day I got a cold chill.

"Whatever happened that night, Dobbins and his little family—including their maid and her son—were packed up and sent to Black Mountain for good. To me, that indicates something bad happened. I figured his father pulled some kind of strings to get Charles off the hook. Then put him in a safe place where he couldn't do much damage. You can't get more isolated than the mountain. Also, Mr. Dobbins had a reputation in New Orleans for his taste in colored maids, if you know what I mean." He looked at me. "What did you find in the church records?"

"Mostly deaths and births, but I did find out there was a Negro girl who came up missing in 1870. She was loved so much by Amelia Daniels that she put up signs attempting to find her. Kind of strange for the times." The angel came to mind and I smiled.

Zach wore an intent stare. "It seems your concerns are correct, Maude. Now tell me what you think the good pastor did."

I waited a minute. Once my thoughts were out, I couldn't put them back, or as Mama used to say: Open a can of worms, and you can't close it again.

"George Connor told me Lydia Dobbins left the mountain in a hurry. The woman never leaves the mountain."

"You can't arrest a man because his wife leaves him." Zach frowned at me. "Tell me."

I took a deep breath. "Arleen Brown died in childbirth in the summer of 1935."

"That's been four years ago. Why now?"

"Her death seemed a simple case caused from childbirth gone bad. But she told me something right before she died." The words hung in the air between us.

"What did she tell you?"

"That she was forced into having relations with the baby's father."

He looked at the ceiling. "And that is, who? And why now? Why not five years ago when it happened?"

"I didn't have a real reason. I didn't know the person responsible."

"And you know now. You think it is Dobbins? Why? You didn't just pull him out of thin air."

I looked away. Faith didn't need trouble from Zach. "Something isn't right about him. It's a feeling."

"Feelings don't count as proof, and you know it." He cocked his head to the side. "You're giving me the runaround. Why?"

"I'm not."

"Maude, what else?"

I reached into my pants pocket and pulled out the cross, dropping it on the desk. "This was Arleen's. Her family never knew how she got it."

He turned it over in his palm. "The Browns are pretty stretched, right?"

"Yes."

"No one on the mountain has the means to own such a nice piece of jewelry except you and of course Charles Dobbins."

I laughed. "You know it's not mine."

"I have to cover every possibility. You know that." He smiled. "So, we have a cross and a dead girl's last words."

"In the church records, Amelia Daniels's brother mentioned a missing cross with a diamond in the middle, but that was 1870," I blurted. All of a sudden I wanted him to believe me.

He turned from the window he was looking out and stared at me again. "Maude, how did you get this cross?" The question stood between us. "I know you're not telling me everything."

I looked away from him and waited, waited because I wanted to save, to protect, Faith. "Faith brought it to me yesterday."

His face remained neutral. "Where did she get it from?"

"I really don't know, Zach. But I do know Arleen had it around her neck in the casket at the funeral. But I know Faith could never take it off. I know this about her."

He plopped down in his chair. "Maude, we have a mystery but I'm not so sure it only involves Pastor Dobbins."

"We have to leave Faith out of this. You have to trust me. If anything, she is a victim too."

He slapped his hands on his knees. "We have a mother who may have taken her daughter off the mountain. We have a dead girl's cross and her confession of being raped. We have to have proof. The cross isn't proof." He thought a minute. "Does Faith know if anything was going on between her father and Arleen?"

"I don't know. She is a private girl. I do know he bought the girl a brand-new casket and brought it up the mountain. It was the talk for some time. And the Sunday before her funeral he tried to give the Browns the offering collection. Mr. Brown refused because of pride."

"While all interesting, nothing proves he is a rapist, not even the information we got from New Orleans. He's a pastor and we have to tread lightly. We have to pin this cross to him, and that will help a whole lot."

"You know if Charles Dobbins forced himself on Arleen and she became pregnant, then in a way he is responsible for her death."

"No jury would convict him." Zach shrugged. "I'm going to do more snooping. Maude?"

"Yes?"

He frowned at me. "Do you think Dobbins is a threat to his daughter?"

"I've always seen him as a stupid man, an idiot, but yes, I think he could hurt someone, especially Faith, maybe even Shelly, his maid's daughter."

"Then you have to be careful."

I looked away. "He won't hurt me."

"Just be careful. I've got to give this some thought. I'll come up to see you in the next day or two. We can decide what the next move will be."

"I'll come down here."

He smiled. "Still worried about what others think?"

I frowned. "No, I don't want to tip off Dobbins."

He nodded.

Arleen Brown

Mama's words was all over me when I closed the door to Faith's room and pulled the desk chair in front of the window. This way I could keep a watch on Pastor, who was stretched out in the backyard, yelling at the sky every once in a while. The charm quilt was spread out on Faith's bed, and the old sewing basket sat next to it. What that basket held was part of the magic: a thimble, a pair of shiny little scissors, and lots of thread, some homespun and so old it broke when I pulled too hard while stitching. The thread colors, pale red, gray-blue, yellowing white, and coppery brown, painted the feelings being sewn into the pattern. Mama said in the old days a quilt was much more than a blanket to throw on the bed in the winter. A person's story was sewn right into the design. A wedding quilt most of the time was made from scraps of clothes that once belonged to the beloved couple. A baby quilt gave hope to the sweet parents bringing the child into the world. And a charm quilt could be a lot of things. This one was a death quilt and told the story of my death at the hands of all those who played a part. Death didn't always come to a person in a straight line. Those involved sometimes didn't even understand they had a place in the circumstances.

Mama was not part of my death quilt. I thought I'd get something of hers and add it, but after the visit I knew she believed me to be good. If she did one thing wrong, it sure wasn't her fault. Every good Christian woman believed in her pastor. They was supposed to. Mama was no different. So she couldn't be faulted. But I had me a real list of folks that had gone into this work. Faith left the finishing touches to me. One more thing had to go into the quilt—a soul. And that soul was wicked. A death quilt had a sleep charm woven into the materials. When placed on that soul, it gave sleepy calm. It was then and only then a girl could go after her revenge.

In a small cup was buttons Faith stole from the wash that hung on the lines out behind the main house. She snipped them off without anyone but me seeing her: a sunny yellow one from Mrs. Dobbins's robe, three red triangle buttons stolen from a satin blouse hidden away in a cupboard in Amanda's cabin—a blouse she had forgotten, wanted to put out of her mind—and last a bright blue button belonging to Miss Tuggle's fancy dress along with some hair from her brush. Everybody that needed to be included in the making of the charm was right there.

The buttons made little clicking sounds in my hand. I would stitch each one on the quilt, a part of each person. I hummed one of them lullabies Mama sung to me as a little girl. A fluttering moved up my chest as I hummed louder. Faith wasn't going to put up with me taking over her body for a long time. Her thoughts was tangled up with mine so tight I started to wonder which was hers and which belonged to me.

The house was silent and empty. The women was plotting how to save us all from Pastor so we'd be leaving soon. Of course, if Pastor fell through the hole in his mind and started killing everyone, that would be a sight. The quilt held a secret pocket that Faith had sewn into the hem. She was one smart girl, and I guessed that was one of the reasons I picked her. Folded into the pocket was a sheet of soft blue tissue paper with a lock of black hair. Hair always looked the same no matter how long it'd been around. All them bodies in Daniels Cemetery probably still had hair. I bet my baby boy was still curled in my arms out there in the ground.

A shadow moved across the glass in the window. A cloud hid the moon, and I couldn't see Pastor. A strawberry moon looked like any other full moon, but it came in June just as the strawberries began to get ripe. It was a forgiving moon. Not one part of me was up for that, for forgiving.

That silly colored-girl haint, Armetta, stood in the corner of the room. "You working?"

"I guess so." I touched the blue velvet hem of the quilt.

"A charm quilt." She moved closer to the bed. "I could sew real good when I was alive, but I didn't like it none."

"I don't like sewing either, but this be my way of fighting without no one knowing," I whispered. "That girl, she did most the work. She likes to sew."

"No forgiveness in this room." She ran her fingers over the part of the quilt with the stolen words from my marker.

"Don't have no room for such." I shrugged.

"Maybe not." She moved close to me. "You be one powerful spell, girl. We could help each other. I want what you want." She looked at the hair in my hand. "Who that belong to?"

"Me."

She turned quiet and looked at it. "No good going to come from you working alone."

"Don't intend no good. This here is a death quilt. I'm sewing a death and a truth at the same time."

She stared at the quilt a minute longer and then threw her head back and laughed. A thick scar circled her throat. "Teach me how to have a body so I can finish my story."

"This ain't some trick I can give. She called me, the pastor's daughter, Faith. She needed me to save her from herself."

The cloud moved away from the moon.

"You got powerful mojo," Armetta whispered. "You got a backbone too."

"Why you stay with Pastor?"

Again she let go with that ugly laugh. "Our stories are all twined together like a fine horsehair rope. Me, you, and that girl inside of you, we all tangled." And she was gone.

There was a time in my life when seeing that girl would have scared me into a early death, but now what scared me most was Pastor. He was real, solid, and pure mean. Those were the most fearful things. If he decided to pay Faith a visit, there was that razor in my pocket. That was the best kind of spell I knew. Faith needed a lesson in how to use a blade in the proper way.

Shelly Parker

I WOKE WITH MY HEART BEATING so hard in my chest I couldn't think, and for a minute my breath was squeezed right out of me. My mouth tasted like sand, and my hands shook. I remembered how we'd be leaving anytime. The cabin was quiet, and the sun stretched over my bed. Maybe all of it was just a bad dream.

"Shelly," Nada called from the front porch.

Mrs. Dobbins, her face bruised and beaten, was asleep in Nada's bed. A chill walked through my body, a warning that something bad was sitting, waiting on all of us. "Yes, ma'am."

Nada drank her coffee and looked at the yard.

"You ain't really going to make me go, are you?"

Nada didn't look at me. "He's gone for now. Mrs. Dobbins will be wanting to leave when she gets up. She's going to take the car without him knowing. Get your stuff ready. Take it all, Shelly, especially your money. You might need it before this is over. I told you it be your running money."

"I'll go if you go."

"This ain't no bargaining table, girl. Go take yourself in there and get your things ready. When I call you, it'll be time."

I wore my meanest look.

"No fussing. Go."

"Why you want to get rid of me?"

Nada gave me her most sorrowful face. "Girl, you know better. Be watchful. That's something you've never been. Use the smarts God gave you and don't listen to your heart all the time. It'll fool you in a minute. I'm taking care of you by sending you off. That's what a mama does." She huffed and turned her attention on the cup of coffee. "Go on, now."

It took me about five minutes to put my extra dress, my books, and my money in my feed sack. There was that stupid old book of Armetta's under the floorboard. I grabbed it up just so I could say I had it. Part of me didn't want to admit just maybe she could help me.

I scooted out the door 'cause I had two places to go before I left the mountain.

WHATEVER I THOUGHT I was going to find by hoofing it over to Miss Tuggle's I sure didn't get. Her house was shut up tight like she'd done left the mountain for a while. A note hung on the door.

> *Gone for a walk in the woods. Be back soon.*
> *Maude*

She was gone. I dug in my bag and pulled out my little pencil. It was mighty unfortunate she chose the day I was leaving to go take some dumb old walk. So I decided to tell her what happened and where I'd be.

Miss Tuggle:

By the time you get back, I'll be gone from this here mountain on a trip that will probably last a month of Sundays. See Mrs. Dobbins is taking me and Miss Faith away from the mountain. We're all going to hide at her brother's on the Georgia coast. We got to sneak off with the car, so Pastor is going to be hot and he'll come looking for you. Nada won't go and I'm horrible afraid for her. He's done lost his mind this time, ma'am. If you need to hide from him, there's a cemetery up the mountain that is lost. Nobody goes there no more. It's called Ella Creek and Pastor won't never think to look there for you. See, he's going to think you helped us get away. He don't like you one little bit. Be careful going through them woods 'cause they be filled with lost souls. I know you be rolling your eyes, but for once just listen.

Shelly

I folded it real neat and slid it under the door. Instead of heading back to the main house, I took the trail leading further up the mountain. Maybe Nada would send Mrs. Dobbins and Faith on their way if she couldn't find me. The woods always looked different. In the summer the trees was so thick it could come a hard rain and the water hardly touched the ground. The mountain laurel was in bloom and I wouldn't get to enjoy it. That wasn't fair. I loved the clusters of flowers. They didn't have no smell to speak of, but the soft pink and white petals was real nice to look at. The deeper I went into the woods, the more heaviness settled on me. The dark spirits lived in those parts. Sometimes I'd stand on the back porch of the cabin and hear them whispering and moaning. Haints a girl didn't want to meet up with, especially on a lonely trail going up the mountain. Haints like them watched from hidden places, waiting. No telling who they were and why they stayed out of sight. But they had to be better company than Mrs. Dobbins and Faith on the run.

Sunshine sprinkled across the path ahead. I knew where I was going. It was my quiet place. Ella Creek Cemetery was safe for now. I wanted to see Daddy's grave one more time before I left. The last time I was there, a fine patch of wild daisies had sprung up on his grave just like someone had planted them.

A FINE-LOOKING RED BIRD landed on one of the old headstones. He cocked his head to the side. Nada said red birds meant a person would see someone unexpected. One of them haints from the woods was watching me. I felt them. I squatted in front of the stone, and that dern bird stayed right there. LOST was carved in the granite. ARMETTA LOLLY was carved underneath.

A statue of some kind was on its side covered with kudzu vine. Then I saw wings. One was perfect and one was broken. They looked about as real as anything could look. I touched the feathers. Angel. A marble angel. The kudzu held her tight.

"That be the grave meant for me."

I jumped a foot. "You scared me to death."

"Ain't that what haints do?" Armetta smiled. Up until then, Armetta's yellow dress always looked dirty and stained. But it was like brand-new, and her face had turned all soft like a light was under her skin. "This cemetery be a busy place these days."

"What you mean?"

She smiled. "Never can tell who might come up that path and visit."

"My daddy is buried over there close to you."

"This is the place Miss Amelia put up for me. She didn't know about him and what he did." Armetta turned a mean look on me. "No one ever knew what happened to me or where my body ended up. No one knew my story."

"Who hurt you?" Fear crawled up my arms.

"I ain't telling you. You got to read my book, girl."

"I got it here with me," I admitted. "Can't you just tell me so I won't have to leave? Can't we just get this all over with?"

"You want to rush my story? Nope. You got to read it. And you got to go. It's part of your story. But I got to tell you some things before you go." Armetta came closer.

"I ain't leaving."

"Yes you are. Your mama be determined, and there ain't nothing like a determined mama."

"I can't leave her." I stood up straight.

"She needs to go with you, but she won't. She's got things to take care of here." She studied me a minute. "You know your trouble, Shelly? You be pretty to look at but not a bit useful, like that bottle tree you made. Read the book."

"Okay, I'll read it, but help me stay here."

She laughed. "There was only one person that knew most of my story, Shelly. That be Ma Clark over at Ella Creek."

"Who was Ma Clark?"

"Oh, girlie, you got to find that out on your own. And you will when you read the book. Her real name was Celestia and she was a slave with my mama, Liza Lolly. Liza, Celestia, and Emmaline, they was best friends."

"Slaves. Lord, that was a long time ago."

"I was born a slave but saw freedom just like Mama, Daddy, and Ma Clark." Armetta moved right next to me. "Here's what I have to tell you. My story be one big mess, girlie. That's why I'm stuck here. You got to untangle it. Someone's going to die and I want to stop it. I'm not sure I can." Her words hung in the air like a sheet on a windless day. "You best get back. They need to leave soon to miss Pastor." A hard gust of wind hit me in the face and Armetta was gone.

NADA HAD STOOD on the cabin porch, stiff, straight, soft as the color blue. The smell of rain hung in the air. The last I seen of her she was twisting the corner of her apron in her hands.

The road went on and on. The car rocked, and I settled in that comfortable place of dreams. *A boat rocked back and forth on what must have been the ocean, but seeing how I'd never seen it, I couldn't be sure. A man stood on the deck, wearing a worn-out gray cap. He just stared at me like he was waiting for me to start talking first.*

"It's hotter than hell in here," Faith complained from the front seat. The wind rushed in the open windows, but the air was sticky.

I opened my eyes, and my face was stuck to the back car seat. Drool ran from the side of my mouth. Faith sat with her leg hiked up and her thigh showing, watching out the window.

"That's not decent talk. And cover your leg, sweetie." Mrs. Dobbins wore dark glasses, but her face still showed a puffy mess.

"God," Faith fussed.

"We'll have to drive all the way through."

"How far is it?" Faith asked.

"Too far, but we have Shelly and no motel will let us stay." Mrs. Dobbins looked at me in the mirror. "It's not your fault, Shelly. It's just the way things are."

Like that made some kind of excuse. I didn't say a word.

"If I get tired, I'll just pull into a parking lot and sleep for a while. We'll be fine. This is our adventure." She sang out like everything on the mountain was fine and dandy.

So she drove and drove. The wind blew hot, hotter than I'd ever felt. I could have cut the air with a knife it was so full of rain that wouldn't let loose. Nada crept into my bones and knotted my stomach. One of Pastor's hymns about a bright sunny day hummed in my head until I felt more like myself. The road turned long. I could have hugged Mrs. Dobbins when she pulled into a service station. I was about to pop. By the door hung a neatly painted sign: NO COLORED BATHROOMS HERE. MOVE ON. WHITES ONLY.

"Come on, Faith." Mrs. Dobbins turned to me. "Shelly, you stay put. Don't talk to a soul. They eat coloreds for supper down here."

No matter what skin color, a girl had to relieve herself, but I was left with no choices. There was a good stand of trees out to the side of the store. I slid out of the car and scooted across the gravel parking lot without a soul noticing. As soon as I was hidden, I hiked up my skirt. It was plain out sinful to treat a person like I was being treated. Nada would say it was just the way things was, but she was wrong. I pulled down my panties, dancing a little to hold back. It wouldn't do to wet my clothes. Flies and mosquitoes buzzed around me.

"You! You!"

I cut the stream off just like a water faucet and yanked up my underclothes.

"What you be doing, girl?"

The voice was coming out of the trees. "I'm sorry. I had to wet."

A colored woman hobbled out from behind a tree. Her clothes looked like they came from a long time in the past. She reminded me of someone. "Do you know what them white folks in that store will do if they catch you here? They'll kill you dead, girl."

"I had to go, ma'am. I couldn't hold it no longer."

"Ha. You don't know nothing about taking your fill of something, child. You be young and weak. You take yourself on back to that white family that brought you here. And girl, things never be what you think. Remember that. You got a journey to take."

"Who are you?" The hairs on the back of my neck stood straight up as the old woman moved close.

"Just when you get soft and easy, something flies at you sideways. I know where you from. Blood be thicker than you think, girl. It flows like that big old river that pulls water out of the land and rushes it to the sea." The old woman just shook her head and kept on moving. "Go on, now. Go back to them white women." She laughed. "The child don't even know what her eyes be telling her half the time. You know me. I'm the one who's been watching you all the time. Think on it." And she went so far into the trees I couldn't see her.

Mrs. Dobbins and Faith came out of the store with green-colored bottles. Faith pushed one at me. "Drink this. It's got to be the best thing I've ever put in my mouth."

Mrs. Dobbins frowned. "Faith, you act like you've never drank a Coca-Cola before."

Faith just grinned at me like we had some big old secret and I guessed we did. "Try it, Shelly."

The bottle was icy cold, and the brown liquid bubbled in my mouth, turning it both hot and cold at the same time, taking away my breath.

"I told you." Faith turned her own bottle up and drank the last of it.

We drove and drove and drove. Sometime during the night Mrs. Dobbins pulled the car over on the side of the road. I woke up to them two women's heavy breathing. At first I thought I was stuck in some crazy dream, but then I saw the stars in the sky. Some old night bird was out there calling and calling. I went back to sleep.

THE NEXT MORNING as we drove, the clouds changed from white and fluffy to dark layers stacking on top of each other. All the shades of gray showed against the blue sky. At home, clouds sat on top of us like big, heavy blankets that hid the sky for days. Now, the thick air turned so salty I could taste it. Around us the red clay gave way to sand. But mostly it was the long, gray, tangled hairlike stuff hanging in the sprawling oak trees that made me stare. I thought about the old woman spirit back at the store. Maybe she had been a tree come to life.

"How much longer?" Faith asked around a yawn.

"Almost there." Mrs. Dobbins turned and smiled at Faith. Her look said we was almost free.

The sign to Darien pointed to the left over a bridge. A snaking, wide, calm river came into view. Nothing like Dragonfly River, all in a hurry. No, this river was strong and quiet. The old woman's words came into my head: *that pulls water out of the land and rushes it to the sea.* Nada would say the old woman spirit was an omen of some kind.

There was a bunch of boats at the long dock. "Those are shrimp boats, girls," Mrs. Dobbins said.

"Where's the beach? Where's the ocean? I thought we would be near the ocean." Faith looked around.

"Your uncle Tyson's house is on the marsh that opens up to the sea. It is beautiful. I think you'll both be happy there."

Faith frowned. "One place is as good as the other."

The shrimp boats all had names: *Miss Marie, Polly, Anne,* and *Sweet Jesse.* "Why are the boats named after girls?"

"That's a good question, Shelly. Tyson says it's because a boat is a thing of grace and beauty."

A good-size alligator was stretched across a dead log, floating near the bank. It slid off into the water and floated away with a back-and-forth swish. As the road left the river behind, I turned around and got one more look. The boat named *Sweet Jesse* was easing away from the dock.

PART FIVE

Fiery Sign

❧

August 1935

"Hot, dry, and barren. Not so good for planting and transplanting."

—*Old belief on Black Mountain*

Faith Dobbins

"FAITH, YOU BE CAREFUL about them plants. Give them plenty of water. We're going to have us a drought," Amanda warned.

So I listened. I tried to listen to everything Amanda said, like how I needed to give Will some room for working and thinking.

"Pastor don't take kindly to him. You don't need to be causing him trouble. It wouldn't take much to get your daddy building stories in his head."

Heat spread up my neck into my face. "I don't want to hurt Will." My voice broke.

Amanda looked up from slicing the fatback for the green beans. "Child, I know that, but you don't understand that Pastor's thinking is different than all of us. He be a one and only, that's for sure. When we look at Will, we see a fine young man. When Pastor looks at him, he sees a back to break and the color of his skin. He don't care much for mens, especially if they be colored. He likes to be boss, and he loves to be the boss of women. If he figures out you care about Will, God help you both. See what I'm talking about?"

"Yes, ma'am."

AMANDA HAD FORBIDDEN ME to go in the woods near her cabin, but I went there all the time. I was fifteen, not some old baby who would get lost. When I stepped into the trees, a calm spread over me. The whole place was a bright green with vines and flowering bushes here and there. Miss Tuggle had taught me a lot of names, but I couldn't seem to hold them in my mind as long as I could the names of birds. A little of the blue sky showed through the thick trees. I found the big oak and sat down just to think, just to be quiet. The wind was hot. The heat had turned worse when Arleen was buried, like the mountain was angry. That's what Amanda believed.

A branch broke somewhere nearby. The tops of the trees moved back and forth. The bird songs lulled me into a deep, quiet place. The intruders crashing through the woods were on me before I understood what was going on. Will stumbled out of the thick brush. At first I thought he was playing some dumb trick on me for being in the woods. But his face was a mask of rage, and right behind him charged Daddy. I crawled behind the large tree trunk and flattened my body against the bark.

"I don't know who you think you are, boy, but what you insinuated back there I take as fighting words." Daddy stepped closer to Will. "Why are you running? Because you know you're a liar, that's why. See, I think you were that baby's father. Arleen was trash and we both know it."

I couldn't see Will's face but I could hear him breathing, and I could see him opening and closing one hand in a fist.

"I was Arleen's pastor. I knew her better than her mother did. I saw just what she could do from the beginning."

"She wasn't like that and you know it! You're the liar."

"What did I do, boy?" Daddy boomed. I could only imagine how red his face had turned. Will was a brave, good person and no match for Daddy.

"I want to know exactly what I did, boy!"

There were scuffling and grunting sounds. Daddy would kill Will over Arleen. I'd seen her on the edge of the woods talking to Will more than one time. When I asked him about their conversations, he told me Arleen was upset and in need of someone to talk to. I believed him. Will was not a liar. He was my best friend and told me everything.

"Tell me, you sorry ass!" Daddy yelled. "You abomination! You make me sick!"

"You're the one." Will gasped the words. "You put your baby in her. You forced her to do things she didn't want to do. I seen you follow her through the graveyard into the woods. She told me what you did. If she had lived, she was going to tell the church."

The sound of a fist breaking a nose is a horrible crack. I ran out from behind the tree and flew into Daddy with my fists. I hit him in the back. Will's face was covered with blood.

"You hurt him! Look what you did!" I hit him harder. "You're supposed to be a pastor but you hurt Will!"

Daddy swung around and grabbed my arms. "Get out of here, Faith. This isn't any of your business."

"Why? Why should I listen to you? I won't go. You can't make me. Hit me. I don't care. I won't leave him. I won't let you hurt Will."

A dark shadow moved through Daddy. "What did I tell you, Faith?"

"I'll tell the church what I know. I promise if you hurt Will, I'll tell, and they will make you leave the mountain." I was crying but it didn't matter. I would take the next blow for Will if I had to.

Will stood up. "I know a lot more. I know what happened before Faith was born. I bet these folks here would like to know too. They'd like to know about all your lies and not just about Arleen." Will stepped closer to Daddy, who was still watching me. "See, Pastor, I got something that would put you in jail."

Daddy turned and grabbed Will's throat. "You think that you're anything to me? Nothing, boy! Nothing."

"I'm going after Mama." I turned my head and screamed, "Mama!"

Daddy continued to hold Will by the throat. "See, I've decided not to hurt you right now. No. But if you don't leave this mountain for good, I'll kill your mama and that little sister of yours too. Then who is going to tell what? If you're still here by sunup, I'll keep my promise." He shoved Will back into the brush and stomped off through the woods without saying another word to me.

I ran to Will. Some of what he said began to sink into my bones, aching. Don't get me wrong. I had always known Daddy was capable of bad things, but still the thought of him with Arleen sickened me. "Daddy would have killed you if I wasn't here."

He touched my shoulder. "You shouldn't be in these woods."

"Well, good thing I was." I folded my arms across my chest.

"I'm glad you was here," he admitted.

"Daddy had his way with Arleen Brown?"

His expression turned into a gray shadow. "She told me that story, and she told the truth."

The words I wanted to scream were rocks in my chest, sobs in my mind.

"I got to leave, Faith. But first we have to have a long talk. You got to know the whole story. Everything. Then I'm leaving."

"I'm coming with you." Until that moment, I never thought I had the courage to leave Daddy, the mountain.

Will squeezed my shoulder. "No. Now, listen. 'Cause I'm going to tell the whole mess to you and you got to be strong."

The hot wind moved through those haunted woods. Somewhere a girl sobbed, and it wasn't me.

WE SAT IN THE VERY WOODS where I was forbidden to go, so my life could be shifted, changed, ruined in many ways. But the truth is always,

always easier than the lies. The lies tear a person in half. No one came looking for us. I thought at least Amanda would have searched. Maybe Shelly. Will talked until no more words would come out of his mouth. At first I put my hands over my ears, but Will pulled them away, insisting I hear every word he had to say, the whole history. Finally when I couldn't take any more, I stared at the blue sky peeking in and out of the tree-tops as if I were listening. The wind settled into a hot, dry cry roaming through my thoughts.

"Listen, Faith." Will said this so many times I wanted to cry out for help, for rescue. "Shelly will only have you. Just you. You have to be strong." He went on with his crazy talk.

"She hates me, Will. You know that." I sounded like a young child.

"Naw, she just thinks she does. Shelly cares about you, Faith. She's going to need you. Are you listening? Do you understand what you mean to her? You'll be my voice she can't remember." He looked at me with that sad look of his, the one that tore my heart from my chest.

Both hate and love crashed through my body. "I'll die if I stay here, especially now that I know all this. I can't. I'll lose my mind. I may any-way." A dark cloud of feelings settled on my brittle shoulders.

"You can't just leave Mrs. Dobbins. You got to keep what I told you a secret, Faith. It could tear lives into shreds. It could cause a death. It may anyway. You promise?"

This swear wouldn't be hard to keep because why would I ever speak of the things he told me his last afternoon on the mountain? I wished away the whole day like casting one of Amanda's conjures. But a spell couldn't repair a story. "Yes, I promise."

"Good."

"What about money? I have some money at the house, Will."

He shook his head. "No. I won't take what you may need down the road. This ain't over just 'cause I'm leaving, Faith."

"Where will you go? How will Amanda live through this?"

He stood. "You go on, now. I'll take care of myself. Go back to the house. Don't look back at me, Faith. Go on. Remember all I told you. It links us together."

I opened my mouth but I closed it back.

"Go on, now." His voice broke.

The first three steps made me stumble like a child taking her first walk. Then I broke into a run. Never, ever again did I want to think about the day I lost my father and my best friend. Will yelled something, but I kept running.

"God, are you real? And if you're real, why would you make him leave? Why? He's all I got now. Are you there?" I yelled at the sky like I'd seen Daddy do. God didn't answer.

The kitchen was empty so I went straight to my room. I had to do something. Then I remembered the dream about Amanda's grandmother and the sewing basket.

PART SIX

Finders Keepers

June 1939

"If you find something, it's all yours whether you want it or not."

—Shelly Parker

Ada Lee Tine

SWEET JESSE BOBBED UP AND DOWN in the water. Will stood in the cabin. On his head was a tattered cap with his bushy hair pushing out from underneath. Tough times or not, the boy had to have him a real haircut. All the money from our catches went into his college jar. He was in his third year and I was right proud of him. We'd made do when he was away and he came home during the summer to help me fish. My life started and stopped each day with the thought of him.

The air was heavy with a weather line coming in on us from the west. A land storm. They could be the worst and we had white folks coming too. I shook my head just thinking on it. A shadow stood just behind Will, near the boat's wheel. There Roger was looking after my boy. Had he lived, we would have looked after Will together and things would have been a lot different, but I couldn't bring myself to think on it. Will brought hope and love into my life when there wasn't a bit more left. That made him my angel. Not many women had an angel.

"Ada, what you smiling at?" Will laughed.

"Just a thought scooting through this old brain of mine." I stood on the dock.

"I got us a good catch today, best of the whole month. Now we need us a good price on shrimp."

"Lordy be, you right about that," I said. The shadow stood there like he was listening to us. "I'm thankful. Lots of folks don't have nothing at all, Will. I heard yesterday they done busted up a Hooverville in Brunswick, near the tracks. God bless. That's got to be the saddest thing ever. I never thought I'd see a day when folks went without eating in our parts. There's always a catch, has been since slave days."

"Hard times, Ada, will cause folks to do things they wouldn't normally do."

"I'm right proud you going to college. Did I tell you that?" I grinned.

"Yep, you sure have, but just keep saying it."

"What you see for the next year, Will?" I stepped into the boat.

He started the engine and scooted *Sweet Jesse* out from the dock, headed upriver. "You know it don't work like that. I can't see my own future. Don't want to. And I never know how far ahead I see. It's too messy to put any store in."

I squeezed his hand. "What you see for me?" The tingling began in the tips of my fingers.

His eyes went kind of glassy. "Peace. No matter what. You're a peaceful soul, Ada."

I let him go. Peace. Now, that was a good thought to carry through the summer. Peace. But Will was the peaceful soul, not me. He was my boy, but he was a strong man.

"I see this white family getting on your last nerve." He laughed.

I play-slapped at him. "That ain't seeing no future. That's just fact."

"It might take me longer than I thought to finish college." He grinned.

"Why?"

"I've been thinking big. That's all."

The gulls flew overhead looking for some leftover catch.

"Did you know there was a colored man killed for no good reason right here the same year I came?"

I laced my fingers together behind my back.

"And that same night a white man and his colored girlfriend died."

"People tell stories. They add on something with each telling."

"Yep. And they told me plenty about the colored man who was killed for nothing. He sounds like a fine man to have known."

The water of the Altamaha River was deep, dark, and still with a hidden current underneath. I heard tell there was places upstream where it moved like the mighty hand of God, but for me, it owned the souls of history in Darien. And that day it lapped against *Sweet Jesse,* keeping time with Will's words.

"Folks in Darien think you're a good woman, Ada Lee."

"That story works under my skin like that mountain of yours does you," I said. "Something I want to put behind me."

"This island is my home. Always has been even if I didn't know it. Does that make sense?"

"Maybe not book sense, but perfect sense to me."

Will's face was still. "Mama's right where I left her. I'm sure of that. Working for the white pastor and looking after his wife and girl, protecting them with her hoodoo. She's good at that. She's got ties to them that run too deep to leave." He looked at me hard. "I'm thinking the way Negroes are treated is wrong. White people do what they want when they want. Not all of them are bad. And even the good ones mostly don't see us for who we really are. They see skin. They can go to the bathroom anywhere they want. They can eat where they want. They can buy a business or land anywhere they want. They sleep in the hotels they choose. Well, I want to change the situation." He finished out of breath.

"Don't start that mess. You don't need to die young. That talk will get you in trouble real quick. Shoot, there's a law against what we're doing right now, talking about the wrongs. *Talking,* boy. Mr. Jim Crow ain't for fun."

His look darkened. "I'm not standing by and living my life in fear, Ada. I met some people at college in Atlanta."

"Well, you leave them alone. You understand? What happened to you on that mountain to stir you up so much?"

"It's not just about what happened up there." He was quiet, thinking. "Here's the thing: we both have our secrets we keep close to our hearts. I want to do something, Ada, so Negroes don't have to keep those kind of secrets. I want to change things."

This mess of a boy was turning into a full-grown man before my eyes.

"Ada?" He kept his stare on the crooked river.

"Yep."

"Yesterday when I got on *Sweet Jesse,* I saw, plain as day, a man standing at her wheel. He was tall and thin. He turned and tipped his cap at me. He knew me."

I just watched the marsh.

"I figure he's the colored man that was killed for no good reason. And I think you knew him well, since he gave you this boat."

"If I counted all the coloreds that have been wronged, Will, I'd be counting till doomsday." I sighed. "Nothing ever going to change that."

"I had to leave my family behind. A sister too young to understand that Negroes are just doomed to be wronged in a white world. The day I left, I understood what being a Negro meant. That man who owned *Sweet Jesse* came to point me in a new direction, a direction of change."

"What you know about him? Look where he went." I spit the words. "His death didn't help one person here in Darien, black or white. He left a hole. A big one. You get them big old thoughts about saving folks out of your head. He didn't have them, never would risk his life for something that just couldn't be done. He was a good man. That's all. A good man. We are who we are here. Saltwater Geechees from Sapelo, peoples of Biali. He be a slave, Will, a slave that led other slaves on Sapelo. He taught them how to live a good life and be in their lives with as much grace as possible. A slave who was educated. Wrote a book of prayers."

"Ah, Ada, I'm sorry to worry you. You got them new nets ready for casting tomorrow?"

"You're changing the subject. I see what you be doing, Will." I let him ask about them nets, but inside, them worried thoughts turned into a prayer.

Lord, Will be needing you something terrible. He's got this crazy notion that he's going to save his people like Moses, but he ain't Moses, Peter, or Paul. He's just a boy you sent me when I thought I'd die. I give him to you. Keep him safe. Amen.

MR. TYSON LET ME KNOW up front his sister and niece was coming in a rush and it wasn't planned. He said they wouldn't be a bit of trouble, though. That business about leaving home in a hurry tipped me off. I wasn't no fool. See, I hadn't messed with his house since I got the boat, since them murders. But Mr. Tyson was stuck. He had been good to me, especially after Roger was killed, so I owed him some help.

"You have to keep an eye out for her husband, Ada Lee. You have to know he's nothing but trouble. I want you to call the sheriff if he shows himself on my property." Now, this wasn't like Mr. Tyson. That husband had to be one mean man.

A shiver walked down my backbone. "I ain't worried about her husband none. He don't want to mess with me."

"He knows he's not welcome, but call the sheriff if he shows up." Mr. Tyson smiled. "I wouldn't mind seeing him tangle with you, Ada Lee." He laughed. Him and missus was on the way to their new house in Maine, late leaving. Mr. Tyson had somehow managed to do good even though there was a depression. Darien in the summer was too hot for them now. The old brown house pretty much stayed empty year-round. But it was an old family house from way on back, so he would never sell it. And I was glad about that.

There I was in the big brown marsh house when Mr. Tyson's sister came rolling into the yard in some old car that would have made her brother frown. Mr. Tyson loved him a nice car. The sister wore a scarf on her head and big sunglasses like she be Carole Lombard. But she didn't hide a thing from Ada. I seen them bruises and thanked God that her husband wasn't with her. Next out was some little white girl, who had a thick black cloud around her. Then out popped some old colored girl all arms and legs, but pretty in a plain way, like a woman who knows how to dress quiet and peaceful. As soon as she stepped out onto the driveway, I saw spirits walking out of the marsh to meet her like they had known she was on the way. Sweet Baby Jesus, this girl had the sight something strong.

Miss Hollywood behind her dark glasses stepped toward me. "Ada, I'm Lydia, Tyson's sister." She held out her hand. Them fingers of hers looked like they might snap in two. Everything about Miss Hollywood made me think of those thin teacups Mrs. Tyson kept in the sideboard, gathering dust after years of never being used.

Without thinking much about it—and that wasn't like me—I took her hand in mine and shook it. "Yes, ma'am, we met a long time ago, when you was a young thing." She was just a slip of a girl in a woman's body.

"You remember me, Ada?" She said this like no one cared after her. She turned toward the little white girl. "This is Faith, my daughter."

Now, something about that name released into the air made me let go of Miss Lydia's hand. When I looked at this Faith, I seen more stirring around in that head of hers than I wanted to know about. Two girls brooding in the same skin. One was pale with dark eyes in a blue-eyed family, fading in and out. The other girl came from a hardworking life and sly. Lord, she was sly like a fox or maybe a weasel. Time would tell just who would be the owner of that pitiful body. I heard tell of people with several spirits inside of them. This girl was one.

"You want to walk through the house and get acquainted?" I offered Miss Lydia. That's when I saw her, Miss Mary Beth Clark, standing on the landing of the second floor. "Go take a look around." I nodded to Miss Lydia. When they walked by and got out of earshot, I turned to the colored girl. "I be Ada."

"I'm Shelly Parker." She watched the spirit, trying not to keep her eyes on it.

"This is the first time I've been back here since she died." I spoke low. Something quiet grew inside of me without a name or a face, like a dern old kudzu vine choking out the pretty with its fat green leaves. "You can stay with me at night." I watched this girl with interest. Something about her was almost familiar, like I ought to have known exactly who she was and what she wanted in Darien.

She turned that look of hers away from the haint. "I guess."

"Well, you can't be staying on the Ridge at night, child. You be colored. You can come home with me. I got me a place in town for weeknights and then on the weekends, like tonight, we'll head on back to Sapelo Island. You ain't never seen nothing, nothing like it."

"Shelly can just stay with us at night here, Ada." Miss Lydia stood halfway up them stairs and heard every word I said.

"I'll be needing help in the evenings at my place for the next day. The weekends just give her a break. This girl needs to be around young people." I smiled real big. "My boy will pick me and her up at the dock this evening. I live on Sapelo Island, ma'am, in case you don't remember."

"Yes, that's right. And you have a son, Ada? I thought you never married."

"He be close family and staying with me now. He's going to school to be a lawyer."

Miss Lydia smiled. "Is that what you want to do, Shelly?"

Lord help, that poor girl looked confused like she hadn't had many choices. "Yes, ma'am. I'll stay with her." Shelly cut a look at Miss Mary Beth's spirit still standing on the stairs.

"Well, that's settled. Faith and I will go choose our rooms. Ada, you fill Shelly in with what she needs to know." Miss Lydia started up the stairs again and walked right through Miss Mary Beth Clark's spirit, but that Faith girl walked around the haint. Lord help me, she could see the ghost too.

"She's a fine-looking for a haint," Shelly said.

"Oh yes, she be fine, all right, and she thought that when she was alive. It's probably what got her killed." I turned to leave.

"You know her?" Shelly asked. "I never know the spirits that come see me."

"I guess you could say I knew that one. As you get older, you'll know some of the haints that come your way." I walked back to the kitchen. "We ain't got time for an old-home week with them kind of spirits. We got to get this supper fixed. I leave here every day at five and no later. Today be Friday, I'm going to take you to Sapelo with me. And I like to cook supper for my boy."

She nodded and followed me into the kitchen.

Shelly Parker

ADA LEE TINE was one of the strangest colored women I'd ever met, but then I'd only known Nada. She wore a feather and four colored beads tied around her neck with a piece of leather. Her dress didn't have a bit of shape and was gray with no color at all. On her head was a black scarf. But it was the way she watched me—like I was the most interesting thing she'd seen. She was bent under the sink in the kitchen when someone came knocking.

"Get that door, Shelly."

A tall, lanky colored boy not much older than me looked surprised. "I was looking for Ada Lee Tine." He held a big wire basket with two horrible-looking creatures inside.

"Sam!" Ada yelled as she stood up. "You got my lobsters." She stepped in front of me and took the wire basket. "I guess it's a dollar apiece, like usual?"

"For you, Ada Lee." He smiled.

"Get on out of here." She laughed and shut the door. "He be one of the fishermen," she explained. "Come on over here." Ada placed the wire basket on the table. She checked on a big, tall pot full of water, heating on the stove. "Now, this here is lobster. God's most beautiful creatures."

I frowned.

"Oh, don't you be making them kind of faces. I'm going to teach you to cook them. We'll have some of our own tonight and later take us a walk on the beach. You like the ocean?"

"Never seen it, ma'am." The water began to steam.

She shook her head. "Ain't nothing about you that's right." Her smile was big. "Next week we'll stay in my aunt Hattie's old house. She's been dead for a few years now, but I use her home when I got to be here in Darien. Never seen her spirit."

I let a breath out and nodded.

She put her hand into the cage and brought out one of them ugly creatures. "He's going to make a fine, fine supper. Don't you think?"

"He be ugly," I said.

She laughed. "Yes, ma'am, they are ugly creatures, but they taste better than a king's supper." She lowered the thing into the pot of hot water. A hissing cry filled the kitchen.

I must have looked scared, 'cause Ada Lee Tine shook her head. "It ain't really crying, child. Just sounds like it." This woman had the darkest skin I'd ever seen. "You know how to fry cooked corn?" She pulled five ears of corn out of a cloth bag.

"Yes, ma'am."

"Good. You be useful." She handed me the ears. "Then get to it. The butter's in the icebox. We leave here at five on the dot."

Mrs. Dobbins came into the kitchen. "You can stay here if you want, Ada. It won't bother me to have the extra company."

Ada Lee Tine kind of laughed. "No, ma'am. Like I said, it be Friday. I go to the island on the weekend." Then she looked at Mrs. Dobbins real serious. "This is the Ridge, Miss Lydia. I ain't never staying here after dark."

Faith came into the kitchen. "Can't Shelly just stay here?"

That's when I understood I didn't want to stay. I wanted to go with this strange woman and find out what else I could know from her. "I'll go with Ada."

Ada smiled at me like I passed some kind of test. "We have some business this weekend, and it ain't cooking and cleaning here on the mainland." She laughed.

I thought Mrs. Dobbins would puff up, but she smiled real big. "Shelly needs a good adventure."

There we was all acting like we was on a vacation, just happy as could be except for Faith. I think that girl really wanted me to stay. Well, even if she was Arleen Brown, I wasn't going to be her friend and babysit her either.

"Go on and wash up, you two. I'm going to leave you enough food for a army. You can fend for yourself for two days. Can't you?"

Mrs. Dobbins still wore that silly grin. "Yes. That'll be our adventure." She reached over and squeezed Faith's hand. I don't ever remember seeing that woman touch Faith. It's what mamas was supposed to do, but Mrs. Dobbins never showed no kind of touching in front of Nada and me. But she was softening to this new place. And that was the best thing of all. If she started loving this place with her whole heart, maybe Nada would come live here too. And maybe just maybe that silly old Arleen would let go of the real Faith. And I still didn't know why I cared.

When they was gone to wash up, Ada looked at me. "You got you two doozies there."

My cheeks heated. "They ain't mine."

She laughed. "I know just how you feel. You're here now, and we're going to make the best of it until you go home. I'm going to teach you all I know about cooking and the island. Two of the things I love best. We're going to have us a feast on the island with my boy. You ever been on a real boat?"

I laughed 'cause the answer to that question stuck in my throat. A real boat.

"You going to have you a fine time, girl. And since you live alongside them folks, I got a feeling you need it."

This trip wasn't going to be so bad after all. Maybe I wouldn't even bother with reading Armetta's stupid old book. Maybe she was just stirring stuff up. Nope, I'd put that thing away and not think about it no more. The thing wasn't nothing but her selfish way of getting her story told. How could a story save anyone? Anyway, Armetta couldn't even bother me in Darien. But I kept thinking on that pretty haint upstairs.

Armetta

I WOULD WATCH MAMA for the longest in her garden when I was a little thing. The way Shelly's mama sat with her legs folded under her and dug her fingers into the fresh dirt made me miss being alive. Mama had been the cook in the main house and loved her garden better than anything, just like Shelly's mama.

When Pastor found out the womenfolk was gone, Lord help, he got all upset and took off down to Asheville, probably hunting down the sheriff. But not before he threatened Shelly's mama for playing like she didn't know anything. But still the air turned softer, easier, almost happy with him gone. And a little tune no one alive could hear scooted through the wind. If I hadn't known a whole lot better, I would have believed he was gone for good. Shelly's mama had the strength to stand alone on the mountain. She could face Pastor head-on. But to stop him, it would take a whole lot more than a strong colored mountain witch and a white granny woman. Maybe a little craziness.

"You're here. I feel you." Amanda's words was soft, kind. She had never tried to talk to me before, not even when I blew in her ear that night her boy ran off. Nothing could have stopped him. His leaving was written across them stars in the sky. "You're the girl spirit, the lost one. Shelly's gone. I sent her away. No need to worry. She be safe for now."

"Nobody safe."

"Maybe, but I had to try. He's gone." She clipped mint leaves and dropped them in her basket.

"Not for long."

"I guess you be right."

"Can you see me?" I asked.

She shook her head. "My sight is weak as water. Sometimes if a spirit is real strong, I can hear them." She moved to her lavender bushes that had seen better days. "The story is that you be good with growing things. The flowers still turn out real pretty in that old cemetery every spring."

"It be my home."

Her hands looked much older than her face. "I miss New Orleans bad enough to cry sometimes. I guess that's where my spirit will go when I pass." Shelly's mama looked out to the west.

"Maybe you'll go on into the light 'cause you'll be finished in this world. That be the best thing. I didn't because my story is all tangled."

"Depends on what happens before I die. Lots of untold secrets sit on my back." She gave a short laugh.

"Your back sure be straight if it's carrying a load."

She looked in my direction. "You come when someone is going to die."

A tiredness soaked me all the way through like I still had bones and skin. "I'm stuck to him, always have been."

She nodded. "You was here when Will left."

"Yes, ma'am."

"Did he die?" Her fingers shook.

We all got our weaknesses, the place where we feel the hole open and suck us in. "Not yet. We all got to die, though."

"What you mean?" She sounded angry.

"Just what I said. None of our bodies will last forever."

"Will is a good boy."

"From what I seen, he sure wasn't no boy. He acted like a man. Not many men do that." We both got quiet.

"Shelly's daddy acted like some dern old boy running up and down the mountain, selling moonshine for Hobbs Pritchard. Always smiling at me, telling me not to worry. Then he got himself killed."

"Men can't never be believed." I spit them words.

She nodded. "One minute they tell you something, and then they change what they be thinking and go in a different direction, like we women be the craziness that caused it. We give all ourselves to them, and they take without giving nothing in return but lies."

"Amen!" I yelled.

She stood, and I could see all them little lines on her face, one or two for every year her boy had been gone. "So why you here?"

"He's got to tell my story, he be the keeper." That's when I asked her the question I'd been thinking on for a long time. "Why you stuck to him?"

She shook off a shiver. "I'm just like you. I've had burdens placed on me."

Something thick and heavy formed in the air. Fear swept over the sky. A hot wind that blew before a funnel cloud was bringing him. Nobody was safe. I seen them all four: Shelly and her mama, the white granny woman, and that girl of his. His evil wanted to bury them in the ground before their time to go. I had to find out which ones he was going to hurt. I had to help them.

Maude Tuggle

WHEN I GOT HOME, I found Shelly's note. So she was gone with Lydia and Faith. That was probably for the best. She spelled out a warning, though. I stood in the doorway with the paper in my hand, thinking about how to handle the situation. Should I go see Amanda? Find out what happened?

Charles Dobbins pulled into my drive in his old car. I had the irrational feeling that our good pastor knew that I knew about his past. Crazy thinking.

"Can I help you?" I stood with my feet apart, hands on hips.

He stood at the bottom of the stairs. "My dear Miss Tuggle, I hope this fine day is treating you good."

"It is a pretty day, Pastor Dobbins, but you haven't come to chat about the weather. We're just not on those kind of terms."

As I expected, his cheeks turned red. "Where are my daughter and wife?"

"I really don't know. I haven't seen Faith since yesterday morning. Has something happened?"

"Please do not insult me, Miss Tuggle. I know your involvement in this disappearance. Lydia couldn't leave this mountain alone. You helped Faith leave once. Why not the both of them? They are all gone but that maid, even her daughter went with them."

My smile came through. "I'm so sorry to hear of your worries, but I'm sure your wife can take care of herself, or is that what you're so worried about, Pastor Dobbins? She may have decided to leave you for good?"

He walked up two of the three steps. "Don't be smart to me."

When I was young, Mama taught me if a stray dog came after me, growling and baring its teeth, I had to stand up to it and use a firm voice. So I took her advice to heart in that minute. "Pastor Dobbins, I warn you not to come any closer to me. I do not know where your wife and daughter are. I don't blame them for running away from you. You deserve it. But I did not have the pleasure of helping them. I will kindly ask you to leave."

He took a step back. "I heard you were reading the church records. Have you finally become interested in finding a place in the church, Maude?" He twisted my name with tone in his voice.

"Please leave."

He stood there a minute like he might just slap me silly. "I know your soul. You're black-hearted. Stay out of my business and away from my family. Do you understand?"

"I don't see how I can get close to them. Neither of us know where they are."

He stormed away from me to his car, started the engine, and spun rocks leaving the driveway. I only hoped he wouldn't take out his anger on Amanda. I decided to go warn her and talk to her about what I knew.

* * *

AMANDA MET ME on the porch of her cabin. She watched my every move. "It be good to see you, Miss Tuggle."

"I've just had a visit from Pastor Dobbins. He is a very angry man."

"Have a seat in the rocker." She gave me a long look. "He thought you helped them? Right?"

The note from Shelly was on the tip of my tongue, but I bit it back. "Yes, you are correct. Are you going to be okay with him here?"

She gave a tired smile. "I'm used to his ways. He won't hurt me. Hasn't all these years and I've seen him in all kind of moods."

I nodded. "I've also come to talk to you about the abandoned cemetery up the mountain, if you have a minute."

She stood, leaning against the railing. "I can tell you mostly about Ella Creek, the settlement. I don't know so much about the graveyard." I must have shown my disappointment, because she shook her head. "Not a soul alive that knows much about that graveyard. The Danielses are gone. The coloreds that lived in Ella Creek left here a long time ago. You was born and raised here, Miss Tuggle. You ought to know all this."

"Mama never talked about the Danielses. They were gone by the time I got old enough to know about that part of the mountain."

"But the coloreds weren't. Shelly's daddy grew up there. He was one of the last families to leave. They all worked for the Danielses. Them folks owned a lot of slaves before the War Between the States. When the last of the Danielses left, the coloreds held on and tried to farm 'cause the Danielses had given them the land. Owning land was and still is like money or better." She looked out at her garden. "All of the coloreds had hightailed it off the mountain by the time I showed up. Clyde had moved to Asheville, but he was working for Hobbs Pritchard. That's how I met him. Us being the only two colored adults within miles of here. I was lonely; otherwise, I would never have got tangled with him. Shelly owns her daddy's land parcel now, but I ain't bothered telling her. What good would it bring her?"

"It's land." This woman was a mystery to me. Part of her was head-strong and the other seemed to hide from what she saw as difficult.

"Maybe so. Why you asking about the graveyard, anyway?" Her tone told me she was going to send me on my way.

"I went there this morning."

"What you doing way out in them bad woods, Miss Tuggle?"

"I've been walking this mountain since I was a young girl. I'm not afraid and do not allow stories to rule my decisions. But somehow I missed this most interesting cemetery."

"That cemetery don't care a bit whether you believe in the haints up there or not. I hear the whispers from the woods, Miss Tuggle. I don't make up stories."

Now I had offended her. I looked at the woods.

"I respect your not believing, Miss Tuggle, 'cause you respect me," Amanda continued. "But believe it or not, them spooks in the woods be real and dangerous. Be careful."

"In the church records, I saw where a Negro girl was lost. She's buried in the Daniels family plot. That is unusual for now, but especially back then."

A flicker of something flashed over Amanda's face. "I don't know about any of that."

"There is a Paul Dobbins buried in the same plot. Did you know that?"

She looked away. "I don't know nothing about that."

"Dobbins isn't an uncommon name."

Amanda studied her shoes. "I guess you be right."

"Did our good pastor have family that lived up here before you came?"

"Not that I know, but that man be as secretive as he be mean." She looked troubled.

"Any strange stories about this Ella Creek Settlement or the people that lived there?"

A quiet settled between us for a minute. "The only thing I can think of was Clyde talking about the Clarks. They lived next to him and had a little girl. There was a story about how the little girl's grandmother, Ma Clark, had been a slave and good friends with the lost colored girl's mother. Clyde said the little Clark girl was always complaining about a haint coming into her bedroom at night to look at her. That wasn't the strange thing, though. Clyde kept up with the girl. She grew up and could pass if she tried hard enough, so she moved to New York. She called herself Mary Beth Clark and dressed real fancy. Right before the bad storm five years ago, she came breezing through looking for Clyde. I told her he had died a while back. Something about that girl just rubbed me the wrong way, and I wasn't jealous. It was like she held herself above me. But she was right sad Clyde had died. Tight on her arm was a white man, so I figured she'd been playacting in her new life. Seems she'd come to Black Mountain to visit her grandmother's grave and something about needing to look through the old house. Well, nobody cared a dern thing, so she snooped around up there. I guess she got what she came for, 'cause she left right off this mountain and never came back again. Like I said, something about her was wrong. Off." Amanda looked at me. "That's the only story I know about Ella Creek."

THE NEXT MORNING, I woke up with the feeling someone had been in the bedroom with me. How silly. The sun streamed in the window and the sky was blue. My boots sat next to my desk. On a blank sheet of paper was childlike writing: THE ANGEL. Now I was writing in my sleep.

A knock on the door made me jump. "Wait just a minute." I slid on my pants from the day before and tucked in a clean blouse. "I'm on the way." Someone had to be sick. I grabbed my boots, frowned at the sheet of paper again, and went to answer the door.

Zach stood there in his uniform.

"What's wrong?" I said.

He smiled. "I can't just show up for a visit?"

"You wouldn't," I answered, and motioned him into the front room. "What is going on?"

"Well, first it seems your friend Pastor Charles Dobbins—"

"He's not my friend."

Zach gave me a stern look. "I know that. He came into the office late yesterday afternoon to report his wife and daughter had been kidnapped. He suspects his maid has hurt them."

"Amanda? How stupid." I sat down and began to put my shoes on.

"I suggested maybe they left of their own accord. He became quite irate. He also said he believed you had something to do with their disappearance."

"Oh my gosh. He was here yesterday afternoon. I told him I didn't even know they had left. I went to see Amanda. She was fine, but not very helpful."

"I warned him to leave you and his maid alone. I didn't mention our suspicions." He looked at me. "I have more of the story."

"Oh, really?"

"This part came from my sister, who always remembers things better than me. She remembered the story our grandmother told about the Danielses." He watched me close. "It's about Amelia Daniels."

"Really, she's the one who lost the Negro girl who worked for her."

"She's your connection to the good pastor."

A prickle ran across my hair. "How?"

"She married Paul Dobbins, a fourth-generation Episcopal minister. He was here visiting the church and met Amelia, marrying her within a year. Then he took her off to New Orleans. He was an oddball, just like his grandson Charles Dobbins would be."

"Paul Dobbins?" I echoed.

Zach nodded. "Sis said. He insisted on being buried near Amelia when he died. She's buried in the family plot up the mountain a little. Paul Dobbins wasn't much of a minister or husband. There was a lot of talk about him killing a Negro girl who was pregnant. Of course that was just part of the story Grandma told, along with him having a cross stolen from him, a cross with a diamond in the center." He looked at me. "It seems two of the current Dobbins men come off unstable. Charles Dobbins's father is known for his like of other women. He's also terrible to his sons. Like father, like son. Maybe."

"Makes sense."

Zach nodded.

"And we know he was sent here to the mountain for his possible involvement in the death of the young Negro girls in Georgia?"

"No, that's not the whole reason. I heard back from my friend in New Orleans. He did some more snooping around. Charles Dobbins was accused by a member of his father's congregation of making un-healthy advances on a fourteen-year-old white girl as soon as he came back from his revival in Georgia. The girl's father was well-off. Within a day, Charles's father had decided to ship him off to Black Mountain."

I couldn't speak.

"He's a loose cannon. It seems he threatened to kill the youngest brother, Lenard, who happened to visit a week or so ago. Told him he'd kill him rather than let him stay on the mountain."

"I never even heard they had a visitor." I frowned.

"I think we have to be careful. We have to find out if that cross you have is the same one Grandma's story mentions. That will give us some solid proof."

"Amanda's not going to talk to you, Zach. I'll go back to see her to-morrow." Maybe he needed to see what I had found. "Are you really busy?"

He looked at me strange. "Why?"

"I want to show you the abandoned cemetery where the Danielses are buried. Paul Dobbins's grave is there. There's something I want to do up there too."

He nodded. "I'd like to see the place."

And we walked through the woods in silence. That was one of the things I always liked about Zach. He enjoyed quiet and didn't need to fill the air with small talk.

"Look at the ironwork on those gates." He walked in the direction of two large gates I had somehow missed the morning before. "Artwork at its finest."

The letters across the top of the gates spelled ELLA CREEK. I stood beside him. "I brought you here to help me with something."

He gave me a wary look. "Those words always get me in trouble."

What I wanted most of all grew inside my chest, a pressure against my ribs, a completely unhealthy desire. "Over here." Part of me believed the angel wouldn't be there, that I had imagined it. A shadow scurried across the corner of the Danielses' plot. I stopped walking.

Zach nearly ran into me. "What's wrong?"

"Nothing. The sun got in my eyes." I refused to see ghosts everywhere. The sun cut through the trees in bright swaths.

"There." I pointed to her.

Zach knelt down and ran his hand across her face. "She's beautiful."

"I want to sit her up. I found her yesterday. Actually, I want her for my garden."

He gave me a stern look.

"Don't look at me like that. No one is looking after this plot. I want her."

"It's still theft, Maude."

"What a fuddy-duddy." I squatted down beside him. "She deserves to be on her feet."

"Be careful. Her wing is broken, but here's the piece. She could be repaired." His stare settled on Paul Dobbins's gravestone just across from the angel.

"I don't want you around Charles Dobbins." He pulled my angel free of her vines with one smooth motion. "Grab her good wing."

I did.

Zach righted her that easy.

"I will see if Amanda knows anything about the cross."

"Okay, but I swear if you get hurt—"

I laughed. "Then what?"

"You know what I mean. You'll come see me right away?"

"Yes."

"Promise?"

"Yes."

"Okay."

We walked down the mountain.

ON TOWARD EVENING, I pushed my wheelbarrow up the path to Ella Creek Cemetery. I worked with the angel until I had her propped in the wheelbarrow. Going downhill with her wasn't as bad as I thought. By the time the gray of dark washed the yard, I had her righted in the middle of my garden. I could have sworn she smiled at me. In her beautiful marble hands sat a perfectly carved rabbit. I touched it. Somehow I hadn't noticed it until that moment. Cold drops of rain began to hit my angel. The drought was breaking. I stood there with my hand on her broken wing. Tomorrow I would go see Amanda with the cross. Then maybe Shelly and Faith could come back to the mountain.

Ada Lee Tine

"WE GOT TO TAKE the old truck and leave it at the dock so we got a way back Monday morning." Lord, Shelly looked like she might break in half, no meat on her bones at all. But she was right handsome to look at. She didn't know how she looked, and that was best kept as it was.

"It's pretty here 'cept for the gray stuff." Shelly pointed at the Spanish moss hanging off the old oak trees. "That makes me think of dried-up hair like goes in a spell."

I laughed. "You talking about root. What you know about that?"

Shelly looked at me like I lost my mind.

"Root is what we on the island call voodoo, spells, you know, conjuring, magic." I gave her one of my real laughs.

She smiled. "Nada been conjuring since she was little. She comes from New Orleans, and it comes natural to her."

The top of my head tingled. "This be moss." I pulled a string off the big twisted oak near the truck. "See?"

She took the curly gray piece. "It's soft like hair."

"Yep."

"The air smells like salt here. I ain't used to that."

"Yes, ma'am. I never get tired of it. You be a long way from home, but old Ada here will help with that loneliness. Before you know it, you'll be headed back. Where does Miss Lydia live, anyway? Mr. Tyson never said."

"Black Mountain, North Carolina."

"I heard of that place. I just can't place who told me about it."

That girl watched out the old truck's window. I couldn't quite figure her age, maybe fourteen or fifteen. "You have good friends back home?"

"Only one. She be a white granny woman who is teaching me to read better. So I guess she ain't really my friend, but she believes I can become a writer one day." She gave me a shy look.

"Lord, girl, why you ain't got no colored friends?"

"No coloreds on the mountain but me and Nada." She waited a minute like she was going to say something else and then shrugged.

"Then you going to have the time of your life here. I'll make sure." I touched her shoulder and a tingle went through my arm. "It's hard being away from home. I remember the first time I worked for Mr. Tyson and left the island for a whole week. Lord have mercy, I was the worst thing. I cried myself to sleep each and every night. Aunt Hattie petted and talked to me, but it didn't make no mind. Every chance I got, I stood in the topmost room of Mr. Tyson's house and looked out that little round window and caught me a glimpse of Sapelo. I'd feel better for a while."

"So you never slept in the house?"

"No, sirree. Not me or no other colored in Darien. None of us will stay on the Ridge."

Shelly turned her pretty gaze on me. "You be stuck in that darkness at Mr. Tyson's house."

I let her words settle in me. "How you mean stuck?"

"Part of you is held there 'cause of what happened. The knowing hit me as soon as I walked in the door. Then I seen that dern ghost." She smiled. "That fancy ghost ain't come back for you. It be me. I don't know why. I just know."

"You got some powerful sight."

"Yes, ma'am. It be strong, or so Nada says. She should know."

A chill blew over my arms, and I rubbed it off the best I could. "I had me a run-in with that haint when she was alive. That's probably what you're feeling. You stay clear of her and pray she don't want you."

Shelly cut me a look. "It already be done."

"What you mean?" This girl was starting to wear on my nerves.

"You're thinking you were part of her passing, the fancy ghost, but you wasn't. I know this. You was close but not part of it." She looked straight ahead.

As silly as it sounded, I believed her. I took comfort in those words. But a part of me worried. I never could remember what happened that night. All I knew was the old woman spirit used me. Took me with her to that house. "So who killed them two if I wasn't part of it?"

Shelly watched the road. "Don't know. Just know it wasn't you. I got a feeling."

"What would that feeling be?"

She shook her head. "Something is coming at me. It's moving as fast as fast can be."

The air felt different. That girl was something else. "That white girl with you is strange."

"Yep."

"I seen her sewing things."

"She calls herself a quilter. The quilt she be working on now is the worst. It be charmed. I seen her taking the hair from the white granny woman's brush. I don't know what she's up to."

"I had me a look. It looked strange." I gave a little shiver. "We got us a shrimp boat to catch."

She gave me a straight-face look.

"You be liking to ride on a boat. *Sweet Jesse* is solid." The dock was in plain view. "There she is." I parked the truck near the edge. Will stepped out of the cabin of the boat the same time as Shelly got out of the truck. I told him he had no business fishing when he was almost finished with his degree, but that boy loved the sea. He even slept on *Jesse* some nights.

That dern girl had stopped dead in her tracks.

"Come on. What you doing way back there?" I pointed at the boat. "That be my boat and my boy."

Her shoulders relaxed and she took a few steps. "I thought it was someone I knew a long time ago."

My fingers went numb. "You don't know my boy."

Will cupped his hand over his mouth to yell but went stone-still. He was staring at Shelly.

"This here . . ." I yelled a little too loud for how close we was.

"Lord," he said.

Shelly stopped walking. I was about to start throwing me a fit. This was my boy, and they wasn't going to start getting goo-goo eyes for each other. Then I seen her hands shaking something terrible like she was seeing her first haint.

"Lord, Lord, Lord." Will smiled bigger than I'd seen him do.

That's when I knew something was going on, something bigger than a summer love.

Arleen Brown

"THIS IS SO GOOD," the missus moaned as she stuck a piece of lobster meat into her mouth. Butter dripped from her fingers.

I had to find my guts to taste the stuff, but when I did, the bite melted in my mouth. Shoot, sweet potatoes was the best thing we had to eat in my family. I smiled thinking on it.

"There's my girl. She's been hidden for the longest time behind frowns. This meat is so rich. I'd forgotten how good it was."

"Like folks with lots of money." I smiled. She was softer since she ran off from Pastor, and I knew she was going to figure out—if she hadn't already—that I wasn't Faith. A mama always knew her own child better than anyone else.

"Yes." Her laugh sounded like tinkling glass, and I felt Faith stir around inside her hiding place. "Open the window wide, Faith. Let the salty air in. The marsh comes alive in the evening. It's too long since I've been here. This is my peace and I have forgotten about its existence."

That Ada woman had closed most of the windows probably 'cause she was so scared of spirits, something I sure didn't worry on. I pushed the large kitchen windows open wide, and a breeze came through like it had been waiting. The house's ugly brown made me think of our old farmhouse on the mountain. Daddy had given it a fresh coat of paint right before I died. His boss at the quarry told him to take the gallons 'cause they ordered the wrong color.

"I love that smell. Thank you. I can't imagine not staying here tonight. What is there to be afraid of, Faith?"

"I don't know. I don't have one reason to fear some ghost."

"Here, eat." The missus dished yellow rice on my plate.

It was spicy, and I closed my eyes as it sat on my tongue.

"And look, fried corn, just like Amanda's. It's like having her right here." She spooned corn on her plate and pushed the bowl to me. I knew all about fried corn and dipped out three spoonfuls. A warm loaf of homemade bread sat on a heavy brown plate. I cut a piece off and spread butter, warm honey butter, on it.

"Aren't you glad we left your father, Faith? We needed to just get away from him and the mountain."

"I can do without him, but I love the mountain." I looked at the missus across the table. She was wearing a bright-red wraparound skirt and a white blouse tied in a knot at her waist. Her hair was pulled back in a ponytail. She looked like a child. Like me when I died. This made me about as sad as the day I woke up holding on to that baby boy, both of us dead. Funny how I could love him so much, seeing how I came about having him.

"Eat. You're too thin," the missus said.

"It's right good."

She gave me a sharp look. "Something is so different about you, Faith. Nothing bad, just different."

"Thank you." A pain, maybe love, jabbed in my ribs. I had no time to be sloppy.

"We have some decisions to make. You and me. Because it has always been you and me. Hasn't it? We're the product of everyone's deeds. Aren't we?" Her smile was sad.

"I guess."

She nodded. "Did you bring the quilt you're working on?"

"Yes."

"Go get it."

"It's not nothing."

She looked at me with an odd catch in her expression, almost like pity. "Nothing? It's you, Faith. Of course it's something. Go get it."

"After I finish eating." I took a big bite of the butter-coated meat and tried to smile.

She nodded. "Do you still have the old sewing basket you took from Amanda?"

Now I didn't even know what she was talking about. "Only that one basket with all the old thread."

Missus touched my arm. If she kept it up, Faith would come back before I made everyone safe. "You deserved that basket. You didn't do wrong for taking it. Don't ever let anyone tell you different."

I looked away 'cause, Lord, I didn't want her to know I didn't understand. Part of me wanted to tell her who I was, what happened to me, and who did it. But I wasn't sure how much that woman could take. I wanted to tell her about the death quilt, the buttons and the hair. But all that talking would give away what would happen. See, my death quilt had one key ingredient sewn into the making: magic. My quilt had the best of some people and the worst of others, little pieces that made up their souls. When woven together, they brought the most powerful protection.

Missus talked about being a young woman and coming to stay in the big, ugly brown house. She talked about seeing blue herons in the marsh, of snakes ten feet long. I ate and listened to her words. The marsh played music that slipped in the windows. Somewhere a night bird called as if to say good-bye to the sun. No haunted woods here. Only the marsh and the big, mighty river.

After I finished cleaning off my plate, Missus began to run water in the sink. I couldn't help but wonder if she'd ever washed a dish. "Go get your quilt. You can sew while I wash."

"I want to help."

She looked at me with a sweet smile. "I want to wash them and look out the window. Go get the quilt."

Upstairs in the room I picked to sleep in, I unfolded the quilt from the cloth sack that I brought it in. All different colors. Some bright, some soft, some dull. Outside in the backyard two alligators moved into the marsh from the tall grass. I pushed open the window and sat there watching the water way in the distance. And beyond was Sapelo Island. Shelly was there, probably having the time of her life. But Ada was strange, maybe a witch, a lot like Shelly's mama in many ways.

"Maybe," I heard over my shoulder. I spun around and saw the pretty colored woman I'd seen earlier.

"You're a haint."

She threw her head back and laughed at me. That's when I seen her scar across her throat. "You're from Black Mountain." The woman watched me.

"Yes, ma'am. I'm a long way from home." I picked up the sewing basket Missus had been talking about earlier.

"Yes you are. You have a memory box." She looked at the basket.

"It's not a box and there sure ain't no memories of mine here."

"It's memories. I can almost see them. Old memories." She looked back at me. "And you're not a bit afraid of me. How can you see me and your mama can't?"

"I'm different."

The woman wore a fancy city suit, nothing a colored woman would wear in the mountains. "There's something not right about you, girl. Are you crazy? I've been around crazy." Faith's fear bubbled up in my chest. For a minute the whole room spun around. She was listening to every word. She wanted to come back.

"Why you bothering me?" I asked.

The woman took a step in the door. "I have a story on Black Mountain. Did you know that? I know more about that place than you think."

"How?"

"My granny lived there. Shoot, I lived there as a child. That Negro girl with you."

"Shelly?"

"Yes, I played with her daddy when we were children. Part of my story is right there on that mountain. What's your name?"

"Faith Dobbins."

She got the most hateful look on her face. "Liar. Don't mess with me. I don't have time for lies." She turned to leave.

"Arleen. Arleen Brown. I'm using Faith to finish my story."

"Yes, the truth will set you free. So you're a spirit?"

I nodded. "Come here." I stood in front of the looking glass.

The woman looked and saw the real me in the reflection. "You got a story as big as me. I'm Mary Beth Clark. My grandmother was known as Ma Clark. Did you ever hear of her?"

"No." But I answered to an empty room. The woman was gone. Time was running out. Faith wanted free, and if she came back now, things would be a mess. The story would never be told.

"EXCUSE ME, MA'AM!" I yelled from the top floor of the big house.

"I'm in the kitchen, Faith. I've made pancakes and soaked them in butter. Come on down." Missus walked into sight. She was wearing men's pants and a sleeveless blouse. "Bring down your quilt. You fell asleep on me last night. I want a good look at it."

"Yes, ma'am." I went back for the charm quilt. She might as well see it up close. I buried my nose in it and took in the lavender smell from Missus's own perfume.

"A quilt?" Mary Beth Clark was blocking the door.

"More than a quilt."

She nodded. "What kind of spell?"

"A death spell."

Mary Beth Clark watched me. "I'm here for a death too. I wonder if it will be the same death."

"Maybe."

"But I have come to talk to Shelly. She has to hear my story. I might just have to use your trick to tell her."

"What do you mean?" I said.

She laughed. "Your trick of sharing a body. I like the idea of that. Then she'll have to listen to me."

"You don't need to do that. Shelly can hear and see us spirits just fine."

"Faith? Are you talking to someone up there?" Missus yelled.

Mary Beth Clark was gone.

"No, ma'am. Just talking to myself."

"I do that all the time." Missus laughed.

PART SEVEN

Death Quilt

June 1939

"Two things make a death quilt work: blood from the one that got hurt and blood from the one who did the hurting."

—*Arleen Brown*

Shelly Parker

WHAT WAS I SUPPOSED TO THINK about a brother who was living down here on some island and never ever sent me a letter? I know those weren't the thoughts I should have been pondering. He was older, grown, and I wondered if maybe I just imagined he was Will.

He caught me staring at him. "What do you think about the boat ride?"

Now, any other time I'd be dying to talk about the ocean, but my mind was slap full. I shrugged. Why in the world wouldn't he have at least sent a letter? Why?

"I guess this must feel strange." He guided the boat toward the island.

"Maybe." I said that word with a attitude full of sass.

He was quiet.

The water turned smoother as the boat neared shore.

"I guess you have lots of questions." He scooted right up to the side of the dock like he could do it with his eyes closed, like he'd been doing such things all his life.

The Will I remembered couldn't drive a boat.

"It's not as simple as writing a letter." Will looked straight ahead.

"Really?"

"You got to show Shelly the island this weekend." Ada moved close to us.

Will looked away from me.

"That's okay. He doesn't have to show me anything." I guess part of me wanted to hurt Will 'cause I sure was aching.

He didn't say a word.

MY STOMACH RUMBLED at the smell of onions and green peppers cooking. "Here, you chop," Ada said, handing me a clove of garlic and a sharp knife.

I chopped just like I did in Pastor's kitchen on Black Mountain.

"This smells good." I didn't look at her.

"You listen to me, girl. You don't go judging him. You and him has a lot to talk about." She looked at my hands. "You finished with that?"

"Yes, ma'am." I passed her the garlic.

Three scoops of yellow rice went in a pot of simmering chicken broth. "I see that look, young lady. I know what be running through your head. He ran off and never got back to you. Find out the story first. What kind of boy was he when he was home?"

"Quiet and sweet most of the time."

"So you think he just up and changed into some mean old person? You think he didn't want to see you?"

I shrugged, even though she knew exactly what I was thinking.

"You got a lot to learn about growing up." She wagged a finger at me. The kitchen was so hot, sweat poured down my back.

"He should have let Nada know where he was. Them two had a

way of talking that only they understood. And he just up and left one afternoon."

Ada looked at me. "Must have been mighty lonely."

"What do you mean?"

"Well, your mama and brother talking between each other like you not even there." She stirred the garlic, onions, and peppers, adding a little extra butter.

"Ah, it wasn't like that."

"Maybe not." She shrugged. "But they had something to talk about that you wasn't a part of. That's what I heard you say. What was it?"

"I don't know. I was younger by a lot."

"Shelly, your room is ready." Will stood in the door.

My cheeks warmed at the thought of him hearing us talk. "Thank you."

"We'll be through here in a bit. You go take your walk on the beach."

"Can I steal Shelly?" He gave Ada a big smile and she glowed.

"Go on, Shelly. Take you a walk with Will."

No one asked me if I wanted to go. Maybe I didn't want no part of him.

"Only if you want," he said, sensing the pause I took. I'm sure he was surprised that I didn't just cow down and show him how happy I was to see him alive. That old Shelly would have followed him to the end of the earth. That's what I always did, follow him, sucking them two fingers, thinking he was just as good as Pastor's Jesus that walked on water.

I washed my hands under the faucet. "I guess."

"Good." He turned.

"You be nice to him," Ada whispered. "Just think on this. Why hadn't your mama gone looking for her boy? Hm?"

I left that kitchen as fast as I could.

Will waited for me in a truck. "Come on. There's nothing like a little talk while walking on the beach. You'll see." The drive was short.

The wind blew so long and hard I could barely hear Will.

"This is Nanny Goat Beach. I like to walk this way. Mr. Reynolds and his friends use that part."

The white sand was warm but not too hot to bare feet. The sun was over to our left and hit the water here and there with sparkling light. Everywhere was shells. I picked up one that was perfect and smooth with a pink inside.

"That's a pretty shell." Will touched the smooth circles that began in the center and worked out.

"It's for Nada." I couldn't look at him, so I watched the water rushing into the beach, creating a louder sound than the wind.

"You turned out to be a beautiful young woman!" Will yelled with a smile on his face.

I almost kept quiet. It seemed too much to speak with the wind pushing at me. "Why you say that?"

He looked at me funny. "You really don't know how pretty you are."

I laughed long and loud. All those years of trying to be noticed, to get Nada to see me as something besides a little girl, folded out in front of me. Pretty was long blond hair and white skin. Pretty was lacy dresses and blue ribbons hanging down my back. "Nothing pretty about me."

He shook his head. "You can't see who you are."

Now he was working on my last nerve. "Well, you sure don't know. Do you? You ran off. I clean and cook just like Nada. That's my life. I take care of selfish old Faith and Mrs. Dobbins, dodging Pastor when I can." The words were so angry they were louder than the hum of the ocean.

He touched my hand, not a bit mad. "I have the gift of reading. Two children with gifts that are more like plagues. Nada turned us out special. I read you today on the boat. Do you want to know what I saw?"

And there it was. My future offered to me. What fifteen-year-old girl wouldn't want to know? But a feeling was building inside of me, a feeling that men only cared about themselves. "I can't know nothing. It'll be too hard to go on living my life on that mountain with Nada. I won't run off and leave her, Will. She needs me."

"That's not much of a life, Shelly. And it doesn't turn out like that." He walked on ahead.

"SHELLY, GET UP!" ADA YELLED from the front room. "Will wants you to go with him somewhere."

Will didn't even look at me good. "Come on," he said.

So why did I follow him?

He parked the truck in the same place as we did the evening before. "Come on. Hurry." He jumped out, and I ran behind him.

He nodded to what looked like really long pieces of half-dried grass, swaying in the dern wind that blew all the time. "These are sea oats. They grow in the sand dunes."

And really, why would I care? But I did. Miss Tuggle would love some of them in her garden. The water rushed in and out, rocking me. This was the kind of place I could live if I let myself. Will sat down on the sand and pointed to the place beside him. I gave us some extra room. He watched the gray-brownish water move in and then pull out. Then he looked out further like he might be searching for the flat end of the earth.

"Now watch." He leaned over to me without moving his stare.

Where the sky touched the ocean turned a thin strip of orange. The orange grew wider and turned brighter.

"There." He pointed like some little boy.

The waves far out into the sea grew bigger. The orange turned into the sun and stretched its yellow fingers across the water, sparkling. Then what I thought was a wave twirled into the air and then another. The ocean was coming alive, dancing in the twinkling bright light. I could only stare. The waves were alive, sparkling when the sun hit them. Creatures, large fish. Their bodies were shiny and wet.

Two jumped into the air at the same time and twisted before disappearing into the water again.

Will smiled. "Dolphins. They put on a show each morning." The sun was full and bright. The dolphins seemed to dance on the water. "They're called angels of the sea in many books."

Books. I looked at him. Yes, angels.

He unfolded a cloth with two biscuits coated in sweet, dark syrup.

I took one and allowed the bite to soak in my mouth until it was nearly gone.

When we finished eating, the dolphins had left. They faded away one at a time like I had been dreaming.

"I have something else to show you."

I never opened my mouth on the truck ride down a bumpy road that seemed to cut straight across the island through the woods. Every kind of strange bird I could think of and some I sure didn't know showed themselves. Then the trees disappeared and the marsh grass waved back and forth near a dark, wide, still creek.

Will parked the truck close to an old wooden dock where there was a net. "Take a look at this."

The water was moving in a quiet, strong way.

"Tide's coming in." Will picked up the net. "This is a seining net. Do you know what that is?"

"No."

"This is how fishing started here with the Geechees."

"The what?" I looked away before he met my stare.

"Geechees. That's what the Negro people on Sapelo Island call themselves. See, these families, my father's family, go all the way back to slave days and further here on this island. They didn't have a way to own a boat back then. So they fished the way the elders did in their homeland." He looked at me quiet-like. "They all ended up here because they were stolen from their land and made into slaves. And that isn't right."

Part of me was just too stubborn to agree.

"Everyone was poor and still is, but they knew how to take a catch from the ocean even if they didn't have a boat." He picked up the net with little weights tied to the edges and a long rope that he tied around his arm. "I'll show you how they fished. Then we are going to take our catch and eat lunch." He took a piece of the net and placed a weight in his mouth. The thing opened like a flower when it was in full bloom and landed on top of the water, sinking. Will held the rope. He waited and then tugged. He waved me over to help him pull in the net even though I had a feeling he could have done the work all by himself. The net dropped on the dock. Inside were shrimp and a couple of good-size crabs with shells that looked blue in places.

"See, the water gave us our lunch just like it did the Geechees a long time ago."

That simple. I took a breath and sat down on the dock without thinking. The water seemed to hum with a slow movement.

"My daddy, William Tine, was a netmaker until he left the island and met Mama in New Orleans. Ada still uses his nets, mending them when a hole opens. I guess it's her way of honoring her love for him. Brothers and sisters are like that even when they don't agree."

Someone loving a person that much was hard for me to hold on to. And I wasn't going to talk to him about brothers and sisters, 'cause he didn't know a dern thing.

"Let's go to eat our catch. Ada will cook it up." He turned and looked at me. "So Faith is in Darien?"

I stiffened. "Yep."

He nodded.

"Nada's doing real good, Will, in case you were wondering." My words came out mean.

"Things aren't simple."

"You're not the only soul who had hard times, Will."

"My leaving wasn't about hard feelings."

"What about Nada?"

A big bluish-gray bird flew to stand on the bank.

"That's a blue heron. It's catching food for the day."

So we wasn't going to talk about Nada.

"YOU GOT TO DROP US at Miss Laura Wool's house," Ada told Will. Then she looked over at me. "She be one of the best root doctors on the coast."

Will nodded. "I'm going to *Sweet Jesse.*"

Ada smiled. "I wondered how long it would take." She smiled at me. "He spent the whole day with you yesterday, missy. Most days when he's home from school, he's on that boat. It be like them two are married."

Will only smiled.

He dropped us in front of a tiny green house that sat on the edge of the community Ada called Hog Hammock. "You want me to come back for you?"

Ada laughed. "We can walk. Do us good."

As I stood waiting on Ada to slide across the truck seat and get out, Will smiled at me. "I have a good life here, Shelly."

And I knew he did. It was probably what made me the maddest at him.

After he pulled away, Ada looked at me. "What's wrong with you, girl? I wouldn't blame him if he didn't talk to you again."

I looked away. "He left me, Ada. He left Nada."

She snorted. "So no forgiveness coming out you, girl. Good thing most folks don't think like you. I don't think your mama would want you acting like this."

And she was probably right about that.

Ada pushed an old wooden door open, tapping on it. "Miss Laura, how you doing this fine day?"

The room was dark and tiny but clean as a pin. A big chair sat under the only window. The old woman sitting there looked at me. "Who she be?"

"No worries. Miss Laura, this is Will's sister, Shelly."

Miss Laura gave me a hard look. I wanted to tell her I didn't want to be there any more than she wanted me.

"We came to see your quilts. I want Shelly here to see your charm quilt."

Miss Laura took her mean look off me. "It be right over there, Ada, in the trunk. But you know how powerful that thing is. Be careful."

Now my full attention was on the trunk and Ada.

"Yes, ma'am. But I want Shelly to see it 'cause she won't believe me if she don't." She shot a tolerant smile at Miss Laura. "She's been raised in the mountains of North Carolina and don't know a thing about the old ways."

"Lord, do I know what you be talking about, Ada. The only reason we still honor the ways is 'cause of being right here on this island. But now that Will, he be good. He understands."

"Yes, ma'am, but he's one of a kind." Ada looked at me.

The quilt was wrapped in old, soft tissue paper. Ada brought it to the table in the middle of the room.

"Careful, Ada," Miss Laura said. "I don't touch the thing much."

Ada folded the tissue paper back, and there was a faded blue, red, and green nine-patch pattern. There was a picture and handwriting on a piece of muslin right in the middle. The thing looked as old as Miss Laura Wool.

She handed me a corner. "Feel it."

When I touched the quilt, my fingers tingled like one of Nada's spells. I seen a young black man dressed in an old suit of clothes. He faded in and out.

Miss Laura Wool struggled to stand.

"You don't have to stand, ma'am," Ada said. She moved to help her, but Miss Laura Wool waved her away.

"You'll find what you're looking for on the mainland, girl. Then you'll go home, but ain't nothing ever going to be the same."

I looked away from her watery hazel eyes.

"Your brother will live out his life here."

The quilt burned beneath my fingers.

"This quilt was made into a charm to punish my man. He died in his wedding suit."

Ada tapped the quilt. "This is the same kind of quilt Faith be making. The one you told me about." She continued to stare at the quilt. "I seen it up there in that room folded all nice and neat in her cloth sack. You're right, Shelly. She's got a charm quilt."

I looked at the middle of the quilt, where there was a picture of a gravestone. *He died too young.* I jerked my hand away.

Miss Laura Wool laughed, a crackling sound. "You be right about that, girl. Don't be touching it much. It's the touch that brings it alive. Depending what this girl has sewed into her death quilt, it could kill you."

"How does it work?" I asked.

Miss Laura Wool looked at me for a minute like she was trying to decide if I was worth telling. "A soul is locked into the sewing. Who be sewed into this girl's quilt?"

Who would Faith hate enough to sew into a spell quilt? But Faith wasn't herself. She was Arleen. So who in the world did Arleen hate enough to help sew them into a death quilt?

"If a soul be picked, they're doomed to die. Ain't much you can do to save them." Miss Laura Wool smiled real big at me. "Lots of desires, pain, hate, and love goes into the making. You got to know the story to understand the use intended in the charm."

And in Miss Laura Wool's words I saw Armetta. I had managed not to think of her too much since I left. I hadn't even touched that stupid book of hers, but I knew I had to read it and sooner than later I had to know the whole story.

Arleen Brown

AROUND MIDNIGHT ON SUNDAY, I woke up to Missus standing by my little bed. "You were crying in your sleep, calling me."

Faith was stirring around inside of me, but I shoved her down. "I had a bad dream," I said.

Missus pulled back the cover. "Scoot. This is what my mama used to do when I had nightmares." She crawled in beside me. I tried not to touch her but that was hard. Then Faith stilled and sleep slid through me. I relaxed next to Missus's warm body. Nobody ever did this for me before. Maybe if they had, I wouldn't have been hurt by Pastor in the first place.

Now, the rules for a spirit taking over a human body was simple. The human had to take help, and if the human wanted to come back, the spirit had to step aside. But I wasn't having none of that. Faith wasn't ready. One thing had to be taken care of before I left. And I wasn't giving one bit until that thing was finished.

ONE LOOK AT SHELLY on Monday morning, and I knew something big had happened. It was spelled right across her face. She was softer, kinder. She stood at the stove cooking alongside Ada Lee Tine like they was something to each other. Just two days on that island, and she was gone from Black Mountain, gone from Missus and Faith. Maybe it was as simple as that, leaving. "These pancakes are so good, Shelly."

She half smiled at me. "Ada's recipe."

"We got to get us this recipe, then." I smiled real sweet at Ada, who looked at me like I was some big old bear coming after her.

Missus wore a full red skirt with a blue sleeveless blouse. She took a bite of her pancakes. "Yum. Maybe we'll never leave this place, Faith. Maybe we can always have Ada's pancakes."

"I'll not be working more than a month, ma'am. But I have a feeling a woman like you could make out just fine on her own." Ada smiled at Missus.

Missus looked at me. "I think we should explore today. Why don't you go change into some comfortable walking shoes."

I was wearing Faith's fancy heels that was blue to match the dress I had on.

"Yes, ma'am." I left the kitchen and ran smack into Mary Beth Clark.

"You understand that nothing soft and sweet can come from this moment forward." She rushed up the stairs in a way that proved she wasn't of the earth but a ghost. A picture fell from the wall, shattering.

"What was that?" Missus came into the hall followed by Ada.

"The picture up there just jumped off that wall." I pointed.

Ada looked at me like I was a liar. That woman didn't like me one bit. "I'll get something to clean it up, Miss Lydia."

Shelly looked at me like I was growing horns from my head. You would have thought she'd never seen a spirit.

"I'll go get my other shoes." I ran up the stairs.

Mary Beth Clark waited in my little room at the very top of the house. "They are happy here. No one should be happy in this house."

"Why?"

She stared at me and came closer. "Do you know how pretty you are?" She nodded at the looking glass. "Not that girl's body, but *you*?"

"I'm way prettier in death than I was alive."

"There's a reason for that. Death isn't all bad, you know." She came so close I should have felt heat from her body. "I studied Greek mythology when I was alive. I tried to outrun my little family. I didn't know a thing. Do you know what a myth is?"

"No."

"It's a story with a hero. In the country called Greece, they told myths about their gods, and they had a lot of gods." She pointed to the real me in the looking glass. "My favorite is the one about a mother and daughter. Persephone and her mother, Demeter."

I stepped away. "The last thing I want is a story about mamas."

"You need to listen to this one. It's important."

I looked at this beautiful colored woman. "I got to hurry. Missus is waiting on me."

"Persephone was out picking flowers one day when she came upon the most beautiful of flowers, a flower placed there on purpose to lure her. See, someone wanted her very much, enough to trick her. When she picked the flower, the earth opened up and Hades—Persephone's own uncle and god of the underworld—grabbed her, taking her back to his home to be his queen. Now, Demeter never noticed Hades's obsession with her daughter. She closed her eyes to it. She became so depressed when she discovered her beloved daughter was lost that she did nothing but search. Her job was to keep the crops plentiful, among other things. She stopped taking care of the earth. She was so upset, she caused a terrible drought to fall on the earth, so bad that Zeus,

Persephone's father, told Hades to let his Persephone go before Demeter destroyed everything. Hades didn't want to let her go. See, there's good and bad in everyone. Hades was no different. While he was the god of the underworld, he had good parts to him, only the bad outweighed them. So, instead of just letting Persephone go free and clear, he tricked her into eating pomegranate seeds. This way, several months out of every year she had to come back to the underworld and be his queen. Demeter was angry her daughter had been deceived and decided those months Persephone had to go to the underworld would be bleak and dead. Everything died out, slept, and turned dull. But if Demeter had been on guard, her daughter would never have been taken and fooled." She looked at me. "What do you think the story means?"

I walked to the window overlooking the marsh. "It's a story about how we got winter." I shrugged. "The old folks on the mountain talk about planting by the signs. You just told a story about the barren sign."

"What's the barren sign?"

"Never try to plant seeds, harvest, or do anything besides weed and clear when in the barren sign, 'cause it will all come to naught. It's like coming on a barren soul, wandering around the earth in hopes of living in someone else's body. No good can come from it, naught. If you're not careful and don't let go when it's time, you'll become a barren soul." The island where Shelly stayed was just visible. "I have to use my death quilt on a soul. Then I'm finished."

"Who is the soul?" Mary Beth Clark asked.

"He is my Hades."

She nodded. "Then you have to leave. Understand?"

Maybe.

Armetta Lolly

HE MOVED AROUND THE MOUNTAIN in the black of night. I seen him, a dark shadow against the smoky moonlight in the backyard. The souls in the woods, the ones stuck like me, began to moan. Shelly's mama didn't even know he was there, scooting across her porch while she and that white granny woman talked. The angel be gone, and that woman took her. Why oh why would someone want my angel? Things were going to go bad before they ever got good. That woman loved my angel, needed her, but she took something that wasn't hers to take.

The white granny woman was busy showing Shelly's mama something she had spread out on the table. Me and Shelly's mama was one and the same in many ways. She was thinking on how she could catch him once and for all. So was the white granny woman. The light from the overhead lamp hit what they was staring at on the table and it sparkled. And there it was, bigger than that whole mountain and tiny enough to fit in a pea pod, the cross. No wonder Pastor done lost his mind, staring in the window, almost pressing his face against the glass like some desperate boy. The cross.

"Stupid, stupid women," he hissed.

Them two women was walking on a sheet of thin ice, and their feet wasn't even feeling a bit cold.

"I seen this thing many a time." Shelly's mama touched the cross. "That be his." A chilly wind blew in out of the west, wet with a summer rain. Lordy, I knew all about that cross, way too much.

"Them two won't do this to me," Pastor whispered, and took a step back.

And that was the end of that. Those two fine ladies was going to pay, and if Shelly was here, she would too. That girl still hadn't opened that book. 'Cause I would have felt the knowing scattering in the air. I thought I could count on her. She be the one who can tell.

"God, I am a soldier in your army," Pastor whispered. He moved across the yard into the solid darkness of the storm headed toward us.

I pushed every bit of power I had at him.

He stopped still. Then turned. "I know you, girl." His voice was silky-sweet. "I see you. I know why you're here. It was told to me as a bedtime story, so I would learn never to cross the line and stand against God. I know the damnation you brought to our family." He pointed at me. "My soul is like Paul Dobbins's. That's why you are with me. You're looking for him." He laughed hard and crazy. Could have been because he'd already started his crossover. Sometimes that happened to the worst ones.

"You and me aren't so different, girl. We're both looking to end something."

Maude Tuggle

"AMANDA?" THE CABIN WAS EMPTY, and she wasn't in her garden. Charles Dobbins's house was quiet. I opened the door to my truck, and Amanda stepped onto the back porch of the big house. She waved and walked toward me.

Her smile was kind, like an old friend. "Hello, Miss Tuggle." Something had passed between us that eased our differences.

"I'm going back to Ella Creek Cemetery. Do you want to go with me? I want to show you something."

A shadow crossed over Amanda's face. "It's getting late. We'll have to hurry. I don't want to be in the woods after dark. Haven't seen a thing from Pastor since he found out Mrs. Dobbins and Faith was gone. He hasn't even been home for the food I've left out. It's too easy. I keep looking over my shoulder for him to show up." She gave me a stern look. "I ain't never been afraid of no one in my life. Couldn't. But, Miss Tuggle, I believe I'm afraid of Pastor."

"I think you have good reasons to be afraid, Amanda. Can I leave my truck here while we walk?"

She frowned. "Park it out back of the cabin. I keep feeling like he's out there watching me." She gave a little shiver.

We walked the path in silence. The birds sang in the trees. Amanda gave a little jerk.

"What's wrong?"

"A shadow crossing my grave, I reckon."

I smiled.

"Smell the rain?" She looked at the snatches of blue sky showing through the treetops. "I can't help but think on Shelly and what she's doing. I miss her."

I sniffed the air but failed to smell rain. "If I know Shelly, she's doing fine, reading her heart out on some book she's found or took with her. She's such a smart girl."

Amanda beamed. "She is smart, but lately she's had her heart in struggles on this mountain. Maybe it comes with her age. But we've always had something that held us at arm's length from each other. Could be it's 'cause I'm the mama and she's the daughter."

"I remember fifteen was the age I began to question my mother. I no longer believed everything she said. I had to find out on my own."

"Yes, ma'am. That's Shelly. Finding out on her own." She shrugged. "But I ain't no perfect mama, mind you. I've done my stuff. She lost her brother and I wasn't worth a diddle to her. That was the summer she found out she had sight."

I looked at her. "Is there a perfect mother? I think the world would like to paint mothers as perfect and place that expectation right on our shoulders, but we're just human whether we're mothers or daughters or both."

"I guess some is worse than others."

"Yes."

Dragonfly River was loud, and the cool breeze blowing across the water soothed me.

"Something ain't right." Amanda frowned at me.

"What do you mean?"

She held her finger to her lips. "We'll talk at the cemetery. These woods got ears. This place is tainted with a spell." Her words mingled with the sound of rushing water. Tainted. Maybe that was the right word. Tainted.

A shadow scurried across the path ahead of us. I stopped.

"What be wrong? What'd you see?" She frowned.

"Nothing. The light is playing tricks."

She laughed quietly. "Tainted."

The path wound away from the river. "What is between Pastor Dobbins and you, Amanda?"

Her face became guarded. "I think the better question is what settles between the missus and me. That be the question."

I kept quiet.

"A story way too big and full of omens to tell to you. But it's what makes me a mama with a passel of shame."

The sun hit the black iron gates of the cemetery. "Amanda, I took an angel from here and put it in my garden. A marble angel."

Amanda studied me with an odd expression. "Sometimes we just got to follow our wants. But how did you get her down this part of the mountain?"

"Wheelbarrow." I motioned her around the gates. "There are some graves I want to show you."

"I dearly hate the gravestone of the lost girl. Don't take me to her. It be too sad. Nobody ever found her." Her words echoed through the cemetery. Somewhere an animal made a moaning sound. Or maybe it was the wind in the top of the trees. "That's why her spirit roams this mountain." She looked off into the woods.

"Do you really believe that, Amanda?" I tried to be quiet, but I just couldn't help myself.

"You took her angel, Miss Tuggle. She was known to sit at its feet in the evening. Some hurt went all the way to that girl's bones." She looked at me as we stepped close to the gravestone. "They found a missing necklace that belonged to Miss Daniels hanging on that angel's wing when the colored girl disappeared."

"What kind of necklace?" I asked.

Amanda looked at me. "I don't know. But that Miss Daniels up and married a pastor from New Orleans. Your Pastor Dobbins that be buried over there."

"So you knew about his grave."

"No disrespect, Miss Tuggle, but I had to think on your intentions before I talked." She gave me a wise smile.

"Do you think he is related to Pastor Charles Dobbins?"

"Lordy be. My heart can't take these stories like it used to." She laughed.

"Amanda, do you think Pastor Dobbins could have forced himself on Arleen Brown?"

Amanda backed up a step. "You got to know something. You talk first."

I looked away.

"Is that why you brought me up here? To ask me that question?" She waited. "Pastor could just about do anything to anybody. Anything. Arleen wouldn't have been no problem for him."

I shivered. "I have something to show you." I pulled the cross out of my pocket.

Amanda frowned at me. "What you got yourself into, Miss Tuggle? Let's go to my house and have a better look. Not here in this place."

WHEN WE GOT TO THE CABIN, it was nearly dark. "Come on in here and let's talk about what you got."

I followed her. Amanda lit the gas lamp hanging over her little table and the room glowed.

I spread the cross out, and Amanda took a deep breath. "Pastor's cross. How'd you get this, Miss Tuggle?"

"Would you tell the sheriff this was Pastor Dobbins's cross?"

She narrowed her look at me. "Answer my question."

"I got the cross from Faith before she left the mountain."

Amanda stood still, arms folded over her chest. "How?"

"I don't know where she got it."

Amanda frowned at me. "Miss Faith wouldn't steal a thing, Miss Tuggle. She just wouldn't do it. She ain't been herself. He be bad, Miss Tuggle."

"I'm trying to help Faith and her mother. I'll make sure all of you are safe."

She gave me a disgusted look. "You sure can't keep me safe from him if he decides he wants to do something. I ain't no fool."

"But he has to be stopped, Amanda. I want Shelly and Faith to come home to a safe place. I think he could kill them."

She looked away. "You be right about that. But first he'd do a lot worse than kill. I reckon I have to help you, but no good will come of any of this mess, Miss Tuggle. You remember what I said."

The pitch black of night stood outside the cabin. I saw my reflection in the window. My face looked different. Maybe it was fear.

I DIDN'T SLEEP AT ALL that night. At one point when the moon was straight up in the sky, I went out to sit with my angel in the garden. Her beautiful milk-white marble face stirred something inside of me. The half-moon's light washed over her. A fresh rainstorm had come and gone, weaving cool air over the summer heat. Clarity was a sweet drug, a peace I hadn't felt since before Arleen's death.

The young colored girl stood near the big oak. I went to her, thinking that Shelly would be proud of me for accepting what I saw.

"Shelly has the book, ma'am," she said. "She has the story. It be up to you to stop him without knowing the whole reasons. Use that cross of his. Punish him with that."

"Who are you?"

The girl shook her head. "I be the one stuck to Pastor. I know his whole story." She began to fade, and the trees behind her showed through. "I be the one who owns that angel you stole." And she was gone.

She owned the angel. I was losing my mind, but I would tell Zach that Amanda confirmed the cross belonged to Pastor Dobbins. Now I was seeing ghosts. What could I say about that?

Ada Lee Tine

"THAT GIRL BE THE TIDIEST I've seen any white girl," I said as I walked into Faith's room behind Miss Lydia.

She nearly jumped a foot. "You scared me, Ada." She laughed. In her hand was that hateful quilt. "You must not let Faith know I was handling her work. See this silk?" She rubbed the center of the quilt. "That is mine. I had it put away in my room. This cloth belonged to my mother. I always thought I'd make a baby blanket from it, but I never found the time." She looked off, kind of dreamy.

Lordy me, I'd only seen the thing in passing on Friday when they arrived. The picture of the gravestone was perfect. Some old girl named Arleen Brown. Little buttons and lace were sewn here and there. From the looks of that quilt, there was a powerful spell that went into the sewing. Shelly had been right to worry over it. "It be a strange quilt, ma'am, even though it is pretty."

"Oh, I know what you mean. At first I thought it was odd she would put gravestone rubbings on a quilt. But now I'm attached to her work." Miss Lydia shook her head. "She doesn't get it from me. I sure don't sew."

I touched the old lace, and an angry feeling hit me. Somebody had been done wrong. The quilt was a story of pain. I looked closely at the picture from the stone. The hand of God was reaching down and breaking a chain. "I don't like that picture."

"It is horrible. I'm not sure why the Browns had that put on their daughter's marker. She was only fifteen when she died. Maybe they felt broken by God."

"What girl would be roaming around a graveyard taking the pictures off the stones?" This just popped out before I thought on it long.

Miss Lydia smiled, so I guessed she didn't take no offense to the question. "I don't know. There is a lot about Faith I don't know. She has always been quiet and stayed off to herself."

"We got strange gravestones on the island. She'd have a time with them."

"I bet your island is pretty, Ada."

"Yes, ma'am. I'm partial because it is my home."

"I don't even know where home is anymore. I wish I could go to your island." She began to fold the quilt.

"It's the best place in the world. You get ready one Friday morning and I'll take you. My boy can bring you back before dark." I said this without even thinking. This woman had managed to get on my good side.

"Would you? I bet Faith would love it too."

Now, just the mention of that white girl's name set my teeth on edge. "We'll do just what I said. I'm going to clean your room, ma'am. This one is too clean to mess with."

The biggest cold chill settled on me in that little room at the top of the house. Once, it had been my favorite room 'cause I could see the island on a clear day.

"I'll see you downstairs, Ada." Miss Lydia left me standing there.

"That be one strange white girl that keeps her room like this," I mumbled to myself.

"Yes, she is strange," said a voice behind me, one I recognized straightaway.

I didn't turn to look. Nope, nothing at all I wanted to see. "Don't be bothering me after all these years. I ain't got a thing to say to you."

"You blame me for your beau dying." She still talked in that proper way of hers. Death didn't take that away from her.

"I don't blame no one for nothing." Still I looked out the window.

Her laugh was soft. "You're afraid of me, Lou." She said that name with a hard edge.

"Not much I'm afraid of these days." Boy, that was some kind of lie. I flipped the lock on the window and forced it open. The salt air filled the room, clearing my head.

"Why didn't you like me? I never did a thing to you. You could have saved me. I died too early."

This made me turn around. I couldn't help myself. "You're still some kind of fool, girl."

"Me? You still work here."

"Why are you here?"

She smiled. The mark on her neck made my stomach turn. "Me and you have a story together, Lou, but my being here doesn't have one thing to do with that. I have a story to tell, but not to you. You didn't care when it counted. I'm here to tell someone else that will listen."

"You brought all that mess on yourself, Mary Beth Clark," I shot at her.

"You're right about that. But tell me, was it because I was with a white man? Or because I was dressed nice and talked decent that you were mean to me?" She crossed her arms over her chest. "What makes you any different than a white person passing judgment?"

"You ain't the only one who lost something that night. I lost my life when Roger died. They killed him 'cause of you."

She tilted her head to one side. "Yes, ma'am, but he came here at the wrong time. Me and him were having a conversation. That's all."

"Stop." I held up my hand. "I don't ever want to know."

"You're part of what happened that night, Ada Lee Tine. You are part of that night no matter whether you want to be or not." She waited a minute. "The old woman ghost used you to get here, to get into the house. That's the way she moves from one story to another. She uses a live person who can see her and hear her. And there you were. Benton T. Horse killed me. He killed me, and the old woman ghost didn't save me." And she was gone.

"None of it had a thing to do with me." I said this too loud.

"You don't know." The words sat in the room. I stepped out on the landing and seen Shelly standing at the foot of the stairs. Faith came into the front hall and cut a look up at me. For a minute I saw two girls in one. That's when I understood I was looking at that girl from the stone, Arleen Brown.

PART EIGHT

Memory Box

1869–1870

"Memory box: a box made of anything that holds a girl's trinkets, dreams, and secrets."

—*Armetta Lolly*

Shelly Parker

THAT SUNDAY AFTERNOON when I seen Miss Laura Wool's death quilt, I knew I had to read Armetta's book, knew I'd been wrong not to read it before then. Arleen, Faith—whoever she was—had a streak of bad running through her. I told Ada I was going to walk on the beach. I took Armetta's book with me, safe in the pocket of my skirt. I settled on the part of the beach that met the hills of sand. I let the wind blow across my skin and the water sing to me. Maybe it wasn't too late to find a answer.

April 3, 1869

I live in a small shack tucked in one of the corners right close to the bend in the river, not far from the Danielses' plot. The shed was meant for tools, but I cleaned me out a space and ran a pipe out the wall for the old wood stove Smug Platt hauled over there for me. All I need is a warm room with no one bothering me. I've given up on living in the world and decided to stay tucked away in the cemetery for the rest of my life.

On the left side of Ella Creek Cemetery is nothing but woods and the road leading down to the white farmers. On the right is Dragonfly River named by the Danielses. Mr. Daniels's place is out behind the graves, about a half a mile in the woods. Folks on down the road believe the woods that separate them from Ella Creek Cemetery be full of haints. I reckon they know just what they're talking about 'cause I see my share of spirits roaming the family plots, but me and them share the place with no problem. Those spirits don't even surprise me no more. It's the river that drives me slap crazy, the way it churns so loud, filling my head with long, mournful sobs. But mostly all those graves bring me some peace in this old world.

I take care of the graves: planting, raking, and all the things that make the dead seem looked after. It keeps me busy. I know lots of whispering is going on about me living in a cemetery. But here's the thing: folks be real bad about throwing stones without looking at their own ways. See, I have me a good reason to be living right here. My daddy wandered off down the mountain and fell off his old mule into the river. He drowned. I was standing in the front yard of our old house when the mule came wandering back. I knew something terrible was wrong 'cause Daddy was attached to that old mule like a boy to his dog. Mama had only died a couple of months before, so I was alone when I went searching for Daddy. My mama, Liza Lolly, was something special. And if the truth be known, I loved her better than Daddy. I put him in a grave right beside Mama in the cemetery. Mr. Daniels don't have a gripe with coloreds burying their dead there as long as they choose a plot in the corner away from the white family plots. Imagine a graveyard being separated into skin colors. Lordy, what does he think? That we will rub off on him in death?

So I took me some slate and buried part of it in the ground so it stood nice and straight at the head of his grave. But for some reason, I couldn't bring myself to leave the slate blank like he had Mama's. I spelled out his name with a piece of white chalk that I kept in my memory box. The first decent rain would wash him away.

My memory box is the one thing I keep from my old life. Inside is that chalk, a button from the shirt Daddy wore when he drowned, Mama's real gold wedding band, a ribbon from her hair, and a note some old boy gave me when I was thirteen. He died a year later when he fell off a crazy horse while working on a farm down the mountain. And that was that for me. And if the person reading this right now wants to know how a old colored girl learned to write, the answer is Amelia Daniels, but that's more of a story for another day. The good thing about living and working in the cemetery is I can do pretty much what I want. I like it that way. But them haints do get under my skin sometimes.

April 10, 1869

All I am good for is planting. I can plant anything and it will grow like some dern weed. Now, a few years back I had me a idea to go down the mountain and see the Swannanoa River. That is a decent-sized stretch of water. I can tell 'cause when I stand in the west corner of the cemetery, right on the edge of the woods, I can see it snaking on the valley's floor. I bet it is quiet and lazy, not all riled up like Dragonfly River. But I never went. Couldn't leave. That dern old mountain has me around the feet and planted me right here. So sleeping in my old shed comes to me just as natural as wildflowers coming back to the meadow each and every spring. I like that word meadow. It sounds all nice and kind. Not much of that here on the mountain, kindness, not for coloreds, anyway. Each day I get up and work until dark, but always I wander over to Mama's grave and have me a conversation with her. Sometimes I can hear her sweet, clean voice. She was the best cook ever. That's what Mrs. Daniels said when Mama died. "That orange cake she made was divine, Armetta." A cake. A stupid old cake. My mama was something more than her cooking. She was the air in my lungs and the push in my step. That's why it didn't take me no time to bring that cemetery into a show place. Folks, both white and black, walk by and whistle at the work I've done.

So it was all my hard work that brought me to Miss Amelia Daniels. See, she be crazy. That's what everybody said, especially the coloreds that worked there. I knew her when her and me was little things. She started teaching me to read then. Later she learned me to write halfway. Mama said she was touched, but Mama was always kinder than most. Amelia stayed upstairs in the house all the time, but I'd seen her sneak out late in the evening and dance without any shoes in the meadow while the sun went down. Mr. Daniels, her daddy, up and died from a heart attack, and that changed the whole place. Most of the coloreds started worrying that living on the Daniels place was going to end, but then that lawyer man read Mr. Daniels's will—I even had to go stand in the yard and listen. He left each colored family their old house and a plot of land. Folks said he was still trying to make up for slave days.

When Mr. Daniels died, things changed. Miss Amelia began to come out of the house anytime she wanted. The day I started knowing her, really knowing her as a grown-up, she wore a pink dress covered in tiny rosebuds. On her feet was a pair of soft pink slippers like flowers in bloom. She moved around like a fairy in one of Mama's stories. Her dark-red curls fell down her back. I wanted so bad to touch that hair. Mama always said red hair be the sign of luck and favor. I've never been anything to look at, not like Mama. This gives me three wrongs: a girl, colored, and ugly. And everybody knows three be a bad number. Most folks say I looked like some old boy.

Miss Amelia carries herself like a butterfly that caught a good wind. What I would do for that kind of grace in my soul. Now, a soul be a funny thing, all tangled up in this worldly life, speaking in the most quiet words that can't be heard by the human ear. Once in a while a soul takes up housekeeping in a person's mind and steals all her practical sense. Miss Amelia has that kind of soul. You can tell by looking deep into her eyes.

My soul be old, old, old. Nothing fanciful. So it was a true wonder that I walked right up to Miss Amelia that day. Most of the time I kept off in the woods when others came visiting the graves.

"There you are." It was that simple, like she'd been knowing all along I'd come to her.

I stood there like all my sense had drained out of my feet.

"What are your plans for Daddy's grave? I think . . ." Her voice broke in half. I wished her silent. Her pain soaked into my bones and ached just like Jesus hurt when he saw Martha crying over her brother, Lazarus. "I think he needs something real pretty," she finished.

Life could rip a girl up and leave her to defend herself. "Some wildflowers." I dug the toe of my old work boot into the loose dirt.

"Please." One long curl pushed down over her eye.

"I'll work on it today."

She looked at the pure blue sky. "Daddy called that a glass sky, Miss Armetta."

My name sounded like musical notes coming out of her

mouth. Imagine a glass sky. Not a thought I would ever find on my own.

"I always remembered you. I taught you to read. Daddy would have killed me if he knew. He never believed in smart coloreds."

I nodded.

After she left, I sowed a whole slew of seeds into Mr. Daniels's mound, working my fingers into the cool dirt. I'd been catching plenty of seeds for a while. Only fitting to give them back to Mr. Daniels. The knees of my overalls had big dirty patches. The evening sun stretched out and touched my shoulders as I worked. My job was to make them seeds stay put until they took hold. That was the most important job.

April 14, 1869

And we set into a pattern for the next few days. Me working and her talking.

"I had me a beau once. He was pretty as he was tall." Miss Amelia watched as I tended the seeds with water I hauled from the river.

"If we don't get some rain, these flowers will never grow." I kept my look on the ground.

"He had eyes as blue as robin eggs. Do you know that color, Armetta?"

I met her stare. She talked to be talking, and listening to her soothed the hurt I didn't even know was there.

"He just up and left for Atlanta. I don't blame him none. I was more your age and the dumbest girl around. Lord, Daddy kept me closed and didn't even let me live. The boy just wanted me. You know what I mean?"

The river was calm from lack of rain. "I reckon."

"Well, he used me right up. I never had another thing to give to a boy. You need to be careful, Armetta Lolly. You are alone in *the world. Men are snakes. Don't trust them." She dug her bare feet into the dirt. "Mama says I need to find me a man and just get married. She says there ain't no use in loving someone. She says I'll be twenty-five soon and nobody will want me."*

The words in my mouth tasted like gravel, and I forced them down. I care about you. *That thought floated right through my mind. But her mama was right. Amelia needed to find a man and marry. What was love? I'd never known one thing about it. Mama loved me, but shoot, she was so busy taking care of us to show me much touching. Daddy was Daddy, all about himself, like I wasn't even part of him.*

"Love be right here." I opened my arms to the graves.

She pulled her feet close to her and studied me. "Maybe. But that's so sad, Armetta. Real sad. The dead give us love. Too sad." She shook her head. We could disagree and still be together there, among the graves, the dead. Me growing things and her talking things out.

April 18, 1869

Miss Amelia came knocking at my door today, a good week after I planted the flowers on her daddy's grave. She had found the seedlings peeking up even though we was still in a dry spell, not to mention the hot wind.

"Mama has taken sick. I think it's this crazy weather. Not a cool day in sight." She nodded at the ball of sun in the sky.

"Nothing I like about this weather," I said.

"I made you some fresh bread and gathered some eggs." She pushed a pretty brown basket at me. "I have this too. I want you to take it." She pulled a package out from behind her back. It was wrapped in pink tissue paper and tied with a yellow ribbon.

My stomach got to fluttering. The tissue paper was the prettiest thing I'd seen in my whole life, prettier than the white

Bible Mama gave me one Christmas. It be in the memory box too.

"Go on, silly. It's just plain old paper." But she wore a big pleased smile on her face.

The paper be soft like a piece of fancy cloth, maybe softer. Pale-yellow material with tiny white dots was folded in the neatest of ways. The color against my dark skin makes it look beautiful. A dress. The skirt is flimsy and fluffy like a cloud settling on the cemetery after a rain. They say the valley pulls the clouds down and when the sun hits them it be the prettiest sight looking down from Black Mountain. My one dress is meant for scrubbing floors at some white woman's house. And it is this very reason bile pushed in my chest and up my throat. The new dress is a heartbreak waiting to be thrown on me. That's exactly what Mama would have said. It is so pretty, sin is written all over it. Miss Amelia thought she be doing good, trying to make me better, lift me up in the world. A white woman with good intentions is the worst thing to come up against in life.

Miss Amelia took the dress from me and gave it a good shake. "I think it will be a perfect fit. You'll look so nice, Armetta."

My name coming out of her mouth sounded like a soft wind rippling through the leaves. I held on to the pink tissue paper.

"I know you're thinking you don't need to look pretty, but that's just not so. Every girl should look her best. Anyway, surprises happen every day. You never know when you might need a good dress."

Now, that was the apple on the tree of knowledge tempting and taunting me. "I'll wear it to the next party I'm invited to." I cut her a grin so as not to show disrespect or hurt her feelings.

"You never know, Armetta. We can meet someone special in the oddest of ways."

"I ain't looking for nothing to make me pretty, Miss Amelia."

There were some things this girl just will never understand. Like what it is to be colored on a mountain in North Carolina. Not only colored, but ugly and built like a boy.

When she left, I noticed a big greenish dragonfly dead on the step leading to the shack. Could be good. Mama said dragonflies brought change. I scooped it up and placed it in my memory box.

Tonight I spread the pink tissue over the one window in the shack. The evening sun turned the room a fancy red. It was a bad omen to add color to such a plain, peaceful place. It was like the offering in the church plate waiting to be used by those do-gooders, all showy and praiseworthy.

May 5, 1869

An angel showed up. The steady rain had been falling a week. Dragonfly River was lapping at the trees near my shack. The weather was cold. Mama called those kind of spring days "blackberry winter." "Days you just have to trudge through, Armetta. It's the devil that sends us the frost after the flowers start to bloom. He's trying to break our spirit. But remember, life always comes on anyway, even after a frost." *Maybe I'll find the guts to leave the cemetery for good, making me a life somewhere else—that's just what that pink paper has done for me, made me restless.*

A wagon stopped at the big double iron gates in the afternoon like it might pull straight through. It was plain as day that the wagon came from somewhere off the mountain, a city. Someone yelled, but I just held my ground. Maybe they'd leave. A man dressed in a town shirt and pants jumped down from the seat. His hair was the color of honey.

I stepped out of the shed 'cause he looked like the type to snoop.

"Excuse me!" he yelled through the gates. "I'm supposed to speak with Miss Armetta Lolly, the caretaker of Ella Creek Cemetery."

Lord, I sounded so important. I lost my thoughts and stood in a puddle halfway up my boots. "That be me."

"You're the caretaker? Miss Lolly?" He smiled. A colored man held the reins on the horses.

"Yes, sir, I be Armetta Lolly." The wind cut through my flannel shirt. "I'm hoping this rain don't freeze and kill my plants." Now, this was the most I had spoken to anyone outside of Miss Amelia.

The rain stood in his hair, little drops here and there. He took his time looking at the cemetery, like he wasn't even getting wet, like it was the finest place in the world to be standing. "I don't regularly care for graveyards, but this is nice, real nice."

I studied the ground. "The river is high."

He kind of laughed. "I can see why. Ever since I've arrived from New Orleans, it's been raining." He smiled at me in a soft way.

It was him who brought the rain and the cold.

"I'm escorting a gift here for Miss Amelia Daniels. She said you knew where their family plot is."

"Yes, sir, I do."

"I'm Paul Dobbins, Pastor Paul Dobbins. Why don't you come out here, and I'll show you what I have." He circled the wagon.

I opened the iron gates and followed him.

She was as tall as me. Her wings were almost as long as her body. They arched back as if she might be showing them off or about to take to the sky. I could count the feathers overlapping. A belt was tied around her small waist. In her arms, she held a bunny. Mama always said white rabbits was special and

*shouldn't be bothered. They brought good luck. Without
even thinking, I reached out and touched the pure-white
dress.*

"She's a beauty. Don't you think?" The pastor smiled.

Heat moved up my neck, and I thought of how that fancy
dress Miss Amelia gave me might just fit. "Yes, sir."

He touched the angel's arm. "I wish I had carved her. She's
made of marble. How far have we got to move her?"

"A ways."

The man who called himself Pastor Paul Dobbins smiled at
the angel. "We'll get her there." He grabbed a hand truck off
the wagon.

The rain wasn't even bothering me anymore. "We could try
using some wood planks I got behind the shed."

"Now, that's a girl who knows what she's talking about."
Pastor Paul Dobbins nodded.

The big colored man worked with getting the angel off the
wagon.

She looked like she might speak to me. I shook off the shiver.
"I'll go get them boards."

The job was slow. I took the wide boards and placed them
edge to edge as far as they would reach. When we got to the
end, I'd bring the planks around and start again. This went on
for a while, and somewhere along the way the rain stopped.
Just as we got to the family plot, a gust of wind pushed a cloud
to the side and one ray of sun spilled onto the ground. "We got
to put her there so the sun hits her." The sun went back behind
the clouds.

"You know, Miss Lolly, you might just understand this angel."

"You can call me Armetta."

Pastor Paul Dobbins winked at me and pointed to the spot
where the sun had been. "Let's put her there."

In no time the angel was standing proud and gentle. The sun

broke out again and washed over her like a holy light. A tingling started in my toes and spread up my body into my mind. Something changed in the air, and a chill squeezed through my heart.

When the angel was standing in place, we walked back to the wagon, Pastor Paul Dobbins and me.

"Is there a place where I can clean up before I go to the Danielses' house? I don't want to track up their floors."

My feelings hung all over my body. "You could use my shed. I could spare you a bit of supper. It's simple, nothing fancy, Pastor Dobbins."

"Paul, please." He touched my elbow like I might be something. He looked at the wagon driver. "You can go home." He reached into his pocket and handed the man some folded bills.

The driver smiled, nodded, and jumped up in the seat of the wagon. We walked off in the direction of my shed.

"I take my baths in the river. It's right high now. You'll have to watch yourself. And it will be plenty cold." The river had slowed some. "I got some soap and a towel you can use. Them pants is terrible." Mud soaked all the way up to his knees.

He followed me into the damp dark of my shed. I handed him my rosemary soap, and he held it to his nose, taking in a deep breath. "Smells good."

My cheeks turned warm. "I made it. Here's the towel." It hung right by the dress Amelia gave me. The room filled up with silence.

When he was gone, I had to stand still for another full minute and smell him, dampness mixed with a musky man scent. The room was fully pink as the late afternoon sun worked its way in. I moved the tissue paper and looked out. The angel, in all her beauty, stood watching me. I could feel her. The river moved steady. There he stood in the water up to his waist. The

cold didn't even bother him. Soapsuds clung to the curly hairs
on his chest. Time stood right there. Nothing in my whole life
will be that way again. I turned from the window and removed
the dress from the nail. The softness slid over my head and stuck
to my body, becoming a new skin. I smoothed my hair as best I
could, pushing it into a piece of string.

He walked into the room wearing his clean wet pants.

"You be too wet."

He smiled.

I took his shirt from his hand and hung it on a nail near the
stove. Then I took his pants.

His touch was like a hot coal against my arm. "Mama said
my calling to God was a gift. I didn't believe her. I'm not and
never will be good enough. Where is God in this world, Miss
Lolly? But today I met you. You're an angel. You're my pure
inspiration to speak God's word."

I ran my hand over my hair. My skin was so dark next to him.
He kissed my fingers one by one. My mind turned still. The dress
fell into a puddle on the floor. The angel was cut from marble,
but Pastor Dobbins carved me from his details: my skin, that
had seen only hard work, my bushy hair bouncing free from the
string, my wings, angel wings, beginning to grow. They came last
in layers and layers of feathers. Each one beautiful and ready to
take into the air.

Pastor Paul Dobbins was gone the next morning. For the longest
time I stayed on that cot. The cold soaking into the walls, into
my skin, into my heart. Toward evening I got up and put that
dress over my head. The blackberry bushes were in full bloom,
white-pink with the sweetness of snow. The river had moved
around to the front of the cabin and lapped at the front stoop.
I walked through the water to dry ground, barefooted, until I
reached the angel.

"Come," she whispered into the air. "Come to me, child, and rest."

I curled up at her feet.

September 25, 1869

For months, Pastor Paul Dobbins showed up in my cemetery any old time he felt like coming. Things had changed between us after that first night. It was like I didn't have any choice but to let him visit me. He was rough, mean, and quick to leave. You would have thought I would think more of myself. But I was always on the lookout for him. He was to me like a pint of liquor had been to my daddy. Each time he came, I figured it was the last. After all, I was just a colored girl, and even though I was on Black Mountain, that didn't keep me from knowing I was messing with pure fire. Still, I had me a stack of dreams. And him loving me was one of them. But Lord knows some dreams never come true.

It was four months after I met him—smack at the end of the hottest summer ever—when I came to know something just wasn't right. Not just about him but my monthly business had been missing for a while. I was pretty dumb, because I couldn't figure out why. I thought maybe I had the sickness that ate away at Mama until she died. I went to see Ma Clark. She is the colored mountain witch and is good at what she does. Her and my mama came to Black Mountain together as slaves from some island on Georgia's coast. That was one story Mama promised to tell me but never did.

Ma Clark and Mama had been best friends, and their stories was all tangled up. That's why I could go to Ma Clark for anything.

I found her sitting on her porch shelling crowder peas. Her

husband had died before Mama of a snakebite, so like me she was all alone. "What you need, Armetta?" Her face looked younger that morning, and I almost forgot she was way older than me.

"I ain't been well, ma'am. Could you check me?"

She placed her bowl on the floor beside the rocker. "Come on in here and let's see what's ailing you."

Ma Clark had her a pair of spectacles—Mrs. Daniels had bought them for her—pushed down on her nose so she could see up close when she needed. That day I just remembered her looking over the top of them with a worried stare. She poked around on my stomach. "Lord, Armetta, you're going to have a baby. Who you been laying with, child? I didn't think you left the cemetery or had nothing to do with folks." The judgment slid through them words aimed at me.

So what I'd been doing with the fancy white preacher caused a baby in me. "He's gone off this mountain," I lied.

She looked at me sideways. "You got to think on this one, Armetta. If he be a white man—and I think he is—you be in trouble with him."

I looked at my hands.

"I know all about white men and what they do to colored women. I know it can't always be helped, and there ain't a thing you can do about it now. All we can do is pray this baby don't make it."

I sucked in air. "There's not a prayer like that in me."

She looked at me. "You so much like your mama, girl. You come on down off your high horse and understand what you about to do to this child."

She was right. A cemetery wasn't a place for no family, especially if my baby turned out white. Somebody would have something to say, and Pastor Paul Dobbins would be the loudest.

* * *

That night Pastor Paul Dobbins came right after dark like most nights, and for the first time I saw him, really saw him. He was just a mean white man using me up each and every night. That knowing must have shown on my face.

"You're the one who keeps bringing me here. You're the sinner." His words rushed at me as he pulled my dress off.

He was spouting craziness like a person with a fever. How long had his loving been like a beating for me? I kept my baby a secret. It was mine, not Pastor's.

September 27, 1869

I was trimming monkey grass today when Miss Amelia and Pastor Paul Dobbins came strolling up to the big iron gates like they was on some afternoon pleasure walk.

"Armetta." That fool girl was waving at me like we be best of friends. Trouble was written on Pastor Paul Dobbins's face.

I straightened and nodded at her. "Miss Amelia." I couldn't help but notice Miss Amelia's arm hooked through his.

"Armetta, I have the best news." She looked like a girl at her own birthday party, waiting on all the presents.

"What that be, Miss?" I really wasn't interested to hear a thing she had to say. Pastor Paul Dobbins wasn't worth nothing, but I still knew his smell, the way his muscles in his arms and down his back stood out, the tiny mole on his left shoulder.

"Well, I want you to come to work for me." Her cheeks were pink, her blue eyes too bright. Around her neck was a cross with a diamond in the middle. She touched it and rattled on. "See, Paul, I mean Pastor Dobbins and I are going to marry. Can you believe it? I won't be an old maid after all."

The good pastor couldn't look at his sin, me. I was nothing but a passing hour, maybe two each day. "That be real nice, Miss Amelia. I know your mama be proud, and a man of God to boot." And *the crazy thing was I hurt for her. I wanted nothing but for Miss Amelia to be happy, but he wouldn't make her that way. He was one big heartbreak. I had to make me some plans and quick.*

"Armetta, you look like you've put on some weight." She touched her cross. "I always worry about what you're eating. It looks like that's been for nothing."

Pastor Paul Dobbins's hard stare cut into me.

"You have to come to New Orleans with me. We'll make the garden of all gardens. I promise." She made that life sound so sweet I almost believed her.

The love I wore in my heart for Miss Amelia bubbled up.

"Paul says we will have the best soil in the country there. Isn't that so, Paul? Help me convince Armetta how important it is for her to come with us. I can't go without you, Armetta."

"You must give my Amelia what she wants." He patted her hand but looked over the top of my head.

Pastor Paul Dobbins was a walking, breathing lie. "I got to stay here, Miss Amelia. I can't go traipsing off the mountain. This be my home."

Her eyes turned wet, and she looked over at Pastor Paul Dobbins. He only shrugged. She came close to me. "Please, Armetta, I can't leave here without you."

"What you thinking, Miss Amelia? We ain't nothing to each other, nothing at all. We can't be." It near broke my heart to lie, but that devil stood there like a big stone wall blocking my way to her.

"You think on it. I know you'll see reason. You're just scared. We'll have the best garden, me and you. You got time. The wedding isn't until after Christmas. We won't leave for New Orleans until February or March. I can't leave you here, Armetta."

"That be a long time, Miss Amelia. Things could change between now and then."

"Two things will never change: my upcoming marriage to
Paul and my love for you, Armetta."

"I think we should go, Amelia." His words hung in the air.

He never visited me again at night. I didn't expect him to.
Miss Amelia had done shown me just who he was.

It's bedtime now, and I'm sitting on the little stoop of my
shack and watching the green corn moon. We call it that 'cause
it's time to harvest. This moon always makes a soul restless. The
river is churning and rushing behind the cabin. I can feel the
baby moving inside of me, wings fluttering. Life from sin. Ain't
that what Mama always talked about? Jesus died for our sins and
gave us life. A baby isn't bad, but a half-white baby with a colored
girl will make living hard, worse than just plain dark skin.

March 5, 1870

*His hot devil's breath hit me full in the face last night. The
night was so dark I couldn't see nothing about him. But I knew
it was him even though I hadn't seen him in five months. I'd
hoped him and Amelia had left after marrying at Christmas,
but I knew better. Pastor Paul Dobbins clapped his hand over
my mouth. "She's coming here to see you soon and thinks I've
been trying to convince you to go to New Orleans with us. You'd
better not say anything different." He poked me in the stomach
with his finger. "If you have to hide then hide, but she can't
know about your condition." He came in closer like he might
suck the air from my mouth. "I'll make sure you pay if you tell
her about this. You need to disappear off this mountain while
you can." He left without me opening my mouth. The place on
my stomach burned with pain.*

*I kept my eye out for Miss Amelia, and sure enough this
afternoon while I was on my knees weeding some flowers, I seen
her red hair shining in the sun that cut through the trees. I'd*

taken to wearing some of Daddy's baggy overalls that hid my
stomach. My heart wasn't wanting to hurt Miss Amelia. She was
a good soul, and the one person in the world who cared after me.

Her face was creased with worry. "Armetta, I need to talk
to you."

"I'm working on this flowerbed, Miss Amelia. Come on down
here and join me like you used to."

She smiled and dropped to her knees. "Paul said he begged
and begged you to come with us to New Orleans, but you just
flat refused. I've never known you to be out-and-out mean,
Armetta." Those blue eyes of hers was the saddest I'd ever seen
them.

"It won't work. You need to make a life with him. You can't if
I'm there."

"Armetta, I need you. You're my real family. Please come with
me. I can't live with him unless you're there. He won't even let
me walk on the mountain. He's like Daddy. Mama agrees with
him. I can't go back to being locked in a house. I need you to
help me."

My heart cracked some.

"Paul isn't who I thought. It's too late. I'm stuck."

The baby kicked me. "I'll have to think."

"You can't. It's now or never." The sunlight hit the diamond
on the little cross and sparkled. "I'm going to have a baby. He
doesn't know." Amelia smiled.

"I'll go, but first I got to finish something."

She smiled so big I thought her mouth had to hurt. Her
perfume smelled of honeysuckles blooming. "We leave at the end
of the month." She stood up. "I knew you would do it if I talked
to you."

"Miss Amelia, how about we not tell him I'm going? I got a
feeling that wouldn't be smart."

Her look settled on my shoulders. "I think you're right. I

*won't tell, Armetta. You're saving my life. But what do I say
when he asks about my visit?"*

*"Tell him I refused because I'm going down the mountain to
work in town." Evil begot evil.*

"The end of the month, Armetta." She smiled.

"Yes, ma'am. I'll be all ready by then."

March 19, 1870

*My pains started near dark. They cut across my belly like a
knife. I thought of making my way to Ma Clark, but I knew
I never could. So I worked through those pains on my own.
Sometimes I screamed so loud, I was sure someone in the
settlement would hear me, but no one came. I was on my own.
When the pushing started, I was near out of my mind. How
could I get the baby into the world alone? I screamed again.*

*"You can do this, Armetta. I'm right here." Mama's voice was
the sweetest sound I had ever heard. "Squat. Then push with all
you have, baby."*

*I did exactly what she said. A horrible pain wrapped around
my body, bearing down on me like a knife cutting me in half.
This went on for a while, and each time I thought I couldn't
push again, Mama's voice brought me back. Finally a boy, Lord
Jesus, a boy, a fine baby boy came into the world.*

*On toward daylight I set out walking to Ma Clark's. See, I
had me a plan. I'd begin a new life with Miss Amelia. I'd make
every living day of Pastor Paul Dobbins's life miserable. I'd
protect Miss Amelia. The good pastor would wish he had never
crossed me.*

I kept my baby close to me inside my thin coat.

*Ma Clark answered the door before I knocked. "You be mess-
ing with fire, Armetta."*

"I know."

Ma Clark knew what she called "root" from her island. She
sometimes knew things without a soul telling her. "You can't go
off with that girl. He won't let you. He be after you if you do."

"Yes, ma'am, but I'm going to make him pay. I got a plan."

"Revenge is the Lord's, child."

"No, ma'am, it be mine."

"You'll pay for that kind of thinking."

"Yes, ma'am."

Ma Clark looked at my coat. "What you got hidden?"

I opened the faded cloth and brought out my baby boy. My
heart wanted him so bad I nearly dropped to my knees. But his
life wasn't worth a plug nickel with me. "I be giving him to you."

Her face went soft. Ma Clark never could have a baby.
"Child." She took him. Her face went blank for a minute.
Then her eyes cleared. "He'll grow up to be a good man, but his
daughter won't be nothing but trouble. She'll break my heart
with her foolishness. Mary Beth be her name."

"How you know all that?"

"Just do. It's in the touch. It runs all through my peoples.
I be Geechee from Sapelo Island. Your mama, Liza, was from
Savannah. She never understood me and Emmaline's root from
the island."

"Who is Emmaline?"

"She was my sister, kind of, like your boy will be my son.
She's been dead for years now. Died in the walk. During the War
Between the States, the master on Sapelo, along with a couple
of masters in Darien, decided they would save their property,
slaves, by walking them all the way to Macon. Many of them
died. But she still walks the coast, a place called the Ridge. Her
spirit will never rest 'cause she's a storycatcher."

"A what?" I snorted.

"That's someone who untangles the wrongs plaguing others.
Some people be born that way, some are only burdened after

*they die. You never want to be a storycatcher, Armetta. You'll
spend your life giving things up for other people."*

"Yes, ma'am."

*"I left that island and never saw Emmaline again. The last
thing she said to me before I left was 'I love you, Celestia.' And I
believed her."*

*"Here." I pushed my memory box at her. "This here is my box.
One day he might want to know about me."*

*"You don't worry none on this boy. His daddy won't even
know I'm here with him. This baby will grow to be a strong
man. No evil will touch him. I'll give him the box when the
time comes."*

"Yes, ma'am." My stomach hurt so bad I thought I'd die.

*Then I walked back to the cemetery 'cause Miss Amelia
would be ready soon.*

March 29, 1870

*The day before it was time to leave, I was thinking on how I
could just stay on my mountain with my boy.*

*Pastor Paul walked up beside me. "The angel looks nice with
all the daffodils blooming around her." His words was like a big
spoonful of honey.*

*I didn't look up at him 'cause I was purely afraid of how I'd
act. "It be my job."*

"Really, Armetta? I heard you had a new job."

*I figured Amelia had done gone and told him. "I don't know
what you mean." I pulled weeds around the headstones. The
heat from him worked up my back, but I still didn't bother
looking.*

"I heard you were a mother."

*Now, Mama had taught me not to lie, but there were times
when a colored girl didn't have no choice; plus he was lying,*

'cause nobody knew about my baby but Ma Clark, and she sure wouldn't tell. "I don't know what you're talking about. I ain't married." I knew the last words would crawl under his skin.

"Don't be uppity with me, girl." His words curled around the peaceful graveyard like black, oily smoke.

I moved away from him without speaking. If I looked at him, he'd read the hate and loss in my eyes.

"I have something for you."

Again the fool was trying to trick me. "I don't have no baby. Lord help."

"Don't use the Lord's name in vain, Armetta."

This was when I looked at him. "It ain't a crime for a colored girl to talk to God."

His eyes flashed with meanness, but he stayed calm. "Me and Amelia want you to have this no matter whether you're telling the truth about the baby or not. We want to leave you something since we are going away." He held out his hand, and there was Miss Amelia's cross. "Amelia is very upset because you won't be going with us. She insisted. She can't come to see you. She's too fragile right now. You hurt her so bad when you refused to come with us."

He was a fool and a liar. I only stared at the little cross.

"Take it. Don't tell me you're going to refuse my, our, gift. I'm not heartless, Armetta. You had my child. I just need to know where he or she is."

"There ain't no child. I told you that. I'm not a liar, like you." All the hate I owned came out in them words. "So I don't need no gift. Go leave me alone. I have no link to you." I stood right there and stared him down.

He made two steps toward me. "Don't lie to me." He grabbed my wrists. The power in his hands could break the bones like twigs. "I want to know where the child is." The cross, wound in his fingers, was cutting into my skin.

"There ain't no child." I said this nice and quiet. Why did he want the baby so bad? It sure wasn't love.

He let go and walked behind me, and put the cross around my neck, hooking it in one smooth move. "Now, that looks nice." He came close to my ear. I could smell him, the sweat, the pine trees. "You just better stay away from Amelia. We're leaving soon. No seeing her."

"I ain't got a reason to see her," I lied. "I just want you and her to go."

He pushed me hard and I fell on the ground.

I grabbed me a rock in my hand.

"Stay away from her." He turned and left. I should have came up behind him and hit him on the head.

The necklace was hot on my neck. That man had something way up his sleeve, and it wasn't good for me either. That afternoon the rain came. It was so hard and long I figured I didn't have to worry over the good pastor 'cause I was going to float down the mountain. Dragonfly River was so high it worked around my shed and came in the door and cracks around the floor. There was some kind of doom in the air. The cross hung around my neck. If I lost it, he'd blame me for stealing, and Miss Amelia might believe him. Nobody could be trusted.

Miss Amelia showed up two hours later. She never saw the cross 'cause it was stuck down my blouse. "Armetta, we're leaving in the morning." She looked so young, too young. Never ever would she understand his kind of bad.

"Let's stay, Miss Amelia. Make him go without us."

"Paul won't have it and Mama would throw a fit."

I let my breath out.

"Be out behind the house at seven tomorrow morning. I'll surprise him then. We have a train to catch."

"How am I going to catch a train, Miss Amelia?"

"I bought you a ticket, silly. I got me some running money

hid away. Charley went for me. I swore him to secrecy. He prom-
ised." Charley is a good man but he just drinks too much.

"Okay."

"Be there. Promise?"

"Yes. I promise, Miss Amelia."

"It's going to be the best garden ever, Armetta."

"I know it will, ma'am."

I been jumping at every little sound tonight. There isn't a bit
of sleeping to be had. I opened the door to the shed and let
the chilly air inside. My last night. A wind picked up, and I
breathed in the smell of rain. That's when I saw a barn owl
sitting on one of the headstones. Now, some folks thought an
owl was a devil sign, but Mama said owls was the messengers.
When a person came upon an owl that wasn't afraid or shy—
like the one I saw—it meant the person would be a teller, a soul
who brought the truth to those who didn't hear or see things
from the beyond. That barn owl sat right there watching me. A
cold chill walked over my head. My life there in the cemetery is
fading away, and I know I will leave the baby with the light skin
forever. Ma Clark already spun her story about a brother who
lived on the Georgia coast. All I can do is pray. The next time I
write in the book, I will be in New Orleans. Maybe I will have
good things to say.

I CLOSED THE BOOK. Armetta never wrote another word. Now, how was
that story supposed to save anyone? It wasn't even finished.

PART NINE

The Grim Reaper

June 1939

"When Death is ready for you, he comes in his hooded cape, and there ain't a thing you can do."

—*Ada Lee Tine*

Shelly Parker

I SEEN DEATH with his black hooded cape walking in the backyard of the Tyson house. I stood on the back step, and the specter walked toward me. I closed my eyes tight. I needed Nada.

"Shelly," Ada called from behind me in the kitchen.

"Yes, ma'am."

Death raised his head and looked right at me. Then he disappeared.

"What you doing out there?" Ada asked.

"I need to talk to Nada."

"Ain't you too old for this mess?"

"I seen something. I need to check on her."

"That old woman spirit?" Ada stood behind me.

"Worse."

"What, then?"

I turned around. "Death. I seen the specter walking in the backyard."

"You seen him?"

"Black cape and all." I pointed. "Right there."

"Hush, child, hush. Talking about him could bring him our way." She pulled on my arm. "Get in here."

In the bright kitchen my thoughts on Death began to settle. "I want to check on Nada."

"I know you do, child, but how? We got a phone but does your mama?"

"No, but the main house has one."

"We got to ask Miss Lydia about calling, unless you know the number."

My heart sunk. "No, ma'am."

She patted my arm and looked out the window into the empty yard. "Your mama's fine. This be about that quilt. I'm telling you that Miss Faith is something else. Have you looked at that clean room up there? That ain't normal."

"I told you that quilt is bad. Miss Faith is charmed. She ain't never been clean a day in her life but when she started making that quilt. When things began changing."

"Like how? Something ain't right with her. I think it has something to do with that girl on the marker, the one on her quilt."

"Arleen Brown. Maybe."

"Ain't no maybe to it. That Arleen Brown has got a black soul. She be owning Miss Faith."

I wasn't never one to take up for Faith Dobbins, but I found a lot of firsts in Darien. "The real Miss Faith ain't all bad, Ada."

"Then tell me who this Arleen Brown is."

"Some old girl back home on the mountain that died a few years back. I don't know why she's got Miss Faith other than she's got unfinished business with the pastor."

"What kind of business?" Ada asked.

I shrugged. "Don't know that."

She looked out the kitchen window one more time and shook off a shiver. "Let's go get some fresh flowers for Miss Lydia. They be gone 'exploring' the town."

"You don't fool me, Ada. You like Miss Lydia."

Her face softened. "She be a decent white woman."

"Yes, ma'am." And I realized that's what she had become since leaving Pastor.

WE WAS IN THE FRONT YARD near the road gathering flowers from the beds. A car went by with a white lady driving—and that wasn't no big deal—but I had to look twice.

"What you looking at this time?" Ada asked in a nervous way.

I shook off the willies. "I thought I knew that white woman, but it can't be no one from Black Mountain down here. Wouldn't be no reason."

Ada looked at the car. "That be Pastor Harbor's car. He's the pastor of the white Episcopal church in Darien. He got him a new wife. She ain't from here, but I can't tell you where she's from. She keeps to herself a lot. She's young and pretty. Don't want a bit of help. Does all her work herself."

It couldn't be Nellie Pritchard, the woman I worked for who murdered her husband, but it sure looked like her for a minute. Wouldn't it be something if Nellie was living right there in Darien? If she only knew I still had my two hundred dollars. If I wanted I could go anywhere 'cause that was a lot of money. It was enough to help me live for a long time. If I wanted I could leave Black Mountain. But Nada would be left all alone. One child running off was enough.

"Make things right with Will. He be your only brother. And brothers are hard to come by." Ada looked at me like she had read my last thought.

The air already felt like a furnace. "I don't want to talk about it."

Ada stopped what she was doing. "Time ain't your friend, girl. Clean up how you feel. This ain't about you. It's about Will and what happened to make him leave his mama and home. Show him some respect. He's showed you."

I huffed.

"You think you don't have to respect him? You got a lot to learn."

The old woman spirit was standing near the house. "I got a job for you, girl," she said.

"Lordy be," Ada whispered.

"You got something to do for me before you go home. Get ready. You understand? You wasn't protected all these years for nothing."

"I can't do nothing for you, ma'am. I'm not even from here."

The old woman laughed. "You be silly. You be perfect because of where you came from and where you going."

"Come on, Shelly." Ada started walking fast.

"You can't run away from me, Ada Lee," the old woman called after her.

Ada kept moving to the back steps of the house.

"She be afraid of you because of that night," I said. For some reason the old woman didn't scare me.

"That girl's been through a lot." Then she looked at me. "I'll talk to you soon. When we get done, you can go on back home." And the old woman was gone.

"Get on back here!" Ada yelled.

I went to her.

"She be bad, Shelly. Something terrible going to happen. Get ready. And you be a part of it. What was she talking about protecting you?"

But I couldn't speak. Mrs. Dobbins pulled back into the driveway. She was all smiles but she was alone. "Ada, the town is wonderful. I left Faith at the dock looking at the boats."

Both me and Ada looked at each other.

"What she want with boats?"

Mrs. Dobbins frowned. "That's a good question. She said she liked looking at them."

"I just bet she does." Ada frowned.

Maude Tuggle

ZACH LOOKED UP when I came into the office. "Well, what did you find out?" He put down his pen and took off his wire-frame glasses.

"I talked to Amanda."

"You have my attention."

"Amanda said the cross belonged to Charles Dobbins. She's agreed to talk to you."

Zach shook his head. "I should hire you." He stood. "Come on. We have to go see her now."

Life can change in a moment while waiting on a promise to be fulfilled. I never told him about the angel. I never told him about seeing and talking to a ghost. I kept these things tight in my chest. Had I told, maybe things would have turned out different.

Arleen Brown

I WATCHED THE MISSUS DRIVE AWAY before I walked down to the dock. The old woman spirit that kept following Shelly around stood off to the side.

"I'm here to tell you, girl. You need to go back from where you came. That quilt won't stop a thing 'cause you can't be the one to use it. Don't you know that? A spirit can't harm a soul. We only start the telling of the story and watch, and it don't matter that you be in that girl's body. She can't do a thing you want unless she wants it." She cocked her head sideways at me and disappeared.

"Faith?" And there stood Will on one of the shrimp boats.

"So you're what brought the change in Shelly."

"I guess I am. Except she's not really happy to see me." He walked to the rail of the boat.

"Sure she is. She's just being Shelly." I looked away. I didn't want him to know it wasn't Faith.

He laughed.

"You've been here all this time?" I said this more to myself than him.

He stood on the deck of the boat called *Sweet Jesse.* "Yes."

"What about your mama? She nearly died of heartache. I know this. I seen—" I stopped, knowing I didn't sound like Faith at all.

Will looked hard at me. "Something is different. What's wrong with you, Faith?"

I turned away from his hot stare. There wasn't no use in trying to fool him. "I'm Arleen. I came back to clean up what you left behind. I came to catch this story gone all wrong."

"Arleen?" He looked at me like I'd lost my mind.

"She couldn't handle all your truth-telling. You men are all the same when everything is said and done," I said.

He was quiet. "Arleen? How can this be?"

"Easy enough. You should know that, seeing how your mama's a conjure woman, or has your new life made you forget the important things?"

He studied me. "I don't know what to say, Arleen. What happened to you was wrong."

A screeching sound went off in my head. "I don't want to talk to you now." I began to walk away.

"Wait. I need to talk to you and Faith."

"Not today."

"How about meeting me tomorrow?"

I turned around. Faith's heart slowed. It was dangerous. She wanted out to talk with him so bad. "Maybe."

"Go to the dock close to the Tyson house in the morning at sunrise. I'll meet you there. We'll talk, Arleen. I'll explain what happened to bring me here to live." He sounded like he was telling the truth. "And you can tell me how you ended up being Faith."

"Okay."

He smiled.

THE NEXT MORNING I left out before Ada came pulling into the drive from town. The dirt road out to the dock was bumpy, and my driving wasn't the best. Shoot, all I'd ever driven was Daddy's old tractor in the field, but I managed 'cause there wasn't a soul to be seen. Missus would be worried over Faith taking her car, but I'd settle that when I got back. As a strip of orange showed where the sun met the marsh and water, the putt, putt of Will's boat let me know he wasn't far off. The gray of morning was almost gone.

By the time he slid that boat up to the dock, I was standing there. The water lapped against the dock's poles. "Now we talk, Arleen?"

"Okay."

He sighed. "I had to leave. Faith knew that. Why are you stirred up? Why did you take Faith's body? That doesn't make sense. Faith knew the whole truth. I never lied to her. There was a lot more that caused me to leave besides what happened to you."

"I got something in the car to show you." I couldn't help but smile. "I need to tell you what Faith was doing and why I took her body. I have to finish something and then I'll let her back. I will."

"If someone sees me with Faith, trouble will start." He looked over at *Sweet Jesse*. "Why don't you come on the boat and I'll take you out for a while. We'll ride."

I looked at all that water and marsh. "I guess, but let me get something from the car." If I had lived, I could have loved Will with my whole heart. I ran to the car and got my package.

Will held out his hand as I stepped onto the dock. "What have you got there, Arleen?" He helped me onto his boat.

"Something special I've been working on, the whole reason I'm here in the first place." I kept the quilt against my chest. "So you live with Ada Lee Tine?"

"Yes." He smiled.

"Lord, she truly hates me. I can tell by the way she watches me, so don't deny it."

He started the boat and began to pull it away from the dock. The floor rocked under my feet and the boat parted the water, spraying it up on my face.

"Hold on to the rail until you get your sea legs!" Will yelled over the engine. "Ada doesn't hate anyone. She's the kindest soul I know." He nodded at my quilt wrapped in the old blanket. "She's afraid of your charm quilt. Yes, I've heard all about it." He smiled.

"What about your own mama, Will? Why did you leave her?"

He frowned. "It's a long, long story, but sometimes mothers aren't who they are supposed to be."

I laughed. "Lord, Will, if I had lived, I'd be younger than you, and I know mamas aren't perfect. Sometimes they be downright stupid, but everybody loves their own mama."

"I love her, but well, lies have a way of driving people apart, Arleen. The bigger the lie, the further the distance."

"Faith would love to have a mama like you have, and you just threw her away."

"That's not so." His face became serious.

"This is why I took over Faith's body." I pulled up the skirt I was wearing and showed him Faith's legs.

He looked away.

"It's okay to look. You got to see what she did so you understand why I'm here."

His face became still when he saw the scabs.

"This is what she started doing to herself. Ever since you left and told her all your truths, she lost her mind in bits and pieces."

"Cover them."

I dropped the skirt. "We both know how to twist and turn a story. Don't we?" I laughed. "I had to catch it and turn it right. I had to think fast. See, I wanted to pay you back for helping me like you did. You stood up for me even after I was dead and gone. I wanted to take care of her for you." I unfolded my quilt. "See, you be here. Right here in the hem."

He looked over to where I pointed. "I don't see anything."

"Of course not. You're hidden in there. It's your goodness that helps give power to this charm."

"Arleen, I want to talk to Faith." He gave me his soft, serious look.

Faith stirred, but I was boss. "Did you know that Faith is a quilter? Her quilts are special. She started sewing when you left, and she stole the sewing basket from your mama's cabin. The gravestones are what makes her quilts so important. She adds them to her work."

Will looked at the quilt. "But Ada says this quilt is bad."

"A death quilt is for protecting one who has been wronged. Lord help the person who did the hurting, though. She be right about that. See, I got to tell my story. Me and Faith are telling it through this here quilt. Then I'll be through and I can leave."

He watched the water as we bumped across. "If Faith understands what needs to be done, then let her come back."

"She's too good, Will. I have to make sure the rightful owner gets this death quilt. I thought you'd be glad to see me. You of all people." I smiled at him.

He pushed that boat out to open water.

"Where are we going?" I touched his arm. A heat came into Faith's fingers. I'd been real careful not to touch many humans, just the missus. For some reason she didn't drain my power. Probably because her heart was the purest I'd seen, besides Mama's. Not even Will could match Missus.

"Brunswick. Nobody knows you there."

"You're not going to make me let her go right now. It's not time."

He frowned. "I know what happened to you, Arleen, was unfair and hard, but taking Faith's body hostage won't change that."

I laughed. I had to laugh. "I loved my life, hard or not. You and

Faith get to walk around doing what you want. Not me. So don't go telling me about unfair."

"But Faith didn't ask you to take over her body."

"You're wrong. She accepted my help. She had to ask me to come. That's the rule."

We were in the ocean water and the boat rocked and bumped. The air was so salty I could almost taste it. Maybe I could stay here. Missus was thinking she'd stay. She told me. I liked her, the new her out there in the marsh away from Pastor. Maybe she cared. I closed my eyes and allowed the wind and spray from the waves to move over me. What would happen to Faith? "Will, I already know why you left. I know the lies and the truths. There are no secrets where my spirit lives. Pastor Dobbins is not the only rotten apple in this big barrel of lies."

Will looked over at me. "Maybe you do know."

"Let ye not judge." I closed my eyes again.

Faith struggled to the surface, but I pushed her down. The salt washed over my skin. "I know everything," I whispered.

Ada Lee Tine

MISS LYDIA STOOD at the window. "That tree reminds me of an old woman."

I looked out. There stood the old woman spirit in the backyard by the big twisted oak Miss Lydia was talking about. "Lots say that."

"Where's Shelly?"

"She's changing the sheets on the beds, ma'am."

Miss Lydia frowned. "Faith took the car early this morning. Has she come back?"

The wind was whipping the treetops. "No, ma'am."

"Ada, I've never seen a quilt like the one she's working on. Have you? I can't imagine where she got the idea for this one. There doesn't seem to be a real pattern."

"Don't need a pattern for that kind of quilt. You make it up as you go."

"I would have to have a pattern."

"Lots of women work better with a pattern to go by. We need some direction. Miss Faith strikes out on her own. That be both a good and bad thing."

The old woman was still waiting.

"I'm going out for a walk before it rains." Miss Lydia turned from the window. She left out the front door. Shelly bumped around upstairs. Girls now just didn't move silent like they did in my day. The old woman hadn't moved. I took off my apron and threw it on the chair. Enough was enough. I charged out the back door before I lost my nerve.

The old woman kept her sight on the upstairs windows and didn't pay me no mind. Pure sadness mixed with a little anger showed on her face.

"We got to talk."

She kept looking at the house. "I don't like this house. It was too hard to live in." She waited. "I ain't here for you, girl."

This flew all over me. "What do you mean too hard to live in?"

Still she watched the bedroom window that Shelly must have been in. "You don't know me. You should. I be from the island a long time before you was born. I've been gone from this earth since the walk."

"So you lived here," I said.

"Yes, ma'am." She still didn't look at me.

"You need to listen to what I got to say to you. It's been a long time coming. I'm sorry you was a slave and died away from home, but we got to settle what's between us."

This made her look at me. "I don't reckon we could ever settle what's between us, Ada Lee Tine."

"You leave Shelly alone."

"That's what you had to tell me? That's what was between us?" She cackled.

"You took the only thing that ever matter to me. Did you know that? Roger was mine, and I loved him with my whole heart. You hear? Part of me is missing and always will be 'cause of you."

"I didn't do nothing."

"You caused him to die. You could have saved him. He was mine."

"Girl, how could I save him?" She came closer.

"It was you messing with other people's lives that caused this whole mess."

"How you figure that, Ada Lee? I was here because of Mary Beth Clark, not him. She was and is tied to me 'cause I was close to the woman that helped raise her, Celestia Clark. Helped her real great-grandmama, Liza, out of a story. Celestia was like my sister. We was raised together. Close as two peas in a pod until Liza came along, but she turned out to be okay. It was you that caused him to die. He came looking for you, not her or me." She laughed.

"I loved Roger." My voice cracked.

"That's what you say, but girl, why you never tell him that?" She waited a minute. "I'll tell you why. 'Cause you thought you had the whole world in front of you, that you could be slow and settled. Life ain't about being slow, girl. You dragged your feet and he left this world. Not by me. Folks leave when they are finished, when their job be done."

"No. That ain't so, 'cause he left me unfinished." The tears was there. Tears I had held in for so, so long.

"Lordy, girl, he finished you. Can't you see that? His job was not to be your man but to teach you how to reach out and love. He opened the door for the boy that came to you. Before him, you wouldn't have been so trusting, so eager to love that boy."

My heart cracked open out there by that big old oak tree.

"You can't own something that's not yours to have, girl. He wasn't yours. He was the doorman."

The marsh grass rustled in the wind. A storm was coming, but there was time before it hit. Maybe it would go around.

"Good and bad things happen in our lives. We can't control either. Bad will come to you, girl. It always does. How you think you could outrun it? But here's how it is, you walk right through."

"I miss him."

The old woman nodded. "He was a good soul. You come from good family. The Tines be caring, loving folks. I know. See, they be my family. Your granddaddy was my boy. I loved him with my whole heart and he lost me, Ada Lee. He lost me out there walking. My name be Emmaline."

I shook my head. "Why you want Shelly?"

"You think you was part of that killing. You got it in your head because of your old auntie that you might have helped me. You thought I killed them two and you was part of it. You had it wrong. I used you to get here and left you at the door. You never stepped foot in the house. Lord, girl, they did that killing mess to themselves. Mr. Benton T. Horse of New York City was evil to the bone. Devil bound. You felt it. He killed Mary Beth Clark. He was so mad about her talking to Roger that he finished losing his mind. He killed Mary Beth before I could get to her. Mr. Benton T. Horse was standing over her with a knife. I just whispered in his ear, and he took his own life. He took Mary Beth out of this world before I could set her story straight." The woman spirit was quiet a minute and then in a low voice she finished what she had to say. "Celestia and me had a long story full of lies told to protect. Those be the best kind of lies 'cause they aren't mean and hateful. Celestia, me, and Liza was all friends. That be Liza Lolly. I don't reckon I was always friends with Liza, but Celestia held us together. We was slaves on Sapelo. They was sold to Black Mountain, North Carolina. I was sold to Darien. Shelly is going to finish the story for my friends Liza and Celestia. She's got to. Then they will all rest."

"Leave Shelly alone. I don't want her hurt."

"You going to talk to me that way?" She gave me a mean look. "Your Roger was avenged when the man took his own life. That you owe me for."

"I want Shelly to go home to her mama."

The woman laughed. "I ain't got no control over that. Death is a being that roams this earth. You got to take that up with him. We sure can't control him. I'm here to finish a story. You go on, now. Take care. Remember what I said about Death. He be of his own mind." She walked right into the house and left me standing there.

Shelly Parker

I WAS STRUGGLING with putting new sheets on Faith's bed up in the small room at the top of the house. The roof slanted near the little bed, and I'd done bumped my head three times.

I looked up and saw Mary Beth Clark standing in the doorway. "The hot, steamy rain that falls at the end of June always lifted my spirits when I was alive," she said.

"I like the rain on the mountain. It always cools the air," I said.

"You know that horrid man killed me, cut my throat from behind. I never even saw him coming."

"Who was he?" I stopped what I was doing.

"A banker from New York. I hated him, but I was determined to have a better life."

"How, with a man you hated?"

She laughed. "You have a lot to learn, little girl."

"Maybe."

"So you're just stuck here because you was killed here?" I thought of Armetta's book and how it just stopped, how she was tangled up with a bad white man too.

"You're thinking about her. The girl who wrote the book you were reading the other day."

"Yes." I don't reckon I would ever get used to a haint reading my every thought.

"I'm still here because of her."

Now, this got my attention. "What do you mean? Armetta?"

"I never knew her name. Ma Clark didn't talk about her, but she was my grandmother. I found out about her after Daddy and Ma Clark died."

"She's a right hateful ghost."

"Really?" Mary Beth Clark thought on this a minute. "I got my own story, just like you."

"Well, I don't have a bit of time for listening." I started back in on the sheets.

"I'll finish before you're through with this room." She smiled.

I just huffed.

"My daddy was the prize of our family. It was easy to see why, because he was an only child who came to Ma Clark late in life. My mama always said Daddy couldn't live up to Ma Clark's expectations. And Mama also pointed out that Ma Clark's whole story about Daddy's birth was suspicious. See, Daddy had light skin like me. He could have passed. Ma Clark said that could come from way on back in the family, but like my mama, I had to wonder. Then one day Ma Clark looked at me out of the blue—this was after Mama passed from a blood disease—and let a truth slip. I was chopping onions for hushpuppies, and Ma Clark was simmering a gumbo. It was an old recipe she brought from her island.

"'You love to cook just like her. It breaks my heart,' Ma Clark said with the sweetest expression on her face.

"'Who?' I honestly thought we were talking about my mama.

"'Liza Lolly.'

"The name didn't ring a bell with me. For a long minute all I could hear was the sound of my knife cutting the onions. 'I don't remember her,' I said.

"Ma Clark shook her head. 'You didn't know her. She was buried a long time before you come into this world. She was one of my best friends from the island. We got a story together.'

"I kept quiet when I should have asked for more. Not long after that I found a box in Ma Clark's old keepsake trunk. The thing felt warm when I picked it up like maybe there was a promise inside.

"Ma Clark walked in, looked at me kneeling at her trunk, and slapped my face so hard I dropped the box. 'You're headed down the wrong road, Mary Beth.'

"In the second our stares met, I knew I would outgrow Black Mountain, that somehow I didn't belong there, never had, and I wasn't connected to Ma Clark. I left home as soon as I turned seventeen. I didn't even come back when Daddy died. I couldn't. I was afraid I would be stuck there. Turn out like your daddy, Shelly."

I looked at her funny.

"Yes, I played with him as a child. Anyway, I made my own life with fine things and money. Men are just waiting to give you money, Shelly, if you're pretty like you are."

"I ain't pretty."

"You'll find out one day." She took a step toward me. "Not long before I left on the trip that brought me here to Darien, I had a dream about Ma Clark. I hadn't seen her in too many years. I kept dreaming about the box. Dreaming so much, I asked the man that brought me to Darien to stop at Black Mountain on the way down from New York. He did. Ma Clark had died, and no one knew how to find me. I talked to your mama. She didn't like me one bit. Most women didn't because of my looks. She told me to go up to Ella Creek Settlement because no one lived there anymore. Ma Clark's house looked like always. All her stuff was right there like I remembered.

"The box was all I took. When I left the cabin, I heard a mournful cry. I didn't like believing in all of Ma Clark's stories, but the truth was as soon as I took her box from the mountain, my life turned upside down. Me dying was going to happen anyway, but I know there is a story tangled around that box. I just never found out what it was."

"Where is the box?" I asked.

She only shook her head. "Don't ask me that question. I will not tell." And she was gone.

BLACK MOUNTAIN GHOSTS was much easier to deal with than the spirits I was meeting in Darien. I went down to change Mrs. Dobbins's bed. The house was quiet. Faith was gone and so was the car. I couldn't help but wonder where she had to go to in Darien with no friends. Wherever she went, she took that creepy quilt of hers. That suited me just fine.

"Girl!"

I nearly fell over Mrs. Dobbins's bed. The old woman spirit stood in the door. She looked like a real person.

"You got something to do for me. You understand?"

A sigh left my chest.

"Don't get sassy. I ain't your regular old haint. You got to take something away from here with you."

"What?"

"It be hidden and you got to find it."

"What's hidden?" I looked around the room.

The old woman smiled. "You be a good girl. You listening without arguing."

All the fight was out of me. I just wanted to go home to Nada. Will and I hadn't had much to say to each other since the day he took me on the beach. What was there to say when I was so mad at him for not coming home?

"You could listen to him, child, really listen to him," the old woman said. "You ain't done nothing but bellyache with yourself about not having him. When you find him, you fight him."

"He left me and Nada."

"Ain't nothing like it seems, girl." She pointed at the bed. "Now, look under there against the wall on the floor, near the headboard."

I stood where I was.

"Now, girl."

The dust tickled my nose, but I pushed under the bed on my belly.

"See them boards that are loose?"

I tapped on the boards, and two moved.

"I told her to hide it there 'cause he was coming. She listened to me."

The two boards came up with a little tug, reminding me of my hiding place at home.

"You find it?"

"Yes." The last thing I wanted to do was reach in the dark hole under the floor.

"Go on. Ain't nothing going to bite you." The old woman laughed.

Something hard and square was in the hole.

"Take it out."

I pulled out a small wooden box.

The old woman spirit moaned. "Yes, ma'am, that be it. Time to take it back home." In the daylight of the room, I seen two letters carved into the lid: A. L.

"Open it. You know you want to see in it. You be a brave girl, so you deserve a look."

I sat on the floor with the box in my lap and pulled the lid off. A cry escaped.

"What you see?" The old woman moved closer.

In the box was a lock of fine dark hair tied with a thread, a faded piece of pink tissue paper, a small square of white dotted yellow cloth, a piece of white chalk, a gold wedding band, a brown button off a man's shirt, a small Bible, and a dead dragonfly. I spread the things on the floor. The need to cry washed over me. "A life," I whispered.

"Yes, ma'am. You be a good girl. Take the box back to her, and the story will be over."

"Who, Mary Beth Clark?"

"Lord, no." The old woman cackled. "You got her book. It's all been about her story, child. Too late to fix what happened to her, but you can stop the evil in its tracks." She nodded to the box. "It's a map, a deserving map, to the truth."

And she was gone. *A. L., Armetta Lolly,* I thought to myself. This was her box just like she talked about in her book. Maybe all this mess had been about bringing her box home. That's why she wanted me to read her book. She wanted her box back home. I'd do my best.

Armetta Lolly

HE MADE EVERY STEP Shelly's mama made, and the fool didn't hear him or see his signs. Evil walked the mountain that day. God help her soul.

PART TEN

Ebb Tide

June 1939

"The wind becomes still and the water pulls back. It be so quiet you can hear the birds breathe."

—Ada Lee Tine

Shelly Parker

THAT WIND STOPPED BLOWING and the water got still when I found the box. I left the bedroom in a run and almost knocked Mrs. Dobbins down.

"Shelly, where is Ada?" she asked.

Her face was lined like it stayed when she was on the mountain.

"The last time I seen her, she was in the backyard."

Her frown got deep. "Go find her. There's a man here about her boy. He's been hurt."

I pushed down them stairs two at a time with my hand shoved in the deep pocket on my skirt, holding the memory box safe. My plans was to hide it in my bag at Ada's house in Darien.

"Be careful, Shelly. You're going to hurt yourself."

It was time for some truths. "Her boy be Will, Mrs. Dobbins."

"What?" she yelled.

But I couldn't stop running. Will was hurt, and I hadn't even taken the time to tell him I did love him.

Maude Tuggle

I LOOKED OUT THE WINDOW of Zach's truck, trying to shake the dread easing down my scalp for no good reason.

"Maude, this woman is colored, and it will be hard to get a court of law to take her testimony serious, especially against a pastor. I wish we could talk to his daughter. What is her name?"

"Faith, but she's gone. They're hiding. Shelly's note said they went to the Georgia coast. Amanda is trustworthy, and she went to work for him before Faith was born."

"It doesn't matter, Maude. Some people will not care about anything but the color of her skin." He turned into the drive.

The big house was quiet. "His car isn't here. I haven't seen him since he came to my door raving like a crazy man."

"That is odd. I expected to see him again. He was very angry." Zach stared at the house.

"Let's go to Amanda's cabin first." I had a feeling someone was watching our every move. When I knocked on the door, it swung open. Zach touched my hand and shook his head. He took a step inside.

"Amanda?" I called. "Maybe she's up at the main house." Then I saw all the bottles on her shelf in the kitchen scattered over the floor. The shelf hung sideways on one nail. "Something bad has happened."

"Maybe the shelf just fell. It looks like it was loaded down." Zach eased into the kitchen. "Let's look around."

This didn't take long. "She's in the main house." I said this around a knot in my throat.

When I stepped into the yard, a wave of pure panic washed over me. My hands shook.

"Her be lost." The words floated through the air.

"Did you hear that?"

Zach looked at me funny.

"I thought I heard a voice."

"I didn't hear a thing," he said.

I nodded.

The back door to Charles Dobbins's house stood wide open. Cabinet drawers were pulled out and the contents scattered all over the floor.

"Maude, come over here." Zach pointed to the floor.

Sugar was spilled. Someone had written a message: FIND HER.

I shook my head.

"I think our good pastor has lost his mind."

I saw Faith's face in my thoughts. "He's left. He's gone after Faith and Lydia, Zach. He's going to hurt them like the others, like Arleen."

Zach's face turned red. "I have a friend who is the sheriff of McIntosh County, Georgia." He moved to the phone. "Maybe he'll know where they're staying. He has connections up and down the coast."

"What about Amanda?" My stomach churned. "I shouldn't have left her. He came after I was here."

"He could have taken her with him."

"Maybe." But I knew he hadn't. "Let's go to my place. Maybe he's been there too."

WE STOOD in my garden.

"The angel was here?" Zach pointed at the flattened grass. "I thought I told you not to bother it, Maude, that it was stealing."

"I know."

"Who helped you?"

A butterfly caught a breeze and glided along to the next bush. "I did it with my wheelbarrow."

He shook his head. "So Charles Dobbins could have seen you bring it out of the woods?"

"I guess, but why would he care about the marble angel with a broken wing?"

"I'm not sure, but I have a gut feeling he was watching you and this angel is important. Let's go to the cemetery."

I led him up the path into the woods. All was still.

"She be lost." The voice was loud this time. Zach still didn't seem to notice.

Arleen Brown

"HERE'S YOUR COFFEE." I handed Will the steaming paper cup. "It's wrong that I can go in there and buy coffee and you can't."

Will looked at the shrimp boats from where he stood on the side of the road. "Lots of wrong things, Arleen. You should know that. It's the way things are right now, but maybe not forever."

"We're the same, Will."

He placed a finger to his lips. "Arleen, be quiet. You have to let Faith come back into her body. You understand. I don't know why you think you are helping her. It sounds like you're just helping yourself."

"That's not true." I wasn't going to listen to him. "She can't do what has to be done. I have to use the death quilt. There's a soul sewn into it. That soul will die when I finish."

"So you sewed the pastor into the quilt?" He frowned. "If he dies,

Faith will be the one blamed. That cannot happen. Let her go." His voice was mean.

I stood up. "No. I won't. This is my time. Not hers. I'm owed this."

He reached for Faith's hand.

I pulled away. And just like some ten-year-old girl, I ran. I'd go back to Missus.

"Arleen!"

Tires screeched and a violent shove sent my world spinning. Then all I heard was the loud thud. Footsteps all around me.

"Someone call an ambulance."

I tried to open Faith's eyes.

"That's Ada Lee Tine's boy. Check on him." Hot breath hit my face. "Ma'am, ma'am?"

I managed to open Faith's eyes. A man with a dark beard stared into my face. "Will," I whispered.

"She's talking!" he yelled over his shoulder. "They got to take him to the colored hospital," he said.

"He saved my life. He pushed me out of the way." The siren came close. Then I could see the red lights. Two men jumped from the cab and ran to me.

"Go check on Will! He got hit by the car. Not me." A wild-animal sob escaped my chest.

I got to my feet. "Will?" He was in the middle of the road. Two white women stood on the curb watching. No one was helping. "Help him!" I went to him and squatted down. "Will!"

He looked at me and smiled. "Damn girl, you stay in trouble."

"Help him!" I screamed at the ambulance guys. "What hurts?" I looked Will in the eyes.

"My knee feels bad." His eyes were bloodshot.

Around his head was a puddle of blood. A wild scream worked inside me, but I kept it down. There. There. A cut near his eye. Not his head.

The men began to work with Will.

"We're sending word to Ada." This came from a colored man who seemed to have just appeared from nowhere. "He's got to go to the colored hospital, ma'am."

"No! He needs the nearest hospital. Do you hear?" I screamed.

The knocking in my head took up all the thoughts, and I fell down the dark black hole. Faith wanted to come back, and I had to let her. It was the rules.

Armetta Lolly

THE SOUND OF BONES CRACKING shook my dead soul. It was one of those sounds I knew and wished I didn't. When he was done, he crashed through the woods with my angel. The white granny woman never heard him take the dern thing from her garden. He even watched her through her bedroom window while she undressed. Now he was trying to put the angel back before someone found the hidden place. The man was a devil.

"You be in trouble if you hurt the granny woman."

He laughed hard and long. "You silly ghost, I'm the one with the power, not you, or her or the other bitch. Me! It's over. The angel goes back where it belongs. It's over. I have the power. Now Faith has to stay with me forever."

* * *

I MET HER SOUL when she left her body—Shelly's mama—a bright glow. That meant she be lucky. All was at peace and out of her hands.

"Watch my children, Armetta," she said. What made her think I was going to stay on the mountain that long? I wanted to leave just like her. It was way past my time. Then she turned into a golden crystal light and soaked into the sky. What made her soul different from mine? And then I knew. Forgiveness. She forgave herself for all she'd done. If I did that, could I leave? Could I go, even though I was still lost? Or did I have to be found?

"Where's the cross?" he screamed as he went through her cabin.

This made me laugh. I laughed and laughed. His time was near.

Ada Lee Tine

THERE HE WAS all shining and new. His leg wrapped. A cut here and a bruise there. He was whole like no truck ever hit him. Shelly stood on one side of the bed and me on the other. That Miss Faith stood in the room like she belonged. They said she caused a ruckus, not wanting him to go to the colored hospital.

"I told them to get Will the best white doctor in Brunswick, Mama." She looked at Miss Lydia. Something had changed about this girl. Before she made me think of little irises that come up in the woods when it still be cold on the island. Quiet, studying, like she be thinking about her next move. Now she'd done turned into a bright red rose full of thorns and sneaky. Yes, sneaky. Something told me nobody knew just what might go through that one's mind.

"She be back, the real Faith," Shelly whispered to me across Will like he couldn't hear a word.

"I need to talk to you, Shelly," Will spoke softly.

She nodded.

"A white doctor ain't going to see my boy." My head was pounding with nervous pain.

"He's not your boy," Faith whispered. "The best doctor in Brunswick is coming. I insisted."

"When's he coming? Two days from now? His leg needs to be checked by a doctor today." I know I sounded sassy to my boss's daughter, but it didn't matter.

"I promise he'll be here. I just want the best care for him. He's like family to us." Faith said this nice and quiet. She wasn't a bit sassy. Something had to be wrong with her.

"Will, did you ever let Amanda know where you were?" Miss Lydia spoke for the first time, studying my boy.

"This is my boy, Miss Lydia. I don't mean no disrespect, but don't go in our business. I'm going after our doctor."

"Ada, I'm fine. My knee hurts but they wrapped it good."

"I think Amanda deserves to know her son is alive."

The whole time I'd known Will, I'd never seen him with a mean look on his face. He only had kind, soft words for folks. Now he shot Miss Lydia a hateful look, full of spite. The very spite I'd seen on Shelly's face when she first saw him.

Miss Lydia looked like she might say something but she backed down.

I broke the silence. "I'm going to see Dr. Thomas. I'll be back. Shelly, you stay right here with Will."

Miss Faith looked at me with pity, and that made me madder than anything. She thought I didn't understand who Will belonged to. She was the one who didn't get it. He didn't belong to his mama, Shelly, her, or me. He belonged to Sapelo Island.

"Don't worry about me, Ada," Will said.

"You hush and let me do what I'm supposed to do." I left him in the room. Dr. Thomas stood at the end of the hall near the nurses' station. Our little hospital wasn't nothing to look at, but the care we got from Dr. Thomas was the best on the coast.

"Hi, Ada."

"Can you come look at my boy? He's the one who got hit by the truck, saving that sassy little white girl."

"Yes, ma'am. The whole town is buzzing."

"Could you look at his knee and eye?"

He ran his fingers through his hair. "I can't, Ada."

I had to take me a breath. "Why? Is it money? I can pay. I won't leave no bill."

His face turned straight, almost sad. "You know I don't worry about money, Ada."

"Then what?"

"That white girl done called in Dr. Ballard, the white doctor. I can't step in front of him."

"I give you permission to treat my boy. I don't want no white doctor." My voice was getting loud.

"Ada, it's not a bit about what you want, or I want, or even what your boy wants anymore. Dr. Ballard could close this hospital down just 'cause he feels the notion. He doesn't like treating coloreds, but the niece of the richest family in Brunswick called him. This is serious business, and I have this whole hospital of patients to think about."

"That fool girl."

"Yes. I think her heart was in the right place."

My thoughts rushed around my head.

"From what I've seen, Will is stable. Ballard will be here. It seems he's having lunch with the mayor."

"Lord." I needed to put that Miss Faith in her place. "Thank you, Dr. Thomas." I stormed back down the hall.

"Things are going to be just fine." Will was talking to Shelly. Miss Lydia had taken that daughter of hers out of there.

"We got to wait on the white doctor thanks to little Miss Busybody."

"Ada, she wasn't trying to cause trouble. She's from Black Mountain. Things are a little different there." He looked over at Shelly. "We can't blame Faith for the way she acts. She doesn't know all the rules."

Just then the white doctor entered the room. "Okay, folks, I was called by Tyson's niece. She wanted me to check out some colored boy that saved her life," he said, looking at Will with a big old rich plastic smile on his face.

"This here be Will," I said.

"Understand, I don't make a habit of treating coloreds. But Tyson is an old friend. I can't do it again." He looked over at Will. The light reflected off his shiny bald head. "Now, what's the problem?"

"He was hit by Parker Lock's milk truck, saving Mr. Tyson's niece." I wanted him to know I didn't no more want him there than he wanted to be there.

He looked at Will. "A truck, you say?"

"Yes, sir."

"That's a nasty cut there. I'll have a nurse stitch you up. Any other complaints? You look good to me for someone hit by a truck." He laughed at his own joke and looked at a gold watch on his wrist.

"My knee hurts." Will frowned.

Dr. Ballard pulled back the sheet and began mashing Will's knee.

Will sucked in air.

"Bruised. Stay off of it for a week. I guess I'll leave you to the capable hands of the nurse. She'll stitch you and rewrap that knee. You can go home first thing in the morning." He smiled. "I have a meeting. You have a wonderful day." And out of the room he walked.

"See, I told you, Ada. I'm fine."

Will looked over at Shelly. "What do you say when I get out in the morning, we go to Black Mountain? I think Mama should be part of our talk."

Shelly broke into the biggest smile. "She'll be so excited, Will."

My heart bottomed out. "I guess I'd better go fix Miss Lydia's supper before it gets any closer to dark."

Will turned his smile on me. "You're going with me, Ada. I'm not leaving you behind. Then when I'm finished, we'll both come back. I told you the island is my one and only home."

The nurse came in with a tray.

"You and Shelly go back to Mr. Tyson's. Tell Faith we're going back to the mountain tomorrow. Mrs. Dobbins might want to stay behind. I got the feeling she has left Pastor for good."

"You have to stay off your knee," I fussed.

"It will be fine in the morning. Don't you think?" he asked the nurse.

She smiled. "I have a feeling with you it will be in working order."

I gave him a big old hug. "I love you, boy."

He squeezed my hand. "I love you, Ada," he whispered in my ear.

I had to turn my head to keep him from seeing the tears in my eyes.

"See you tomorrow, Shelly."

She took two steps toward the door and ran back to him, hugging him too. "I'm sorry to be so mad at you."

He smiled. "Ah, I would have been mad at you if you did what I did."

And that was that. We left.

Miss Faith and Miss Lydia stood by the car in the back parking lot. Nothing about them made me think of mother and daughter.

"Did Doctor Ballard come?" Miss Faith asked. There was a calmness in her eyes that hadn't been there when she came.

"They letting him come home tomorrow morning."

Miss Lydia touched my arm. "I'm sorry, Ada. Faith acted without my knowledge. She just wanted the best for Will. Those two grew up together. Faith nearly grieved herself to death when he left."

Now, in all my years of working for white folks, not one ever said they were sorry for something they did to me.

"It all worked out." That girl of hers could learn something from her mama.

"I don't know what I'd do if something happened to Faith. She's everything to me."

Faith looked at her like she couldn't believe her ears.

"I got to buy some supper fixin's. You go on home. Me and Shelly will catch us a ride."

"No, Ada. I'll drop you at the market in Darien."

And for once I just let go and allowed somebody to help me. My boy was fine. He was coming home, and we'd take off tomorrow morning for Black Mountain.

WHEN WE WAS FINISHED at the market, I told Shelly we was going to walk on back to the Tyson house. She whined a bit but followed me.

"You go on upstairs and make sure Miss Lydia's clothes are hanging on hangers. She changed today. I'll get supper started."

"Yes, ma'am." She stood in the door a minute. "Ada."

"Yes?"

"I'm glad Will's okay and I'm happy you're coming with us tomorrow."

My heart flipped over. "You be a good girl, Shelly. Now, run on before Miss Lydia gets back."

Shelly didn't no more get up the stairs good when I looked out the kitchen window and seen a tall man walking toward the house like he walked right out of the marsh. Once when I was ten, I seen me a haint in the hall of my house on Sapelo. She was the scariest thing to look at, all blond and pale, sitting on the floor of the hall with her knees drawn up to her chest. Her eyes was sunk back in her head with black circles under them. Nothing but bones. That girl was bones with a little skin stretched over them. She watched me with this hopeless look and then vanished. I ran to tell my mama, who told me it sounded like something had eaten away at her spirit from the inside out. This man headed toward the house on that summer day looked just like that spirit girl. His death was showing on him before he quit breathing. A skull replaced his face for just a second, but it was enough to make me look away.

Shelly Parker

I HAD TO PUT THAT BOX in a good hiding place. Nobody had noticed
it yet in my skirt pocket. I was going to put it back where I found it. No
more spirits. I was going home with Will, and we was going to see Nada.
That Armetta would just have to figure out another way to get her stupid
old box home. I walked into Mrs. Dobbins's bedroom. All of her jewelry
was spread out on her dresser. A shadow moved across the mirror. Mary
Beth Clark came to stand behind me. Her face was like a mask of hatred. What had I done? I closed my eyes tight, wishing her away. When
I looked again, there Pastor stood.

"What are you doing, stealing my wife's jewelry?"

"I'm just putting it away, Pastor."

He was crazy looking. "Are you calling me a liar?"

"No, sir."

"You have no right to touch her things. You're just like your mama." He stepped closer to me.

There wasn't a place for me to go. I was hemmed up against the dresser.

"Did anyone tell you that you're pretty, Shelly?"

He smelled of sweat.

I kept quiet.

"I bet you haven't even kissed a boy." He pulled at my blouse, popping all the buttons.

I dug my nails deep into his arm. Where was Ada? She was supposed to be cooking supper. He grabbed my wrists, and there was a cracking sound. Pain, red hot, shot through me. He shoved me on the bed and pushed my skirt around my head. The box in my pocket pressed into my cheek. I screamed out all the pain inside me, but still he forced his body on me, in me. My soul split into a million pieces. He'd killed Ada. He must have.

"You son of a bitch!" The words cut through the air. A woman's voice I didn't know.

He was off of me.

I couldn't move.

"You abomination!" he yelled, almost like a woman, and then there was silence. Three heavy thuds followed. Quiet. I pushed my skirt—I'd thrown up in it—away from my face.

There was that quilt of Faith's wrapped around what must've been Pastor. A wide stain of red spread over the cloth, soaking into the stitches, into Arleen's name.

Two strong hands grabbed my arm. "Go." The old woman spirit was there. Mary Beth Clark was beside her.

"I can't." One of my hands wouldn't move.

Ada came into the door. "Shelly?" She looked at the pastor. "Oh Lord in Heaven, what have you done? Come on. We got to get you out of here before Miss Lydia comes back. She don't even know we been here." She looked at my wrists. "They're bad, Shelly. Come on. We got to leave." Ada bent over and buttoned Pastor's pants. Then she gave a shiver.

"Your head is bleeding, Ada."

"Yes, I know."

She made me walk down the stairs. "We're going to say you fell and hurt your wrists. Okay? On the way up the road. We got to get away from here, Shelly. Hurry. I know you be hurting."

"Did you kill him, Ada? Did you bring the quilt?"

She looked at me funny. "Go. No more talking." She took her sack of food we bought at the market with her.

We got on down to Fort King George before Ada stopped. "I think this is far enough." She looked at me. "I know you hurting. You've been so brave. But we got to walk back now."

My head spun. The pain wasn't even there anymore. I felt like my soul might walk on the outside of my body. That's when I seen Nada. She was standing in the field where the fort once stood. "Thank you," I said to her.

"What you thanking me for, child?" Ada had my arm.

"He be dead. I'm glad he's dead. He hurt me. He hurt me bad." Now I was talking to Nada, but Ada couldn't see her. Probably 'cause she wasn't there anyway. My mind was on fire.

"Lord, child, he hit me in the head when he come in the back door. I never even had a chance to stop him. I was out cold. I didn't kill him, but I wish I had." She touched my shoulder. "Come on. We got to walk back to the house and hope Miss Lydia be there by now."

I DON'T EVEN REMEMBER how I walked back to Mr. Tyson's house. We was just there, standing in the backyard, and Mrs. Dobbins busted out of the door white as a sheet. "Ada." She looked over at me. "God help us." Mrs. Dobbins came to me. "What happened to you, Shelly? Have you seen Faith? She jumped out at the café and said she was going back to the house. Did she come here?" She looked back at Ada. Her face went calm and serious. "We have a problem upstairs in the bedroom. I've called the sheriff. Have you been in the house?"

"No, ma'am. Shelly fell something bad down the road. I was trying to get her here. Her wrists be broken." Ada lied that easy.

Mrs. Dobbins looked at my hands and shuddered.

"We left Nada back at the fort. I seen her there. Can you please go get her, Mrs. Dobbins? I need her something terrible."

Mrs. Dobbins nodded to the old truck. "We have to get her to the doctor. I can't leave before the sheriff gets here. Can you take her, Ada?"

"Yes, ma'am."

She looked around. "Go on before the sheriff gets here and wants to question you two."

"What be wrong, Mrs. Dobbins?" I was talking out of my head.

"No worries, Shelly. Ada is going to take you to the hospital. If you see Faith, make her go with you, please. She doesn't need to be here." The phone started ringing. "Go on now, Ada. I'll tell them you've had the truck all this time. Now go." She went in and answered the phone.

"Come on, Shelly. I ain't stopping for no Faith. She ain't nothing but pure trouble," Ada whispered real loud.

"Yes, thank you. Yes. I have the sheriff on the way here." Mrs. Dobbins got quiet inside the house.

"Let's go, girl."

Mrs. Dobbins stuck her head out the back door. "That was the sheriff in Asheville, and he warned me Charles was headed our way. I'm not worried about who did what was done upstairs. I will protect them." She looked hard at Ada. "There's blood on Shelly's apron. Take it off and throw it away somewhere before you get to the hospital," she demanded. "And Ada, your head is bleeding. Clean that up before you get there. Come up with a better story on how both of you got hurt."

Ada nodded and opened the door to the truck. I sat down. She took the apron off, and that's when she saw the box in my pocket.

"Please don't let nobody touch it. The old woman spirit said I have to take it back to the mountain. I'm finishing what that Mary Beth Clark done."

Ada touched the box. "That be a devil box. I'll keep it with me while you're being looked at by the doctor." She looked at me. "Shelly, did you kill Pastor Dobbins?"

"No, ma'am. I reckon Mary Beth Clark did." Then everything went black.

WHEN I OPENED MY EYES, my head pounded like a railroad spike was driven down the middle of it, but my wrists didn't hurt a bit. They both had some hard white stuff on them. Faith sat in a chair.

"Where's Ada?"

Faith's face was sad, quiet. "She's taking care of Will."

Then I remembered Pastor.

"Mama's taking us back to Black Mountain tomorrow. Too much has happened. Then she's coming back to Darien to live. We can stay on the mountain or come back with her."

"Will wants to go with us. He's bringing Ada. He's got to talk to Nada himself."

"He can't." She didn't look at me.

"Why?"

"He's got problems, Shelly. Just be quiet for now, okay?" She sounded like some grown-up.

"Nada will be so happy that Will is alive. I can't wait to see her face. We can live anywhere we want. We could come back here and live on the island. I'm sure Ada will let us. I got the money. Got it right in my things. No more Pastor." All his blood.

She must have seen the look on my face, 'cause she touched my hand. "He tore up the house before he came here. Mama talked to the sheriff in Asheville. He can't hurt anyone anymore. The sheriff from Brunswick said he killed himself up in Mama's bedroom." She didn't look at me, and I was glad. I wanted to tell her I was glad he died.

"Does Miss Tuggle know about Will?"

Faith looked at me. Her deep-brown eyes reminded me of someone, but I couldn't think straight. "Shelly, I got to tell you because there is no one else to do it. Mama is busy with the sheriff. Ada is with Will. It's just me. Miss Tuggle says Amanda is missing."

My head went ice-cold. I seen her at the fort. The words stabbed me like a knife. "You're a liar! She's fine! I want to talk to Will now!" I was screaming over the roaring sound in my head.

"He just got out of surgery with a ruptured spleen. Dr. Thomas finally stepped in. He lived but he could have died because of me butting in." She sobbed.

"Does he know about Nada?"

Faith shook her head. "He was in surgery when Ada brought you here. He can't go with us." She held something out to me. "Here, Ada said you had to do something with this." She placed the wooden box on the bed beside me.

I was alone, all alone. I didn't have a person. Not one. Nada was lost. Will was sick, and Ada was with him.

"We have each other, Shelly," Faith said.

Was she crazy?

WHEN MRS. DOBBINS WHEELED ME into Will's room, he smiled. "There's my little sister. What were you doing?" He looked at my arms.

I couldn't talk; instead, I put my forehead on his bed.

"You got to be brave one more time, Shelly. I'll get there just as soon as I can. You go to Black Mountain and find Nada. Tell her about me. I'll be there as soon as they let me out of this hospital."

"You can go home with me, Shelly. Just wait on Will to get better. Then we can go together." Ada smiled, but it was a real sad smile.

A big sob caught in my chest.

She put her arm around my shoulders. "Your mama knows what a good girl you are, Shelly. You go on home and find her. But remember she's always right there in your heart." She touched my chest.

"I got to find Nada. I got to find her."

"You listen"—she took my face in her hands—"we'll be up there as soon as we can. You understand?"

"Yes, ma'am. I love you, Ada."

"Now, hush that mess."

And that was how we parted.

I PRAYED THAT NADA would be standing on the porch when we pulled up, but she was nowhere to be seen. I didn't feel her. She was gone. That was settled. Beside me on the seat was my bag with the box and my money. I had enough to make a living for a long while.

Miss Tuggle walked down the back steps of the main house. She was all the hope I had. "We haven't found her yet." She stood between Faith and me.

Faith started crying.

I looked at my wrists. "She might be gone."

Miss Tuggle didn't give me that doubtful look that I thought, hoped, she would. She'd seen something that changed her ways of thinking. We was both changed. "You can stay with me, Shelly."

"We need her here," Faith said.

Miss Tuggle nodded.

"I'll stay in the cabin. Nada might turn up and be looking for me. This story ain't over until she does."

That night I stayed by myself—I wouldn't let Mrs. Dobbins or Faith stay. On the kitchen table I had the box. So, what was I supposed to do with it? I'd brought it home like the old woman told me to do. All that seemed years before.

* * *

THE SECOND NIGHT I woke out of a deep sleep. The moon was full. On the little table by my bed was the box.

Armetta stepped out of the shadows. "I know where that goes." She nodded to the box. "You read my book. I be proud of you, Shelly."

"I don't know how it ended," I said.

"Come with me."

I did what she said. "You going to show me where Nada is?"

"First you got to know the end of the story. The morning I was supposed to meet Amelia I left early. Pastor Paul Dobbins stepped on the path and asked me what I was doing out so early. I thought on running, Shelly, but I didn't. He told me he knew all about my plan to go with Amelia and that he ought to beat me, but instead I could just go back to the cemetery if I went then. I turned and took three steps. I was thinking of my baby boy and how I'd get him back. Then there was a pressure on my neck and across my throat. That last thing I saw as a live person was blood all over my hand where I tried to stop him. My spirit woke up at the cemetery. The cross was clean and hung from my angel's wing. But she stood in a new place. I screamed into the air and used all my anger to run at my angel. The last little bit of living power tipped her over and broke her wing. Do you know that Pastor Paul Dobbins gave that cross back to Amelia? She never, ever knew that it hung around my neck when I died. And it ended up in your pastor's hands, passed on to him, a keepsake." She looked at me. "Now we got to go."

I followed her barefooted through the woods. That's how I figured I was dreaming. She took me down a path to the old cemetery. Then we walked in the big gates. "Here." She pointed to a bunch of trees near Dragonfly River. There was vines and brush all over, and I couldn't see the water but I could hear it. "There." She pointed at the mess of limbs and brush. "In there. That's where you need to be."

I looked in between the limbs and saw something white. Now I was dreaming 'cause it was night. When I reached out to pull the limbs away, a bright-green snake hung in front of me. I woke up and it was sunny as sunny could be.

* * *

I WALKED OVER to Miss Tuggle's house. She smiled when she caught sight of me. "Have you seen any sign of Amanda, Shelly?"

"No, ma'am, but I need to take this box somewhere and I don't want to go alone."

"Okay. Where are we going?"

"To that old cemetery up on the mountain, near Ella Creek."

Miss Tuggle blinked. "I've spent too much time up there, Shelly."

"It's where I got to go. Will you come?"

"Yes, but let's take my truck to the church. That will make the walk shorter for you. Is Will coming soon?"

"In a week."

The church looked the same. Nobody was around, but talk was a new pastor was on his way. From where wasn't real clear. Pastor's body was picked up by his brother and taken back to New Orleans without Mrs. Dobbins, who refused to make the trip. It seemed Pastor had stabbed himself in the throat. But I knew that was a lie. I figured that was more proof Mary Beth Clark did it, since that same thing happened to her. Either way. I was alive even though he hurt me bad.

"Shelly, what happened when Pastor Dobbins died?"

Now, up until that point I hadn't had to lie. "Don't know."

We walked on through the woods that was moaning and creaking. I held tight to the box.

"What's in that box?"

"Just some simple stuff. I have to put it where it belongs, Miss Tuggle. Don't ask me questions unless you be prepared to believe."

She hushed.

When we walked in the cemetery, Miss Tuggle looked over at some of the graves. I took out across the plots just the way I'd dreamed. The pile of brush and trees around it was there all the same, but the limbs and some of the vines had been torn away. I looked inside. There was the angel and a building. The brush and vines covered a old shed. The angel was staring right at me.

"Open the door, Shelly. Put the box in there. Be careful. You won't want to look too hard," Armetta whispered close to me.

"Shelly, where are you?" Miss Tuggle sounded worried.

The door to the shed gave way a lot easier than I expected.

"Shelly." Miss Tuggle—right behind me—sucked in air. "She's here. Get out, Shelly. Get out now."

But it was too late. I seen something, a body wrapped in a blanket.

Miss Tuggle pulled my arm. "Come on. I'm going to call Zach, the sheriff in Asheville."

I let her pull at me, but I sat the box on the rotted floor. Bones were scattered to the side of the body. Bones that had been there for a long time.

"He killed her." I looked at Miss Tuggle. "I seen her arm. He killed her." That's the last I remembered until I woke up near the gates.

Miss Tuggle was holding me in her lap. "We got to get out of here. Can you walk?"

I nodded.

WHEN THE SHERIFF came down the mountain from the cemetery, Miss Tuggle was sitting with me on the front porch of our cabin. He was a man about the age of Miss Tuggle, and they seemed to know each other pretty good. He liked Miss Tuggle a lot.

"It's what we thought." He looked at me.

"Nada?"

His face went soft and sad. "Yes."

I nodded, trying hard not to cry. I was a orphan with nobody, nobody but Will. Mrs. Dobbins and Faith came out of the house and walked to us. Somehow keeping quiet made all that had happened not true. Something inside of my chest cracked so loud I was sure the sheriff and Miss Tuggle heard, but they didn't.

"I don't know how he got the angel in there without leaving a trail for us to follow. We looked up there. Remember?" He looked at Miss Tuggle.

"I don't know, Zach."

He waited until Mrs. Dobbins and Faith came walking up. "We found Amanda Parker. He killed her and hid the body in Ella Creek Cemetery."

Faith burst into tears, and for the first time, I truly didn't hate her for loving Nada so much. Mrs. Dobbins put her arm around her, and they walked away back toward the house, a house they probably couldn't stay in much longer because Pastor was dead. And me, I was alone like some sorrowful tune floating through the trees.

"We found the remains of another body."

There was silence.

"It was old and had been there a long time. The body had been shoved into a wood box in that shed. The side was knocked out from a tree limb."

"The Negro girl who was lost." Faith was standing there again. Her eyes red.

"Armetta, she be the ghost that belonged to the box I took up there."

"She wanted to save us, and it was Amanda all along," Faith whispered.

"No, it was all of us," I said. "Nada stayed behind."

WE BURIED NADA next to my daddy. That was the saddest day in my life. I was still staying in Nada's cabin. Faith was going to live alone in the main house. It turned out Pastor had built the house with his daddy's money, and it now belonged to Faith. Mrs. Dobbins begged us to come to Darien with her, but neither of us wanted to. Miss Tuggle promised to keep a eye on us. So I was in Nada's garden when I heard Miss Tuggle's truck come up the drive. When I looked up, there stood

Will, my Will. There was a time in my life that I didn't believe I'd ever see my brother again, that he was lost from me, and I accepted this. There he stood bigger than life, older, new, with a small limp from his accident. And as much as I loved him, I knew he was different, grown into a man that I didn't know. My brother—the one who looked out for me when I was little—was lost for good. I wondered if he felt the same way when he looked at me. We would have to get to know each other all over again.

"Shelly, no matter where you are or I am, we'll always be together." He squeezed me close to his chest. I knew he meant every word.

I smelled the marsh salt on his shirt. He was a Geechee from Sapelo Island.

"We've lost time, but we have each other now. I'm your brother, and I love you with my whole heart, always have." And I knew I loved him too.

Sap Moon

March 1940

"A time when the sap runs in the maples and folks can make the best of syrups. A sweet time."

—Amanda Parker

Shelly Parker

My baby boy was born the next March, in the sap moon. There was this cold snap that made us all think spring was backing up and leaving. Miss Tuggle caught him early in the morning. He was so beautiful I fell in love that very minute. Faith stood right there with me through the whole thing. She'd learned a lot about taking care of the sick from Miss Tuggle. The folks on the mountain said this was best, seeing how Miss Tuggle didn't have no children to pass her doctoring off to. Faith hadn't touched a needle and thread since the pastor died. She just didn't need it anymore. She was going to be a granny woman.

"What is this little boy's name?" Faith cradled him in her arms. For a second, I saw she would never marry. She would be just like Miss Tuggle, and happy for it.

"William Clyde Parker. I'll call him William."

Faith smiled with tears in her eyes. "Will is going to be so proud. I've called his college and left word. I'm sure he'll be here in a day or two." This new Faith, neither the mean girl who tortured me nor Arleen who replaced her, was kind, quiet, and hardworking.

Will showed up at the end of the week with a big bunch of flowers. "Ada said you would have a boy and for you to never ever think about how he came to be. He's the good from all the bad." He held his nephew close to him.

"Ada is right. How is she?"

"Same as ever. I'm going home this summer for good."

"You're finished with school?" Will was trying to be a lawyer.

"I just want to be a shrimper, Shelly. That's what I want to be." His face was so beautiful and at peace. We talked about the day he left, how Pastor threatened to kill me and Nada if he didn't. How Faith was there and was told to protect me. There was peace between us even though I felt like there was parts of the story he had left out. I didn't care anymore. I had him, and that was enough.

THE DAY MY BABY WILLIAM turned a month old, Faith came to my cabin. "Shelly, I have something to tell you." She was so serious I thought maybe Mrs. Dobbins had died. "I want to tell you what happened the day Will left. I want to tell our secret."

A cold chill walked over my whole body. "Will told me."

"There is more. He left this part to me. Some secrets are so bad they can kill you. I know. The day Will ran away, I lost myself."

"You mean when Arleen came."

"But you see—you don't understand—Arleen wasn't the whole story. Her spirit was stuck in the woods, waiting. Daddy raped her. The baby that died was his. Will knew about it because Arleen told him before she died. Will went to Daddy when Arleen died and told him what he knew. Daddy threatened to kill you and Amanda if he didn't leave the mountain. Will had no choice but to run. He loved you two that much." She took a big breath and waited.

"Will told me all that."

She held up her hand. "That's when Will told me the truth."

I waited.

"My father was Pastor Charles Dobbins, and he was Will's father too. My real mother was Amanda. Will and I are full brother and sister."

My head roared. How? How could I not know such a thing? "You don't look—"

"No, I look like my father, just like him except for my brown eyes. Amanda gave me to Mama when she lost her baby boy during birth. Mama didn't even know. Mama almost died from the birth. But then she pulled through, and Amanda decided to give me a better life. I was so white no one knew. She'd hid me for a couple of weeks. But my father knew, even liked the idea. But not poor Mama. She didn't know until later, way later, when Uncle Lenard came to visit before we took off to Darien. She heard him and Daddy arguing, and she put the whole mess together." She looked at me. "Mama thought if she held the secret over his head, we would all be safe. That turned out to be the very thing that made Daddy finally lose his mind. When Will ran, he made me promise not to tell what I knew. He also made me promise to look after you. I stole the sewing kit because Amanda's grandmother, our great-grandmother, came to me in a dream and told me to take it and make a quilt. Amanda figured out that I knew, but not once did we sit down and talk. She did the best she could, Shelly. I don't blame her. Mama will always be my mother. And you can't be mad at Will."

"Nada lied."

Faith nodded. "Yes, she did. But we all do, and you don't know what you would do for that baby boy."

I looked at him. She was right. I would kill for him.

"One more thing." Her cheeks flushed and her voice sounded tired. "I want you and baby William to live in the main house with me. But you have to know this: I, not Arleen or Mary Beth Clark, killed Daddy that day. I left Mama at the café so I could get to the house. I could feel him coming. I just knew. I was too late. Ada was on the floor knocked out cold. I grabbed one of her carving knives. I found him on the floor with the quilt wrapped around his head. I saw that he did to you the same thing he did to poor Arleen and no telling who else. I killed him. He never moved, and I would do it again." Her hands shook.

"You didn't put the death quilt on him?" I asked.

She looked at me oddly. "No. But it made killing him easy. He never fought me. It was like he was already dead or asleep."

"That quilt had a powerful spell."

"I know." She ran her hand through her blond hair. "All I know is, Shelly, if you can live with a murderer, I want you in the house with me. You are my sister. We have each other."

THERE WAS A TIME IN MY LIFE I hated Faith Dobbins for everything she was. That afternoon I knew I would go live in her house, and we would be close as close could be. And I never seen what she did to Pastor as murder. I seen it as self-defense. And I knew who brought the quilt. The old woman spirit, Emmaline. The storycatcher. It was her job to finish the story.

Will came to be with his nephew two or three times a year, and when my boy, William, was old enough, he went to spend summers on Sapelo. But William was raised by two women. A granny woman and a colored girl, who finally went off to school and learned something. Only to come back and live out her life on Black Mountain. Sometimes I could feel Armetta there in the woods, but that wasn't bad. Her story had been told. She was at peace at long last.

The way I see it, life is made of choices. Both Faith and me chose to live.

Acknowledgments

The Storycatcher would not exist if not for many people: God gave me the talent and love to put words on the page. Jack and Ella inspired me to write the best book I could. Ayana and Merrariyana by their sweet existence drove me to step out of my carefully constructed box and write Shelly, Ada, and Emmaline's story. Morgan and Matthew, who I hope know are an important part of this family's future. Melissa, Cassey, Beth, Ella, and Stephen, you are my heart. Thanks to one of my dearest friends and best fans, Myrtis Doyle; Hollywood is waiting. Susan Lenz, whose art saved Faith Dobbins from being cut out of the novel. I'll treasure our newfound friendship forever. If not for Bill Merriman at the Sapelo Island Visitor Center, I would not have made it on the ferry to Sapelo Island. His tour so changed the writing of this book. Thanks to Darlene Rogers, my faithful reader. Alyse Urice and her Homecoming Queens. You guys held a mirror in front of this author's face and changed my life. I love you all. Ms. Renea Winchester, who bribes me with dilly beans and keeps me on the straight and narrow. Karen Spears Zacharias taught me through her writing and life examples that the truth should always be told. And most of all, Emilia Pisani, my editor at Gallery Books, who worked her art on this story, and for that I will always be in awe. For all of those who are not mentioned by name, you know how important you are to me.

THE STORYCATCHER

Ann Hite

Introduction

Shelly Parker, a sixteen-year-old servant who works for the tyrannical Pastor Dobbins and his family, has the gift of sight. She's grown accustomed to coexisting with the spirits of the dead who roam Black Mountain, telling Shelly their stories and warning her of the dangers that surround her. When the ghost of Arleen Brown, a poor woman who died on the mountain during childbirth five years earlier, begins to pursue Pastor's daughter Faith—hell-bent on revealing a terrible secret that she took to her grave—Shelly is the only person who can help her. The two young women soon find themselves tangled up in a web of secrets and lies that takes them from Black Mountain to the murky saltwater marshes of Georgia, uncovering long-hidden truths that put their own lives in danger.

Book Club Discussion Questions

1. *The Storycatcher* is told by multiple narrators and out of chronological order. How does this affect your understanding of the events that take place in the novel and your opinions of the main characters? How do you think the story would be different if it were told from just one perspective? If you had to pick just one narrator to share her story, whom would you choose?

2. Which character do you sympathize with or connect to the most? Why? Which character are you personally the most similar to?

3. The spirits of Black Mountain and the Ridge in Darien, Georgia, interact with several of the living characters and influence the events that unfold. Compare the way each living character responds to the ghosts. Consider how the ghosts directly affect each character's actions.

4. Of all the supernatural gifts of the characters, which would you most like to have? Why?

5. Discuss how each of the characters in *The Storycatcher* approaches the ideas of justice and revenge. Which characters represent a traditional justice system? Which characters represent vigilantism?

6. In the aftermath of Arleen Brown's death, Shelly Parker observes of Pastor Dobbins: "In that music was the man a woman would want to marry, the softness, the person who could mourn a young dead girl. Everyone had a decent side" (page 24). Is Shelly right about Pastor Dobbins? Does everyone have a decent side? How does this manifest in the other characters?

7. The various relationships between women—whether between mother and daughter, white and colored, or employer and employee—are central to *The Storycatcher*. Discuss how these women make up the backbone of the Black Mountain community. Why is it important for these women to act as confidantes for one another?

8. Discuss the significance of the names in *The Storycatcher*: Black Mountain, Faith, Will, Nada, Miss Tuggle. Why do you think the author chose each of these names?

9. Consider the alliances on the mountain. Who is loyal to whom? How do these loyalties change throughout the novel?

10. According to the spirit Emmaline, everyone has his or her own story to tell. What do you make of the ending to Armetta's story? Was Arleen's story truly finished? Mary Beth Clark's?

11. How does Will's character act as a bridge, a connection, between the women in the novel? Compare and contrast his relationships with Faith, Shelly, Ada, and Nada.

12. Shelly's exposure to the poetry of Langston Hughes opened up a new world for her and contributes to her evolution throughout the novel. Which novel, short story, or poem has most significantly influenced your own life? How?

Enhance Your Book Club

1. Have you ever had a paranormal encounter? Share your own personal ghost stories with your fellow book club members.

2. Ann Hite's first novel, *Ghost on Black Mountain*, introduces readers to the inhabitants of Black Mountain, focusing on the relationship between Nellie and Hobbs Pritchard. Read *Ghost on Black Mountain* for a future book club meeting; discuss the similarities and differences between the two novels set on Black Mountain.

3. Visit www.realhaunts.com to find a local haunted house in your hometown. Plan a visit with your book club for your next meeting and come up with your own ghost story.